RED HAIL

JAMIE KILLEN

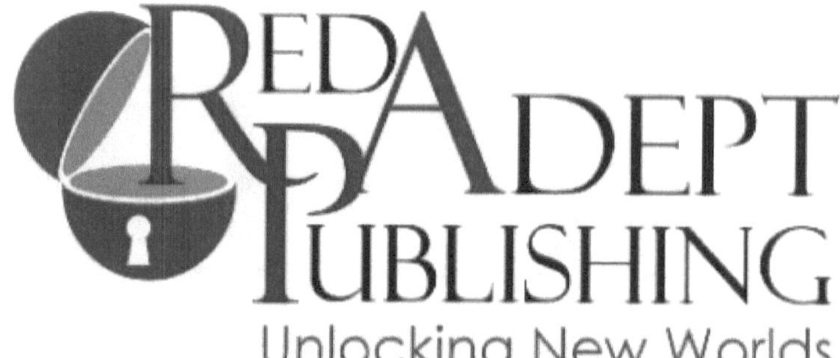

Red Hail
Red Adept Publishing, LLC
104 Bugenfield Court
Garner, NC 27529
http://RedAdeptPublishing.com/

First Print Edition: February 2020
Cover Art by Streetlight Graphics

This is a work of fiction. Names, characters, places, and incidents either are the product of the author's imagination or are used fictitiously, and any resemblance to locales, events, business establishments, or actual persons—living or dead—is entirely coincidental.

For Mom and Dad

CHAPTER 1: 1960

Anza stood at the window and watched her father's truck bump down the driveway. It passed through the honeysuckle-draped front gate and turned onto the road to town. Anza knew the unpaved road just beyond their driveway was actually called Rio Avenue, but no one ever used that name. It was always just "the road to town."

Once the truck curved around the edge of the mesa and out of sight, Anza slipped away from the window and retrieved her wide-brimmed hat from its peg on the hat rack. It had been Mama's once. Dad had presented it to Anza on her fifteenth birthday. In truth, it was a little too small, and she would have preferred a different color, but it made Dad happy to see her wearing it.

She started to sweat as soon as she stepped from the swamp-cooled air of the house into the sweltering May sun. She pulled the hat low on her head and set off along the side of the road. She didn't go toward town as she normally would have, but in the other direction, where the spaces between the houses grew wider and there were more horses and sheep than cars.

No one was on the road this time of day. The men were at either the mine, the saloon, or the cantina, while the women were doing housework or at their jobs in diners and banks over in Bisbee. The children and teenagers lay low, waiting until the sun dipped close to the horizon before they made their way to the drive-in or the ice cream parlor. Unless someone went out for an unexpected errand, Anza could count on not being seen.

She'd never visited Dove McNally's old adobe house, but she knew the front gate. It was marked with two horseshoes welded together, each one cupping a letter *M*. Anza didn't remember Mr. McNally's first name. She knew only that he had died years before she was born, just a few weeks after marrying Dove.

A powder-blue truck sat in the driveway, but no one answered when Anza rang the bell. She rang twice more before wandering around to the back. A tidy vegetable garden huddled in the shade alongside the house, where almost-ripe bell peppers hung heavily on the chicken wire fence. No flowers, though. Anza tried and failed to think of another woman in Galina who didn't at least keep a pot of geraniums by the front door.

She spotted Dove a short distance from the back porch, heaving a bale of hay from a pallet onto a teetering haystack. A horse nickered from the nearby barn.

"Oh, hush. You had breakfast already," Dove said.

"Need a hand?" Anza called. She'd hoped it would sound confident and jaunty, but instead, her voice quaked.

Dove straightened up and turned around, pushing her hat higher on her forehead. She stared for a long moment. "Esperanza Kearney," she said at last, the name passing through her lips in slow, careful syllables. "Well, aren't you just the spitting image of your mama."

Anza had heard that before. She'd seen from pictures that she had Mama's straight, waist-length black hair and her deep-brown eyes. Maybe some similarities in the facial features. But Mama sported a womanly figure, while Anza had a short, wiry frame. She'd assumed she would fill out more, but she was already sixteen and a half and could still fit into boys' clothes, so it probably wasn't ever going to happen.

Dove was tall and rail-thin under her denim work shirt and thick gloves. Her red hair, threaded with gray streaks, was pulled back into a braid at the base of her neck. Her skin was rough and lined with sun, but underneath were the fine features she'd supposedly used to bewitch Mr. McNally on his deathbed: razor-sharp cheekbones, cupid's-bow lips, and vivid blue eyes.

"I guess," Anza replied. Then, as an afterthought, "Morning, Mrs. McNally."

"Oh, now, call me Dove. I wasn't married long enough to warrant the title." She pulled off her gloves and made her way toward the house's back porch. "What brings you out here?"

Anza hesitated. She'd rehearsed this moment, thought about what one was supposed to say in such a situation. Her carefully planned words melted like frost on a windowpane. "I heard girls come to see you sometimes. About... women's troubles," she said at last.

"That, they do." Dove fixed her with an unblinking stare. "What sort of trouble are you having?"

"I..." She bit her lip and blinked against the sudden tears. She hadn't said the words yet, not to anyone.

Dove sighed. "Come on, come inside."

Anza sniffed and followed. The interior of Dove's house was smaller and more cramped than Anza had imagined. The living room overflowed with books. Shelves covered every wall, each stuffed with paperbacks. Other books sat stacked on the coffee table and in little towers next to the old sofa.

"You decided if you're keeping it yet?" Dove asked as she made her way to the kitchen. When Anza hesitated, she added, "I only ask so I know whether to make tea or pour you a whiskey."

"Tea, please," Anza said, voice trembling. She sat on the edge of the sofa and listened to the clanking of the kettle.

Dove came back to the living room and set a steaming teacup in front of Anza. "Now," she said, settling back in an armchair. "How long has it been since your last period?" Then, at the look on Anza's face, she rolled her eyes. "Now's not the time to get prim and proper. You want help, you gotta be straight with me."

"Seven weeks. And I've never been late, not once in four years."

Dove stirred her tea. "Well, that doesn't bode well. And I take it this isn't an immaculate conception? Figure you'd lead with that if it were."

Anza let out a little bark of laughter. "Nope. Nothing immaculate about it."

"How many times? Since your last period?"

"Uh... five. But we used a rubber for three of them."

Dove nodded and sipped her tea in silence.

Anza raised an eyebrow. "What? No lectures on how stupid I was?"

"Well, you already know that. No sense in me repeating it." Dove balanced her teacup on a stack of paperbacks. "Here are your options. We can't be one hundred percent sure unless you see a doctor, but it sure sounds like you're knocked up. So... You can bite the bullet and keep it. That's if you don't mind breaking your daddy's heart and you're content to marry a boy who can't be bothered to wrap up his package even when he knows damn well where babies come from."

Anza's face heated up. "Hey, he's not—"

Dove held up a finger. "Or I can help you nip it in the bud, you can get smarter about rubbers in the future, and just maybe you'll finish high school and make something of yourself."

"I get straight As. My teacher thinks I can get a scholarship to college." Anza lifted her chin, meeting Dove's gaze.

"Well, in my eyes, that settles it. Course, some people get sentimental about these things." Something angry came over Dove's face, the blue of her eyes icing over. Then it passed, and she seemed disinterested again. "You get rid of it, best never to tell the boy. Men tend to think they deserve some kind of say in these matters."

Anza realized that she hadn't even considered telling Fernando about it. She tried to imagine his face when he heard the news, and just the thought filled her with dread. "I..."

The light in the room had changed. Although stark sunlight had spilled through the open living room window a few seconds ago, the room had gone almost too dim to see.

"What on earth?" Dove asked. She stood and crossed to the window. "Well. Goddamn."

Anza joined her, pulling aside one of the curtains. Outside, deep-purple clouds hung heavy in the sky. They formed a solid blanket from horizon to horizon, so thick Anza wouldn't be able to guess what part of the sky the sun was in.

"Huh," Dove said. "I've seen storms roll in quick before but not this quick."

"Too early for monsoon, anyway." Anza jumped as thunder cracked right above them.

A metallic plinking sound drifted down from the roof. It sounded awfully loud for raindrops.

"What in the..." Dove squinted and pushed her nose close to the windowpane. After a moment, she picked her way around the stacks of books and headed for the front door.

Anza followed. As Dove reached for the doorknob, the tinny sound of individual drops sped up and became a roar.

Anza froze as the door opened, and the smell hit her. It wasn't rain. Not the comforting, loamy earth-and-creosote smell she loved falling asleep to. No, this was something coppery, musky, and so heavy, she could taste it.

"Hail," Dove said, voice almost drowned out by the roar of falling ice.

Anza moved forward slowly, eyes locked on the ground. It was hail, all right. Most of the chunks were the size of her thumbnail.

Some were as big as golf balls. A pile of them was already melting into slush where they had rolled against the front step.

Instead of the pale color of fresh ice, though, the hailstones had the raw crimson hue of uncooked meat. As Anza watched, they piled and began to melt while new stones fell onto the slush. It only took a minute for Dove's front yard to transform into a red mass of gore. It sluiced down her driveway and into the road, forming a river of blood flowing down the slope.

"You know," Dove said, holding the edge of the door with one hand. "If I were the superstitious type, I might be tempted to read this as a bad omen."

Anza's throat tightened. "Where's your bathroom?"

Dove pointed at a door down the hall. Anza just managed to make it to the toilet before she fell to her knees, gagging on the smell of blood.

"WELL, PHONE'S STILL out," Dove said, returning to the living room.

"Don't know what I'd say to my dad anyway... about why I'm here," Anza replied, fidgeting and tapping her fingers against the coffee table.

"Easy. You were out for a walk, the storm came in, and you ran for the nearest house, which happened to be mine." Dove set a kerosene lantern in the middle of the coffee table and lit it with a long match. The walls flickered with orange light.

"What do you think it is?" Anza asked, looking out the window again. The hail showed no signs of letting up. It was getting darker as the day moved into late afternoon. The road had become a stream of fast-running red water, at least a foot deep, judging from how it lapped at the gate posts of the house across the road. "Think the Soviets finally dropped the bomb?"

"Nah. We'd all be vaporized already if that were the case." Dove spoke absently, staring up at the clouds.

"Then what?"

Dove said nothing for a moment. Then she shrugged and turned away from the window. "No idea. I'll let you know if I manage to come up with some brilliant answer." She grimaced and dropped into the chair again. "I'm sure whoever the hell the preacher is these days has all kinds of thoughts about what's going on."

"Pastor Benjamin or Father Santiago?"

"What's the difference?" Dove gestured at the kitchen before Anza could answer. "Be a doll and fetch me the whiskey and a glass from the cabinet on the far left. Or two glasses, if you've made up your mind in that direction."

Anza found the half-full whiskey bottle right away. She stared at the row of round, squat highball glasses. One was clean, but a thin layer of dust covered the other five. She took a deep breath and pulled two glasses out of the cabinet, dusting the second one off with the tail of her button-down shirt. Dove said nothing when she set the glasses down and poured a generous dollop into each.

"I'm not sure I like whiskey," Anza said, sniffing the glass.

Dove let out a dry little cough of laughter. "You're an Irish copper miner's daughter. Whiskey's your destiny. You can trust me on that." She paused, considering the drink in her hand. "Of course, you're also a nice Mexican teetotaler's daughter, so I guess it's a coin flip."

Anza sipped the whiskey, trying not to make a face. "Ugh." It tasted the way nail varnish smelled. After a second, though, a pleasant warmth spread out from the base of her throat. She sipped again. "I don't know if my mama was a teetotaler."

"Oh, she was. I tried to change that on more than one occasion, but she wouldn't budge. One stubborn lady, your mama was." Anza thought she caught that quick moment of anger again—tension around the mouth—but it was hard to tell in the syrupy glow of the kerosene lantern.

"So you and Mama were friends?" Anza tried to remember if Dad had ever mentioned Mama's friends. She must have had them, but Anza had never thought to ask who any of them were.

Dove took another gulp of whiskey. "Let's get back to our discussion of your predicament. We were interrupted by this Biblical nonsense outside."

"How..." The whiskey seemed to swirl in her stomach. "How are you going to do it? Are you going to... to cut me?"

"No, darling, nothing like that," Dove said, her voice gentle for the first time since Anza had arrived. "Women have been finding ways to deal with this since the dawn of time, since before surgery was a thought in anyone's head. There are medicines that are supposed to be for other things, but they'll do the trick. They're pretty safe if you know what you're doing, although they don't always do the job. Those fail, I can do it the other way. I still know some people from my nursing days. They can get me some things for the pain. Ether, maybe. And it's quick as can be, quicker than you think." She shook her head. "There's some who think women should be awake to feel the pain, like it'll teach them a lesson. I say we got enough pain just being in this world. Might as well avoid it when we can."

"I don't have much money." Anza tried to sit up straight and not let her shame show. "I make some money babysitting but not much. But I can work. Mucking stalls, pulling weeds, whatever you—"

"Stop." Dove winced like Anza's words hurt. "You don't have to pay me anything."

"But my friend Paula said—"

"*You* don't have to pay me anything. The deal I have with anyone else is none of your business."

Anza didn't know what to say to that. Finally, she just shrugged and thanked her. She didn't understand the thoughts flickering across Dove's face, but she knew they weren't for her.

Some sound made Anza jump. She looked around, realizing that the room was growing brighter. She followed Dove back to the window.

A crack of clear blue sky split the storm clouds down the middle, almost directly overhead. As Anza watched, the crack expanded, pushing the clouds away and toward each horizon. Within two minutes, the sky was completely clear again.

Dove and Anza blinked at each other. For a moment, Dove actually seemed a little unnerved. Then she shrugged and turned away from the window. "Well, that's passed. Best get you home before we get hit with locusts or plague boils or whatever else is next."

Anza finished her whiskey as Dove fetched a set of keys from a bowl near the door. "So when do we... you know?"

"There's some things I have to get together," Dove replied, opening the front door. "Your daddy work Monday?"

"Yeah. Eight to five o'clock. Usually, he gets home around five thirty, unless he stops at the saloon."

Dove said nothing for a moment. Both women stood in the doorway and stared out at the bloody landscape. The gravel, the dust of the driveway, even the pale blue of Dove's truck, all were stained a deep red.

"Come by first thing Monday," Dove said at last, leading her to the truck. "More time we have, the better."

Anza flinched as her boot squelched into the mud. Red liquid flowed into the hole made by her heel. She tried to shake off her boot before climbing into the cab of Dove's truck, but the red muck clung and refused to let go.

From the truck window, Anza watched the houses and fields as they drove past. People stood in their driveways, stared out at their gardens, or gazed up at the sky. She scooted down and pulled her hat low over her face, praying no one saw her.

"Thank Christ, Dad's not home yet." Her breath rushed out in a sigh of relief as she caught sight of the empty driveway. "Guess they didn't send them home from the mine."

Dove pulled up in front of the house. "Remember, Monday. Bright and early. Don't eat anything before you come over."

"I'll be there." Anza climbed out of the truck. She turned back, hesitating. "Thanks, Dove."

"Sure thing, darling." She put the truck in gear and drove away without a backward glance. Anza watched until the truck disappeared, a vanishing dot on a bloody road.

CHAPTER 2: 2020

"This is the most horrifying thing I've ever seen."

"It's not horrifying. It's beautiful." Colin wrapped his arms around Alonzo's waist. Before them, the kitchen overflowed with boxes, trash bags, and an old pillowcase stuffed with utensils and dry goods. Some of the new appliances remained sealed in their boxes, yet to be assembled.

Alonzo shook his head. "The house is beautiful. Unpacking all this shit is the stuff of nightmares." But he leaned back against Colin's chest as he spoke.

"Let's just leave the mess for tomorrow. We can unload the coffeepot and two plates and just order a pizza for tonight. What more do we need?"

"Beer."

"Okay, point."

Alonzo stepped away and turned to face him. "Good plan, though. Let's leave the unpacking for later. Tonight, we celebrate." Stocky and broad-shouldered, he was about four inches shorter than Colin. He had to tilt his head up a bit when they kissed. Colin drew back to see him a little better. He was going prematurely gray, which Colin knew he was self-conscious about, but he liked the look of the silver streaks sweeping back from Alonzo's temples.

"Yup." Colin grinned. "I don't know what *you're* celebrating, but I'm celebrating the fact that it's too late for you to change your mind."

Alonzo smiled back at him, teasing but tired. "Well, if I'd remembered how much of a pain in the ass it is to move, I probably would have stayed where I was."

"Ooh, are you picking our first big fight?"

"Nah. Too tired. We'll do it tomorrow. Along with everything else." He turned and started clearing a path to the fridge. "I'll crack open the beers. You go order the pizza."

"On it." Colin picked his way through the chaos of the main hallway, past the spare room that would be his home office, and into the jumble of furniture that would eventually be organized into their living room. It was one of the main reasons they'd picked this place; the kitchen led directly into a high-ceilinged living room with exposed beams and natural light spilling through the sliding glass door. It felt big and airy, even when full of clutter.

He found his phone on the coffee table they'd scavenged from Goodwill and called in an order for way more pizza than they needed. Then he joined Alonzo on the house's little back porch, which was bare but for two deck chairs and two beers. Colin dropped into one of the chairs, suddenly realizing how tired he was once he sat. His back and shoulders ached from wrestling the couch and dining room table up the front steps. He sighed and lifted his bottle. "To cohabitation."

"Cohabitation," Alonzo replied, grinning as their bottles clinked together.

"And," Colin said, holding up a finger, "to the sixtieth anniversary of the Red Hail. Although technically, the anniversary started at 9:42 a.m., so we're a little late."

"Jesus, how do you remember this stuff?"

"Because writing a dissertation means spending years learning way too much about one incredibly narrow thing no one else gives a shit about."

"It's just so fucking weird that you know more about my family history than I do." Alonzo sipped his beer and paused. "Okay, so how old was Grandfather Fernando on that day? During the Red Hail?"

"Fernando Cardenas, born 1942, so eighteen or so?"

Alonzo shook his head. "Can't imagine that. He always seemed so old, even when I was a little kid. And so serious. Guess surviving what he did does that to you."

"Yeah, there's some interesting research on the psychology of people who spend time in mass hysteria zones." Colin stopped, reminding himself not to go off on a research tangent.

Alonzo sighed. "Yeah. I always got the sense... I mean, we talked about this already, but I always got the sense there was stuff they didn't want the rest of us to know. You know, my grandparents and old friends from Galina would be talking, and they'd stop when I came into the room. That kind of thing."

Colin nodded. "Most mass hysteria cases are like that. People lash out, blame someone, turn against each other. They tend to have a lot of shame afterward." He thought about some of the terrible things his older interview subjects had admitted to doing or seeing during the Galina Plagues, so many years ago, they didn't care about keeping it secret anymore. Some of them had given him nightmares.

They settled into comfortable silence, watching the little yard with its desert willow and a handful of lantana plants. Lizards scurried up and down the yard's brick wall then dashed across the pale-pink gravel, but aside from that, everything sat lazy and still in the late-afternoon heat.

The doorbell rang.

"Pizza's here," Alonzo said, setting down his bottle. "Be right back."

Colin leaned back in his chair and smiled, letting himself bask in the moment. They'd finally done it. They'd gotten through the uncertainly of the early days, learning each other's limits and faults. Now they would wake up next to each other every morning, in a place that belonged to both of them.

He heard indistinct conversation, the door closing, then footsteps down the sidewalk beyond the garden wall. A car started and drove away. He tried to remember if he'd set out the plates or if he should go in to help out. No sound came through the open patio door. No rustling of a pizza box or the clatter of silverware. Colin cocked his head, listening. "Lonzo?"

Alonzo spoke, his voice low and indistinct.

"What?" Colin said.

The voice remained low, the rhythm almost monotone.

Colin waited for another minute before he stood and went back into the house. The plates still sat empty on the countertop. The sound of Alonzo's voice drifted from the entryway. Colin wondered if Alonzo was on the phone and he should give him a minute, but it didn't sound like a conversation.

He found Alonzo standing just inside the front door, holding the pizza boxes in both hands. There was something odd about the motion of Alonzo's head; he moved it slightly, muttered something, turned it again, then repeated.

"Lonz?" Colin moved closer. "Lonzo?"

Alonzo muttered more words, too quiet for Colin to make out. His eyes stared, glassy, at nothing.

Colin's heart beat faster. "Alonzo? Babe, you're scaring me." He stepped forward and touched his arm. "Come on, stop doing that." Then he remembered why the situation was so familiar, and he nearly gasped. "Alonzo, please." He squeezed his arm tight and gave it a little shake. "Hey!"

Alonzo spoke one last word, blinked, and smiled. "Hey. Can't believe how much pizza you got." The smile faded. "What's up?"

"Do you remember all that stuff you were saying just now?" Colin asked, fighting to keep his voice level.

He frowned. "To the pizza guy?"

"No." Colin swallowed. "You were just... zoned out. Muttering to yourself. I was talking to you, and you didn't respond."

"Really?" He shrugged. "Well, I feel fine. Probably just dehydrated and tired from hauling stuff around all day. My electrolytes must be out of whack. Plus I'm starving. Speaking of which..." He hefted the boxes. "Let's eat."

As Alonzo moved past him and into the kitchen, Colin thought about pushing it, saying more about what he'd heard. But as Alonzo bustled around with pizza slices on plates and another couple of beers, it almost seemed like he might have imagined the whole thing.

Almost. He might have convinced himself if not for the last three words Alonzo said before he woke up. The three he'd spoken while staring right at Colin were the only ones he'd heard clearly. Those words kept running through Colin's mind for the rest of the evening, even as they ate, drank, laughed, and drifted off to sleep surrounded by the wreckage of their move.

Colin. Lover. Human.

SONIA SLOWLY TRACED a spiral in the corner of her notebook page. A lyric floated just out of reach, a phrase that would give the song an edge. She almost had it, something about hard steps on a hard road—

"Hey, Sonny. Another pitcher." It was Greg, or maybe his name was Eric, one of the construction workers who always played at table 5.

She forced a thin smile as he ran a suggestive hand up and down his cue, like she hadn't seen that same stupid move ten thousand times.

"You sure do wear that tank top well." He leered as she set down the pitcher of Corona.

Sonia bared her teeth, not even trying to make the expression pass for a real smile. "Keep trying to look down my shirt, and I'll show you something *really* nasty I can do with that cue."

She went back to the bar without another word, leaving the guys at table 5 to mutter about feminazi bitches who couldn't take a compliment. Picking up her pen, she went back to staring at the unfinished song. But the lyric she'd been chasing was long gone, and she tossed down the pen in disgust.

Will came out from the back room, carrying a case of Modelo. "Can you replace that Maker's?" he asked, gesturing at the nearly empty bottle behind the bar.

Sonia nodded and headed for the storeroom. She rummaged around until she found the Maker's Mark on the bottom shelf, then she straightened up and started back to the bar. She blinked, and Will suddenly stood in front of her, hands on her arms.

"Jesus!" She jumped, almost dropping the bottle. "Where'd you come from?"

Will stared at her with wide, frightened eyes. "Are you back, Sonia?"

She nudged him with an elbow until he got out of her way. "What's your problem?"

"Sonia, you were just spaced out for like five minutes. I was about to call an ambulance."

She replaced the Maker's and rolled her eyes at him. "Ha-ha."

"No, Sonia, I'm totally serious. I think you might have had a... I don't know. A seizure."

Sonia stopped and studied Will's face. Not much of a joker, he was all business even when she and the other servers goofed off and gave him shit. And she didn't know many people who would drag a bad prank out this long. "Wait, seriously? What happened?"

Will hung back a little, as though unnerved by her presence. "You were taking a while, so I went back to check, and you were just standing there, staring into space. And you kept, like, chanting. Or reciting."

"Reciting what?" Something cold gripped her stomach.

"Just words. Like *box*, *wall*, *paint*, just stuff in the storeroom."

"Well, I don't... I feel fine." She hesitated, trying to detect nausea, a headache... anything.

The phone rang. Will picked up the old cordless receiver. "Billy's Billiards." He held out the phone. "It's for you. Dylan's school."

"Christ." She pressed the phone to her ear. "Yes?"

"Hi, Mrs. Rollins?"

"It's *Ms.* Rollins. But yeah. Is everything okay?"

"Dylan seems to be just fine now, but a few minutes ago, he had something we think might have been a neurological event. The ambulance is on its way."

"A 'neurological event'? What does that mean?"

"He... Well, he seemed to lose consciousness or go into a trance. Just for a few minutes. And now he seems perfectly fine. But the paramedics should be here soon, and—"

"Don't... Have the paramedics look at him, but don't let the ambulance take him to the hospital. I'll be there in ten minutes." Heart pounding, she hung up on the woman. "Dylan's sick," she said. "I gotta go to the school."

Will frowned. "Of course, I mean, yeah, you can go, but should you be driving?"

"I..." The thought of going blank again stopped her. "I feel fine. I have to, I mean." The medical bills were going to be bad enough without having to pay for the ambulance ride as well. She gathered her things, trying to remember what was fully covered by their insurance, what required a co-pay, and exactly how much she had in her checking account.

She made it halfway to the door before she stopped and ran back for her notebook.

"YOU SURE YOU DON'T mind?" Alonzo asked. "Because I can skip a week. It's not a big deal. They've got enough other volunteers to keep an eye on things." He wore his old, frayed boxing shorts and shirt, his bag of gloves and gear under one arm.

Colin held up his hands in a placating gesture. "I promise, I don't mind. That's the beauty of academia: summers off."

Alonzo rolled his eyes. They both knew Colin was working harder over the summer than he had during the school year, scrambling to finish his manuscript by the publisher's deadline. Still, he could spare a day to unpack boxes and tidy up.

Colin waved at the door. "Go. Teach America's youth to punch each other better. There'll still be plenty left to unpack when you're done."

"Okay, if you're sure." Alonzo checked his watch. "Gotta go. Love you." He gave Colin a quick kiss and headed for the door.

"Love you too."

Colin glanced around at the silent, cluttered house. It still felt like he was trespassing. It didn't smell like their place yet, and the layout wasn't second nature. He kept turning left instead of right to go into the bathroom from the hallway, kept pivoting the wrong way to get to the sink from the coffee pot. Even so, he knew it wouldn't be long before it felt like home.

He spent the morning getting the kitchen set up. Once it was done, he turned in a slow circle, searching for anything he'd missed. The mix of items kept standing out: his plates, Alonzo's coffee cups, and the new blender they'd bought for the move, all side by side.

A pair of hideous cow-shaped oven mitts his sister Tori had gotten them hung on a hook next to the stove. Colin was pretty sure they were supposed to be a gag gift, but they were funny enough to keep.

He wondered how long it would take for them to forget who had brought what into the household, for it all to just become *their* stuff.

Deciding the other rooms could wait until Alonzo got back, Colin set up his laptop and research folders. He could at least get a little editing done. He scrolled through chapter one, settling on a new paragraph after a section break:

When asked about the name of the town, the residents of Galina and their descendants offer two possibilities. The first and more plausible explanation is that the town was named for galena, the silver-rich lead ore many nineteenth-century prospectors sought as part of their mining efforts. In that version, the name of the town is a simple misspelling. The second and more romantic story holds that the town was named for the beautiful Russian wife of the community's nineteenth-century founder. Older residents of the town claim that the desert air cured her near-fatal case of tuberculosis, which she had contracted on the long journey to the United States. She vowed never to leave the dry, arid mesa where she came back from her brush with death, demanding that her husband establish a town to attract other settlers. She lived to great old age, insisting on being buried in an unmarked grave on the mesa, and (according to some accounts) haunting it to this day. Like most of Galina's stories, the truth probably lies somewhere between these two wildly different tales.

Colin moved on through the chapter, tracking down rogue citations and fleshing out footnotes. Then his eyes fell on the word *glossolalia* as he skimmed through an article on language phenomena in mass hysteria cases. He remembered Lonzo's weird episode the night before. Biting his lip, he opened his transcribed notes on the first serious incident of the Galina Plagues. The first file was from his interview with an elderly woman named Paula Porter, who had been a teenager when the Plagues began.

The first one was called the Naming Disease. People would just go into a trance, you know? Like the rest of the world wasn't there. And they would name everything around them. The ground, people, food, cars, whatever they could see. Of course, it wasn't as bad as the later ones, but since it was the first, it seemed scarier at the time.

Colin shook his head and closed the file. There was no way. It couldn't be a physical disease and certainly not a hereditary one. People had done questionable research before his, hacky pseudo-scientific journalism instead of sociological or historical analysis. They'd tried to make a case for the Plagues being caused by some toxin, maybe something from the nearby mine spilling into the groundwater. They dug up references to poisons and hallucinogenic substances with vaguely similar side effects, like seizures and incoherent speech, but they also glossed over all the symptoms that didn't match. And as he argued in the book's introduction, they all ignored the most important fact of all: the effects of toxins and bacteria don't instantly vanish overnight, after one terrible day of rioting and murder. Only social illnesses evaporated that quickly.

Colin nodded once and resumed his editing. It was a mass hysteria case, kicked off by strange environmental phenomena, economic strain, and racist paranoia. It wasn't a physical illness—and certainly not one that could resurface in the grandson of one of the survivors. It couldn't be.

"WATCH YOUR FOOTWORK, Jessa. Don't overextend. Good." Alonzo turned his attention to another pair of sparring partners. "Nice right hook, Stevie, but don't drop your shoulder."

The kids on the practice mats looked gawky and awkward, as always. The red padding of their gloves dwarfed their skinny arms. The ones who had been coming to the program for a year or two had decent focus and knew how to pace themselves. The newer ones tired themselves out in minutes, throwing around sharp elbows and wild punches, forgetting to conserve their energy. Alonzo remembered when he'd been at that stage, the first few weeks he'd gone to the boxing gym back in tenth grade. Every bag and mat had taken on the form of a jeering kid from school. He'd flailed away at them with rage but no technique, at least until the gym's owner talked him into lessons.

The equipment was newer now, but the gym still smelled the same—of sweat, old socks, and the polyurethane of the gloves. For just a moment, standing on the edge of the old practice mat, Alonzo wished he could go back and tell that earlier version of himself how things would change, how he would get past those early years and through to the other side. If that pissed-off kid had only known about the days to come...

Alonzo shook off the odd feeling, half morose and half nostalgic, and brought his attention back to the practice mats. He clapped his hands. "Time. Now switch. Daryl, pick up the pace on those jabs."

As the kids switched sparring partners, Alonzo glanced back over his shoulder. The newer volunteers hadn't yet developed the ability to monitor a whole room full of teenagers at the same time, so he checked for brewing fights or trouble every few minutes. Everything seemed calm now, though, and he turned back to the practice session, only to find the students standing in a loose semicircle, staring wide-eyed instead of sparring.

"Yo, what's going on? It's not break time yet," Alonzo said, gesturing for them to get back to the mat.

"You okay, coach?" Jessa asked, shifting her weight from one foot to the other.

"Yeah..." He looked at each of them in turn. "Okay, what's going on?"

Daryl bit his lip. "You were just being weird, Coach. We were worried."

"Weird how?" Alonzo tried to sound bored, skeptical, even, but something tightened in his gut.

"Just, like, spaced out. Like, you just kept saying words, but you weren't talking to anybody," Jessa said after a moment. "It was, like, a minute or two."

"Yeah, you been hitting the bong before practice, Coach?" Stevie said it with a grin and a playful nudge toward Daryl's arm, but none of the other kids responded. They still watched Alonzo with quiet unease.

"This doesn't look much like practice to me," Alonzo said, clapping his hands. "Thank you all for your concern, but I know you're just trying to take an extra break. Jig's up. Get back out there."

The kids reluctantly returned to the practice mats and got back to their sparring. He watched them and called out instructions, trying to ignore the growing tension in the back of his mind.

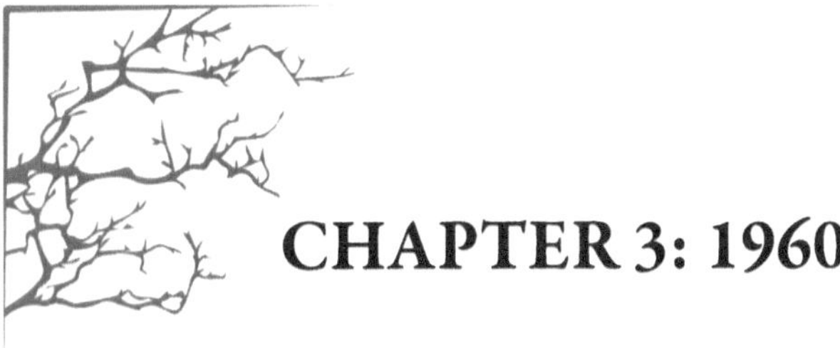

CHAPTER 3: 1960

"Where the hell were you? I've been calling and calling." Dad's voice echoed through the receiver as soon as Anza picked up the phone.

"I'm sorry. I got caught in that storm, and I had to wait it out." She held her breath and waited for him to ask questions. *Why were you out? Where did you wait? Why?*

Instead, he just said, "Stay inside until I get back. No one seems to know what the hell that storm was. Don't want you out in it if it might be poison."

"Okay. But the clouds are all gone." Anza checked the clear sky through the kitchen window.

"Still. Stay inside. I'll be home soon."

Anza hung up and stood still for a moment, staring at the phone. She wondered if she should call Fernando and talk to him about what was going on. But Dove was right. Fernando would just interfere, and the whole time, he would think he was doing the right thing. She shook her head and went to the kitchen to make dinner.

Dad got home just as the cornbread came out of the oven. Usually, he went straight to the bathroom to wash up before dinner, but today, he came into the kitchen. "You sure you're okay? Didn't get any of that stuff on you?"

Anza shot him what she hoped was a convincing smile. "Nope. I saw the clouds coming while I was out walking and ran into Dove McNally's house. She let me stay until it passed." She figured he might hear from someone who saw her in Dove's truck, so she might as well stay ahead of it. "What was that stuff?"

But he just looked thoughtful for a moment. "Dove McNally, huh?"

"Yeah. Her house was closest, so... What's wrong?"

He smiled the big grin that made him look younger than he was. "Oh, nothing. She just don't like me much, is all. Never could figure out why." He seemed to remember her first question. "I got no idea what that stuff was. Scared the heck out of some of the guys at the mine. Some of 'em, the churchgoing ones, they were talking about it raining blood in the Bible and such. That's nonsense, far as I'm concerned, but there was no reasoning with them. Maybe we'll see something about it in the paper tomorrow."

"Maybe. Dinner's ready."

He washed up and returned to the table. He opened a beer and poured a thick stream of molasses over his cornbread before digging in. "Your cornbread is damn near as good as your mama's these days. Beans is good too."

Anza nodded and smiled. He said the same thing about everything she cooked. She suspected one of her aunts or maybe Mrs. Cardenas must have impressed upon him the importance of complimenting her cooking, even when it was the same cornbread and beans a five-year-old could make.

"Any more word about the layoffs?" she asked, spearing a cube of beef hidden among the beans. The sight of the meat made her think of the bloody hail, and she hesitated.

Dad shrugged. "Same gloom and doom, as always. There'll be layoffs. That's for sure. I mean, hell, they're converting the Copper Queen mine into a tourist attraction. God forbid we actually keep producing things in this country."

Anza frowned. "Why would anyone want to go on vacation to a mine?" She looked at his hands and the calluses permanently ingrained with dirt and grime no matter how well he scrubbed. She remembered the handful of cave-ins and scares, when she'd held her breath until she got word that he wasn't among the dead.

He snorted. "Who knows? East Coasters, I imagine. Those folks never have any sense. Anyway, Copper Queen's not gonna be hiring anytime soon, unless you think I'd be a good tour guide. Heh. But maybe if they get this new open-pit mine up and running before too long—"

The phone rang. Dad dabbed his mouth with a napkin and went to answer it. Anza stared at her plate, hoping it wasn't Fernando calling. He usually called every night, if she didn't call him first. She'd never given it much thought before, but now it occurred to her that it was almost always him who called her.

"Hang on a second. Anza?" Dad cupped his hand over the phone. "Anza, you seen the Garces kids today? Pablo or the girls?"

She frowned. "No. Last time I babysat was three days ago."

He nodded and turned away. "Bert, Anza says she ain't seen them for three days. Did you call the sheriff?" There was a long pause in which he just made little uh-huh and nuh-uh sounds. "Well, we'll be out to help in a few minutes. Don't you worry, Bert. I'm sure they just hid from the storm and they're scared to come out. Uh-huh. Bye."

"What's going on?" Anza asked as Dad came back to the table.

"Finish up your dinner. The Garces kids are missing. Bert and Maria need help searching."

She stood, food forgotten. "What happened?"

Dad sat in his chair and started lacing up his boots again. "Well, no one's sure, but Bert thinks they were out on the mesa when that hail hit." He bit his lip. "No one's seem 'em since."

THE DRIVEWAY OF THE Garceses' house was already packed with cars and trucks by the time Anza and Dad got there. Anza caught sight of the sheriff's car, two deputies leaning aimlessly against the side. Sheriff Brandt stood near a cluster of men and women holding flashlights, pointing at something out on the rocky mesa.

Fernando's beanpole frame emerged from the crowd, his parents trailing behind him. Anza's heart sank, and she thought again of how often he called her, how tired the idea of talking to him made her feel. "Damn," she muttered.

"What? You and Fernando have a fight or something?" Dad climbed out of the truck and passed a lantern over to her.

"Not really. He just got on my nerves the other day."

"Well, you don't put up with nonsense, and teenage boys are pretty much nothing but." He raised his hand in response to a wave from Fernando's father, Mr. Cardenas. "Still, go easy on him. He's a good kid."

Anza stole a peek at Dad, imagining about how fast he would change his tune if he knew what was really going on.

"Sheriff says the kids were playing somewhere out on the mesa when the hail hit, near the edge of the property," Mrs. Cardenas said as Anza and Dad joined her in the crowd. "So we're supposed to walk a few feet apart and keep an eye out for any footprints or clothes or shoes or anything." She stole a glance over her shoulder. "Poor Roberto and Maria. They're just a wreck."

"I'm sure we'll find them," Dad said.

"Want to walk with me, Anza?" Fernando asked, giving her puppy-dog eyes, even with their parents standing a few feet away.

She swallowed the urge to snap at him. No sense blaming him for something that was just as much her fault as his. "Okay."

Everyone formed a ragged line behind the Garceses' house. Their property was the last one before the fringes of the town dissolved into a flat mesa stretching out across Cochise County and toward the New Mexico state line. A few ranches were scattered here and there, and if they went far enough, they would hit Interstate 80. Mostly, though, it was a whole lot of nothing between Galina and the Mexican border twenty miles to the south. Anza thought about Margarita, Luz, and Pablo out there, maybe hurt, maybe trapped. She swallowed and blinked fast.

"Okay, everyone," Sheriff Brandt called through his cupped hands. "Take it slow. Keep an eye out for anything that might belong to them. Call me over if you find something. Listen for them. And watch out for rattlers and holes in the ground. Last thing we need is someone getting bit or breaking a leg."

Maria Garces let out a wail, and Sheriff Brandt looked pained.

The searchers set out across the mesa. Anza kept her eyes on the ground, sweeping her lantern back and forth. The line began to drift apart almost right away. Despite the searchers' best efforts, boulders, arroyos, and patches of teddy bear cholla kept them from maintaining a straight line.

Fernando inched closer to Anza as they pulled away from their parents. "That was pretty crazy earlier, huh? That weird hail?"

"Yeah. Pretty crazy." Anza's heart leapt a little as she caught sight of something she thought was a snake, but it was only a half-buried stick.

"So, uh..." He glanced over his shoulder. "I know this isn't really the right time to ask, but you want to go to the drive-in tomorrow? I had a lot of fun last time." He smiled.

So had she. She'd thought about it for a week afterward, how good it had felt to straddle him, his hands under her shirt. Her orgasm had been so powerful, it made her dizzy. But also... "I don't know. You gonna forget to bring a rubber again?" she asked, and it came out meaner than she intended.

"I already said I was sorry about that. And we don't have to, you know, if you don't want. We could just see the movies." His lower lip pushed out in a pout as his eyes fixed on the ground.

Anza cringed at the hurt in his voice. She reached out to touch his arm. "Sorry, Nando. I'm tired. Sure, let's go to the drive-in."

He grinned at her, teeth white in the lantern light, and for some reason, him forgiving her that quickly made her want to cry. She focused on picking her way around a mesquite tree and between two stands of prickly pear cactus. The fruits were still small and green, a couple months off from ripening. Once they turned purple, there would be a flurry of harvesting and canning with the other women in town, making jam and candy and trying to keep the translucent little splinters from finding their way into her skin.

Someone hollered in the darkness. Anza whirled around and held up her lantern, trying to see where it had come from. Flashlight beams bounced and flared crazily across the mesa as people ran toward the sound.

"Stay back, everyone. Just stay back," Sheriff Brandt said as everyone converged on one spot.

Mrs. Cardenas stood stone-still, flashlight pointed at something on the ground. Murmured comments drifted back from the huddled crowd:

"Now, that don't make no sense."

"What in God's name..."

Anza stood on her tiptoes, trying to get a look. Finally, she just ducked between two men with lanterns and peered over the outline of Sheriff Brandt's hat as he knelt on the ground.

She clapped a hand over her mouth when she saw what lay in the dirt. She recognized that dress, those shoes, and the patched pair of boys' pants. The clothes of all three children rested on the ground. They weren't crumpled or piled up like they had been discarded. Instead, they lay flat in a neat row, shirts and dresses at the top, pants and shoes beneath them. They looked as though the children wearing them had gone to sleep on the ground and simply vanished, leaving their clothes behind.

Mrs. Garces fought her way through the crowd. As soon as she saw the clothes, she let out a shriek of grief, collapsing into her husband's arms. Her scream echoed across the mesa. On the very edge of Anza's hearing, a pack of coyotes howled in response, filling the night with the sound of fear.

# CHAPTER 4: 1960

Dove opened the door before Anza had a chance to knock. "Come in. Sooner we get started, the better." She led the way into the kitchen. "Your daddy going to be at work all day?"

Anza swallowed and nodded. She'd barely slept the night before, and her stomach had twisted into nervous knots on the walk over. She knew her hand would shake if she held it up. Now, though, she stood up straight and tried to sound as calm as Dove looked. "Yeah. I was worried he wasn't, because we've been out searching for the Garces kids all weekend. But he can't afford to skip work."

Dove filled the tea kettle with water and set it on the stove. While the kettle heated up, she measured a spoonful of white powder from a little brown jar into a cup. "Well, this'll be the third day. Can't imagine they'll be turning anything up at this point."

Anza stared at her, shocked. "You don't think they'll find them?"

"Not alive."

Don't say that, Anza almost said, but then she imagined how it would sound—like a little girl not ready to face the truth. "Well..." She folded her arms. "What do you think happened?"

Dove paused. "I think the world's full of terrible men who do terrible things, sometimes to children. There ain't much mystery to it." She fell silent until the kettle whistled. "Best thing to hope for now is that someone catches the bastard who took them and cuts his pecker off." She poured the water into the cup and motioned for Anza to go to the living room.

For a minute or two, Anza had been distracted enough by thoughts of the Garces children to set aside why she was there, but her hands trembled again, and her throat went dry as she sat gingerly on the edge of the sofa. She pressed her palms against her thighs to make them stay still.

"Now," Dove said, setting the cup on the coffee table. "Couple of things before you drink this. First of all, there's some risk. If you got a weak heart, it can make you sick. Palpitations and the like. Some women die, although not as many as those who go to some butcher with a knitting needle." Dove sat in the armchair, leaning her elbows on her knees and folding her hands. "Now, I've never had a girl get too sick yet. I've always got the dosage exactly right. Doesn't mean I won't mess up one of these days. So, think long and hard before you drink that."

Anza stared down into the steaming cup, thinking about Cindy Nelson. At sixteen, Cindy had been a rodeo queen, a shoo-in to win the state fair. At seventeen, she'd had a growing belly, a hasty wedding celebration, and a hollow-eyed look she'd carried around town ever since. Anza had never particularly liked Cindy Nelson, but something about the other girl haunted her every time they crossed paths.

She picked up the cup and chugged the hot liquid down as fast as she could. It didn't taste like much, just water with a little hint of bitter flavor underneath. Wiping her mouth on the back of her hand, she asked, "Now what?"

Dove put her feet up on the coffee table and fished a pair of reading glasses out of her shirt pocket. "Now, we wait. I'll take your pulse and respiration every half hour, but if it does what it's supposed to, then you should start to cramp and bleed before too long." She gestured toward the bathroom with one hand and picked up a book with the other. "I've got sanitary towels in there for when the bleeding starts. Let me know when it does. Meantime, pick a book."

Anza couldn't imagine settling in to read a book right now. Already, she searched her body for the first hints of cramping, like the familiar pulling ache in her pelvis. Nothing. She wondered how badly it would hurt when it started. She thought about asking but decided she'd already swallowed the stuff, so there wasn't much point in asking more questions.

She got up and went to one of the shelves, intending to grab a book at random so she could hold it up in front of her face and pretend to read. But she soon found herself intrigued by the titles and the cover illustrations. Half of one shelf was full of crumbling magazines, their cheap covers showing lurid scenes of rocket ships and tentacled creatures reaching for women in scanty golden armor. They had titles like *Astounding Science Fiction* and *Planet Stories*.

"You got a nephew or something?" Anza asked, holding up one of the magazines.

"No, Miss Smart Mouth. Those are mine. And if you had any taste, you'd give them a try."

"They look a little silly to me."

"Oh yeah?" Dove glanced up and pointed. "Top shelf, fifth book from the left. Take a look at that one."

Anza stared at the cover: *I, Robot* by Isaac Asimov. She and Fernando had seen a B-movie about robots at the drive-in one time. It had been ridiculous. Still, she took the book back to the couch and flipped it open.

She expected to get bored right away or to be too nervous to read at all, but within a couple of pages, she found herself pulled in. When Dove reached down to touch her arm, she started and blinked in surprise at how much time had gone by.

Dove held her fingers against Anza's wrist for a moment, staring into space, before picking up a stethoscope from the side table. "Breathe normally. Now deep breath. Good." The cold metal of the stethoscope felt like a coin resting just over Anza's heart.

"You're doing fine so far," Dove said, setting aside the stethoscope. "How you feeling?"

Anza paused, trying to listen to her body. The trembling in her hands had subsided, along with the nervous twisting in her stomach. "My back aches a little."

"Good. Won't be long now."

Anza went back to the book, wanting to see what happened to the little girl and her robot nanny. She'd just finished the first story when she felt the pain in her abdomen. Wetness between her legs followed a moment later. "Ow. Think something's happening. Ow!"

Dove smoothly rose and helped Anza to her feet. "Okay, darling, don't worry. Let's just get you to the bathroom."

A FEW HOURS LATER, Anza sat on the toilet and tried to take deep breaths. Her face felt clammy with sweat, but the pain in her gut seemed to be easing. Dove tapped on the door and came into the bathroom. Anza looked up at her, beyond embarrassment over being seen sitting on the toilet and naked from the waist down.

Dove set a glass on the edge of the sink. "Brought you some sun tea with lots of sugar. It'll help with the wooziness."

Anza managed to take a few sips. "I think it's getting a little better."

Dove nodded. "Worst part's over. And now you got your whole life ahead of you." She fixed her with a flat stare. "So no mucking it up, young lady."

Anza laughed for some reason she didn't really understand, a laugh that went weepy at the edges. "Yes, ma'am."

They waited a while longer, until Anza was a little steadier on her feet. Then Dove helped her into the truck to drive her home. Leaning back in her seat, Anza thought about the last time she was in the truck, everything around them still stained red after the hail. The red had faded overnight, and by morning, there was no sign it had happened.

As the truck slowed and pulled over to the side of the road, Anza opened her eyes, expecting to see her house. Instead, they sat on a bridge about halfway between Dove's property and her own, a spot overlooking a shallow sand wash that sometimes flooded when it rained. Dove stared past her, through the passenger window. "Anza, do you see that, or am I just losing my mind?"

Anza peered out the window. At first, she didn't understand what Dove was talking about. Then she looked at the big rock formation looming over the wash. "Oh, sweet Jesus," she gasped, opening the door and stepping out of the truck.

There, on the top of the rock formation, stood the three Garces children. They were naked and completely covered in mud, but Anza recognized them, all the same.

"Luz!" she shouted, trying to find a place to climb over the guardrail and down into the wash. "Pablo! Are you okay? Get down from there!"

The children didn't move or even acknowledge her. They stared straight ahead, hands hanging loosely at their sides.

"Hey! Can you hear me?" Anza waved, but they didn't respond.

Dove reached the boulder before Anza did. She paused, peering up, hands on her hips. "You know what troubles me about this, besides the obvious?" she asked, voice pensive.

"What?" Anza winced as she picked her way across the rocky ground. Each step made her back hurt worse.

"How do you suppose they got up there?"

Anza stopped. It took her a moment to see what Dove was getting at. The boulder was perhaps ten feet tall. One side formed a sheer drop into the sand wash below. The other side was almost straight up and down, with just the tiniest crevices one could use for handholds. Anza didn't think she would be able to get halfway up.

Circling around, she saw that the other two sides were almost as bad, with no large grips and very little slope leading up to the top. She could imagine a skilled, strong climber making it up the side of the rock, maybe, but the oldest of the kids was eight. The youngest was only four. And as for carrying the kids up to the top, she couldn't imagine anyone pulling that off.

Dove shielded her eyes from the sun. "If I didn't know better, I'd almost say they were dropped down onto this thing from the sky."

ANZA DIDN'T WANT TO leave the kids, but they couldn't find a way to get them down. And then, as Dove reminded her, they had their story to consider.

"Can't very well say I was driving you home when we saw them," she said. "One time, you taking shelter with me, that's plausible, but two times is fishy." In the end, Dove drove her home and used the house's phone to call the sheriff. If anyone asked, they would say Anza was home all day and that Dove just stopped at the house to use the phone after she found the kids.

Anza waited, biting her fingernails, until she saw the sheriff's car and the volunteer fire truck fly past the house, sirens blaring. Then she walked the ten minutes down the road to join the crowd of gawkers. Her belly still ached, and she had to swallow down moments of nausea, but she needed to see what had happened to the kids. The firemen had already managed to get Luz down when Anza arrived. The little girl stood motionless next to the fire truck, making no move to grip the blanket draped around her shoulders.

"Anza, did you hear? They found all three of them just sitting on top of that rock. They ain't said a word," said Maggie Jenkins, from two houses over.

Anza nodded, unable to take her eyes off Luz. She'd seen from the ground that the girl was muddy, but she got a better look at how thick it was. It wasn't like she had fallen or even rolled in mud. It was caked on, inches thick, and her short curly hair was clotted with it. Even stranger, it still seemed fresh, just beginning to dry and crack in the sun. The last storm had been three days ago. The water left over from the red deluge had long since been sucked into the baked earth of the mesa.

One of the volunteers got Pablo over his shoulder and started back down the ladder. The boy hung like a sack of laundry. Margarita was the same when they pulled her down—as limp as a rag doll until they set her back on her feet.

Anza caught sight of Dove. A little removed from the crowd, she was speaking to Sheriff Brandt in a low voice while he scribbled in a black notebook. She didn't spare a glance in Anza's direction.

A truck screeched to a halt at the edge of the crowd, kicking up a cloud of dust. Mr. and Mrs. Garces jumped out and ran to their children. Mrs. Garces was already weeping. They swept their children up into fierce hugs, demanding to know what had happened, where they had been, and whether they were all right. Anza blinked away tears, a mysterious sharp sadness welling up in her chest.

"Why aren't you talking? Luz! Margarita!" Mrs. Garces shook them while her husband turned to one of the firefighters, someone Anza didn't recognize, probably from Bisbee.

"What's wrong with them? Have they said anything?"

The firefighter assured him that the doctor was on his way and that they would be taken to the hospital shortly. Then Mrs. Garces gasped and stood up. It took Anza a moment to understand what she had seen—or, more accurately, what she'd heard.

The children spoke. Even from a distance, just seeing their lips moving without hearing the words, Anza could tell they were speaking in unison. She took a few steps closer just as the rest of the crowd fell silent and backed away.

"Sky. Blue. Air. Cielo. Azul."

A shiver ran up Anza's spine. She couldn't stop herself from shrinking away from the children. Their voices were just so lifeless, so robotic. She searched their faces for some hint of the personalities she knew so well, but there was nothing.

The three children kept going, naming the dirt, the plants, and the people around them in a slow monotone. A car pulled up, and Doc Allen climbed out. He had a snowy-white beard and deep lines creasing his forehead, as though he'd frowned so much, his face had just decided to stay that way.

He knelt in the dirt near the kids, not seeming to care about getting dust on his suit pants. He flashed a light in their eyes, scraped away enough mud to take pulses, and held their hands up in the air, nodding when their arms fell back to their sides. He acted like the crowd wasn't even there. After a minute of checking the kids, he turned to Mr. and Mrs. Garces. "We'd better get them to the hospital. They aren't hurt or ill, as far as I can tell, but we need to run more tests."

The parents nodded, Mrs. Garces wiping her tears away with a handkerchief. One of the firemen helped them and Doc Allen move the kids into the car. As they moved to put Pablo in the back seat, they passed Mrs. Edmonds and her daughter, Tracey. The girl was about twelve, Anza thought, a few years behind her in school. She stood watching with wide eyes, her mother's hands gripping her shoulders. Just as Pablo passed Tracey, his hand shot out to grip her wrist. She jumped and let out a little gasp. Then his hand hung slackly at his side again, as though it had never happened. However, even after the kids were bundled into the car and Doc Allen had driven away and the crowd began to wander back to their homes, Anza still saw the faint outline of a muddy handprint on Tracey's freckled skin.

CHAPTER 5: 2020

"So. How's the post-move-in cleanup?" Val handed Alonzo the chart for the first case of the day.

"Finally done, I think. It took more than a week. And Colin did most of it, poor guy." He scanned through the chart. "Oh, for god's sake, he ate *another* bath mat? Come on, Boogie."

"Yup. And corgis are usually so smart." She laughed. "Anyway, word of advice, from when me and Amal first moved in together: keep the living room neutral. Someone starts making the main part of the house their own, there will be blood."

"I'll keep that in mind." It seemed like everyone he talked to lately had some new piece of sage cohabitation advice. But so far, it seemed so easy, so comfortable, that it was hard to take seriously all the warnings about how dirty dishes and bathroom towels could become a minefield. "Okay, let's get Boogie in for x-rays, see if we need to open him up or if he can pass it on his own."

"Will do." Val grimaced. "You might want to go talk to his mom, though. She's pretty worked up."

"Okay." He checked his watch. "I'll go calm her down. Tess can get started with the new cat in room two, and I'll try to catch up."

Boogie's mom, a blond woman in her early thirties named Annie, waited in the exam room.

"Let's go, Boogie," Val said. He trotted over to her, appearing pretty cheerful for just having consumed his weight in terrycloth.

"Dr. Cardenas." Annie sniffed. Her eyes were red. "I just can't believe he did it again!"

Alonzo stifled a laugh. "I know, but he's looking pretty good right now, and we might not have to do surgery this time."

"I thought if I switched to the less fuzzy bathmat, he wouldn't be as interested." She dabbed at her eyes with a Kleenex.

"Well, sometimes, they just get their mind on something, and we don't know why. But we're going to do some x-rays, and then we'll go from there. Just try not to—"

Blink.

Alonzo lay on his back, staring up at the examination room's fluorescent ceiling lights. Someone screamed hysterically off to his right. A figure leaned over him. He squinted, and Val's face came into focus.

"Doc? Lonzo, you with me?" She turned and spoke to someone behind her. "I think he's coming around."

"Whoa, whoa, what happened?" He sat up. Val tried to push him back down, keep him from getting to his feet, but he waved her off. "Did I fall or something?"

Val hesitated. Tess dashed into the room. "Ambulance is out front."

"Ambulance? No, no, I'm fine." He glanced around until he found the source of the high-pitched wails. "Annie, are you okay?"

She stood pressed into a corner, face streaked with fresh tears. She nodded, but her eyes were wide with terror. An odd flush of shame came over Alonzo. He didn't think he'd ever inspired that kind of fear in another person.

"Hey, Tess, you want to take Boogie's mom back out to the waiting room?" Val asked.

"Yeah. Come on, Annie."

Alonzo turned back to Val. "What happened?"

She bit her lip. "I'm not really sure. It seemed like some kind of seizure. You contorted into this weird position. You weren't responsive."

"A weird position?" His stomach clenched. "Like a statue?"

"Weirdest damn statue I've ever seen, but yeah. You were kind of... I don't know, on one foot, twisted around. I didn't mean to knock you over, but I was trying to wake you up, and—"

Two paramedics walked in.

"I'm fine," he said before they had a chance to say a word. "Really. False alarm."

"*Not* a false alarm." Val turned to them. "He was unresponsive for four minutes, by my count."

Alonzo refused to go in the ambulance, but he finally agreed to let them take his vitals.

"Everything looks normal here, but you need to go to the hospital if you lost consciousness," one of them said as he pulled off the blood pressure cuff.

"I will. I'll get someone to take me later." He smiled and tried to act like he meant it. "Seriously. I'll call my doctor."

Once they'd finally left and he'd confirmed that the other vets could cover his patients for the day, he called Colin. "Hey, listen, I'm not feeling so hot. Think you can pick me up?"

After he hung up, he looked up to find Val staring at him with her arms folded.

"'Not feeling so hot'?" she asked.

He sighed. "I'm gonna tell him, just not over the phone. I don't want to freak him out."

"Dudes. I swear to God." She sighed. "Okay, you good until Colin gets here? I gotta go check on Boogie."

"Yeah, yeah, I'm good. Go."

Alonzo sat in the empty exam room, waiting for Colin to arrive. He couldn't stop thinking about one of the questions Colin had asked on the day they met. They'd spoken on the phone before then and communicated by email. Colin had been seeking interview subjects, former residents of Galina or people related to them. Alonzo had figured it couldn't hurt to give some sociologist an hour of his time to answer questions about Grandfather Fernando. They'd met at the Epic Café, the favored hangout for hippies and university professors.

The moment Alonzo laid eyes on Colin, he wished they were there to talk about something other than his grandfather. But he answered the questions, managing to slip in one or two of his own to get a feel for what Colin was like.

"So what about the Statue Disease? What do you remember him saying about that?" Colin asked about twenty minutes into the discussion.

"Well, it came after the Naming Disease. I know that." He tried to remember. Grandfather Fernando didn't like to talk about Galina much. Most of the stories about the Galina Plagues came out when he'd had a few drinks or when he reminisced about some older family member. "The first time he saw anyone Statue—he always called it 'Statuing,' like a verb—was at some kind of town meeting. I'm not sure who it was. But he said it was like watching someone who was possessed. I remember one time he said he'd never really heard of demonic possession when he was younger. People talked about the devil but not possession, you know? I think he saw *The Exorcist* when it first came out, and it made him start to think about the Plagues in those terms."

Colin sighed and nodded. "Yeah, it's a real shame no one took interviews right after it happened. Or during. The last fifty years of horror movies have really contaminated memories of it. Just trying to disaggregate—"

Alonzo hadn't really listened carefully after that. He had just watched Colin talk, charmed by the unselfconscious, geeky tangent.

It was a warm memory, one Alonzo had revisited over and over since then. But now, that word, *possession*, coiled around it, like a dark cloud passing before the sun.

"HEY, MOM," SONIA SAID, tucking her phone against her shoulder and trying to maneuver her keys into the lock without dropping the grocery bag.

"Hi, sweetie. I'm almost there. What's going on?"

"Not much." She shoved the door open with a shoulder, dropped the groceries on the countertop, and checked to make sure Dylan had followed her inside. "Listen, the guys wanted to put in some extra time at practice before our gig on Friday. Think you could stay with Dylan until eight o'clock?"

"Oh, of course, no problem." She said that now, but Sonia knew she was sure to find some fault with the house, probably something that wasn't clean enough, and she would have plenty to say at the end of the evening. Still, it was better than paying for a sitter.

"Thanks, I appreciate it. See you soon."

"Grandma's coming over?" Dylan asked, opening the fridge.

"Hey, no snacks. It's almost dinnertime," she said, even though the kid was so scrawny, she couldn't really see the logic behind denying him calories. Dylan's pediatricians just always told her no snacking between meals.

He closed the fridge door without a fight. She cleared her throat, trying to sound casual. "Hey, Dylan. Something I want to talk to you about. Remember that thing that happened the other day? When you blacked out for a bit?"

He nodded. "You too."

"Right. So, I'd like it if you didn't mention that to Grandma."

Dylan frowned. His dad's features showed when he did that. Of course, Denny had rarely had any expression other than bafflement, whereas Dylan actually comprehended things most of the time. "How come?"

"Because," she said, ripping open a box of mac and cheese, "Grandma gets worked up about stuff. And even though we went to the doctor and we know everything's cool, she'd still freak out." As she said it, Sonia wondered if it counted as a lie. The doctors hadn't really given them a clean bill of health but more of a shrug and a "let's wait and see." But there was no reason to worry Dylan with that.

"Yeah," he said with a solemn nod. "Like when I cut my toe, and she screamed."

"Right. Just like that. She's not chill, not like us."

"Okay. But what if she did it too?"

Sonia frowned. "What if she did what?"

"What if she did the naming thing too? I did, and you're my mom, and you did it at the same time, and she's *your* mom, so maybe she did too." He gave her a crooked smile, revealing gaps in his teeth like a jack-o'-lantern. He was shy about how smart he was, but every now and then, he got those little glimmers of pride when he pieced something together, when he got to a thought faster than Sonia did.

"I don't think so." She turned on the burner and poured the macaroni into the pot. It did make her wonder, though, the way she'd been wondering ever since it happened. Something Dylan had said was familiar, something about...

Naming.

Sonia stopped, hand on the cabinet door. Naming. That was one of the things Grandpa Richie used to talk about before he died, one of those bullshit stories he'd told about how a witch had cursed his hometown when he was a younger man. There'd been something about banishment, too, something about how there would be another curse on him if he ever went back...

She tried to remember the details. There was a whole summer of weird shit. The naming thing, then something about the coyotes around the town, and freaky bugs no one had ever seen before, then—

Someone knocked on the door. She jumped, and the thought was gone.

"Hey, Mom," she said, opening the door.

"Hey, Sweetie." Mom stepped inside and set down her purse, a gust of dusty summer air chasing her into the air conditioning. "Ooh, it's warm. Honey, when are you going to get rid of those bangs? You have such pretty features, and you hide them under those bangs and that black eyeliner—"

"And the new land-speed record for unwanted criticism goes to Marnie Rollins. Woo! Go Marnie!" Sonia mock-applauded as Dylan bounced into the room.

"I'm not criticizing. I just—"

"Hey, Mom. You remember those stories Grandpa Richie used to tell about those plagues?"

"The Galina Plagues? A little. Most of what I know, I heard from your father. You know I never got along with his folks."

"Yeah, because Grandpa Richie was an asshole."

Mom glared and gestured at Dylan.

"Sorry," Sonia said. "A butthole. But I was just wondering, you remember anything about it?"

"Like what?" Mom parked herself at her usual spot at the dining room table, where she could see the TV in the living room but could also keep an eye on the stove.

"I don't know. Anything. I'm just curious."

"Well, you know someone's writing a book about it. I told you about that."

Sonia shrugged. "I don't know."

"Oh, you remember. Last year, someone from down in Tucson, some new professor at the university, he called about interviewing us. But then, of course, your father was the only one who knew Richie well enough to know anything about that time, so..."

"That time?"

"The summer when everyone went crazy."

"Can you send me his name?"

Mom blinked. "Who?"

"The professor. The guy writing the book," Sonia said, forcing herself not to snap. Sometimes, she wondered who had the shorter attention span, Mom or Dylan.

Mom laughed. "I think a university professor has better things to do than talk about our family tree."

"I'm not... Just send it to me, please, okay, because I asked, and it would be nice?" Sonia stopped before she said anything else, taking a deep breath and silently counting to five.

Mom pulled out her phone. "Fine, fine, I'm doing it. You get so worked up about things. I'm sure I've got the email somewhere in here. I just need to find it..."

Sonia decided she'd better leave before she lost patience and snatched Mom's phone away to find the name herself. She pulled Dylan into a hug. "Love you. Be back in a bit."

She opened up the to-do list on her phone as she made her way down the driveway. It was maddeningly long, with bulleted and starred items about the dentist, an oil change, and new soccer shoes for Dylan. She sighed and added yet another bullet point: *Call professor re: plagues.* The sight of the entry made her laugh for a moment, until she remembered the twenty other items above it. Then she got into her car and sped away, already late for practice.

CHAPTER 6: 1960

"**A**nza!" Fernando waved from the sidewalk in front of the ice cream parlor.

Anza hesitated for only a moment before waving back. The cramping had passed, and she was only bleeding a little, which Dove had said was normal. Still, seeing Fernando seemed to make her more aware of it on some level.

"Tracey said you were there when they pulled the Garces kids down from that rock," he said as she sat down next to him. He immediately took her hand in his own. On Fernando's other side sat Paula and David, who had been sweethearts so long, everyone assumed they would get married as soon as they graduated high school. Beyond them sat Consuela and Mark, who had managed to parlay their parents' mild disapproval into a tale of forbidden love they shared with anyone who listened. Anza wondered how other people talked about her and Fernando when she couldn't hear. *Probably the same way they talk about Paula and David: as a married couple in the making.* She grimaced at the thought.

"Yeah, I saw them. They were covered in mud." Anza gazed out at the familiar sight of Main Street. The businesses were the same ones that had been here for her entire life: the general store, the saloon, Millie's Café, the cantina, the ice cream shop, the hardware store, Joe's Feed and Tack, the bank, and the dress shop. Most of the buildings had a worn, dusty exterior years overdue for a fresh coat of paint.

"Is it true they were speaking in tongues?" Paula asked, leaning around Fernando.

Anza frowned. "I don't think so. I mean, they were saying things but real words. Isn't speaking in tongues just gobbledygook?"

"No!" Paula said, eyes widening as though she'd heard something scandalous. "It's the language of heaven. People speak it when they've been touched by God. My Aunt Madge used to speak in tongues sometimes."

"Huh." Anza stared out at the street again. Paula and her family went to the evangelical church on the edge of town. The handful of times Dad had taken Anza to church, they'd gone to the Catholic one on Galina's south side. She didn't really understand the difference between the two, except Mass was in Latin, and priests couldn't marry. It didn't really matter, though, because she didn't think Dad believed in any of it. She was beginning to think she didn't, either.

"Anyone heard anything about the Garces kids? Anything new, I mean?" Anza asked.

"My mom said she heard they came home from the hospital. But she didn't know if they were still crazy," Consuela volunteered.

Anza decided to bring them some food. It would be a nice thing to do, but it would also give her a chance to see if the kids were any different.

The conversation eventually drifted away from the Garces kids, moving on to the subject of what to do with their Friday night. Mark thought he could get his brother to loan him his car so they could drive over to Bisbee for a triple date. But none of them could agree about what to do once they got there.

"Maybe we can get someone to go into the liquor store for us," Fernando said.

Paula rolled her eyes. "We don't need to go to Bisbee to drink. I can always take some of Mama's gin. She'll never notice. Why can't we go to the diner? They always have the best music."

The discussion came to an abrupt halt as Fernando's mother pulled up in the family truck. "Fernando, get in. We're going home.

You, too, Anza." Mrs. Cardenas looked even more severe than usual, her hair pulled into a bun, her mouth pressed into a flat line.

She knows, Anza thought, blood turning to ice water. Mrs. Cardenas loved her and had been nudging her and Fernando toward each other since they were children, but that would all change if she knew Anza wasn't such a good girl after all.

"But, Mama, it's only seven thirty." Fernando released Anza's hand and pointed at the watch on his wrist as though it would change her mind.

"Don't argue with me, *mijo*," she said snappishly.

Anza stood, slowly, hearing the fear in the woman's voice.

"And the rest of you, go home. It's not safe to be out on the streets right now."

"Why? What happened, Mrs. Cardenas?" Paula asked.

She hesitated as though unsure how much to tell them. "Two other kids are sick with the same thing the Garces kids have. The Edmonds girl and her best friend. Now, all of you, go home. I mean it."

THERE WERE FIVE MORE cases over the next two days. Dad kept Anza at home, hoping she wouldn't catch whatever it was. But then his friends Doug Collins and George Esquivel came by for a beer, and Doug talked about the way the Costello kids and Francisco Gallardo's youngest had come down with it.

"And they ain't been anywhere near the Garces kids or Tracey Edmonds. So it can't be just from touch." He shook his head and took a long pull on his beer. "I'm telling you, there was something in that hail. Must have gotten in our water. Been scared to let my kids drink from the tap, but where the hell else am I supposed to get water?"

Dad nodded with agreement then shook his head at the madness of it all.

Anza hovered near the doorway between the kitchen and the living room, eavesdropping on the conversation as she dried the dishes. Dad noticed but didn't admonish her. George Esquivel didn't contribute much to the conversation, just nodding along with Doug and Dad and throwing in the occasional remark. He caught sight of her in the kitchen and smiled at one point, making her face heat up. George was handsome in a way high-school-age boys just weren't—strong and steady, with laugh lines and a touch of gray in his hair. She'd started noticing George like that a couple years ago, and she liked watching him even though she knew full well he still saw her as a little girl.

I can't wait to be the same age as grown men, she thought wistfully, turning back to the sink.

Still, even with George as a distraction, Anza kept listening in on Doug's talk about who was getting the sickness and where they'd been and where the hail had come from. "Gotta be the Russians. Gotta be."

"What would the Russians want with Galina?" Dad snorted. "They have a superweapon, it's gonna be over Washington or New York or someplace like that."

"No. See, that's what people would *expect* them to do. So instead, they start in some little town, and by the time it spreads, it's too late."

"I think if the Russkies wanted to kill us with a disease, they'd have picked something a heck of a lot worse than this," George said in his tobacco-scratched voice. "Ever seen typhus? If typhus had started two weeks ago, we wouldn't still be sitting around to talk about it."

The conversation rambled on in circular arguments about what it was, what it might be, and who had heard what. They stopped having anything new to say after a while, but they couldn't seem to move on to anything else. Anza kept listening, but it slowly dawned on her that she would have to search somewhere else if she wanted to know what was really happening.

As soon as Doug and George left, she said, "I want to take some food over to the Garces family tomorrow. Seems like the right thing to do."

Dad hesitated, running a hand over the rusty stubble on his chin. "Folks in town been saying we should keep the kids inside..."

"You heard Doug. That didn't help those others. Besides, I was there when they pulled the kids down. Pablo passed right by me, so no sense keeping me cooped up now."

It took a little cajoling, but Dad finally agreed. The next day, she dropped him off at work and took the truck to the Garceses' place.

Mrs. Garces answered after two knocks. She looked terrible, with dark circles under her eyes and flyaway strands escaping from her braid.

"Hello, Mrs. Garces," Anza said, holding up a pot. "I thought I'd bring by some food."

"Oh..." Her hands fluttered around her face as she opened the screen door. "Oh, you are such a sweet girl." She sounded exhausted, her voice trembling as though she were on the verge of tears.

"It's nothing," Anza said, embarrassed. "Just machaca and corn-bread, nothing special."

"No, it's just... Everyone else has been afraid to come by. Except Father Santiago. Come in, please."

"How are they?" Anza asked as she set the food next to the stove.

The house felt stuffy, and the countertops were greasy and cluttered. The curtains were all drawn, giving the place a cave-like feel.

"Better," Mrs. Garces said. "They... It comes and goes. One minute, they'll be completely normal, just playing, and the next—" Her face contorted for a moment. "Oh god. It's like there are different people speaking through them."

"What did the doctors say?"

Mrs. Garces rolled her eyes. "Oh, they did so many tests. They said there was nothing wrong with them. Nothing... Nothing had been done to them. They weren't given any drugs. I just don't know, Anza."

"Do you mind if I see them?" Anza asked.

Mrs. Garces smiled. "Oh, I think they'd like that." She led the way into the girls' room. Luz and Margarita were kneeling on the floor, playing with their dolls and toy ponies like nothing was amiss.

"Anza!" Luz jumped up and gave her a hug. "Are you here to babysit us again?"

"Not today, sweetie," Anza said, patting her on the back. "How are you feeling?"

"Bored. We're not allowed to go outside."

Pablo appeared in the doorway. "Yeah. We've been inside all week."

"It's just until you get better," Mrs. Garces said.

Pablo rolled his eyes. "I'm *fine*."

But then Margarita sat up straight, eyes unfocused. "Wall. Wallpaper. Blanket. Bed. Wood."

The rest of the room froze, and Margarita's voice seemed louder than it should have been. Anza avoided Mrs. Garces's eyes, unsure where to look. Her heart thumped, even though she wouldn't have been able to say exactly what about the girl's words frightened her.

Margarita said one last word and stopped. She blinked once and seemed to notice everyone watching her. "What? Was I doing it again?"

Mrs. Garces stared at her daughter, something like pain in her expression. Anza understood why. It made the hair stand up on the back of Anza's neck.

"I better go," she said after a moment. "But if you need me to babysit again, Mrs. Garces, just give me a call."

"Thank you, Anza. I will." Mrs. Garces looked like she was about to say something else, but then she just nodded once and led Anza to the door.

Anza stood in the front yard, staring up at the house. It'd felt wrong in there, like there was something rotting she couldn't quite smell. For a moment, she almost knocked on the door again so she could insist on babysitting, letting Mrs. Garces get out of the house for a while at least. In the end, she just sighed and went back to the truck.

MEN WERE JUST STARTING to file out the front gates when Anza pulled up near the entrance to the mine. Dad caught sight of her idling in the dirt lot but didn't wave. He heaved a sigh as he climbed in and slammed the door.

"Everything okay?" she asked, putting the truck in gear.

For a moment, he just stared down at the hard hat on his lap. At last, he said, "It's not just kids."

"What's not just kids?"

He wiped his forehead. "The Naming Disease. Today, we were setting some dynamite, and Carlo Paredes just stopped and started... just naming things."

Anza watched him for as long as she dared before turning back to the road. "You sure it was the same thing?"

"I tell you, Anza, it made my blood run cold. You told me what it was like, with the Garces kids, but I didn't realize... It scared the be-jeezus out of me. I'm not ashamed to admit it." He paused. "And not just me, neither. Couple of the guys down there, before, they were saying it was just kids causing a fuss. Girls wanting attention and the like. Hell, even Carlo was saying that. But that was real. I could feel it."

They fell silent for the rest of the drive. As soon as they got home, Anza set about serving up the stew she'd put in the Crock-Pot earlier in the day. She'd just set some biscuits in the oven to heat up when the phone rang.

Dad answered. "Hello? Well, hey there, Carmen."

Anza looked up. Carmen was Mrs. Cardenas's first name. Dad glanced over at her, frowning. "Anza? She seems just fine. No, none of that. Well... Oh, my, I'm so sorry. Is he okay? No, not yet. I'll let her know. You need anything, you just call, hear? Bye now."

"What?" Anza asked as he set the phone back in its cradle.

He wiped his mouth. "That was Carmen. Fernando just started Naming."

CHAPTER 7: 2020

"Sorry about all this," Alonzo whispered.

"Sorry? What are you sorry about?" Colin asked.

"We've barely lived together two weeks, and you're spending half your time in hospitals and waiting rooms. It's like I was keeping my shit together just long enough to trick you into signing the lease." He smiled as he said it, but there was real guilt behind his words.

"Don't. Don't do that." Colin squeezed his hand tighter. "I want to be here."

He had seen Alonzo Statue for the first time two days ago, on the living room couch, and it had scared him so badly, he'd almost screamed. Before that, he'd nearly managed to convince himself that he was projecting the similarities to the Galina Plagues onto symptoms that didn't really fit at all. But as soon as he'd seen Alonzo's body contorted on the couch, as still as stone, he'd known it was exactly what all those Galina survivors had described. They'd told it the same way, over and over again, interview after interview. And still, he hadn't really understood until he saw it firsthand.

Someone came to prep Alonzo for the fMRI. They let Colin stay behind the glass to watch. Alonzo waved once before rolling into the big white tube like something out of *2001*.

Colin watched the screens, trying to see some pattern in the roiling colors. Some big red arrow labeled "Danger." It all just looked like the same vaguely blobby set of colors he'd seen in pictures of brain scans.

"Huh." One of the techs said, staring down at the screen. "Alonzo, can you tilt your head just a little farther back for this next one?"

Silence.

"Alonzo? Just a little more than that."

"Wait," Colin said. "Is his foot..."

Alonzo's foot, sticking out from beneath the edge of a sheet, twisted at an odd angle, almost backward.

One of the techs rushed into the room as the machine rolled Alonzo back out of the tube. He stared straight up, face blank, arms intertwined across his chest.

"This is what those seizures looked like, before?" the other tech asked Colin.

He numbly wondered what she must see every day, to be so calm right now. Mouth dry, he answered, "Yeah."

She raised her eyebrows and gestured at the screen. "Well, this might just be our lucky day. I think we may have gotten a picture of it."

"THIS IS... WELL, IT'S definitely interesting." The neurologist looked exactly the way Alonzo had always pictured distinguished doctors, tall and gray-haired with a neatly trimmed beard.

"Is it epilepsy?" Colin asked, his leg bouncing the way it always did when he was nervous.

"Um. Well, we can't rule anything out, but this scan isn't of an epileptic seizure. We'd see totally different electrical activity if that were the case."

"So what kind of activity do you see here?" Alonzo asked. He waited for the words he'd been dreading ever since they'd started doing tests, things he'd read about without telling Colin. Atrophy, degrading neurons, plaques...

The doctor frowned. "This isn't very precise, since we didn't do any other questions or tests to establish a baseline, but honestly, this looks like the kind of activity you see in someone accessing visual memories." He turned to his computer and pulled up several images. "Here. This is what we'd expect to see during an epileptic seizure," he said, pointing to a glowing yellow storm on one side of the brain. "And then here..." He clicked some more. "Here's someone being asked to remember something visual, like a movie or a picture. And right next to it, here's yours."

Alonzo leaned forward and peered at the side-by-side images. His human anatomy was rusty, but it was close enough to other mammalian brains to know he was looking at the visual cortex. The side-by-side images were a little different, but both had a butterfly-shaped red glow blooming out across the scan. It had coherent boundaries, nothing like the burst of activity on the image of the epileptic seizure.

"So..." Colin frowned. "You're saying he was remembering something he'd seen, while he was doing that?"

"Not necessarily, but that's my best guess. I'm doing a study on glaucoma patients and visual memory retrieval, so this looks pretty familiar to me." The neurologist hesitated. "My suggestion is that we keep running tests to rule out some other possible seizure disorders. But in the meantime, I'd also like to refer you to a psychologist."

Alonzo felt Colin tense next to him. "You think they might be psychosomatic?"

Out of the corner of his eye, he saw Colin open his mouth. Alonzo put a hand on his knee, shaking his head once.

"It's possible," the doctor said. "I'm not saying that's what I think. I'm just saying we need to look at all the options."

"Okay," Alonzo said. "I'll take the referral."

"SORRY FOR THE WAIT." The doctor sat across from Sonia and Dylan, flipping over a piece of paper on a clipboard.

"No worries. What did you find?" Sonia asked.

After a moment, the doctor said, "The CT scan, EKG, MRI, and blood work all came back normal."

"So that's good, right?" Sonia asked.

Dylan fidgeted in his chair, his foot kicking the desk.

"Well, it rules some things out. But more than one unexplained seizure is definitely a concern, so we have some more exploring to do. The last incident was two days ago, correct?"

Sonia nodded and swallowed. "That's right." She still struggled to keep her voice level and her face placid when she remembered it. She knew it would only scare Dylan if he saw her panicking, but the memory of walking into his room and seeing him frozen into a twisted pose brought the sickly tang of adrenaline up into her throat.

"Then that makes several incidents in a two-week period. Definitely something we need to look into more." She leaned forward and smiled at Dylan. "Hello, Dylan."

"Hi, Doctor..." He squinted at the name tag on her desk. "Colson."

Her smile widened a fraction. "Tell me, Dylan, do you ever have nightmares?"

He shrugged. "Sometimes."

"Uh-huh. And do you ever wet the bed?"

"Not since he was little. He picked up the potty training really fast," Sonia replied.

Dylan squirmed and let out a huffy sigh.

Dr. Colson's expression went chilly. "I'd like Dylan to answer. In fact, Miss Rollins, I'd like to speak with him alone. It's standard procedure."

Something tightened in Sonia's chest, but she turned to Dylan. "You cool with that, kiddo?"

He bit his lip like he wanted to say no, but in the end, he just nodded. "Okay."

She paced up and down the hall of the doctor's office as she waited. A few people passed by with their own kids. Most of the moms were older than she was, dressed in capri pants and pastel blouses.

Yeah, keep staring, bitch, she thought as one woman with nice highlights gave her the side-eye. *I bet you're two Vicodin into the evening at the same time I'm helping my kid with his homework.*

Dr. Colson led Dylan outside after fifteen minutes or so. "Miss Rollins, can I have a word?"

"Can you hang tight out here, kiddo?" Sonia asked.

Dylan nodded and flopped into a chair in the hallway.

"So. Find anything new?" she asked as she returned to the office.

"Miss Rollins, I want to start by saying clearly that I'm not accusing you of anything." Dr. Colson folded her hands on the desk.

"That's good. Glad to hear," Sonia said, making the words a question.

"But in cases like this, we always have to consider the possibility of abuse." Her eyes seemed to focus on some point near Sonia's nose or mouth—some trick she'd learned to confront someone without making real eye contact, maybe.

The bottom fell out of Sonia's stomach. "I—what? Abuse? Jesus, what did he say?"

"Nothing," Dr. Colson said a little too quickly. "But without a physical illness, we have to look at the possibility that this is psychological." She scribbled something on a notepad. "I'm referring you to a very good child psychologist."

"Which I'm sure won't be covered by my insurance."

"He charges by a sliding scale." She passed the paper over.

Numb, Sonia took it. "So I take Dylan to this guy to confirm what I already know? That I'm not hitting my kid? And neither is his grandmother?"

"Like I said, no one is accusing you of anything. But I'm sure you'd want to know if these episodes are a psychological reaction to abuse or trauma."

"You know I'm having them, too, right?" Sonia gestured at the clipboard. "Explain that."

Dr. Colson started to respond, stopped, then forced another smile. "I'm not ruling anything out. But I really feel our best bet is to consider all the options. And that means taking Dylan to see the specialists he needs."

"Got it." She took her time gathering her bag and finding her keys. Her instinct was to scuttle out of the office as fast as she could and to cower under that gray stare, but she kept her spine straight, checked the time on her phone, and sidled out when she was damn well good and ready.

"Did the doctor tell you what's wrong with me?" Dylan asked as they climbed back into the car.

Sonia turned on the engine and put the air conditioner on full blast, leaving the door open while she waited for the air to cool. "Dyl, you'd tell me if anyone ever hurt you, right? You know you could always tell me anything, don't you?"

He rolled his eyes. "I already told the doctor no one hurts me. Except Benny at school, and that was just the one time when he punched me in the arm."

"Okay, good." Something unclenched in her gut. She knew it was ridiculous. It didn't make any sense since she and Dylan were sick at the same time, but still...

"So... did she say what's wrong with me?"

Sonia sighed. "No. I don't think she's very interested in helping us. She thinks I'm making stuff up. Or I'm getting you to make stuff up or something."

"Why?"

She watched the confusion on his frowning, freckled little face. She thought about all the things she would have to explain to him, all the things people would assume about him because he had a single bartender as a mom. Behind that was the old fear, those moments when she wondered if everyone was right. Maybe she was just a giant fuckup and Dylan would be better off with Mom. For just a moment, it made her so tired, she couldn't breathe. "Some people are just stuck-up and stupid, that's all." She unlocked her phone and found the email Mom had forwarded.

"What are you doing?" Dylan asked.

"Emailing someone who might help us out."

CHAPTER 8: 1960

That night, Anza woke up frightened. At first, she didn't know what had woken her. Then she heard the sound that had roused her—a series of rhythmic, pulsing screeches.

Dad was already up and standing on the front porch when she staggered out of her bedroom. "Dad?" she asked, voice high and thin. "What is it?"

He turned, the lines in his face stark in the light cast by the porch's single bare bulb. "It's the birds, Anza."

"What?" She joined him on the porch, folding her arms tight against her body to ward off the chilly night air. Almost no light reached past the front yard. Clouds obscured the stars, and the moon was an anemic sliver above the western horizon. She listened. Dad was right. As alien as those sounds had seemed at first, they were birds chirping, except it wasn't the conversation of birds in the day-light or under an unusually bright moon. No, it was the sound of birds chirping in unison, short staccato tweets as regular as a metronome, from all sides of the yard.

Even now that she realized the sound was nothing more than birds, Anza didn't want to be outside. It was like the night itself had a sound, the screeching of darkness coming closer to their weak little pool of light.

"What's going on?" she whispered.

"Don't know, sweetheart," he said, wrapping an arm around her shoulders.

ANZA DIDN'T REMEMBER the last time there'd been a call for a town meeting. And even though they happened now and again, she'd only ever gone to one. It had been a meeting where Dad and several other miners had spoken, pushing for the town to do more to reach out to new mining ventures. It hadn't yielded any results she'd been able to see, but she'd been proud to see Dad up there, looking Mayor Fuller in the eye and telling him what was what.

That meeting had been bustling and well-attended, but this one put it to shame. Once they got word of how many people planned to show up, the mayor and the town council had moved it to the high school gymnasium. Still, even with the bleachers and extra chairs lined up along the basketball court, Anza thought some people would end up standing. She and Dad arrived early, snagging a section of bleachers near the front to share with the Cardenas family.

Fernando seemed subdued, but he insisted he was fine. "I don't even remember it," he said. "One second I was watching the TV; the next, my mom was screaming and ten minutes had gone by."

Anza caught sight of Dove's red hair as she followed a large family through the gym doors. Anza waved without thinking. Scooting away from the edge of the bleacher, she said, "Dad? Let's ask Dove to sit with us. She looks like she's here by herself."

He smiled wryly, the first smile she'd seen in days. "You can ask, but I don't think she'll want to be around me."

Anza waved until she caught Dove's eye then motioned her over. Dove seemed hesitant, pausing before moving forward.

"How come she doesn't like you?" Anza asked.

"Don't know. Just always got that sense, ever since back in the day when she was friends with your mama. Probably thought I wasn't good enough for her." He smiled wider, nudging her with an elbow. "Of course, she was right about that."

Anza rolled her eyes.

"Oh, stop that now," Mrs. Cardenas said, giving Dad a playful slap on the knee. Then Dove arrived, giving everyone a civil nod before perching on the edge of the silver bleacher like she was planning to run off any second.

"You hear about the birds?" Anza whispered.

"Hear about it? Damn things kept me up all night."

A few minutes later, Mayor Fuller called the meeting to order. He was a tall, skinny man whose bald head perspired constantly. He'd always struck Anza as nervous, and she'd wondered more than once why he kept running for mayor if the job made him so twitchy.

"Now, we all know why we're here. And I know everyone is worried right now, on account of the strange things we've been seeing around town. But let me assure you, we haven't been idle." That sparked a few derisory coughs and laughs from the crowd. Mayor Fuller cleared his throat and pressed on. "I've spent the last few days getting in touch with health and sanitation authorities all over the state. State health department investigators will be coming out within the next two days to see if they can get to the bottom of things. We'll also be getting some visitors from the University of Arizona who have some experience in this area—"

"And what area is that, Mayor?" someone yelled from the back of the gym.

"Yeah, we don't even know what this thing is!"

He tried to smile. "Well, that's why we're bringing out public health workers and scientists. They're going to test the soil, the air—"

"For God's sake, Joshua, it's the water! Everyone knows this started after the Red Hail! Something got into our water!" another voice shouted. Agreement chorused through the gymnasium.

"Please, everyone, we'll open the meeting to public comment in a few minutes. You can make your remarks then. In the meantime, please avoid spreading rumors. Last thing we need is a panic."

The crowd grumbled but seemed to settle down a bit.

"Now, I'd like to ask everyone to cooperate with the state health officials and the research scientists when they get here. I don't know what all they'll want to do, but the easier we make their jobs, the quicker they'll figure this business out. Now, in the meantime, Dr. Allen is here to take any questions you have about what we know so far."

The crowd grew restive again as Doc Allen fielded a few questions everyone already knew the answers to. Had anyone died? No. Were there any other symptoms aside from the Naming? Not yet. Was it true only women and girls were affected? No. And so on.

Then Dove stood and raised her hand. "Doc, what sorts of record keeping are you doing to nail down the outbreak pattern?"

He blinked. "Well, I keep records for all my patients, of course..."

She shook her head. "No, I mean, what are we doing to track the mode of transmission, the incubation period—"

"I think the state health investigators will be plenty well equipped to take care of all that," he replied with a reassuring smile. He started to point to another raised hand.

"Except they'll be coming in with no knowledge of who lives in this town, who knows who, and who does what." Dove's voice cut through the next woman's question. "Folks who live here start gathering that information, it'll go a whole lot quicker."

People all along the bleachers nodded as she spoke, muttering their agreement. Doc Allen's smile went tense around the edges. "Well, I'll do my best, but I'm the only doctor in town, and I have other responsibilities."

"I'd be happy to lend a hand," she replied. "I saw my fair share of outbreaks back in my nursing days. Typhoid and the like. We handled a few quarantines, tracing a smallpox outbreak. It's been a while, but I dusted off my medical books, and I think there's some steps we could be taking."

Something in Doc Allen's eyes went cold, but it was clear the crowd was on Dove's side. "Well, Mrs. McNally, I think it would be a waste of time with the state coming in, but no one's stopping you if you want to do some interviews."

"I'll get started directly." She sat, lips curving up with just a hint of satisfaction.

As Doc Allen wrapped up the last few questions, Anza noticed some kind of disturbance on the other side of the gymnasium. People muttered and exclaimed, turning away from the Mayor and Doc Allen and toward something in their midst. It took a minute for Anza to see what was causing all the fuss.

Paula, sitting with her parents and sisters, stared blankly across the room, lips moving. Anza couldn't hear from this distance what she was saying, but she recognized that slackness in her features. Paula's mother covered her face, shoulders shaking with sobs.

Doc Allen quickly moved up the stairs and to Paula's side. As he examined her, someone else stood and walked down to the floor of the basketball court. Even though they'd never spoken, she recognized him as Pastor Benjamin.

He was a tall, barrel-chested man with a square jaw and a head of curly blond hair. His eyes were a bit too small for his head, his forehead a bit too prominent. He always wore suit jackets, even in the summer. "Mayor Fuller," he said, voice echoing through the gymnasium. "Dr. Allen, thank you for calling this meeting today. And I'm sure I speak for everyone in town when I say we appreciate your tireless efforts to end this plague."

Scattered applause rippled through the crowd.

"But I must say, I'm troubled by how much all of you seem to be ignoring the obvious."

"Oh, no," Dove muttered.

Pastor Benjamin held up a pocket Bible, the gold leaf edging catching the light. "Exodus 7:17: 'By this you will know that I am the lord. With the staff that is in my hand, I will strike the water of the Nile, and it will be changed into blood.' Blood falling from the heavens. Sure sounds like the Red Hail to me."

Mayor Fuller began to rise from his seat. "Now, Ben—"

Shouts of agreement from several bleachers drowned him out.

"Blood rained from heaven, and now our children are tormented by illness. And from what I can see, this is an illness just as terrible and frightening as the Plague of Boils. And the animals around our town wake up in the night and behave in ways no one's ever seen before?" Pastor Benjamin paused, allowing the yells of "Amen" to fill the silence. "It was Pharaoh's arrogance that caused the death of all of the firstborn of Egypt. We can't be so foolish as to ignore whatever sins caused this." His voice had an odd unnatural rhythm, a singsong beat that set Anza's teeth on edge. It reminded her of the acting in bad movies.

"Please, Pastor Benjamin." It took a moment for Anza to see who had spoken. Father Santiago rose from another bleacher. She'd felt odd about calling him "Father" ever since he'd arrived three years ago. She supposed he must be old enough to have been ordained as a priest, but he still looked like a skittish eighteen-year-old boy. Today, he wore his clerical collar but with pants and a shirt instead of the cassock he wore to perform services. "I think we need to be careful about this. We have no evidence that this is anything more than a germ, a... a virus."

"Evidence. How Jesuit," Benjamin said, smiling warmly. "And you're right, Father Santiago, that we need to be careful. But I say being careful means taking action, taking a long hard look at the sins of our town and our people, before it's too late."

Anza bit her lip as a smattering of onlookers stood and clapped.

Father Santiago held up his hands. "This is a town of good, decent people. I don't believe anyone here has done anything to earn God's wrath."

Others were standing and cheering for him, but some of the ones who had clapped for Pastor Benjamin shouted back at them. A few boos echoed through the room.

"Now, this is getting out of hand." Mayor Fuller banged his gavel. "Let's everyone just wait until we see what the state health folks have to say. In the meantime, the last thing we need is people getting hysterical. So, everyone, stay calm and help thy neighbor, and we'll get to the bottom of this."

Pastor Benjamin turned to the crowd. "For those of you who would like to do more than stay calm, I invite you to our special services every night this week. Come to our church, confess your sins, and reject the wicked ways of Satan. No one will be turned away."

More clapping followed. Then someone screamed.

Everyone froze for just a second before the room erupted in shouting. Anza stood, climbing up on the seat so she could see over the crowd. The three Garces children had been sitting with their parents in the front row of extra chairs set up on the basketball court. Just before the meeting began, Anza had watched an elderly councilwoman lead the Garces family to their saved seats. She supposed it was something of a grim place of honor, being the first sufferers.

The children were out of their seats, standing statue still, in positions so contorted, Anza felt queasy just looking at them. Luz balanced on her left leg, her right extending out parallel to the ground, her back arched so far back that Anza couldn't understand how the little girl didn't just tip over. Margarita's knees were bent, her torso and head twisted around so that her face pointed up at the ceiling. Pablo crouched, his upper body somehow tucked under one of his legs.

"The devil seeks to act through our children! See how he reacts when he knows we're onto his tricks?" Pastor Benjamin bellowed, pointing at the Garces kids. "Join me in praying over these poor cursed children. Join me in battling for their souls—"

But as he approached with his arms outstretched, Mrs. Garces turned away from trying to help Luz. She pointed her finger at Pastor Benjamin's chest, screaming at him in a stream of Spanish before switching to English. Anza caught, "You stay away from my children!" before she turned back to Pablo.

Doc Allen and Father Santiago helped Mr. and Mrs. Garces carry the kids out of the meeting, awkwardly trying to move them even as they maintained their sickening shapes. Some in the crowd followed, perhaps to see them loaded into the car. But Anza stayed to watch Pastor Benjamin's face. He stared after Mrs. Garces, eyes cold. Then he seemed to realize someone might see, and he rearranged his features into the same warm, nurturing expression he'd maintained during his entire time on the floor. Something about that transformation scared Anza more than if he'd just stayed angry.

Mayor Fuller tried to bring the meeting back to order but gave up and adjourned a few minutes later.

"Damn. It's started already," Dove said, shaking her head.

"Don't understand it. Why get folks riled up more than they already are?" Dad grumbled.

"Because he can." Dove stood and led the way down the bleachers.

Father Santiago waited outside, still pale and shaken. "Mrs. McNally, may I have a word?"

"It's Dove, Padre. What can I do for you?"

Anza slowed, trying to look like she was waiting for the crowd to clear instead of eavesdropping.

"I'd like to help you take histories. And whatever else we should do to trace the disease."

"I don't know…"

"I visit parishioners every day. I'm usually the first to hear if there's a new case." His voice dropped so low, Anza had to strain to hear. "Please, the longer this goes on, the worse the hysteria will become."

Anza turned around, marched past Dad, and pushed her way next to Dove. "I want to help too."

Dove blinked. Her gaze flicked over to Dad. "Sean? Any objection to Anza taking notes for me?"

"Dad, everyone's too scared to leave their kids alone anyway. I'm not making any babysitting money this summer, and there's no other jobs, so I might as well help out if I can." She lowered her voice. "It's probably going to hit me any day now. Please let me at least help figure out what it is."

Dad sighed. "Guess I can't see any reason why not. I'm down in that damn mine all day, anyways, so she'll do it if she wants, and I'd be none the wiser."

Dove nodded once. "Okay then. I'll be picking you up bright and early tomorrow morning. Be ready to work."

CHAPTER 9: 2020

Half an hour after Alonzo left for his first appointment with the psychiatrist, Colin gave up pretending to do housework and sat down to comb through his old research files. He'd told himself it was best to just wait and see what this latest doctor had to say, that he should try to get his mind off Alonzo's symptoms for a while. He could tell Alonzo was tired of talking about the episodes and wanted to carry on as normally as possible until they had a diagnosis. Colin knew he was right. There was no point in fixating on it or in talking in endless circles about the similarities to the Galina Plagues. Still, it kept rising to the surface, the thought that the answer was buried somewhere in all that research.

Colin opened the document labeled "Master Timeline." It was ridiculously long and detailed, containing every event of the Galina Plagues, with dates and notes referring to other files, the names of interview subjects, and related resources. He stared at it as though something would jump out, some new causal connection he'd somehow managed to overlook in the thousands of times he'd referenced it in the past.

His eyes fell on a bullet point labeled only "Birds (?)." The question mark indicated his doubts that the event had really occurred and that he had placed it under the category of retrospective narrative construction. The same with the "Coyotes (?)" and "Beetles (?)" labels. The book condensed all of those supposed incidents into a single paragraph about retroactive claims of natural disturbances. Most of the interview references had been hazy, but enough people had mentioned the odd behavior of birds and coyotes and the appearance of mysterious red beetles during the Plague Summer that he'd decided he should at least mention it.

Bianca, his girlfriend during most of his second year of his PhD program, had pressed him about those natural phenomena. She'd insisted they pointed to a physical catalyst for the Plagues instead of a purely social one. He'd dismissed the suggestion at the time. Her doctoral program was biochem, so of course, she would favor the toxin or bacteria explanation. She wouldn't accept that people could develop entirely false memories based on popular myth, even though there was case after case from other mass hysteria incidents. Still, as he ran his cursor over the "Coyotes (?)" label, he saw references to some articles she'd sent him before they'd drifted apart.

The first article was called "Anomalous Migration Patterns of Collared *Canis Latrans* Specimens Originating in Cochise County, Arizona." It was about eight years old, published in a zoology journal. Colin read through it, plowing his way through the scientific jargon as best he could. As far as he could tell, the article claimed that coyotes captured and given tracking collars in parts of Cochise County seemed to range much farther than any other coyotes on record, migrating as far east as Arkansas and south well into Mexico, over the course of their lifetime. He didn't really understand the significance of that information, but he found the name of the head researcher and tracked down the man's email address. He'd started out at the University of New Mexico, but now he was right here at the University of Arizona.

Colin spent way too long composing a brief email, including and deleting information about Alonzo several times. Finally, he just asked in the most general possible terms if they could meet to discuss the coyote research.

As soon as he pressed Send, he saw he had something new in his university inbox. It was from an address he didn't recognize. As soon as Colin opened it, he froze.

Dear Dr. (Professor?) Ayres,

My name is Sonia Rollins, and my son and I have been having some weird medical issues lately. I'm emailing you because I'm told my grandfather had stuff kind of like this going on, and you might know something about it. He was from Galina, in Cochise County, and he was there that time the whole town went nuts back in 1960. (His name was Richard Rollins. If you heard of him, it was probably as the town hoodlum or something.) I hear you're writing a book about it, so maybe if you know what's going on, you could give me a call.

There wasn't much about Sonia Rollins online, at least nothing connected to Galina. No helpful forum posts on genealogy boards or anything like that. But he did find a few YouTube videos of a Phoenix blues band featuring Sonia Rollins as the lead singer. Colin watched one. He wasn't much of a blues fan, but she had a nice, throaty contralto voice, and the band's cover of "Pride and Joy" was decent. She had a slightly Goth look—straight black hair with square bangs, dark lipstick contrasting with pale skin, and a tattered black T-shirt. She seemed a couple years younger than Alonzo.

According to Colin's interview list, he'd gotten in touch with someone named Marnie Rollins, but everyone in the family who would have known enough to be worth interviewing was dead, and they hadn't spoken again.

He sat back in his chair. Another Galina descendant in a different city. Someone he didn't think Alonzo had ever met. Someone Colin couldn't have ever accidentally mentioned. They had no connection, except for Galina.

The front door opened and closed. Alonzo wandered in a moment later, visibly tired. "Hey." He dropped onto the threadbare sofa in the corner of the office.

"How'd it go?"

Alonzo shrugged. "She asked me a lot about stress. Moving in with you. Family bullshit." He smiled thinly. "Basically, it seems like she thinks it's all in my head. Just me not handling stress well or something."

Colin hesitated for a moment before speaking. "I don't think that's it. Do you know someone named Sonia Rollins?"

"No. Why?"

Colin opened the email and turned the screen so Alonzo could see. "She's having symptoms too. And her grandfather was also from Galina." He slid his chair close enough to take Alonzo's hands in his own. "It's not in your head."

They stared at each other in silence. Colin recognized the look in Alonzo's eyes, poised on a knife edge between relief and terror.

"WHY CAN'T I GO TO ONE of those schools where you get the whole summer off?" Dylan dropped his bag next to the kitchen table.

"Bag in your room," Sonia said automatically. "Because your school is the best one around here. So we can get you into a good high school and then a good college, and then you can become a billionaire so I can stay home all day." She pulled a bag of brown rice out of the cabinet and tried to find a clear space on the countertop to put it down. The whole surface was cluttered with empty bags and wrappers, the shriveled remains of a broccoli stalk, and spilled cooking oil. The sink smelled swampy too. Sunday was usually Sonia's cleaning day, but she'd spent all of the last one at doctors' offices with Dylan. She shoved some of the wrappers to the side and set down the rice. "Besides, you get as much time off as other kids. Just not all in one chunk. Trust me, when I was your age, I would have killed for a two-week break every now and then instead of just three months in the middle. And summer vacations are a waste in Phoenix, anyway. It's too hot to do anything but learn."

Dylan went just far enough into the hallway to toss his backpack into his room. "I don't want to go back to my school."

She measured some water into a pot. "Why not? What's going on, kiddo?"

"Benny keeps making fun of me for doing the Statue thing." He sat at the table, staring down at his hands.

"I'm sorry. I know that sucks. Just remember to keep telling yourself how things are going to change in a few years." She paused. "Come on. We talked about this. What do you tell yourself?"

Dylan sighed. "I'm going to cure cancer as a science fair project, and Benny's a punkass who's going to wind up in juvie for huffing paint," he recited in a bored voice.

"That's right." Sonia turned on the stove's gas burner and listened to it click until the pilot light caught. She grabbed a rag and wiped down a section of the cutting board big enough for her to chop vegetables. "Do me a favor and grab me some black beans and a can of tomatoes."

Dylan got up and went to the cabinet. She took a moment to marvel at how little he complained when asked to help out. She remembered herself at that age, a whiny brat who couldn't be asked to do anything without throwing a fit. *Proof there is no karma,* she sometimes thought when she looked at him.

Smoke. Smoke and the shriek of the alarm. Under that, she heard Dylan's voice. "Mom! Mom! Wake up!"

Sonia gasped and staggered as Dylan tugged at her hand with his scrawny little-kid arms. A burnt, blackened dishcloth dangled from her fingers. The water in the pot was boiling, barely visible through the smoke. "Jesus! Where..." Nothing else was burning, as far as she saw.

Dylan stared up at her with wide hazel eyes, the only feature that really made him look like Denny instead of her.

"Are you okay?" she shouted over the alarm, checking his arms for burns at the same time.

He nodded, sticking his fingers in his ears. He went to open the sliding glass door while Sonia waved a broom at the air near the smoke alarm until it ceased wailing. Her ears rang after it stopped. Everything around her sounded muted, like she was underwater. "What happened?"

"You did the Statue thing. The cloth was in your hand, and you moved so it was next to the stove." He paused, eyes watery. "I tried to pull you away, but you were too strong."

"Oh Jesus." Sonia covered her face, pulse thudding in her ears. "Come here. Come here, baby."

She hugged him to her waist, caught as always between marveling at how much he'd grown and feeling how small and fragile he still was.

"Maybe we should just microwave food for a while," he said, voice muffled by her shirt.

She snorted with shaky, tearstained laughter. "Yeah. Yeah, I think you're right. Uh, do me a favor and go see if we have any of those sodium-bomb dinners left in the freezer?"

While Dylan dug around in the freezer, Sonia turned off the stove and immediately backed away, not trusting herself to remain next to the pot of boiling water.

CHAPTER 10: 1960

"This is the list of questions we need to ask all of them," Dove said as Anza climbed into the truck. The morning air still felt cool on her skin. She caught a whiff of the honeysuckle climbing over their front fence just as Dove put the truck in gear and started off down the road.

Anza skimmed through the typed sheets, squinting to read them in the dim, lavender pre-dawn light. There were three pages of questions, still smelling of carbon paper from the typewriter. "'List everything you ate in the three days before you became sick'? 'Name of every person you had physical contact with in the week before you became sick'? Dove, are folks going to be able to remember all this stuff?"

"Nope. And they'll lie, too, about things like hanky-panky they weren't supposed to be having." She gave Anza a sidelong glance. "Like that Fernando Cardenas. I expect he'll lie about certain forms of contact with you. He *is* the boy, right?"

Anza was glad it was still too dark for Dove to see her blushing. "Of course. Who else would it be?"

"Hell if I know. Just because he's the one I see squiring you around town doesn't mean he's the only boy in the picture."

"He *is* the only one. So what? What's wrong with him?"

She shrugged. "Nothing. Seems like a nice enough boy. You still seeing him?"

Anza hesitated. "I don't know. I haven't... you know. But I mean, we've been friends since we were little kids. Mrs. Cardenas babysat me whenever Dad was at work, before I could stay home alone, so

Fernando and I were always together, and I don't know... It's like everyone just decided we belonged together, back when we were little. People used to joke, my dad and Mrs. Cardenas, saying we'd get married when we grew up. So we never really talked about going steady or anything. It just happened. And I think I was okay with that, before, but now I don't know." She frowned, trying to pin down the uneasiness—and irritation—she'd felt around Fernando lately. At first, she'd assumed she just resented him for what happened, but now she wondered if it was something else. She'd never daydreamed about their wedding or anything like that, not the way Paula talked about marrying David. But she'd also never assumed that they *wouldn't* end up together; he was the only boyfriend she'd had, after all. It was like she'd never let herself think too hard about that part of her future, but once she'd started, she couldn't stop.

Dove sighed. "Well, what we're told to want and what we really want aren't always one and the same." She pointed at the sheet of paper again. "Which is why we get so many fibs on these questions. Folks sneaking around, doing things they aren't supposed to, and telling us they did the opposite."

"Then what's the point of even asking?"

"Hopefully, people will remember enough and tell the truth enough to give us a pattern. We're looking for things all of them have in common. You ever hear the story of how they figured out how cholera works?"

Anza shook her head.

Dove turned onto Main Street. It was still quiet, mostly empty, except for a handful of folks getting ready to open their stores. "Back in the eighteen hundreds, they still thought disease came from vapors and bad air and nonsense like that. But this doctor named John Snow didn't think that was true, so he did his research on all the folks who got sick in a cholera outbreak in London. He put all the cases on a map, and he did interviews. He looked for the one thing they had in common, until he finally found it."

"What was it?"

"A water pump. The only thing they all had in common was getting their water from the same pump, and that's how we know today that cholera comes from contaminated water." The truck came to a halt in front of Father Santiago's little stucco church. "So that's what we have to keep an eye out for. Our water pump."

"And what if Pastor Benjamin's right?" Anza asked with a little smile, teasing, even though some corner of her mind wondered.

"Then there won't be a water pump. But the day that man's right about a damn thing, I'll eat my hat."

Father Santiago opened the front doors before they had a chance to knock. "Please, come in."

Anza took a deep breath as they stepped into the church. She'd always liked it in there, the couple of times Dad had brought her. It was dark in a cool, comforting way, smelling of incense. She'd seen pictures of Catholic churches with elaborate stained-glass windows and sculptures, but this one just had plain whitewashed walls and exposed mesquite ceiling beams. Even the crucifix above the altar was simple, roughly carved and unpainted.

"The first appointment is in fifteen minutes," Father Santiago said, pointing at a small folding table he'd set up between the wall and some pews. "Mrs. Bauer and her grandson."

"All right, then." Dove passed him the list of typed questions. "Here's what we'll be asking. As you can see, some of those are a wee bit sensitive, so I'm relying on you to make them feel like their secrets are safe with us."

He nodded absently as he read through the list. "Hm. You're thinking this illness can be transmitted through intercourse, not just casual contact?"

Anza turned away, pretending to busy herself with the pens and pads of paper laid out on the table. *A priest, saying that out loud in his church...*

"Unlikely, but you don't rule anything out at this stage. I was working in a charity ward in Flagstaff when there was a typhoid outbreak. Helped trace some syphilis cases too."

"Ah."

"Okay, here's how this is going to work," Dove said, and at that moment, Anza found it all too easy to imagine her as a ward sister in command of a bevy of younger nurses. "Father Santiago will explain the process to them so they don't get nervous. I'll ask questions for the English speakers, and Father can ask for the ones who mostly just speak Spanish, since mine ain't that good. Anza, you speak Spanish well enough to follow?"

"Yeah, no problem."

"Well then, you're our transcriptionist. Number each question we ask and get their answer down as best you can. No need to make the sentences pretty, just get down the who, what, when, where."

"Okay." Anza sat down at the table and arranged the notepad in front of her.

The front door inched open, and an elderly woman with gray hair poked her head inside. "Father?" she asked, voice timid.

"Mrs. Bauer." He smiled and gestured toward the table. "Please, come in."

"Ready?" Dove asked.

Anza nodded. "Yeah."

Dove sat down next to her. "Then let's get started."

"MY HAND IS NEVER GOING to work again," Anza groaned. The muscles in her right palm cramped and ached.

"Told you there was nothing glamorous about tracking an epidemic," Dove said, peering through her reading glasses at a page of notes.

"No, you didn't."

"Well, I didn't think it needed to be spelled out. Now hush."

Anza sighed and went back to staring at the yellow sheets of notepaper containing four days of work. They spilled over Dove's coffee table and into piles on the floor. She'd moved most of the books to some other part of the house, although the shelves were still bursting with them. They'd spent the first two days trying to work out of Father Santiago's little private office behind the church, but as the cases multiplied, they realized they didn't have enough room.

Seventy-seven cases, she thought, gazing at the notes. And that was just from the ones Father Santiago had persuaded to come in for interviews. They'd gotten barely anyone from Pastor Benjamin's church and only a few non-churchgoers from the rest of town.

Tires crunched on Dove's rocky driveway, and Anza jumped up from where she sat on the floor next to the coffee table. She touched her hair, hoping it still looked presentable in its tortoiseshell barrette. She'd worn a skirt and blouse, clothes she barely ever had occasion or inclination to wear. Still, she didn't want the public health inspectors to take one look at her dusty boots and write off all their hard work.

Her heart sank as she peeked out the window. "It's just Father Santiago. No one else with him."

Dove's shoulders sagged a little. "I was afraid of that."

Anza went to the door and let Father Santiago inside. He seemed angry for the first time she could remember, stomping past her instead of pausing to give his usual greeting.

"*Imbécil!*" he snapped as he entered the living room.

"I *beg* your pardon," Dove said, eyes going squinty.

"Not you. I apologize. That arrogant son of—" He noticed Anza and caught himself. "That doctor the state sent to investigate. He wouldn't even listen. He wouldn't even come to look at our notes, even when I told him about all the work we've done." He picked up a stack of notes and waved it around. "Free information! And he wouldn't even look."

Anza stared down at herself, feeling stupid in her ironed blouse. She thought about the hours of interviewing, transcribing, reading, and rereading they had done over the last few days, and she had to fight back tears.

"What are they doing, then? Their own interviews?"

He sneered. "No, not even that. They're testing the water. That's all."

"The water?" Anza stamped her foot. "The water's the one damn thing we ruled out!"

"Language, Esperanza, please," Father Santiago said.

She glared at him.

"She's right, though," Dove said, sighing. "It's not the water. They're wasting their time with that."

That had been the first thing they'd checked. It was the most likely explanation, given the Red Hail. But there wasn't a common water source. Some of the people they'd interviewed got their water from private wells that could have been contaminated by the hail, but others who lived on the other side of town got their water pumped in from an aquifer outside the area that had gotten the hail. And they'd already checked to make sure no one else using that water in other towns had been affected.

"I told them that wasn't it, but they said I didn't understand 'the science of epidemiology.'" His jaw muscles twitched. "Maybe you should have gone. Maybe they would have listened to a nurse."

Dove snorted. "Bunch of men who don't want to listen to a Mexican priest ain't going to listen to some old lady who used to change bedpans, neither."

"What did they say they'd do if there was nothing in the water?" Anza asked, perching on the edge of the couch.

His lip curled. "That head doctor said he suspected 'mass hysteria.' That there isn't really anything wrong."

"*What?*"

"To be fair, he'd be stupid *not* to consider that," Dove said.

Anza blinked. "You think people are just making all this up?" *All that work, all that damn hand cramping...*

"No. I don't. I thought maybe, when it was just the Garces kids and Tracey Edmonds, but not now." Dove pointed at the piles. "Mass hysteria is people seeing one person acting crazy and jumping on the bandwagon. So maybe Tracey sees the Garces kids Naming, and then someone sees her. Sure. But we got at least four cases here where people didn't see anyone else doing it before they started. And at least two of those, Edna and Percy Lenks, didn't even know it was going on. They don't have a phone out there on the mesa, don't talk to their neighbors much, didn't know until it started happening to them."

"And I *told* the inspectors that," Father Santiago grumbled.

"Well, we're on our own, then," Dove said. "Best get back to work."

"So." Anza found the timeline they'd started to piece together from all the notes. "The Garces kids start Naming. Five days later, Tracey Edmonds starts doing it. Then we get a lot of Naming cases, and not all of those had contact with either the Garces kids or Tracey. Mostly kids and teenagers at first but then some grown-ups. Eighteen days after the Garces kids show up, they start having the Statue Sickness. Two days later, other folks start doing the same thing."

"But only after they've started Naming," Father Santiago said. "Naming always precedes the Statue Sickness and continues even after that phase has started."

"Yeah, as far as symptoms go, they're pretty consistent," Dove said. "Naming is always words for stuff they can see or hear or feel at that moment. The Statue Sickness is always holding a pose for three to seven minutes, not being able to remember afterward."

Anza stared at the timeline and the names of the cases that started each new phase. She shuffled through some of the earlier notes. She almost had it, the thing tying them together—

Dove's phone rang. She got up and answered it, pressing the clunky pink Bakelite receiver to her ear. "Yes?" She paused. "Uh-huh. Okay. We'll be right there."

She hung up and stared at the phone for a moment before turning back to Anza and Father Santiago. "That was Lilia Torino down at the café. She says something's wrong with Millie's daughter, but it's not the Naming or the Statue Sickness." She rubbed her forehead. "Looks like we maybe got a new symptom."

THE KITCHEN OF MILLIE'S Café smelled like burnt toast and old sausage. Anza had never been back there and had only ever glimpsed it through the window where Millie's waitresses picked up the orders. It was smaller than she'd imagined.

Millie stood in one corner of the long, narrow kitchen, hand pressed to her mouth. Mascara ran in streaks down her round cheeks. Her daughter, Patty, stood in the center of the room, wearing a dirty apron over one of the white shirts all the Millie's waitresses wore. As Anza watched, Patty did the same thing she'd been doing ever since they arrived. She stamped her right foot. Then she twitched her head to the left twice, a sharp jerking motion that made Anza wince every time. Finally, her left arm shot forward, palm twisting under and up in an unnatural motion as the arm rose parallel to the ground and fell back to her side. Then the whole sequence started over again.

"How long's this been going on?" Dove asked.

"This new thing started right before I called. About forty minutes ago, now. But she started Naming two weeks ago, and then she got the Statue Sickness the week after that." Millie sniffed and stared at Dove with wide eyes. "This is new, isn't it? I ain't heard about this one yet."

Dove patted her on the arm. "Try not to worry, Millie. Nobody seems any the worse for wear, once the fits are over."

"But this one's lasted so long, I don't—"

Patty abruptly stopped and shook her head. "Mama, what's going on?"

"Oh, Patty!" Millie cried, scooping her into a hug.

"Did I go still again?"

"No... No, darling, it was something else." She pointed. "Dove and Father Santiago here need to take your history so we can give it to the public health authority."

Anza exchanged a glance with Father Santiago, but he gave her a quiet shake of his head before going over to help Patty to a chair. Anza thought she understood why he wanted her to keep quiet. She wouldn't want the three of them to be on their own against this thing, either.

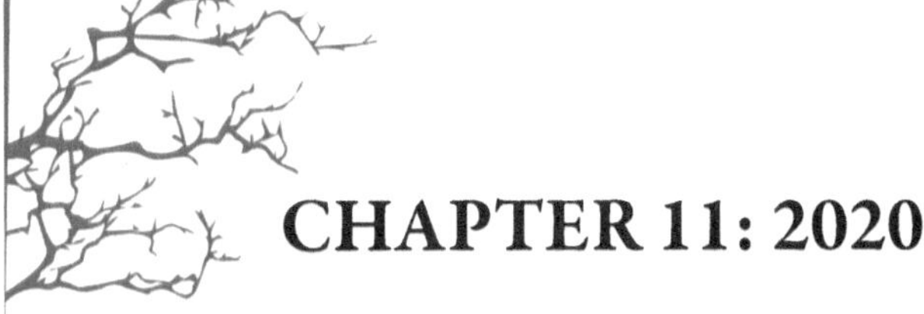

CHAPTER 11: 2020

Sonia checked her email again and stuffed her phone back into the pocket of her jeans. The new girl, Marissa, scrubbed at the bar next to her. Ross finished adjusting an amp and gave her a thumbs-up from the little patio off the side of the building. There was a decent crowd already. Some of the regulars were just wandering outside, but she saw enough faces she didn't recognize to know they'd come just for the music.

"Got this?" she asked.

Marissa nodded, tight-lipped. Last time Sonia had left her alone to man the bar, she'd forgotten how to make a screwdriver and lost someone's tab.

"Yeah, you got this," Sonia said, trying to sound encouraging.

"Yeah. I'm okay. Good luck up there."

Sonia went out to the patio. It was a short set: a couple Billie Holiday covers, then one of the better original songs she and Ross had written a year ago, and finally the new one she'd been trying to capture for the last few weeks. Ross thought it was ready, and Sonia knew their big break wasn't going to happen in a pool hall anyway, so they might as well try it out.

They started easy and familiar, with the cover of "Lover Man." Sonia's voice wasn't much like Billie's, but at her best, she felt like she channeled just a little bit of that heartbreak, like Billie's ghost whispered in her ear just enough to give it some oomph.

After the first few songs, it was an easy transition to "Taste of Cherry," which she and Ross had composed almost entirely on a drive from Phoenix to San Diego. That one got the crowd going, and she finished with an unplanned little flourish on the last note.

Finally, there was the newest one, which was called "Hard Road" until she thought of something better. It was close. She could feel it, teetering on the edge of greatness. But not quite. There was some little tweak the chorus needed, a subtle shift in the rhythm. Even so, the crowd stood and clapped, and the set felt like a job well done.

"Thank you," she purred into the microphone. "I'll be over behind the bar, mopping up spilled beer, if anyone wants to talk about the blues."

She gave Ross a high-five and stepped down from the stage, blood still humming with the rush of performance.

Blink.

"This way! She's over here!"

The audience had moved somehow. They no longer perched on the stools scattered around the porch's high tables. People instead clustered at the far end of the patio, as far from Sonia as they could get. Her arm hurt. She looked down to see Ross's fingers digging into her bicep.

"What the hell are you doing?" she asked.

"Are you back?" The whites of his eyes stood out. Sweat beaded his forehead.

Two paramedics came through the bar and to the porch.

"No, no, I'm fine," Sonia said, ducking away from them.

"You're not fine, Sonia. You were all tensed up in this weird fucking position, with your neck just..." He pulled out his phone. "I got a picture."

She reached for it, but he passed it to one of the paramedics instead.

"Ma'am," the woman said with a glance, "if you were just holding this position, I'd say you had a seizure. It's probably best if we take you to the hospital."

"No." Sonia took the phone and almost screamed at the sight of the image.

She hovered on one leg, which was bent into a deep squat she couldn't believe she'd done without pitching over. Her other leg sat folded over the bent one, like some fucked-up yoga pose. Her neck twisted up and back at an angle so extreme, it seemed broken. Half of her face was hidden, but the other half showed a vacant expression. It didn't feel like seeing a picture of herself. It felt like a picture of someone else who just happened to resemble her.

Blood rushed to her face. She stared furiously down at the screen, thinking about all the people who must have been staring at her while the picture was being taken. If she looked up now, how many people would still be staring?

"Sonia—"

She forced herself to look up at Ross, even though her face still burned with shame. "No. I'm not going to the hospital. Something like this happened before. I already saw a doctor."

"This happened before?" Ross's mouth dropped open. "Sonia, why didn't—"

"Because it's none of your fucking business." She shoved the phone back into his hands and shouldered past the paramedics.

Marissa stood behind the bar, pale and trembling. She eyed Sonia like one would watch a rabid animal.

"Thanks for taking over. I got it." Sonia grabbed a dishrag and wiped down the bar, even though it was already clean. Her skin prickled under the pressure of all those eyes, people at the bar still staring. *If I just ignore them long enough—*

"Marissa, stay with the bar," Will said, motioning toward the taps. "And call Tobi, see if she can come in for an extra shift."

"I'm fine. I got this," Sonia said.

"No, Sonia, come with me." He led her to the storeroom. "Listen, I'm sorry, but I can't have this in my place. Customers come here to relax, not get freaked out by crazy voodoo shit."

"It's not my fault, Will. It's not like I'm doing it on purpose." Her face flared with a fresh wave of embarrassment, and she cursed herself for letting him see it.

"I know, but it doesn't matter. It's bad for business. Like, really bad. Half the people on the patio left already. You know it's bad when something's too freaky for them to even feel like rubbernecking."

"So, what? You're cutting my shifts? What?" Without even meaning to, she was already thinking about her bank balance, the little things she and Dylan would have to cut back on, how low her hours could go before they were in trouble...

He bit his lip. "Sonia, if you get this thing under control, you can come back. The door's always open. But until then, I gotta let you go."

She let out an incredulous cough of laughter. "Seriously? Jesus. You're a real big fucking man, Will. Real man of principle. You can shove this job, thank you very much." She stormed out of the storeroom. "And all the rest of you fucks can just blow me," she shouted toward the pool tables, flipping a double bird as she went.

She managed to get into her car before the sobs started.

"I DON'T NEED TO TAKE time off."

Lianne held up her hands. "Okay! That's fine. Some people think of time off as a good thing, not a punishment. You don't have to."

Alonzo relaxed.

Lianne sat back in her desk chair, running a hand through her frizzy blond bob. Her desk held pictures of her two boxers and a scruffy white cat. Alonzo knew she had a son, but there weren't any pictures of him in the office.

"Okay, so, no time off. But look, Lonzo, I don't have to tell you that you can't be doing surgeries, right? I mean, you get that?"

He focused on his hands folded in the lap of his blue scrubs. "Yeah, I know." He'd already thought about what would happen if he froze mid-surgery, turned into a statue between making an incision and clamping an artery. He would never forgive himself.

"So, we'll just have to shift responsibilities around a little. I already talked to Priya and Margo, and they're fine with taking on more surgeries and giving you more of their clinic visits. Hell, I think Margo's happy about it. You know she prefers being wrist-deep in innards any chance she gets."

He wasn't in the mood to go along with the joke, but he saw Lianne trying hard, so he forced a little chuckle.

It must not have been very convincing, because Lianne sighed. "Alonzo, lots of vets don't even perform surgeries. You know that. I know this sucks, but epilepsy's not a career-ender for you. Cheer up."

"Uh-huh. Thanks." He got up and left before her "buck up, little soldier" routine pushed him over the edge.

Val and Tess lingered in the lab area just outside Lianne's office. They stepped apart quickly enough for Alonzo to know they'd been talking about him.

You're still a vet, he told himself. *You still have your job. You don't even* like *doing surgeries, for Christ's sake.*

"Is my three thirty here?" he asked, only a little louder and more abrupt than he'd intended.

Tess jumped. "Oh. Um. No. Sylar's dad called to say they're running a few minutes late."

"Okay. Let me know when they get here, will you?" He went into his office before Tess could answer, shutting the door behind him.

"OH MY GOD. HOW COULD you not tell me this earlier? And how could you tell Dylan to lie to me? Sonia!" Mom's hands fluttered around her face as though unsure of where to land. Her eyes were already filling with tears.

"Mom, stop. I know. I didn't want to worry you, but I'm telling you now. Listen." Sonia pushed on before Mom had an opportunity to say anything else. "The professor you told me about? I emailed him. He got back to me, and he said there's someone else who's having the same issues as me and Dylan. Someone else with a grandparent from Galina. So I'm going to Tucson to see him and figure out what's happening."

"Sonia, he's not a doctor. At least, not a medical doctor."

"Exactly. The medical doctors haven't been able to tell us jack-fucking-shit, so I might as well go see someone who knows *something*." She sighed. "I talked to Ross. There was a Tucson gig he was originally going to turn down, but I got him to take it. And once I'm there, I can stay with Cara. Remember, from my old band? She said I could do some sets with her new band, and she'd try to hook me up with some shifts at her bar."

"It sounds like you're moving to Tucson."

"No, I'm not. And fuck, don't you think I *want* to take Dylan with me? But I can't drive. I can't hold down a regular job. The best thing I can do is go and talk to the only people who seem interested in figuring out what's actually going on instead of just... just accusing me of *abuse* and throwing drugs we can't afford at us." Sonia blinked back tears. "This isn't the fun option for me. This is what's best for Dylan." Even as she said it, even as most of her knew it was true, some little corner of her mind wondered if she was lying to herself. Wasn't this what all deadbeat parents did? Convince themselves into believing they were doing the right thing, when really—

"Oh, sweetie." Mom pulled her into a hug. Sonia stiffened, but she knew it would be harder to sell her on the idea if she didn't at least hug her back. So she held her mother tightly and tried not to admit to herself how comforting it was.

CHAPTER 12: 1960

Fernando sat waiting on the front porch when she got home. "Hey, Anza," he said, lifting his hand in a tentative half wave.

"Hey, Fernando. How're you feeling?" She joined him on the porch swing.

He shrugged. "Okay. Sometimes I blink, and someone tells me I've been Naming or Statuing for a while. But I never remember anything." He peered at her face in the dwindling evening light. "Are you sick yet? You look tired."

"Not yet. I'm just tired from all these interviews. It's so much work, more every day. And then there's all the reading about epidemics Dove's having me do so I understand it better."

"You don't have to do it, you know."

Anza pulled her hair out of its ponytail and ran her fingers through it. She'd stopped wearing the nice barrettes and blouses three days ago, once she knew for sure the inspectors were never going to talk to them. Now she barely took the time to comb her hair and pull it back before she went over to Dove's place and started working each morning. "I know. But it's important."

For a moment, she wished Fernando would ask about it, so she could tell him all the things she'd learned about diseases, epidemics, and the strange history of doctors. So much of the reading she'd gotten from Dove had seemed dull at the time, but now she wanted to tell Fernando about typhoid carriers, how smallpox vaccines worked, and what white blood cells did when a virus crept into a human body. *If only he'd ask.*

Instead, he just gazed out at the empty lot past the front gate. "My folks are talking about leaving. I mean, they were thinking about it anyway, the way things have been going with the mine. And now all this." He paused. "Maybe you can talk your dad into leaving too. There's a lot of construction work in Tucson. We can live on the same street, go to the same school." Fernando smiled and nudged her with an elbow.

She smiled back and nodded, even though something about that idea made her feel uneasy.

"Seems like a lot of trouble, changing high schools just for my last two years."

The smile faded from Fernando's face. "Well, maybe you'll feel different when you get sick." There was a dark undercurrent to his voice, an anger she had only heard a few times.

"Maybe I won't. Get sick, I mean. With most diseases, there's folks called 'asymptomatic carriers,' and they—"

He cut off her words with a snort and a wave of his hand. "Come on, Anza. Everyone else has it now. At least, all the young people. Paula, Consuela, Mark, everyone in our class. Except you. Bet it'll happen any day now."

Anza scooted away and turned to face him. "Why would you say something like that? You're supposed to hope I *don't* get sick."

A little guilt crept into his features. "Sorry. I know. I hope you don't, really. It's just... You know, if everyone but you gets sick, people would talk."

Something tightened in Anza's belly, and she understood that this wasn't about what people would say, but what they'd already said. She shrugged. "Can't stop people from talking, I guess."

Fernando stared at her for a moment. "Anza... did I do something wrong?"

"No, I told you. I've just been busy—"

"Right, but you don't have to do all that stuff. It feels like you're trying to... I don't know, avoid me or something. I mean... We're going out. We're supposed to see each other. We haven't been out in like two weeks. Are we..." He swallowed. "Are we not going out anymore?"

The words landed like a gift Anza hadn't known she wanted. She took a deep breath. "Maybe that would be best. Until this is over, at least."

Fernando blinked and looked away, a glimmer of tears on his eyelashes. "What did I do wrong?"

"Nothing. You didn't do anything wrong."

"I must have done *something*." He sniffed. "I mean, we go out for two years, and everything's great, and then suddenly, you want to break up? I must have done something."

She sighed. "You didn't. Really. It's just... Nando, we're only sixteen. What's wrong with just doing some other stuff for a while? Thinking about other things?"

"My folks got *married* when they were sixteen."

And there it was—the thing she'd never let herself think about, the future he'd pictured and she hadn't. "That's how it was back then. Nowadays, people go to college. They work first. They don't just get married right out of high school."

Saying nothing, Fernando just stared off into the distance. Misery clung to him like a smell.

She stood. "I better go in."

"Yeah, I should go. My mom wanted me home before dark." He rolled his eyes. "Like we get the sickness from being out at nighttime." It was an attempt at a joke, but his eyes were still damp, his lip quavering.

He hesitated, leaned in, and gave her a light hug and a peck on the cheek. Two weeks ago, that kiss would have been on her lips. *It's supposed to be sad,* Anza thought, *breaking up.* That's how she always heard others talk about breaking up, and it seemed like that was how it was for Fernando. She wondered with a rush of guilt if not feeling sad made her a bad person or if it meant she was selfish.

Anza mulled that moment over as she went into the house. Then she turned the corner into the kitchen and stopped, breath catching in her throat. Dad stood next to the refrigerator, still wearing his work boots. His right arm was looped around the back of his neck, extending toward his chest, so twisted, it seemed like his shoulder should be dislocated. His other arm pointed behind him, fingers splayed out at unnatural angles.

Anza had seen worse poses since the Statue Sickness started, bodies bent into more twisted forms. But seeing Dad that way, with his face blank and empty, brought tears to her eyes. Her back hit the stove, and she slid to the ground.

It only took about three minutes for him to come out of it, although it felt like longer. He straightened up, arms falling back into a natural position. Shaking his head once, he turned and saw Anza sitting on the linoleum floor.

"Oh, goddamn," he said, turning away.

"When did it start?" she asked. Her voice trembled only a little.

He sighed. "Last week. I was in the saloon, and I started Naming. Or so the guys told me." He crouched down to be eye level with her. "I'm sorry, sweetie. I just didn't want to worry you."

Anza took a deep, shuddering breath, wiping her eyes with the back of her hand. She got up and dug around in the kitchen junk drawer until she found an old Steno pad. "Sit down," she said, pointing at the kitchen table. "I gotta ask you the same questions we ask everyone else. Some are embarrassing." She had memorized them by now and had transcribed answers enough times that she knew what the numbers would be.

She sat down across from him and wrote two things across the top of the paper. *Name: Sean Kearney. Number: 102.*

CHAPTER 13: 2020

Sonia wasn't sure what she'd expected a professor's house to look like, but this wasn't it. Medium-sized, Santa Fe-style, the house was small, but it had a neat garden out front. Nothing really screamed money or prestige.

The guy who answered the door didn't seem much like a professor, either. Tall and skinny, he wore an old *Doctor Who* T-shirt and a tidy beard. He was younger than she'd imagined, too, around thirty. Everything about him made her suspect he probably smoked plenty of weed and played Ultimate Frisbee in his spare time.

"Hey. You Professor Ayres?" she asked, trying to sound like she dropped by professors' houses all the time.

"Yeah. But please, call me Colin." He motioned for her to come inside. "This is Alonzo."

"You didn't have to come all the way from Phoenix," Colin said, clearing some papers off the couch so she could sit. "I'm not sure there's much we can do here that we couldn't do on the phone."

"Nah, don't worry about it. My band had some gigs scheduled here anyways, so it worked out." She paused. "Plus, my fucker of a boss fired me for scaring customers with my 'freaky voodoo shit,' as he put it, so I'm free as a bird."

"I'm sorry about that," Alonzo said, grimacing. "I've been having them too. I know it makes work tough."

"So. What are we dealing with, and how do I stop it from messing with my kid?"

Colin exchanged a long glance with Alonzo as he settled down in the chair opposite her. "Uh. Well. Here's what we know so far."

He sketched out the history of the Galina Plagues, the four major diseases emerging over the course of the summer of 1960. Most of it was vaguely familiar to her, if only because she'd spent time researching it online. There were some other things, too, though, things about a race riot and several murders, most likely committed by members of a white evangelical congregation. The Wikipedia article on Galina had glossed over that part, referring only vaguely to "scattered violent incidents."

She snorted. "Wouldn't be surprised if old Richie was involved in that. He was a nasty, racist piece of work."

"Anyway," Colin said, "the Plagues stopped entirely over the course of a single day. After the big riot, they were just over. No one knows why. I always assumed it was because the Plagues came from economic stress and racial inequality and the riot brought those tensions out into the open."

Sonia frowned. "Wait, but what about the other stuff? Like the Red Hail? Racism can't do that shit."

He sighed. "Well, I always thought the Red Hail might not have actually happened. I'm rethinking it."

"Didn't happen? But a whole shit-ton of people saw it. Grandpa Richie never shut up about it." She'd always had an oddly clear, vivid mental image of it, considering there weren't any pictures and she was so young when Grandpa Richie died. She imagined it as gobs of blood-colored ice dropping from the sky, frozen viscera melting and staining the soil red. There was even a smell, something pungent and meaty she must have dreamed up to go with the visuals.

"There aren't any news reports of the Red Hail until a month after it happened. I always thought it was a case of collective illusion of truth effect, but now, I don't know."

Sonia decided against questioning that further. If what he was saying was true, it still wouldn't be even close to the weirdest thing about the Plague Summer. "Okay, so this freaky stuff happens to our grandparents sixty years ago, and now it's happening to us, totally out of the blue." She looked back and forth between the two men. "Tell me you have some kind of theory here."

"Nothing solid. Sorry," Alonzo replied. "Right now, we're still working on ruling things out. We know it can't be all psychological because it happened to you and me independently—"

"And my son."

"And the tests I've had so far basically ruled out epilepsy and most motor-neuron diseases."

"That's comforting, because the tests I could afford on my insurance pretty much just confirmed my head is still attached to my neck."

Colin shuffled through some of the papers at his side. "But the good news is, if this is following the same pattern your grandparents followed, it ends after the fourth illness, and everything goes back to normal." He held out a long printout of something like a timeline, with dots highlighted in yellow.

"So you're saying we just wait it out?"

"No. I mean... there's enough that's different this time around. I don't think we should assume anything. I think our best bet is to contact as many Galina survivors and their descendants as we can, see if we can establish some patterns."

"So..." She leaned forward, elbows resting on her thighs. "If you don't mind me asking, what do *you* think it is?"

Alonzo bit his lip. "The only thing that makes sense is some kind of fungal or bacterial infection with an environmental trigger. Like Valley Fever. People or animals get exposed to the fungus that causes Valley Fever, and it lies dormant in the body for five years, sometimes longer. Then something triggers it, and it becomes aggressive. Granted, this would be a much more extreme dormant period than I've ever heard of. But it's the only way a disease vector makes any sense, and I don't see another explanation."

Sonia nodded. "So you're thinking the Red Hail brought the fungus, or whatever, and our grandparents and parents passed it along, and something happened a few weeks ago to wake it up. And it just happened to go down on the anniversary."

Alonzo shrugged. "I mean, yeah. It's freaky, but I have to think the date is just a weird coincidence."

Colin nodded in agreement.

"Okay." Sonia grabbed her bag. "I gotta go get ready for my gig. But I can start helping tomorrow."

"I thought you lived in Phoenix," Alonzo said.

"I do. But I'm staying here until we figure this out. A friend from my old band lives just a few blocks from here, and she said I could crash with her as long as I need."

Colin's eyes widened. "Oh, you don't have to—"

"Yeah, I do."

"But—"

"Look. Is it fair to say you're the number-one expert on the Galina Plagues?" she asked.

"I don't know about that..."

Alonzo gave him an impatient frown. "Come on, Col, not the time to be humble."

Colin's face flushed a little. "Um. Yeah, I guess. Not the only one, but I've probably researched it more than anyone else. Aside from, you know, conspiracy nuts."

"Okay, then. Here's my situation." She stood. "I got fired. My kid's sick. I'm leaving him with my mom because I don't trust myself not to space out and burn the house down with him in it. This is wrecking my life, and it's only been going on a few weeks. You can't ask me to sit around and not help. And I'd rather try to figure it out with someone who already knows something instead of on my own. Besides, I've been a temp before. Doing the bitch work doesn't bother me."

"I like her," Alonzo said.

Colin laughed. "Okay. Can't afford a research assistant, anyway, so thanks. Come by tomorrow morning. We'll hammer out a plan."

"WHATCHYA DOING?" ALONZO asked, drifting into the office.

Colin pulled a thick volume from the bookcase and added it to the growing stack on the ground. "Setting aside stuff that might come in handy for research. I thought Sonia could start off with some background reading tomorrow."

Alonzo slipped between him and the bookcase. "Okay, no more research stuff tonight. We'll start working hard tomorrow. Tonight, we should relax. Remember, stress avoidance?"

"So, what are we thinking? Ooh, Scrabble tournament?" Colin asked, putting on a pretend excited face.

"Nope." He held up his phone. "They just sent out the announcement."

"Bloom Night?"

"Yeah. Sunset's around seven fifteen."

They stared at each other for a long moment. Colin thought about their first Bloom Night, and he knew from Alonzo's face that he was too. They'd never really decided on an anniversary, neither having any patience for mandatory celebrations of romance, but if Colin had to settle on a day, it would be Bloom Night. He still remembered Alonzo calling to tell him about it and how nervous he'd sounded: "Hey, so... I know you aren't from Tucson, so this might sound really dumb to you, but there's this cactus at Tohono Chul Park that only flowers one night out of the year, and I just got the alert that it's going to be tonight. Interested?"

Before that night, Colin had still been unsure of what was between them. He'd felt the attraction right away, during that all-business interview and the friendly beer a few days later. They'd met and hung out over the next couple of weeks, after he accepted Alonzo's offer to show him around Tucson. There'd been moments when he was certain he saw the same attraction reflected back and times he was sure it was one-sided. So he'd told himself to be patient and not to risk ruining his first friendship in a new city, so far from everyone else he knew.

Then came Bloom Night. They'd walked the luminaria-lit paths of Tohono Chul, saying little. Colin kept wondering how close he should stand and if there was something he should be saying or if the atmosphere and tension hanging between them made it obvious enough. At one point, as they stopped along a deserted side path to watch the blooms, he cleared his throat. "So I notice something."

"Yeah?"

"You're pretty much the only person here not taking pictures." Alonzo's phone had stayed in his pocket and out of sight since they'd reached the park, even as every path around them blinked and shuddered with camera flashes.

Alonzo shrugged. "Taking pictures defeats the whole purpose." He saw Colin's raised eyebrow and went on: "There's nothing really exceptional about how these flowers look. I mean, they're pretty, I guess, but so is lots of stuff. The only reason people are here, the only thing that makes this special, is that they only exist for one night." He glanced down at his shoes, seeming a little embarrassed. "I don't know. It just seems wrong to try to preserve something that's only special because it'll be gone soon."

He started to move away toward another path. Without thinking, Colin reached out and caught his wrist. And then, before he could chicken out, he'd pulled Lonzo into their first kiss.

"That was a good night," Alonzo murmured, bringing him back to the present.

"Yeah, it was. Tonight will be too," Colin said. "Okay, we're on."

THE PARK SEEMED MORE crowded than it had last year, but they still managed to get tickets and find a good spot to watch. The Queen of the Night cactus was completely boring to look at most of the year. It didn't have any of the grandeur of a saguaro or even the Seussian weirdness of an organ pipe or a ladyfinger cactus. Most of the year, Queen of the Night cactuses were just spiny, vaguely sickly sticks. Now, though, luminescent white cracks appeared in the swollen buds dotting the branches. As Colin and Alonzo wandered around the park, the buds opened into brilliant white flowers, so pale they almost glowed in the dark.

Alonzo worked his way through the crowd of spectators to get a closer look at one of the bigger flowers. Colin lingered behind the crowd, staring at the cactus. *There's something... Something about cactus. Cactus, and that summer in Galina—*

"You okay?" Alonzo asked as he slipped back through the cluster of onlookers.

Whatever it was, the thought was gone. "I'm great," he replied, taking his arm. "Let's go see the rest."

LAUGHING, THEY TUMBLED onto the bed. He'd drunk too much wine at dinner, and Alonzo knew he would have a headache in the morning, but for the moment, he didn't care. He kicked off his shoes.

"Jesus, why are you still *dressed*?" he demanded, fumbling with the buttons on Colin's shirt. The thought of the first Bloom Night crossed his mind. It had been so different: tentative, hesitant, learning each other for the first time. That first night, he'd been struck by Colin's narrow hips and waist, as well as the surprising strength in those long, lanky arms.

Even once they'd gone back to his place, Alonzo had still felt drunk on that first kiss—right up until that moment he worried he'd miscalculated. He'd been pretty sure from the way Colin looked at him, but there were still scattered mentions of an ex-girlfriend and a few late-night opportunities in which he hadn't made a move. Then came that first kiss, and all his doubts evaporated.

He came back to the present, on a very different Bloom Night. They managed to get all their clothes off, and he got lost for a while in Colin's skin and smell and the feeling of his tongue. Then he was on top, Colin's legs around his waist. Colin pulled him into a kiss and tightened his legs as Alonzo went inside him, and they moved together—

Blink.

Alonzo lay curled on his side, on the floor instead of the bed. One of his arms was twisted under his body at an uncomfortable angle. "What..." He lifted his head.

Colin sat on the floor across from him. He was still naked, his back pressed to the wall, arms hugging his knees. His face was dry, but the redness in his eyes told Alonzo he'd been fighting back tears. Voice shaky, he asked, "Are you back?"

"Yeah, I... What happened?" He sat up.

"Sorry, I didn't mean to knock you off the bed. But we were in the middle of... And then you Statued, and it was like someone else was there." Colin shuddered. "I didn't mean to. I just freaked out."

"Oh god. I'm so sorry. I'm *so* sorry." Alonzo crawled over and wrapped his arms around Colin.

For just a moment, Colin's muscles stiffened, and he seemed to cringe away. Alonzo stopped, wondering what to do. *Don't leave,* he thought, fighting back the urge to say it aloud.

Finally, Colin relaxed and let Alonzo hold him, hugging him back. But that moment of disgust stayed, stinging like a splinter just under his skin.

CHAPTER 14: 1960

"My sister's getting married in October. It's all the way over in El Paso, so I get to miss two days of school." Consuela grinned as she reached for a can of pears. "I'm going to be a bridesmaid."

"That's great," Anza said. The thought of school gave her pause. She couldn't imagine school days going on with the way things were. Still, she supposed if people were finding ways to work, shop, and while away their Saturday afternoons in the saloon, they would also figure out how to manage school with students and teachers having fits now and then.

"Just hope somebody figures out how to get rid of the sickness by then," Consuela said, smile fading. "If I have a fit during my sister's wedding, I'll just die."

"She'll understand." Anza stared down at the grocery list and tried to calculate if they could fit anything else into the weekly budget. It was smaller than before, what with Dad's hours getting cut. Maybe they didn't need the fruit cocktail, she decided, putting the cans back on the shelf. They would have prickly pears in a couple weeks, anyway. And Mrs. Garces might let her take some oranges from her trees in exchange for babysitting.

Consuela kept chattering about her sister's wedding as they made their way up to the front of the store for Mr. Clarke to ring up their groceries. He'd just finished Consuela's basket and moved on to Anza's when Richie Rollins came around the corner, carrying a bottle of milk.

He stopped when he saw Anza, his lip curling in disgust. "Hank, what are you doing still letting them in here?"

"Richie, come on. Don't," Mr. Clarke said, his face red.

Richie Rollins couldn't have been older than twenty-five, not far into adulthood. Anza vaguely remembered him as a teenager, scrawny and sullen. But somehow, even though he wasn't that old, he'd already taken on the air of a man well past his prime. He was always a little disheveled, stubbly, and smelling of whiskey. Folks occasionally told stories of him spending the night in Sheriff Brandt's cell for public drunkenness, fighting, or some other nonsense. There was a deep anger in Richie that she had never understood. He had a way of glaring at the world and everyone in it.

"We talked about this last Sunday," Richie said. "And now they're still allowed in, near our food?"

"Excuse me? Are you talking about us?" Anza asked, certain he would laugh and clear it up. No, it must be about something else near the front counter, something unclean she didn't see.

But he looked her square in the eye. "Everyone knows it started with the Mexicans. Just like that last influenza epidemic and the big smallpox outbreak back during the war. Now this."

A moment of shocked, horrible stillness came over the store before Consuela erupted.

"How dare you!" she shouted. "You white-trash drunk! You just wait until my father hears about this!"

Anza couldn't move. She stood frozen while Consuela railed and threatened. That gleam in Richie Rollins' eye made her stomach twist. It was like she was a bug, squished on the floor. Anza waited until Consuela took a breath then forced herself to speak. "Richie, there's been just as many white people getting it as us. Maybe even more."

"Course you'd say that." He sneered. "It's been this way for years now, and I'm damn tired of it."

"Now, what's all this?"

She recognized George Esquivel's deep, rumbling voice before she turned to see him standing behind her. His wife stood a bit farther back, watching grimly as her husband ambled over to Richie.

"Is this man bothering you, ladies?" he growled, watching Richie, a thin smile on his lean features.

Anza swallowed. "It's okay, Mr. Esquivel."

"Is it, now, Miss Kearney?" he asked, eyes still locked on Richie. "Because I sure don't think it's okay to talk to two young ladies like that."

Richie seemed to wilt under that stare. He set the milk down on the nearest shelf. "On second thought, Hank, I think I'll drive over to the market in Bisbee. Until you take care of your pest problem."

He walked out, Consuela shouting after him. "Oh, when I tell my father and my brothers about this, that *pendejo* will be lucky not to end up in a shallow grave." She seemed to notice Mr. Clarke staring at her. "Not *really*. They'll just beat him up."

"Thank you, Mr. Esquivel," Anza said quietly.

George tipped his hat as he made his way back over to where his wife waited. "Any time, Miss Kearney."

"I couldn't *believe* the things he was saying," Consuela seethed.

"Is that what people think?" Anza asked, watching Mr. Clarke's face. "That the Mexicans started this?"

Mr. Clarke smiled at her. "Oh, now, don't you worry about Richie. He's as drunk as a skunk most of the time, doesn't know what he's talking about."

But Anza saw the truth in his eyes and the way he waited for her to set her money on the countertop instead of taking it from her hands. She lifted her chin as she gathered up her bags and pushed her spine ramrod straight even though every instinct she had told her to cower and hide. She managed to leave the store and get to the truck before she started shaking.

"ARE YOU SURE YOU'RE all right?" Father Santiago asked again.

"I'm fine," Anza snapped, irritation overcoming her fear.

He hesitated for a moment. "You know... I do understand how that felt. I grew up in Mexico, but I went to school in California. Alma College, in Los Gatos. I was getting a master's degree in theology, and still, there were restaurants I wasn't allowed to eat in. Neighborhoods I couldn't walk through. Stores with signs out front that said No dogs or Mexicans."

"Well, that's not how things are here," Anza said. "They've never been that way here."

He gave her a sad smile, and for some reason, it made her feel very young. "It's easy for people to get along when things are going well. It's when things are difficult that we're truly tested. That's the council I give couples before I agree to perform a wedding. They have to think about how they'll be at their worst, not just their best." He gestured toward the closed doors of the church. "It's the same with towns. Things are worse than any time people can remember, even in the war, and now we're seeing the things that stay under the surface when times are good."

Anza thought about Richie's face again. She didn't understand how that hatred could always have been there without her seeing it. "Well," she said, sitting up straighter in the pew, "either way, we should do something about it, right? I mean, if he's spreading that nonsense around town, it's just going to get people riled up."

"I'll speak to Pastor Benjamin. Maybe he'll see reason." He didn't sound like he really believed that, but she didn't press him on it.

She stood. "We should get over to Dove's place."

As she waited for Father Santiago to blow out the candles on the altar, she noticed some high-pitched noise on the edge of her hearing. "What is that?"

"Is it the birds again?" he asked, following her to the church doors.

"No..." The harsh afternoon light spilled inside as she opened the door.

Anza recognized the sound now, even though the rhythm was all wrong and she'd never heard it during the day. The sound was supposed to come out of the darkness as the pack slipped by the house like ghosts.

As she watched, other people came out of stores and businesses and houses, staring down Main Street at the approaching sound. The high-pitched yips were halfway between hysterical laughter and the sounds someone makes while in pain.

They came down the middle of Main Street, running in a single-file line—coyotes, dozens of them. The only times Anza had seen coyotes during the day had been half-second glimpses of one darting off the side of the road while another disappeared into a ravine. Now she got a good look at their surprisingly shiny gray fur, their graceful motions, the yellow of their eyes. They ran down the white line separating the two lanes of the street, letting out a chorus of yips at regular intervals. None spared a glance for any of the surrounding humans watching their progress.

As the last coyote in the column disappeared into the distance, the bystanders stared at each other. Anza saw a few who might have been praying. None spoke.

"*Calle.* Street. *El sol.* Sun. *Niña.* Girl. Esperanza." Father Santiago stood behind her, just inside the cool dark shadow of the church.

Anza cast a quick glance back over her shoulder. No one seemed to have seen the blankness on his face or the slow movement of his lips. "Come on, Father," she whispered, taking him by the arm and leading him back inside. He shuffled along obediently, still Naming everything in sight.

"WELL, I TALKED TO MAYOR Fuller," Dove said as they sat down. The coffee table and extra chairs that had once held paperbacks and pulp magazines now held folders of interview notes, medical textbooks, and hardcover volumes with cracked spines and titles referring to epidemiology and mass psychosis.

"He said the state finally called him back. They tested the water from a couple of the wells around town, said they came up clean. Same with some soil samples out of a few backyards." She snorted. "Of course, you can't test for something if you don't know what you're looking for. Still, they say they've done all they can, and they're officially writing it off as mass hysteria."

"Even with the strange animal behavior? How?" Father Santiago asked.

Dove shrugged. "We're overreacting. Making things up."

"Mayor Fuller doesn't believe that, right?" Anza asked.

"Course not. He's meek, not stupid. But he couldn't change their minds. He's trying to get the university researchers back out to try again, take some more blood samples and whatnot, but I don't think we should hold our breath."

Anza thought for a moment. "The stuff with the coyotes. Is it other animals, too, you think? What about your horse?"

"Charlie?" Dove asked. "Nothing unusual that I've seen. So far it just seems like birds and coyotes."

Silence stretched out. "So. . . what now?" Anza asked.

"Well... maybe we should consider this possibility, mass hysteria, more carefully," Father Santiago said after a moment.

Dove rolled her eyes and held up a stack of notes. "You know damn well about those cases where folks didn't know about any of it until they started doing it themselves."

"No, we know about cases where people *claim* that. By the time we interviewed them, they'd heard about all the other cases. You said yourself when we began this—people lie. Especially to themselves. And you must admit, this isn't like any physical ailment we've been able to find."

"I knew it," Dove said, lip curling. "I knew, sooner or later, a priest would decide this has to be some kind of spiritual goddamn affliction. What? You think it's demonic possession or something, now that you're showing symptoms?"

"Do *not* put words in my mouth, Mrs. McNally," he said, voice rising. "I never said a word about demons."

"No, you just decided to do what holy men do best, which is ignore stacks of evidence..."

The argument faded from Anza's hearing. She stared at their timeline of the first two weeks. The long roll of butcher paper pinned to one of Dove's shelves listed the names, the dates of first symptoms, and notes about known contacts with other infected. *Then the birds, and now the coyotes.* She saw it.

"Shut up," she said, standing.

Father Santiago stared up at her, eyes wide with shock. "Esperanza!"

"I'm sorry, Father, Dove, but look." Anza pointed at the timeline. "It's the mesa. See? Every case in the first two weeks is a child or a teenager. And all of them were either out on the mesa just after the Red Hail, or they had contact with someone who was. See?" She stepped over a pile of notes and pointed at Tracey's circle. "We always assumed Tracey got it from being touched by Pablo Garces, but her mama was searching with us that night. So was Paula's. Fernando was out there himself. And-and Tracey's friend Becca, her brother came out there too. We didn't see it before, because it started with the younger kids, but all of them had a mom or a dad or a sister or something out there on the mesa the night the Garces kids went missing. And the Garces kids were on the mesa right before they disappeared, before they got sick. And that's where the coyotes live and the birds, so..."

Dove and Father Santiago scrambled through the stacks of notes, pulling out all the cases from the first two weeks. Dove called out a few names. "What about him? Was he out there?"

Anza searched her memory, trying to remember exactly who she'd seen on the mesa that night. "Yeah. And him. Him too. And her."

They ran through the entire list, everyone in the first two weeks. "Twenty-six cases," Dove said at last. "All with a connection to the mesa."

"I always wondered about the Costello children. They insisted they hadn't been near anyone else who got sick, but Eileen Costello was on the mesa that night." Father Santiago flipped through the notes, eyes shining with excitement.

Dove took off her reading glasses. "Well, Miss Kearney, I do believe you may have found our water pump. Whatever this is—virus, bacteria—it started on the mesa. Could still be a disease reservoir out there."

Father Santiago looked up, frowning. "That does raise a question, though."

"What?" Anza tried not to grin even as the glow of pride warmed her cheeks.

"Why aren't you sick?"

Anza felt her smile fade. She thought about who had been on the mesa that night. It had taken the adults much longer to show symptoms, but... "Everyone who was on the mesa has it. Except me."

"That's not unusual," Dove said, dismissing the comment with a flutter of her hand. "A lot of diseases have carriers who never get sick. Like typhoid. Even the worst diseases don't infect everyone. You know that."

Anza nodded and tried to seem reassured. She'd pointed out the same things, back when Fernando insisted she was about to get sick. But now something about it made her nervous, like there was something about herself she didn't know... and didn't quite *want* to know.

CHAPTER 15: 2020

Alonzo barely slept after regaining consciousness on the floor. Colin insisted he was fine, and they eventually went back to bed, but neither tried to resume the sex the episode had interrupted. After a while, Colin's breathing settled into the heavy, slow patterns of sleep. Alonzo just stared at the crack in the curtains until it lightened from black to slate gray. He waited until the clock read 6:30 before he rose, pausing to watch Colin's still-snoozing form.

He went out to the porch. The air was still nighttime-cool. He pulled out his phone and scrolled through his contacts until he found Lianne's home number. She wouldn't be at work for another hour and a half, but he knew she always woke at the crack of dawn to feed her many pets and get her kid ready for school.

She answered on the second ring, voice tinged with surprise. "Hello?"

"Hey, Li. It's Alonzo. Sorry to call you at home."

"No problem. What's up?"

"So... remember how I said I didn't need time off?" He sighed. "I think I was wrong."

Lianne was kind and understanding, assuring him he could take as much time as he needed and come back whenever he was better. It just made the creeping shame in his belly worse.

After he hung up, Alonzo stayed out on the porch and waited for the sky to brighten. Little creatures darted around in the yard, probably lizards and birds, but for just a second, he thought he saw something flash red through a patch of weeds. Blinking, he decided he was just tired.

The porch door slid open, and Colin's sleepy head poked out. "Hey. Shouldn't you be leaving for work soon?" he asked, eyeing Lonzo's sweatpants and undershirt.

Alonzo tried to smile and suspected he was failing at it. "Nope. Just called Lianne and told her I'm researching this full time until we figure it out." He shook his head. "I can't work like this."

Colin gave him a sympathetic nod. "I'm sorry. I know you didn't want to do that."

"No. No, I did not."

"Well, the research should go faster now, at least."

"Yeah." He wanted Colin to come over and rest his hands on his shoulders, give him a hug, or something. Instead, he just slipped back inside the house, leaving Alonzo alone on the porch.

Two hours later, someone knocked on the front door. Alonzo answered, finding Sonia Rollins on the front step.

"Hey," she said, moving past him. As there had been yesterday, there was something familiar about her. He knew they'd never met, and he wasn't a blues fan, so he felt pretty sure he'd never seen her perform with any of her bands. But he recognized something about her voice or her bearing.

As she passed him on her way into the house, their eyes met for just a second. There, he saw that sense of recognition reflected back at him, the quick frown creasing her features as she tried to figure out how she knew him. Then Colin came out to greet her, she turned away, and the moment passed.

SONIA BROWSED THROUGH the folders of research notes Colin had copied over to her laptop, eyes widening as she realized how many there were. She'd signed a non-disclosure agreement and paperwork saying Colin was technically hiring her as an unpaid assistant so he wouldn't be breaking some kind of university research policy. It didn't say what would happen if she repeated anything she saw in the files, but she assumed it would be a lot worse for Colin than for her.

"Okay. So, a dissertation is basically a book, right?" she asked. "You research the shit out of something until you have enough to write a book about it?"

Colin nodded. "Yeah. Pretty much."

"But then, instead of just publishing that, you do even *more* research to make it even *more* of a book, which you then publish."

"That's right."

"So, then why don't you people just do all the research you need when it's a dissertation?"

"Because that would be way too practical for academics. They like making everything harder than it has to be," Alonzo said without looking up from his own screen.

"Okay, I'll admit it's a little bit that," Colin said before turning back to Sonia.

She watched carefully as he answered. People often started using little words and speaking slowly when they found out she'd never gone to college. So far, neither Colin nor Alonzo had done that, but she had some comebacks ready just in case.

"Academics are really good at complicating everything," he said, "but mostly, it's just money. I only got enough funding to come to Arizona for a few weeks back when I was doing the diss, so I didn't have a lot of interviews for it. But luckily, I got a job near where most of my subjects live, so I got the rest of the research done pretty fast."

"So you publish the book, and then you get tenure."

Colin laughed. "Hell no. I need a second book and a bunch of articles and all kinds of other stuff. That's why they give us seven years to do it all."

She shook her head. "Yeah, next time someone gives me crap about being a songwriter, I'm going to tell them what you just said." She scrolled through the folder of research notes again. "Okay, it'll take me five hundred years to get through these. I got a better idea. Just give me the Galina names, I'll take it from there."

"HOW'S IT GOING OVER there?"

Sonia glanced up from the screen. She sat with her back to the couch, laptop resting before her on the hardwood floor. "Good. Did the mass email for the folks on your contact list. Now I'm working on tracking down the ones you couldn't find. Think I found, like, ten so far."

"Ten? Already? How?" Colin asked from his spot at the dining room table. He wore jeans but no shoes, long legs stretched out for most of the length of the table.

He must have a miserable time on planes, Sonia thought. "Facebook. Twitter. Dude, I can't believe you didn't even get on Facebook to find these people back when you were doing research. What did you use, like, carrier pigeons?"

Colin smiled but didn't seem to mean it. Alonzo set a cup of coffee down in front of him and brought another to Sonia.

"Thanks," she said.

Something was going on with those two. She'd figured out pretty quickly that they both lived here, and yesterday, she'd definitely picked up on them being an item. But they avoided eye contact with each other and spoke too carefully, like each was afraid of offending the other. There were some jokes here and there, but of a safe, careful variety, almost forced, and probably for her benefit. It wasn't like the aftermath of a fight. There was no anger, just something else. Something fragile.

Shrugging inwardly, Sonia got back to work. Finding people became harder with each generation, especially when women married and changed their names. She focused on finding Facebook accounts of middle-aged ones whose parents would have been in Galina during the Plagues and whose children would be roughly her age.

Sonia's email dinged. "Looks like we got another 'nope, everything's cool.' But she did give us some more names of folks connected to Galina." She opened up new tabs to start the search for those names.

"Name?"

"Uh, Jennifer Ortega. Her dad was a guy named Mark Zavala. He would have been about seventeen during the Plagues."

"Got it."

A few minutes later, the email account dinged again. "Hey, guys, think we got a hit." Sonia's heart beat faster as she read the email. "This is from Lana Kowalski. Maiden name Kress. Her mom was named Patricia Kress, but at the time of the Plagues, she would have been Patricia Billings. Seriously, god-fucking-damn women changing their names. Anyway, Lana says she's fine, but her daughter Kelsey has been Naming and Statuing."

Colin typed away for a minute. Alonzo moved to look over his shoulder. Sonia caught him starting to lay a hand on Colin's arm before hesitating and letting it drop to his side.

"Okay. I've got Patty Billings. She was there. Her mother ran the café." Colin paused, clicking something. "This is interesting."

"Yeah," Alonzo murmured, nodding. "Weird."

"Hm?"

"Well, so far, every child of a Galina survivor we've heard from says they aren't having symptoms. But every grandchild or great-grandchild is."

"So it skips a generation?" She stood and joined them in staring at the screen. The spreadsheet Colin had pulled up was way too complicated for her to pick up on everything, but she did see the column labeled "Generation" and numbers she supposed stood for first, second, or third.

"We'll need more responses to be sure, but that's what it looks like so far." He glanced up at Alonzo. "How are we doing on the environmental trigger?"

"Got a few ideas." Alonzo returned to his side of the table. "Although I don't see how it would work with this generational thing. But I'm thinking maybe, if we're dealing with a fungal infection, maybe it was this haboob that hit Phoenix five days before the first symptoms."

"What the hell is a haboob?" Colin frowned.

"Not an Arizona boy, huh?" Sonia asked.

"Dust storm. A really, really big dust storm," Alonzo clarified. "We tend to see a lot of pets with respiratory issues afterward, and I bet it's the same for humans."

Sonia's eyes widened. "Hey, yeah! And Dylan and I got caught in that too." They'd been on their way from their house to her mother's place when Sonia saw the wall of dust in the rearview mirror. She'd just had time to pull into a McDonald's parking lot before the wind and dirt slammed into their car, darkening the sky. She'd turned off the AC, but even so, dust particles had drifted into the vents and through cracks in the door. It settled in their eyes and noses, making them cough for a day afterward.

Alonzo ran a hand over the top of his head. "Now, the problem with that is that the haboob didn't get within a hundred miles of Tucson, so it doesn't really explain us having symptoms here. But maybe if the prevailing winds carried just *some* of the dust here..."

It sounded thin to Sonia, but Colin smiled broadly, a little too much. "That's great. Great job."

She went back to her laptop. "I think I'm going to put a call out on some medical forums. That way, even the folks we miss might find us if they're googling their symptoms." She tried to remember the search terms she'd used back when she and Dylan started getting sick and the websites she'd scrolled through while searching for answers.

She'd just finished the first forum post when she got another email. There was a video attached. Sonia clicked it and watched in silence.

"Uh-oh. Hey, Colin?"

He came over to where she sat. "Yeah?"

"Just got another email. But this one has a video, and it's not Naming or Statuing."

She played it again. It was grainy and low-quality, but the motions of the person in it were clear enough. It was a teenage boy, maybe seventeen. He stood in what might have been a living room, the faint outline of a couch behind him. His arm snapped out to the right in a grabbing motion then returned to his side. His jaw swung open and out, so wide Sonia worried it would dislocate. Finally, his entire torso moved in a circle, wobbling like a drunken dance step. Then the entire sequence repeated again.

"This is from another woman whose parents were from Galina. And this is another grandchild," Sonia said. "She says he started with stuff that sounds like Naming and Statuing, but now he's doing this too."

Colin's eyes went distant. "Did she give dates?"

"Uh, yeah." She read them off, and he returned to his laptop.

"What is it?" Alonzo asked.

"I think. Yeah." Colin rubbed his forehead. "It's progressing faster this time. The Galina Plagues were all spaced twenty to twenty-five days apart, as far as anyone's been able to pin down. You and Sonia went from Naming to Statuing in twelve. And now this kid went from Statuing to the Dancing Sickness in eleven days."

"So we'll start getting new symptoms anytime now." Alonzo met Sonia's gaze. She knew that look—nothing she said would make it better.

Colin didn't get it, though. "Hey, it's okay. We're getting a handle on this." His hand stretched out across the table, even though he and Alonzo sat too far away to touch.

For just a moment, anger flared in Alonzo's expression, his jaw muscles clenching. But then it cleared, and he nodded. "Yeah. We'll figure it out."

Sonia turned away, clicking on the video to replay it. She imagined Dylan making those same spastic motions, with that same inhuman stare. Then she swallowed the panic and got back to work.

ALONZO HAD ALMOST GIVEN up and gone to sleep when Colin finally came to bed. He collapsed onto his back with a heavy sigh.

"You okay?" Alonzo asked.

"Yeah. Just a headache from staring at the screen all day." He rubbed his eyes with both hands.

"Are *we* okay?"

Colin finally looked over, his expression softening. "Yeah. We're okay. Come here."

Alonzo curled against his shoulder. It felt better, without the cringing and distance he'd picked up from Colin all day. Still, it wasn't quite the same as it would have been a few days ago. Colin's muscles were just a little too tense, as though he was ready to jump up at any second. Alonzo closed his eyes and tried to pretend everything was back to normal. They said nothing for a while.

"We're gonna figure this out. You know that, right?" Colin said, running a hand along his arm.

"What if we don't?"

"We will."

Alonzo kept his eyes closed. "I'm serious, though. What if we don't? What if this is the new normal for me?"

Arms squeezed him tighter. "Then it's the new normal for me too."

"I don't want that for you." He whispered the words so his voice wouldn't shake.

"Tough shit."

He couldn't help laughing a little.

Colin's body relaxed around him. "It doesn't matter, though. Because we *are* going to figure this out, okay?"

Alonzo nodded, held him close, and didn't argue.

CHAPTER 16: 1960

Anza first heard about the blood beetles while passing a group of women gathered on Main Street. They stood in front of the dress shop, gossiping, as they always did on Saturday afternoons. Instead of laughing and drawing close with a conspiratorial "Well, *I* heard," they hovered in a tense, unsmiling cluster.

"Mel thinks I'm crazy, but I tell you, Laurie, I saw it plain as day. Bright red."

Anza slowed, pretending to peruse her grocery list.

"Like a ladybug?"

"No. Big as a fifty-cent piece. And bloody red, not cheerful like a ladybug. It landed right on the porch railing and sat there for a minute before it flew away."

"I've seen them too," another woman added. "Skittering through the weeds. They're the same shade as the Red Hail, same exactly. And not like any other bug I've ever seen around here."

The women finally seemed to notice Anza eavesdropping. Falling silent, they pulled apart and pretended to be watching something on the other side of the street. She moved on.

The next time she heard about the beetles was that evening. Fernando and the others weren't in their usual spot near the ice cream parlor, so she wandered until she found them in the field next to the school. Fernando stood near a patch of weeds, a Mason jar in one hand.

"What are you doing?" Anza asked timidly. She hadn't seen him since the other night on the porch. He hadn't been angry with her then, hadn't lashed out, but she wondered if he wanted her to stay away.

He glanced up and flashed a quick smile. There was sadness behind the expression, but he tried to hide it. "Trying to catch some of those blood beetles." Squatting, he peered into the weeds. "Folks say they like to hide in the grass like this, where it's tall."

"What's a blood beetle?" She wondered how close she should stand. Talking to Fernando suddenly felt awkward, like neither knew if they were still going with each other or what to think about it either way. Part of her wondered if they could ever just be friendly with each other again, like they were back before they started going steady.

"People have been seeing them around. They're big, like this." He held up his fingers in a circle two inches across.

"Have you seen one?" She folded her arms, trying not to sound skeptical.

"I think so. But I didn't get a good look."

"My mom says that's what's causing the fits," Paula called from the other side of the patch of weeds. "The beetles are biting people and making them sick."

Next to her, Mark nodded in agreement.

Anza made some noncommittal sound. None of the books she'd gotten from Dove had anything about bug bites that could cause diseases like the Plagues, but she decided it would be a waste of time to tell the others that. She waited around for a bit, shifting from one foot to the other. Just as she decided to wander back toward Main Street, something red flashed on the edge of her vision.

"There!" Mark shouted, pouncing with his jar.

"Get it?" Fernando asked.

Mark peered at the empty jar. "No. They're fast."

"I'll see you guys later," Anza said, walking away. That little flash kept running through her mind. She hadn't gotten a good look at the shape, but it had definitely been red. The same shade as the Red Hail.

"SO WHAT ARE WE LOOKING for?" Anza asked, staring out at the rocky ground of the mesa.

"Anything unusual." Dove adjusted her hat. "At this point, I'm thinking maybe a toxin is more likely than a contagion. Maybe the folks who came out here tracked it in on their shoes. Anyway, it would help explain what's going on with the birds and the coyotes. So look for anything unusual going on with plants or animals. Maybe we can at least narrow down the area."

"Yes, and then maybe we can persuade the doctors from the state to come back." Father Santiago snorted. "Or gather the samples ourselves and send them." It was strange to see him in jeans and a straw hat, although he still wore the clerical collar under his yellow bandana.

"Shouldn't we be telling people about it? That it's something on the mesa?" Anza asked.

Dove shrugged. "Don't see much point until we find what it is. People are worked up enough without us making them afraid to step outside. Once we got something solid to show them, then we'll spread the word."

Anza lifted the binoculars Dad had brought back from the war. "Okay, then. So we look for anything unusual. Like blood beetles."

Dove shook her head. "I'm still not convinced those things are real. Catch one, and we'll see."

Anza had scoured an encyclopedia of Southwestern wildlife Dove had brought from the library, but she'd found nothing like the blood beetles people talked about. Dove said it was all just people getting nervous and making things up, but Father Santiago seemed less sure. Anza didn't know what to think.

They set out along the edge of the mesa, planning to cover one narrow band at a time until they swept the entire plain. That would take days, weeks even, especially in the summer heat. She tugged her hat lower on her forehead and sipped from the canteen on her hip before lifting the binoculars again.

Picking their way across the mesa was slow going. They stopped now and then to examine a bird, lizard, or plant that seemed a little unusual. But two hours of walking and searching turned up nothing truly strange enough to be noteworthy. Anza kept looking down at the beige dust beneath her Ropers, wondering what strange spores or chemicals she had carried into other people's homes. She wondered if anyone had caught it directly from her.

"Hey, you see that?" Dove squinted under the brim of her hat.

Anza lifted her binoculars, tracking the mirage along the horizon. "There? That bunch of cactus?"

"Yeah."

"It does seem odd, it being all clustered together that way," Father Santiago said.

They trudged across the mesa, the sun beating down on them. Anza perked up as they got closer, seeing how strangely the cactus grew.

From a distance, it looked like a wall of dusty green. As they got closer, though, she saw that it was more of a circle, a curved shape about fifty feet across. It consisted of a wild mix of cacti, mostly fuzzy teddy bear cholla with the occasional barrel cactus or prickly pear and one tall saguaro growing along the edge. They all grew in one dense, clinging mass, leaving no space between where one cactus ended and another began. Anza rose onto her tiptoes and peered over the closest cactus. The patch continued in a solid mass, covering the entire oval area.

"I've never seen this before," Father Santiago muttered.

Dove folded her arms. "Yeah. Kinda defeats the purpose of being a desert plant, having to fight for water with a bunch of other plants in the same spot." She tilted her head. "One thing's for sure, though. It's one hell of a defense. Whatever's in the middle of this, we ain't never getting to it. I'd rather try my luck with razor wire."

Anza eyed the teddy bear cholla and shuddered. She remembered being a little girl, maybe four, and being drawn to the fluffy, soft-looking fuzz. She'd grabbed it with one hand, and the hair-thin slivers like barbed fiberglass embedded themselves into her flesh. A whole ball of the cholla had come off onto her palm while she shrieked. Dad had to pour cough syrup down her throat to calm her enough for him to pick the spines out with a needle and a pair of tweezers. Then, even though he'd spent an entire night trying to get them all, the rest had taken weeks to work their way out of her skin, and the glasslike hairs had stung every time she moved her hand.

"Yeah. We'd need a chainsaw." Anza looked back toward the edge of the mesa. She frowned, turning in a slow circle and scanning for landmarks. "You know what?"

"Hm?" Dove asked, still considering the patch of cactus.

"I think this is where we found the clothes. When we went out looking for the Garces kids. I remember that arroyo over there, having to go around it. And I'm pretty sure if we walked straight back that way, we'd hit the Garces place."

"What do you think that means?" Father Santiago asked, turning to Dove.

"Beats me. I mean... we know they were covered in mud. How they got onto that rock is anybody's guess, but they must have been in a mudhole or a pit before that. Maybe there was a sinkhole opened up because of the hail? And it's making the plants grow funny." She shook her head once, as though coming to her senses. "No, goddammit, what kind of sinkhole leaves clothes behind, keeps the kids alive, and then spits them back up? Doesn't make a lick of sense, any of it."

"No." He let out an exhausted sigh. "It doesn't."

He stepped toward Dove. As he moved, he brushed close to the outstretched arm of a cholla. Anza opened her mouth to warn him. As she watched, though, the branch pulled away from his hip, retracting deeper into the cactus patch.

Anza froze, and Dove gasped.

"Did you see that?" Anza asked.

Dove nodded.

"What?" Father Santiago frowned at them.

Wordlessly, Dove grasped his wrist and pushed his hand closer to the cactus. Just before his fingertips brushed the spines, it pulled away from him again.

"Dear God." He stepped back, clutching his hand as though the spines had actually touched him.

Dove stepped closer to the patch, reaching for the cactus. It didn't move, even when her finger brushed the very end of a spine. Then Anza tried, wincing as she did at the memory of the cholla in her hand. It didn't move for her, either.

Adam's apple bobbing in a convulsive motion, Father Santiago moved forward again. The cactus immediately shrank away from his body. "I'm going to see if it lets me walk into the center."

Dove bit her lip. "I don't know, Padre. If it decides to close behind you…"

"I'll be okay." He pushed his boot forward into the patch. The ground seemed to ripple, and two cactus plants lurched apart to reveal a section of bare earth big enough for him to step on.

"Sweet Jesus," Anza breathed, even though she knew he didn't like blasphemy.

But he didn't seem to notice. He started to take a second step into the patch, bringing his left foot even with his right. Before he could complete his step, his body lurched into one of the pretzel shapes of the Statue Sickness. His left leg twisted sickeningly up and behind his back. His upper body dipped forward, and for one terrible moment, Anza was sure he was going to topple face-first into the cactus. But he remained standing, perched on one foot, hovering inches from the spines.

NONE OF THEM SPOKE on their walk back from the mesa. They'd tried three times, at three different points, to go beyond the edge of the circle. Every time, Father Santiago had made it no more than two steps before Statuing. And the cactus hadn't shown the slightest regard for Dove or Anza, no matter how many places they tested it.

The sun was beginning to set by the time they reached Dove's truck.

"I think it's time we expand our reading list," she said at last, the first word any of them had spoken since giving up on the cactus patch. "I'm not buying into any supernatural nonsense, mind, but any fool could see this isn't some normal bacterial infection we're dealing with."

"I'll try calling the university again." Father Santiago untied his bandana and used it to mop his sweat-smeared face.

Dove nodded. "I'll drive up to the library in Sierra Vista. See if they have anything on... Hell, I don't know. Plants that like some people more than others. And new kinds of bugs no one's ever seen before. And the world losing its damn mind." She tried to smile but didn't quite manage it.

ANZA WAS READING A book about cryptobotany when the phone rang. She'd had no idea what cryptobotany was until Dove showed up with an armload of books and journal articles about it. The book she was reading, like almost all of them, vacillated between ridiculous and boring, interspersing stories of man-eating trees with dry academic language about the biology of plants. She tossed the book aside, glad for the distraction.

"Anza! Oh my god, Anza, did you hear?"

"Paula?"

"I called as soon as I got home from church. Did you hear?"

"No. What happened?" Her heart pounded. Not a new symptom. Not the dangerous one, the painful or fatal one they'd been hoping and praying wouldn't join the list. *Please just not that.*

"Oh, Anza, you should have seen it! It was amazing!"

The story Paula told was one Anza heard again and again from different people in town over the next week. The details varied, but the broad strokes were always the same. It started in Pastor Benjamin's church. He'd been giving a sermon, an impassioned screed against allowing the devil into one's life and the importance of fighting temptation. Then something changed. He straightened up, body going rigid. His eyes went blank. And then he started Naming. No one remembered exactly what he'd Named. It scarcely mattered, since it was always the same, always just the barest details of one's surroundings. They'd all seen it before by then, at least once.

But then came something none of them had seen before. A few words into the Naming, Pastor Benjamin stopped. Focus returned to his eyes. "No! *Get out*, Satan, get out! I reject you, in the name of Jesus Christ!" As the crowd gasped and stood to get a better view, Pastor Benjamin went back to Naming for a few words. After only a few seconds, though, his body shook in a spasm. He fell to the floor, spine arching.

"No! No, you will not... you will not! I reject you, devil. I..." He let out a horrible scream, which some people described as a howl, a bloodcurdling animal cry. "I said, in the name of Christ, *get out*!" He fell silent. His body relaxed.

His wife, Emily, rushed to the front of the church and helped him to his feet. As soon as he stood, the congregation saw that he was weak and shaky but conscious. His face poured with sweat. Supported by Emily's arms, he held up his Bible in one hand. "Brothers and sisters! The devil came to me, but I cast him out. And all of you can do the same!" The crowd erupted in cheers. Paula's mother cried. People fell to their knees, weeping and praying.

"You could feel it, Anza. The Holy Spirit was there, in that room. Pastor Benjamin found a way to fight the disease." Paula let out a wild, joyful laugh. "You see? We're going to be okay!"

"LEAVE IT TO A DAMN clergyman," Dove fumed, pacing across the small portion of her living room not stacked with notes and books.

"I mean, it can't be true, right?" Anza asked.

Dove's eyes flared. "Of course it's not true!" She took a deep breath and seemed like she was trying to calm herself.

Father Santiago cleared his throat. "I've been hearing rumors of Pastor Benjamin having symptoms for over a week now. One of my parishioners said she heard him Naming at the café."

"So he—what? He fakes a Naming fit and then pretends to fight it off?" Anza asked.

"That's right. Brilliant move. Takes a weakness and makes it a goddamn advantage." Dove's eyes narrowed at the expression on Father Santiago's face. "I'll watch my mouth in your church, Padre, but I'll be damned if I'm gonna follow anyone else's speaking rules in my own house. High time you got used to it."

Father Santiago's lips pressed together, but he didn't argue. "Yes, Anza. He must have known he would eventually be seen by his congregation, so he decided to take control." He smiled ruefully. "Perhaps I should take some notes on showmanship from him. I simply told my flock after Mass."

"I don't care if he's Barnum and Bailey. That bastard's just made our job twice as hard. Now instead of trying out things that might actually work, people are going to be thinking they can magic it away themselves."

Anza sighed. "Well, it's not like we have any better ideas."

"Not yet. We will." She almost managed to keep the doubt out of her voice.

"In the meantime, I'll talk to Pastor Benjamin. Maybe I can persuade him to... tone it down?" Father Santiago said, standing.

Dove's expression softened. "You won't, but thanks for trying." She blinked and let out a dry laugh. "Whole town going crazy, and the only other people left with a good head on their shoulders are a priest and a sixteen-year-old girl. What's the world coming to?"

CHAPTER 17: 2020

Ross looked up from his guitar and smiled. "Hey, Sonia."

"Looks like we got a good crowd out there." She hooked her thumb back toward the front of the bar. The back room was dark and crowded, even by the standards of the gigs they normally played. The unmistakable scent of piss wafted from the bathroom across the hall.

"Yeah. It's a college crowd, though, so I'm not sure they realize we're a blues group."

"As long as me and Kyra show cleavage, it won't matter."

Kyra flipped Sonia off without turning her attention away from her bass.

"Same set as last time?" she asked, scanning the list.

Ross nodded. "Yeah. Feel like we need a little more rehearsal time on that new one before we add it to the rotation."

She thought for a moment. "Hey, what if we threw in 'Careless'? It's been a while. Swap it in as the third song?"

Kyra and Tanya exchanged a frown. "'Careless'? By Billie Holiday?"

"Yeah, who else?" She found her lipstick and bent toward the room's dingy little mirror.

"I don't know that one," Kyra said.

Sonia smacked her lips together and straightened up. "Come on, it hasn't been *that* long, has it?"

All of them stared at her.

"What?" she asked.

"We've never played that. Never even in rehearsal." Ross watched her as though searching for an answer to some obscure question.

"Sure we have," she laughed. "We..." She trailed off as she tried to remember. She knew she'd sung that song many, many times. But now that she was thinking about it, she couldn't recall ever singing it with the band. Not with her old band, either. Her only specific memory was of singing it into the wind, out the window of a truck moving through the night. The taste of whiskey was bitter on the back of her tongue. And her voice. *Was it different then?*

Sonia backed away from the memory. It gave her an odd vertigo that made her anxious. "Sorry." She forced a smile. "Old favorite. Forgot we never played it together."

The conversation moved on to something else, and Tanya and Kyra bantered over each other's taste in clothes. Ross stayed quiet, though. He kept sneaking looks at her, the same ones he'd been giving her since that day at the pool hall. She did her best to ignore him, as well as the looks and the unsettling thought that she'd never actually sung "Careless" herself.

"OH, FUCK ME."

"What?" Colin and Alonzo said at the same time.

"I think our haboob-environmental trigger theory just went to shit," Sonia snarled. She set the laptop down in the middle of the table, where the other two could see it.

Dear Ms. Rollins,

I am writing in response to your forum post on WebMD. I have experienced all of the symptoms you have described, in addition to others involving repetitive muscle spasms. Like others who have posted to this board, my doctors have been unable to arrive at a diagnosis. I do not, however, live in Arizona, nor have I ever been there. I am originally from Munich, but I live in London. I wonder, though, if this might be a genetic condition? I never knew my father, but he was an American soldier who was apparently born in a small town in the Arizona desert. I do not know if it was this Galina you describe, but my symptoms seem too similar to yours to be a coincidence. I would appreciate any further information you have.

Regards,

Leonie Motz

"There's no way." Alonzo ran his fingers through his hair, pulling it back from his face. "There's no way an environmental trigger happens in London and Arizona at the same time. But there's also no way a genetic condition starts producing symptoms in everyone at the exact same time, so—"

"Lonz. Lonzo. It's okay." Colin touched his wrist. "We knew when we put this out on the internet, we'd get some hypochondriacs or people trying to shoehorn their symptoms into a pattern. Sonia, maybe we can set up a Skype appointment with this woman?"

"Aye aye, fearless leader."

Colin stood. "I have to get going. See if this Dr. Nguyen can tell us anything."

"Coyote guy?" she asked.

"Yup. Should be back by two o'clock. Text if you want me to pick anything up."

"Will do," Alonzo said as Colin dashed out the door.

"HI. JASON?" MORE THAN two years out of grad school, Colin still had to remind himself to refer to other faculty by their first names.

"That's me. Colin, right? Colin from Sociology? Come in."

Jason Nguyen was a lot more rugged than most professors, although perhaps it was the norm for zoologists. He was in his early forties, with graying hair and sunbaked skin. He wore a denim work shirt rolled up over his elbows.

Several preserved animal skulls decorated his cluttered desk. Colin gestured to the closest skull as he sat down. "Good for intimidating the undergrads?"

"Hell yeah. I bring out a puma skull for the plagiarism meetings. So, I hear you're interested in the coyotes around Cochise County?"

"Yeah. Specifically," Colin said, pulling out a copy of the old article, "the ones tagged right around Galina."

"Oh man." Jason sucked his teeth as he stared down at the printout. "I fought like hell to get more funding on that one. Even thought about self-funding it before my wife smacked some sense into me."

"Right, so, walk me through this. The coyotes tagged in that area roam farther than usual. That's what's weird, right?"

Jason let out a little bark of laughter. "Yeah, but that's like saying alligators are a little bit bigger than garden lizards. See, most coyote packs have a territory of a couple square miles. Their home range is a little bigger. And then transient coyotes might roam quite a bit farther than that, depending on terrain and food supply. But these guys, I've never seen anything like it. Before we ran out of funding, we managed to collar three generations of adolescents born in Cochise County. All the ones tagged on the mesa near Galina? They all migrated *several hundred* miles, most of the way across New Mexico and Texas, and way down into Mexico. And the craziest thing was, they did it as members of packs, not as transients. It normally takes decades for a coyote population to migrate that far, and that's if there's some predation or habitat loss pushing them along."

Colin frowned. "So, what do you think is causing it?"

"No clue." Jason lifted his palms up in a helpless gesture. "Trust me, that's kept me up nights. But there's definitely something funky about that mesa, man. And listen…" He leaned forward and lowered his voice. "Don't go broadcasting this, because it's far from research-quality data, but I've talked to other biologists working in that area, and they all see weird behaviors too. I was at a conference once, and I talked to a cactus wren researcher from MIT and a guy doing his dissertation work on rattlesnakes in the area, and both of them said migration and territorial patterns were *way* out of whack. And at least in the case of the birds, their calls are apparently weird as fuck." He sighed. "I mean, we spitballed all kinds of stuff—toxin spills from the copper mines near there, human traffic from border crossings—but none of it explains this stuff."

Colin sat in silence. Jason seemed to pick up on something in his expression. "I'm guessing this isn't helping your research at all."

"Um… Hard to say. Thing is," he said, leaning forward, "like you were saying before, don't broadcast this, but I think whatever's affecting your coyotes might influence humans too."

He hadn't planned on it, but the whole story came tumbling out. He watched Jason's eyes go wide, his expression shift from polite skepticism to incredulity.

"Damn, man," he said when Colin finished. "That's heavy stuff." He tapped a pen against a stack of papers, staring off into space. "Tell you what. I can't drop everything and start a new research project, but I *can* reach out and talk to some people who might be working in the area. See if someone can throw some data your way. I mean, it's not like they have to worry about a sociologist stealing their stuff. Besides, if we're looking at the possibility of a zoonotic contagion, we should get the word out."

"Thanks," Colin said. "I really, really appreciate it."

"No worries. Just sorry to hear about your research. That's rough."

"What?" Colin asked.

Jason frowned. "Well, I mean, you said before your research is on mass hysteria. And if this is a pathogen, it kinda fucks the mass hysteria theory, right?"

"Right." Cold realization spread across his chest. He thought about the hours, days, weeks—hell, the *years* he'd spent developing that research. He tasted bile.

"Anyway," Jason said, breaking the silence. "I'll let you know if I hear anything."

Colin managed to smile, say goodbye, and get out of the office. He wandered back to the parking garage, almost dazed. *It doesn't matter,* he reminded himself. *Making Alonzo better is the only thing that matters right now.*

But even though he knew that was right, even though he knew he would choose Lonzo over his work without hesitation, he still couldn't shake the thought that he now understood what it was like to watch his own house burn to the ground.

SILENCE FELL OVER THE house the moment Colin was out the door.

After a moment, Alonzo said, "He's worried something bad will happen if I try to go out for groceries or something."

"Can hardly blame the dude. We're a hot mess."

He grimaced. "Tea?"

"Sure." Sonia went back to her laptop.

A few minutes later, Alonzo brought her cup of tea.

"Thanks."

As she took the mug, her finger brushed his. The moment their fingers touched, every muscle in Alonzo's body stiffened. He tried to take a step back and couldn't. He tried to make a fist, and his hand refused to move. His eyes refused to blink. He'd could only stare at Sonia. She sat motionless, features placid, hand on the side of the mug. She might have been carved out of marble, except Alonzo saw the panic in her blue eyes, a frantic energy like a trapped bird battering itself to death against a window.

Then they spoke together, perfectly synchronized: "I hold my phone. It does not work. I walk and lift it up in the air, and I search for the place where the words that say 'No Service' will go away."

Whatever held them let go. Alonzo took a lurching breath, staggering back.

Sonia shrieked as the mug of hot tea tipped over and scalded her hand. "Fuck! Fucking fuck!" she screamed, and Alonzo knew it wasn't about the pain.

He stood with his back pressed against the far wall, trying to breathe, terrified at the thought that he might lose control of his body again at any moment.

After the panic subsided, they sat waiting at the dining room table. Neither spoke. Alonzo kept trying to think of ways to break the silence, like something comforting or helpful to say. But every time he looked up, he saw that bleak hopelessness in Sonia's eyes, and everything he thought about saying seemed stupid and meaningless.

At last, Colin returned, expression oddly shaken. "What's going on?" he asked when he saw them.

They exchanged a glance. "Something new happened," Sonia said.

Alonzo let her tell the story. He didn't want to say it. Just thinking about it made him clammy with fear.

As she told Colin what happened to them, Sonia sat rubbing at the burned, puffy skin of her right hand. "I didn't think there was anything more fucked up than the blackouts, but those are a million times better than being awake for it."

Colin sank into a chair. "Christ. That's... that's new. No one ever described being conscious during an episode."

"I don't know about you guys, but I'm sort of thinking the whole 'it's a disease' thing might be bullshit." She blinked in the silence. "What? How the fuck does a disease make people's brains fucking sync up?"

Alonzo tried to think of a counterargument, some way it could be a virus, a toxin, or a misshapen chromosome. He shook his head. "I don't know..."

"Well, at this point, I don't give a shit if it's a disease or a demonic possession or a goddamn curse. We have to get rid of it." Her voice went wobbly, her eyes wild. "Do you fucking understand? What you just went through, Alonzo, I *gave that* to my kid. To Dylan. He might go through that at any minute, and it's my fault."

"No, it's not," Colin said, but she was already up and out of her seat. The bathroom door slammed behind her.

They sat still, listening to the bathroom sink running behind the door. Alonzo ran his hand over his head. "I can't imagine. Having a kid and knowing they have this... this thing."

Sonia reemerged from the bathroom, eyes red but dry.

"Okay," Colin said, slapping the table with both palms. "Tomorrow, we change our strategy. Natural explanations, unnatural explanations, fucking UFO abduction, everything is on the table. Anything we find about Galina, we take seriously, no matter how ridiculous it looks." He met Alonzo's gaze. "We're figuring this out. No matter what, we're figuring this thing out."

CHAPTER 18: 1960

"There should still be some spots by the back fence," Anza said, pulling the picnic blanket out from under the seat of the truck.

"Works for me." Dad retrieved the cooler from the back and ambled off toward the field, moving gingerly, the way he did when he'd strained his shoulder swinging a pickaxe.

They picked their way through the crowd. Some sat in the beds of their trucks, while others unfolded blankets on the scrubby grass of the school playground. Anza sometimes wondered what it would be like to sit in the kind of lush grass she saw in pictures of California or the East Coast. Even after a good monsoon season, the grass in the schoolyard felt brittle and prickly to the touch.

They found the Cardenas family sitting near the chain-link fence. Anza hesitated. She and Dad always sat with them, but she hadn't seen Mr. and Mrs. Cardenas since she and Fernando broke up, and she hadn't really discussed it with Dad. She'd wondered more than once since then if Mrs. Cardenas might be angry with her. But both of Fernando's parents smiled and waved, and if Mrs. Cardenas was angry on her son's behalf, she didn't show it.

"Hey, Anza," Fernando said. He smiled a little too widely, as though trying to convince the world that everything was fine. She sat next to him, unpacking potato salad, beans, and biscuits. Mrs. Cardenas had made fried chicken and two pies, and everyone soon had a full plate.

The sun dipped below the horizon. Anza checked her watch. The fireworks were set to start at eight o'clock, although they were usually a little late. She scanned the crowd and caught sight of Father Santiago and Dove standing a little apart from everyone else. Anza set aside her plate and pointed.

"I'm gonna go see if Father Santiago wants to join us," she said to Mrs. Cardenas. "And Mrs. McNally too," she added as though it were just an afterthought.

Mrs. Cardenas's eyes lit up. "Oh, that would be wonderful if Father could sit with us. Tell him there's plenty of food."

Anza crossed the field, glancing at a young man in the throes of a Dancing fit. The family around him avoided eye contact as people watched him snap a finger, shake his head twice like a wet dog, and sway a knee from side to side, then do it all again. Before, that sense of burdened patience was something Anza had seen only on the faces of parents whose infant was making a fuss in public. Now people got that look about relatives of all ages, every time they had a fit.

"Hey," she said as she approached Dove and Father Santiago. "There's lots of food over there if you want to watch the fireworks with us."

"Oh, thank you, Anza, but I already agreed to sit with Mrs. Bauer. Her son left town this week, so she's alone," Father Santiago said. "Give my regards to your father."

"I will. Dove?"

Something about Dove's demeanor was tense and brittle. She looked at Anza, and an odd softness passed over her features. "Sure. Why not?"

Dove barely touched any food after she sat down, but she did accept a beer from Dad. "Happy Fourth, Sean," she said, unsmiling, as their bottles clinked together.

Dad wrapped an arm around Anza's shoulders. She knew what was coming, the same reminiscence she heard every Independence Day. "Ah, this makes me think of your mother. The Fourth of July was Elena's favorite holiday," he said, directing the last statement toward Dove. "She loved the fireworks."

"I know." For just a moment, anger, perhaps even hatred, blazed across Dove's face as she watched Dad. Her eyes shone wet with unshed tears. Then she blinked and turned her face away.

Dad hadn't seen it. He'd already been staring back up at the sky as though to see fireworks that weren't there yet. Anza didn't think anyone had seen except her.

Dad went on, telling the same story he always did, about the day it rained on the Fourth and Elena had insisted on staying out to see the fireworks even as water swirled around their ankles. It was a familiar story, and Anza usually liked the comfort of hearing it. Now, though, she couldn't stop sneaking peeks at Dove, running that glare through her mind like worrying at a sore spot on her tongue.

The fireworks started half an hour late. The grown-ups were a few beers into the evening, some having started on something stronger from their hip flasks. The children were getting restless, jumpy with sugar after all the cake, ice cream, and apple empanadas. Then the first fireworks shot into the sky without warning. White sparks bloomed like flowers right over the playground.

Anza lay back on the blanket to watch. She imagined in these moments that she felt a hint of Mama's personality, some touch of who she must have been if she was willing to stand ankle-deep in rain to see the sky full of color and flame.

The fireworks had been going on for about twenty minutes when a low boom shook the ground and red flared on the edge of Anza's vision. She sat up. "What was that?"

Fernando stood and peered down the field. "I think one of the fireworks blew up on the ground."

"Oh god." Dad jumped to his feet. "Anza, stay here."

Mr. Cardenas ran after him. Fernando tried to follow, but his mother seized his wrist tightly in her hand.

Anza could only make out the barest details from where she sat, but something was burning past the chain-link fence, and at least two figures lay still on the ground. Then there was another boom and another burst of light. Someone screamed, and a stream of people rushed past, dragging picnic blankets and scooping younger children up in their arms. Anza stood and pressed her back against the chain link, trying to stay out of the way of the stampede.

They waited as the crowd thinned out. Anza caught glimpses of Dad, kicking dirt onto a patch of burning grass then dragging one of the still forms away from the remaining fireworks.

"Can you tell who got hurt?" Fernando asked, shifting from one foot to another.

"No. More than one, I think."

Three figures broke away from the dispersing crowd, walking toward them. Anza's throat tightened as she recognized Richie Rollins. There was a younger man, who might have been his nephew or cousin, with him, and J.D. Foster, whom she vaguely recognized as being on Dad's crew in the mine.

"I told you," Richie said to the others as they approached, but loudly enough for Anza to know it was meant for their ears as well. "Told you it was all coming from them."

J.D.'s face was pale and shocked under soot. "My brother's hand is burnt to a crisp, thanks to you people."

"What are you talking about?" Mrs. Cardenas demanded.

"It was fucking Morales," Richie shot back. "He started having one of those Statue fits when he was supposed to be minding the fires. Foster's brother got burnt to hell because of him."

Mrs. Cardenas shrank against the fence, but Anza saw her fighting to keep her head high. "We have nothing to do with that. I don't even know which Morales you mean." Her bony knuckles trembled around Fernando's wrist.

"You people brought this damn sickness into our town. Just like the influenza in '55 and the smallpox outbreak during the war. One of your folks from Mexico probably brought it up, and now good people are getting hurt—"

"It's not us doing it, you ignorant sack of shit." The words were out of Anza's mouth before she realized she was going to speak. Off to her left, Mrs. Cardenas gasped, and for a moment, Anza wondered if she would be in trouble for cussing. But she didn't let herself break eye contact with Richie and made herself take a step forward. "I've seen how you live. People talk about how they can smell your house from a mile away. You're too lazy to even clean up after your pigs. There aren't any Mexicans in this town who just pick up a pen and move it to a new spot because they're too lazy to muck out the pig shit. You're filthy. If anyone in this town is breeding disease, it's you."

Cold rage filled Richie's prematurely leathery features. Anza's entire body wanted to flinch away.

"You mouthy little bitch. Someone needs to teach you some manners." He reached for her arm.

For one panicked moment, Anza wondered what he would do to her. She wondered if anyone would try to help. Then she heard a metallic click somewhere behind her. All three men looked up, eyes widening.

A pistol glinted in Dove's unwavering hand, the hammer drawn back. "You touch so much as a single hair on that girl's head, and I'll gut shoot each one of you. I'll make sure you die slow and screaming."

"You ain't got the nerve," Richie said, but his eyes were full of fear.

"You wouldn't be the first man I shot," she replied steadily, and Anza knew not even a fool like Richie Rollins would miss the truth in those words.

He swallowed. His eyes flicked from Dove to Anza and back again. "I see you picked your side, Dove McNally. We'll remember that."

They walked away without another word. Mrs. Cardenas let out a long, shuddering breath.

"It's okay, Mama," Fernando said.

She said nothing, clutching her son to her chest as though someone would try to rip him from her arms.

ANZA LAY IN BED, STARING at the ceiling. Her hands still smelled of smoke and ash from putting Dad's clothes in the washtub to soak. He'd come back with blisters and small red burns on his hands, along with a singed pant leg. He'd just finished telling them about Bill Foster's horribly burned hand, skin blackened like grilled meat, when Mr. Cardenas returned. Mrs. Cardenas flung herself into his arms.

Dad's face had gone paler and paler as she told the story of what had happened while the men dealt with the fire. When it was over, he muttered, "I'll kill him," and started off toward the remnants of the crowd. It had taken Fernando, Mr. Cardenas, and Anza working together to hold him back.

"That son of a bitch threatens my daughter, and you want me to let it go?" Dad had roared in Mr. Cardenas's face.

"No, Sean, that's not what I'm saying. But listen, man, there's three of them. Our kids are here. We gotta be smart. Okay? They won't get away with this." Something had passed between Dad and Mr. Cardenas, and Anza knew then that neither of them would let it go. But he had stopped trying to find Richie and pulled Anza into a hug.

"Thank you, Dove. I don't know what would have happened if you hadn't been here," he said just as they left.

Dove had said nothing, only nodded once and went to her truck without a backward glance.

Sighing, Anza tossed aside her sheets and got dressed. She scribbled a note to Dad just before she left, praying she got back early enough that he wouldn't have to find it. *Went to see Dove. Took the truck. Be home soon.*

Anza had to knock three times before Dove answered. She wore an old bathrobe, her red-and-gray hair spilling loose over her shoulders for the first time Anza had ever seen. She held her pistol in one hand. "Anza, what happened?" she asked, blinking and rubbing her eyes.

"Nothing. I'm sorry, but... No, I'm not sorry." She pointed at Dove. "You haven't been straight with me. I want to know why you've been doing so much for me. Helping me out with my... my problem for free, letting me help with the research even though you don't need it, and now you pull a *gun* on someone for me—"

"Keep your voice down," Dove said, even though there was no one within earshot. "I told you, I was friends with your mama."

"I'm not stupid, Dove. There's something else. I mean, why don't you like Dad? He never did anything to you." She stamped her foot in frustration. Those looks, those odd moments with Dad, it was like she almost understood it, like it was just on the tip of her tongue...

Dove stared at her for a moment. She sighed. "Come inside. This might take a while."

Anza waited in the living room for Dove to pour glasses of sun tea the way she always did when she had visitors. Instead, she brought two glasses of whiskey. "Trust me, you'll be needing this."

She sat in her armchair and took a long pull on her drink. "Anza," she said after a moment, "your mama and I... we weren't just friends. We were special friends."

There was something odd about the way she said that, some inflection on the word *special* Anza didn't understand. Dove seemed to sense her confusion. She sighed. "Okay, look. Sometimes, women fall in love with each other. The way a man and a woman fall in love."

"But. Well, how? I mean…" Anza thought about what she did with Fernando and the things she knew about sex. She couldn't imagine how it worked with two women.

Dove shot her a hard look. "I ain't gonna tell you all the details about what two women do in the bedroom. But it's more common than you think. Men and men, women and women. There's places, cities where it's not too hard to find people like me."

"Wait, so… You and my mama were in love." Anza gulped the whiskey, coughing and spluttering at the burn in her throat.

"Yes."

"What about Mama and Dad?"

Dove stared at her glass. "Elena loved him too. People are complicated, Anza. I know folks talk like we're all just supposed to pair up two by two like Noah's Ark, but it doesn't always happen that way. Your mama had a big heart, big enough for two. Even though I didn't want to share."

"Did you also love Mr. McNally?"

Dove snorted. "No. But he knew that. I came to Galina to nurse him in his last days. His last days ended up being a little longer than either of us expected. We got close. Not like a married couple, just like friends. He wanted to leave me something as a thank-you for being with him at the end. He only married me so this house and his money would go to me instead of his ex-wife, and that was the easiest way to do it. We were only married two weeks before he died, and we were never husband and wife in the way you're thinking. I'd never planned on staying, but then I had this house and this property, paid off free and clear, and money in the bank. And then I met your mama." A little ghost of a smile touched Dove's features, and for a moment, Anza imagined what she must have looked like when she met Elena.

"We had five good years. Lots of people don't even get that much in this life, so I'm grateful for that."

Anza wondered how she was supposed to feel. Angry or disgusted, she supposed, but really, she just felt stunned. In some corner of her mind, she thought about how nice it was that Mama had two people to love her instead of just one. She stared down at her boots. "Is that why you hate Dad? Because you had to share Mama?"

"First of all, I don't hate your father. I think he's a good man. And I know Elena loved him." She sighed. "I... sometimes get angry when I see your father because she wanted to have babies with him, and he should have told her to stop trying. Not that men ever know a damn thing about baby-making, but he should have known something was wrong."

Anza frowned. "How could he have known?"

"You know how many miscarriages your mama had before you were born? Six. Six miscarriages before the age of twenty-five, and two of those almost killed her." Dove shook her head. "I told her. I even got her to see a doctor to tell her the same thing. She had something wrong with her birth canal, her pelvis. Any doctor could see how dangerous it was going to be for her to carry a baby to term, and all those miscarriages were her body trying to tell her that. But she wouldn't listen. She wouldn't even be honest with your father about how dangerous it was. That's how bad she wanted you, Anza."

Anza's eyes stung. She pressed a hand to her mouth. "Do you ever think about... Is it hard for you, being around me, because of how she died?" she choked.

Dove's eyes went soft. "No, sweetheart. It's hard for me to look at you sometimes. But that's because you remind me so much of her, not because of how she died." She let Anza cry for a little while. Then she cleared her throat and set down her empty whiskey glass. "That's enough of that now. It is what it is. No sense crying over it."

Anza sniffed. "Okay. Don't even know why I'm crying."

"Well, you're sixteen. Crying at the drop of a hat is what sixteen-year-olds do. And this is a lot more than a dropped hat." She paused. "I can't tell you what to do, now that you know. Can't stop you from telling anyone you want to tell. And the truth is you could cause a whole heap of trouble for me if you were so inclined. But just remember: once that cat's out of the bag, ain't nothing going to get it back in. So think long and hard before you do anything."

"I won't tell. Christ, Dove, I don't want to hurt you. It would be like... It would be like hurting Mama too. Besides, it'd probably hurt Dad worse than anybody."

Dove nodded. "That, it would." She rose and pulled her bathrobe tighter around herself. "Now, I'm an old lady. I need my sleep. Stay as long as you need and lock up when you leave."

"I will."

Dove paused on her way out of the room, laying a hand on Anza's shoulder. "Elena would have been proud of how you turned out, Anza. Good night." And then she was gone.

Anza stayed where she was for a time, watching the darkness beyond the living room's picture window. She closed her eyes and tried to feel some trace of her mother in the room, the smell and sound of a woman she had no memory of. But there was nothing, just an empty room with a ticking clock and, beyond that, the call of coyotes on the mesa.

CHAPTER 19: 2020

Cara was watching TV when Sonia got back. "Hey, there's leftover Thai if you want it."

"Thanks." Sonia grabbed the takeout box off the countertop.

Cara muted the show. "Any news?"

"Some new symptoms. And apparently, whatever we have is also fucking with the wildlife in Cochise County." A dull headache pounded behind her eyes.

"Didn't think there was any wildlife in Cochise County besides border patrol."

"Oh yeah. By the time this is over, I'm gonna qualify for some kind of joint history-biology degree, all the useless shit I'm learning." Sonia chewed her food for a moment. "You sure it's still okay for me to crash here?"

Cara rolled her eyes. "For the millionth time, yeah. If anything, I wish you were around more. You spend all your time with the geek squad."

"Yeah, we just—" Sonia's phone buzzed against the surface of the coffee table. "I gotta get this. It's Mom."

Cara waved for her to answer, turning her attention back to the TV.

"Mom? What's up?"

Her mother's voice came through shrill and choked with tears. "Sonia, Dylan's having an episode. I know you said not to go to the hospital, but I don't know what to do, and—"

"Mom, stop. Tell me exactly what he's doing." She sat up straight, her fingers digging into the fabric of the couch.

"He's, oh, he's just making these weird movements over and over. And he won't look at me when I talk to him."

"*Exactly* what he's doing."

"Uh, his left hand keeps clenching into a fist. And after that, his right foot twists against the ground, like if you were squishing a bug. And then he snaps his teeth together, and oh, I'm so worried he'll crack a tooth—"

"When did it start?"

"Uh... three minutes ago."

"Okay. Mom, this is the third stage. He should come out of it in another one to four minutes. Which means you have one minute to get your shit together. I mean it. Do *not* let him see you hysterical when he comes out of this. You're gonna be calm, hear?"

Mom sniffed for a moment. "Okay."

"Okay, now I'm going to stay on the phone until he comes out of it. You focus on getting calmed down." Her hands shook as she spoke.

They sat in silence, Sonia listening as her mother's breathing evened out. Then, in the background, she heard, "Can we watch *Futurama*?"

Sonia let out a long, shuddering breath as she listened to her mother coo over Dylan, asking him how he felt. She covered her eyes with one hand, feeling Cara's palm on her shoulder. "Put Dylan on, please," she said when she trusted herself to speak.

"Hey, Mom. Grandma says I had another one."

"Yeah, I know, baby. She told me. Do you feel okay?"

"Yeah, I feel fine. When are you coming home?"

"Soon, baby, real soon. Remember I told you I'm working with those scientists?"

"Yeah."

"Well, we're learning all kinds of stuff about what's making us sick. We'll figure out the cure any day now."

"Okay. But even if you don't, they aren't so bad."

Sonia remembered the clawing panic she'd felt earlier, as she sat trapped in her own body. *If you're listening, motherfucker, don't you do that to Dylan. Just not to him,* she thought.

And for just a second, she thought she felt something behind her eyes, some new pressure. Then it was gone, and she said goodnight to Dylan and texted Colin to let him know her son had started the third stage.

She looked up from the phone to find Cara staring at her, wide-eyed. "That sounded... intense. Is he okay?"

"Yeah." Her hands started to shake as the adrenaline dissipated. "It's... this new phase is kind of like a seizure. Weird movements and stuff like that. Mom was losing her shit."

"You really kept it together, though. I mean, holy fuck." She reached out and squeezed Sonia's elbow. "You're a great mom."

For just a second, Sonia wanted to hit her. She wanted to grab Cara's hair, pull her face close, and scream, "Are you fucking kidding me? I fucking gave this to him. It's all my fault."

Then the urge passed, and she sat back and took a deep breath. It had been there again, that weird sense of thoughts being pushed into her mind from somewhere else. She closed her eyes so she didn't have to look at Cara.

You aren't mad at Cara, she told herself. *That wasn't you. Cara's right. You're a great mom.*

She almost managed to believe it, to ignore that dark little whisper of doubt in the back of her mind.

"MR. MONTEZ, COULD YOU please slow down? I need you to repeat what you just said." Colin had to talk over the man's rambling monologue.

"I said, my Aunt Krista said it was something in our water. Like, something we're sensitive to because our grandmother grew up in Galina. Is that it?"

"I'm sorry, but I really don't know, Mr. Montez."

"But people say you're the one who's researching it. How can you not know if you've interviewed all these folks?"

"I promise, I'm working as hard as I can to figure out what's happening. As soon as I know anything, I'll get in touch with everyone and let them know, okay?"

"Well, Jesus, what are you doing? I can't be in construction if I keep flopping all over the damn place. It's dangerous."

Alonzo must have caught some hint of Mr. Montez's volume, because he turned away from his computer and raised his eyebrows.

"We're doing everything we can," Colin said. "Now I have to go. Bye." He hung up without waiting for a response.

"Another one?" Sonia asked, wandering out from the kitchen. She ate a handful of cereal straight out of the box, the only thing he'd seen her eat in the last ten hours. Colin made a mental note to pick up more on his way home from the next department meeting.

"Yeah." He rubbed the aching spot in the middle of his forehead. "Another Galina grandkid demanding to know why I haven't invented the cure yet."

"We can start giving them my number instead, if you want," Alonzo said.

Colin rolled his eyes. "We both know you'll lose your temper way before me. And we need these people to keep talking to us."

Sonia sat across from Alonzo and slid the box of cereal over to him. "You get in touch with your friend at the health department?"

"Yeah, but it didn't sound very promising. He said he'd send it up the chain, but they've got a hantavirus outbreak and no funding, so unless this starts looking contagious, it's not going to be anyone's top priority."

"Are you fucking serious?" She spoke through a mouthful of crumbs. "We're up to—what? Three hundred people with symptoms? How does a health department not freak the shit out about that?"

"You know how long the Flint water supply was full of lead before anyone paid attention to it?" Alonzo turned back to his laptop screen. "Years. If most of the people affected are poor and brown, no one gives a shit. And even if they did, their funding's been stripped down to nothing over the last couple of years."

"So we're the last, best hope?" Sonia asked.

"Far as I can tell, yeah." Colin eyed the stack of new books and articles he'd picked up from the library, mentally bracing himself to continue reading.

She raised her eyebrows and gave him a slow, thoughtful nod. "Man, we are *so* fucked."

"I *really* don't want to have this conversation with them." Alonzo stared through the passenger window at his parents' front porch.

"I know. But... look, it's better to just tell them instead of having them find out when you have an episode. And we have to make sure the generational thing holds up," Colin replied.

"Trust me, if Dad were having episodes, I would have heard."

"Still..."

"I know." He didn't make a move to get out of the car.

"You sure you don't want me to come in with you?" Colin asked.

Alonzo grimaced. "Yeah. They've managed to be civil so far because you've never been around them while they're upset, and I don't want that to change." He took a deep breath. "Okay. I'm going in."

"I'll be at the coffee shop around the corner. Just let me know."

Alonzo waited for him to drive off before going to the door. His mother answered so fast, he knew she must have been watching through the curtains. "Hi, sweetheart, come in," she said, beaming. She was still dressed for church, wearing a long black skirt and with her graying hair in a bun.

His dad sat on the couch, watching the game.

"Hey, Pops," Alonzo said.

"Son. Sit."

Alonzo sat down, taking a minute to absorb the feeling of being back in the house where he grew up. He supposed they must have changed things, moved little knickknacks, added pictures, and repainted the walls. But it felt so familiar, the smell and the arrangement of the furniture and the sound of his mother bustling around in the kitchen. Right on cue, she came out with sliced fruit and iced tea.

"Thanks, Mom," he said.

"You should have come earlier. You could have come to church with us." She picked up the remote and turned off the game without asking. Knowing better than to complain, his father just sank deeper into the couch.

Alonzo didn't take the bait. "So, what have you two been up to?"

He tuned out as his mom went on about the volunteer work she did at the school, complaining how much it had changed since his father retired. Dad had been the math teacher for thirty-seven years, two of them with Alonzo sitting in his classroom.

Steeling himself, he waited for a lull in the conversation. "Listen, there's something I wanted to talk to you about." And he told them the way he'd practiced—quick and to the point. It didn't keep Mom from bursting into tears.

"Mom, Mom, it's okay. I'm okay. We're figuring it out." He went to her chair and pulled her into an awkward hug. "Look, I'm telling you this so you know what's going on if something happens, and because we're trying to figure out who else from Galina is having problems."

"I knew it was trouble," Dad muttered.

"What?" Alonzo asked, knowing what was coming.

"Him. Asking about Galina. I knew it was a bad idea to stir all that back up again. Why do you think my father and all those others never wanted to talk about it? And now look what happened."

Alonzo fought to keep his voice level. "Dad, are you saying Colin caused this? Because that's ridiculous."

"All I know is, everything's fine for all these years, and then here comes this guy, asking questions. And now look." He made an expansive gesture with his right arm, pointing at some imaginary piece of evidence.

"Oh Jesus, Dad, you can say his name. Colin, remember? And also, don't pretend you believe this stuff about not talking about it, like it's a curse or something. You're smarter than that." He threw up his hands. "Christ, you were the one who always said it was just people going crazy. You always said the curse stuff was nonsense."

Dad said nothing. Alonzo stifled the urge to yell something else about selective superstition.

Mom sniffed. "Lonzo, you can come home to stay with us. We'll take care of you."

"No. I'm fine," he said through clenched teeth. "Colin's taking care of me. We're fine."

"Oh, he's not good for you, Lonzo," Mom wailed.

Alonzo rolled his eyes. It was the same with every boyfriend he'd ever introduced to them. They always pretended it wasn't about him being with a man, at least not since their slow realization during his high school years that it wasn't a phase. No, it was always *this* man or *that* man they didn't like. But Colin had tried so hard during those stiff dinners and family gatherings. He'd done so many things that Mom and Dad would have loved if they had come from a woman. Nothing worked.

He stood. "This is not a referendum on my relationship. You don't get a vote. And I would have gotten sick anyway, whether or not I was with Colin. Now, what I need from you, Dad, is to reach out to other people you know from Galina, especially people with kids, and see if they're having trouble too. You want to help, that's how you do it." He folded his arms and waited.

Dad stared at the dark TV screen as though watching a show only he could see. "I'll make some calls," he said at last, grudgingly.

Alonzo relaxed. He knew they would still pretend to blame Colin, but they would also go through Dad's entire address book and be on the phone day and night if that was what it took. They wouldn't let him down, not when it came to something like this. Reaching for the remote, he sat down and turned the game back on.

"YO, YO, YO."

"Hey, Tori. What's up?" Colin sat in the parking lot, with the car's air conditioner running. He'd made it to the coffee shop but didn't feel like going inside yet—probably because just the thought of diving back into his research files gave him a headache.

"Oh, not much. Putting the finishing touches on the tenure package. Planning the sweet revenge I'll be taking if they turn me down." She had their mother's voice, the same breathy drawl that made people assume she was dumb until they got to know her.

"You'll get it. You know you'll get it."

"I can't wait for you to go through this in five years or so. Then you'll see how much it sucks to have people throw empty reassurance at you."

He laughed. "Hey, even if you hadn't earned it, which you have, this is a room full of old white dudes who are terrified of women. Just threaten to birth the kid right there in front of them, and it's yours."

"That would be funny if it weren't a real concern. Seriously, Col, I'm huge. Huge and hairy and constantly stuffing food into my face-hole. Rajit's wondering why some moody wildebeest has eaten and replaced his wife."

"I'm sure he thinks you're beautiful."

"Yeah, but only out of contractual obligation."

Colin sighed. "Well, that's the deal. Taking the bad with the good. Sickness and health, and all that."

"Well, aren't we a bundle of merry sunshine today. What's going on?"

He cleared his throat. "Nothing. Got a name yet?"

"Yup. Your new niece is going to be Cicely Kalyani Ayres-Malhotra."

"So you're already punishing her for something?"

"Hey, shut up. That name took six months of negotiations."

"So did the Treaty of Versailles. Look how that turned out."

Tori made a huffy sound, but he knew she wasn't really mad. "So, what's up with you? Lonzo get you pregnant yet?"

"Heh-heh. No, everything's good here. He's doing the usual Sunday-lunch thing with his parents, so I'm just doing work until that's over."

"Still haven't come around, huh?" she asked, voice softening.

"Nope." He'd understood in theory that parents still had issues with queer kids, but his mother had been so blasé the first time he mentioned dating a guy that he never took it that seriously. Not until he spent an entire dinner being studiously ignored by Alonzo's father did he understand how deep it ran.

"Is anything else going on? You sound weird."

He'd started to tell Tori and their mother three or four times, but he couldn't imagine it doing anything but add to the stress. "No, it's all good. Listen, I actually called to talk to Physicist Tori, not Sister Tori."

"I'm not explaining the Heisenberg Uncertainty Principle again. Just believe me. The math works."

"Nope, lower level than that. Okay, so, my question is, hypothetically, if something were being broadcast or transmitted or whatever, and you didn't know what type of signal or what type of frequency it was, is there any way to detect it?"

"Uh, might need some specifics here. Are we talking radio waves?"

Colin swallowed. "Not sure. Anything that could communicate over really long distances without, you know, like, a wired phone. Also, I'm not necessarily talking about communication technology that really exists. I'm just talking any signal that hypothetically could be used for wireless communication." Alonzo and Sonia hadn't discussed the content of their odd synchronized fit, but as soon as Colin heard about it, he started thinking about the idea of trying to get a signal. He couldn't imagine it being about anything other than long-distance communication, although he knew the idea would scare the others, so he hadn't mentioned it to them yet.

"Okay. Huh. Well, first up, all wireless communication technology uses electromagnetic radiation. So stuff high up on the spectrum is, like, gamma rays and x-rays and ultraviolet, stuff that's not good for communications, because it kills people. Then there's the stuff in the visible spectrum, and then below that, there's the ranges where you get microwaves and radio waves. That's where basically all our communications technology is now, although the next phases are looking like a shift toward the visible-light spectrum. You know, encoding data with LEDs and shit like that."

"But if wireless communication is happening, there has to be some kind of electromagnetic signal."

"Pretty much, yeah."

"And is there a way to detect what it is or where it's coming from, if you don't have any idea where in the spectrum it is?"

Tori paused. "Not really. I mean, you could get an EMF meter or something, but those are all going to be for a pretty small range. You could get a broad-spectrum meter and see if anything in the area is giving off more than it should. Could get lucky that way."

"Okay."

"So, what's this about? Think your house is bugged or something?"

Colin shook his head before remembering she couldn't see it. "No. Just working on a theory about Galina."

"Ah. Well, if it's something about microwaves making people crazy and giving them tumors and stuff, don't waste your time. That's all conspiracy-theory crap."

"I know. I've heard Mom say it, so I know it's not true."

She snorted. "I know, right?"

They spent a few minutes swapping snarky remarks about their mother's latest obsessions—crystals, Reiki, and some new thing with a tuning fork. Colin let Tori rant, relieved she'd been distracted from his odd line of questioning. Then he stopped, laughter drying up in his throat. He thought about what it would mean if the solution to the Galina Plagues turned out to be the kind of New Age paranormal nonsense his mother subscribed to. He thought about everything else he would need to question and every other assumption he would have to revisit. Just the idea made him feel exhausted.

His phone beeped in the middle of Tori's description of the new color-coded diet their mother was apparently on. It was a text from

Alonzo. "Hey, Tor? Sorry to interrupt, but Lonzo just sent up the rescue flare. Call you back for more Mom-bashing later?"

"Sure thing," she chirped. "Let me know how the EMF mystery project goes."

He hung up and swung back out of the parking lot to rescue Alonzo from his parents.

CHAPTER 20: 1960

"Esperanza," Father Santiago said, standing as Anza walked through the front door. "Dove just told me what happened. Are you all right?"

Anza stared at Dove, eyes wide. She couldn't believe Dove would tell a priest, of all people...

"Maybe I can have a word with Pastor Benjamin," he continued, fingers picking nervously at the sleeve of his cassock. "I know Richie Rollins attends his church."

Anza blinked, belatedly remembering Richie and the other men after the fireworks accident. She'd scarcely thought of it since Dove had told her about what she'd been to Elena.

"I'm fine," she said at last. The thought of Richie brought back that wave of sickly fear. She'd felt so brave and strong when she stood up to him, but when he'd reached for her, she hadn't felt brave at all anymore, just tiny and helpless.

"Well, even so, this kind of thing can't be allowed to continue," Father Santiago said as she sat down. His fingers stopped fidgeting with his sleeve and switched to tapping against the arm of the sofa.

"You ask me, we're wasting our time asking Benjamin to calm folks down. That man works hard to keep things at a rolling boil." Dove didn't look up from the book in her hand.

"You may be right. But it's not just those men and not just last night. Several members of my congregation have told me similar things. Rumors that the disease started in Mexico, that it was the Mexican and Apache and Navajo families that spread it. Young girls and women being harassed in the street."

"Well, I got a couple spare shotguns in the other room," Dove replied.

Father Santiago frowned and clicked his tongue. "Violence begets violence, Dove."

"Exactly. Anyone decides to hurt any of the girls in this town, it'll beget some violence from me." She closed the book in her hand and reached for a new one, adjusting the reading glasses perched on her nose. "But we can deal with that later. For now, anyone find anything useful in this fascinating pile of research?"

Anza considered the slim notepad in her hand. All the books she'd gone through, all the stuff on the history of epidemics and botany and cryptobotany, and still, she only had two or three pages of notes on things she'd thought were relevant. "Well, I don't have much. Couldn't find anything exactly like the blood beetles, although there's bugs that big in Africa and South America. Just not the right color. But I did read some stuff about how plants can talk to each other. It's pretty interesting, actually. There're trees that get attacked by a bug or something, and they put out some chemicals in the air, and somehow, trees miles away know the bugs are coming. So I guess, maybe, the cactus patch could have come together from plants giving off signals to all come to the same place?" She held up a rough sketch she'd made of a Venus flytrap from one of the books. "And then there's plants like this, that can move and eat things. Bugs, mostly. So plants moving isn't really all that weird, although I can't find anything about cactuses moving. That's about all. Sorry."

Father Santiago flipped through the pages of his own little notebook. "I don't have much more, I'm afraid. I read through all of the books on toxins and plants that can cause madness. There have been a lot of cases, especially from mold on bread. People in the Dark Ages sometimes ate the bread, and then an entire village or town would go mad. One town even had a dancing madness. But none of them are close to ours. People should be more ill, if it were one of these things. People would have died by now."

"And I read about dust-borne disease. Like the Valley Fever and some others. There are diseases that aren't bacteria or viruses. They're mold spores and things that get into dust and then people breathe them in. Especially in this part of the country and in spots like the mesa." Dove shook her head. "But the symptoms are all wrong. All the dust spore diseases are just like consumption, something like that. Things in your lungs and bones. Nothing here about spores that make people crazy."

Father Santiago rubbed his forehead. "It's like all of the pieces are here, but they don't fit together. People can get sick from spores in dust, and there are things that can give a whole town fits, but they aren't one and the same. There are plants that can move but none that also cause these symptoms and none that are cactuses. None of these parts fit."

"Maybe it's just a new spore," Anza suggested. "New diseases pop up now and then, right? Maybe it's a new spore in the dust, and it's something that makes humans and animals and plants act funny."

"Could be," Dove said. "But even if that's true, it's still got to have a source. There's still got to be some reason behind why it makes some people sick and not others, and why it progresses the way it does."

They sat in silence for a moment, mulling over the collection of facts and ideas and books that refused to line up into one clear picture.

"Pardon me," Father Santiago said then went to the restroom.

Anza avoided Dove's gaze. The silence stretched and grew heavy.

"Wasn't sure you'd be back," Dove said quietly.

Anza shrugged. "It's fine. I'm not mad. I just keep thinking..."

The toilet flushed, and Father Santiago returned to the room. Anza cleared her throat and pretended to be engrossed by something on her notepad.

Dove tossed aside another book and leaned forward in her chair. "Okay, then. I think this avenue of research has been a dead end, at least for now. Least until we have more information."

"Where do we look, then?" Father Santiago asked.

"We look into the thing we been ignoring all this time." Dove smiled, but it didn't reach her eyes. "The Red Hail. We figure out what fell out of the sky that day, maybe we just have a shot at calming folks down before somebody gets hurt."

SHERIFF BRANDT EMERGED from his office, meaty features arranged into a broad smile. "Sean, sorry to keep you waiting. I have a stack of paperwork a mile high to catch up on."

Perhaps, but Anza saw the sandwich crumbs in his beard and the grease on his fingers. He shook Dad's hand and tipped his hat to Anza before leading them into the office. "Now. What can I do for you?"

"Well, Sheriff Brandt, I'd like to know what you're doing about the fact that Richie Rollins and his pals are threatening people all over town."

Sheriff Brandt's smile shrank a fraction. "Aw, Sean, Richie's all talk."

"Maybe, but what if he riles up someone who isn't?" Dad's eyes seemed darker when he was mad, a steelier shade of gray. "Sheriff, I'm scared to let Anza do the grocery shopping on her own. Now what kind of town has a man scared about what's going to happen to his daughter in broad daylight on Main Street?"

Anza avoided Sheriff Brandt's eye. She hated the way men talked sometimes, like she was a pet or a piece of furniture. But then he turned to her. "Esperanza, darlin', why don't you go wait outside, let me talk to your daddy for a minute?"

She straightened up in her chair. "No, sir, I think I'll stay. If I have worry about protecting myself against Richie and his boys, I think I deserve to hear why."

His eyes widened even as his smile stayed frozen in place.

Dad folded his arms. He did that when he wanted to intimidate someone; he wasn't a big man, but his copper-miner forearms were bulky with muscle. "Anything you can say to me, you can say to her."

Sheriff Brandt sighed. "Okay, look. People are scared. You know that. Hell, I started Naming last week, so I understand why. And I know all this stuff blaming Mexicans is nonsense—anyone can see that. But you know how people get. So, I tell you what. I'll go visit with Richie. Tell him to cool it with the talk. But I'll tell you the truth, Sean. I'm not the one who needs to talk to them. It's Pastor Ben they listen to."

"You're the lawman in town, Hiram. You got two empty cells right down that hall." Dad pointed toward the door.

"Yeah, and only two deputies to police the whole damn place. Pardon my language. I hear you, Sean—I do—but believe me when I say kicking a bees' nest ain't the way to go. Talk to Ben."

Dad shook Sheriff Brandt's hand but said nothing as they left the building. Anza glanced back at it as they made their way to the truck. It was an ugly brick box set a little ways back from the sidewalk, nothing like sheriff's offices in movies. Those were always old wood buildings with bars on the windows and a post out front to tie up horses. The sheriff in one of those movies either would have died at the very beginning or would win in a gunfight against some sinister man dressed in black. He wouldn't sit in his office, eating a sandwich and saying there was nothing to be done.

Dad sat behind the wheel for a moment before turning the key in the ignition. "Useless," he said at last. "That settles it. I'm going to one of these sermons at Pastor Ben's church this Sunday. Then I'll talk to him, tell him he needs to call off his dogs before someone gets hurt."

"I'm coming with you."

"No. It's not safe."

"No one's gonna do anything at a church meeting. Besides, you're not the one they're saying things about. They might forget you having a Mexican wife and daughter, but they aren't going to forget me having a Mexican mama."

Dad cringed, hands worrying at the steering wheel. "Okay, then." He said nothing more for the rest of the drive home.

ANZA AND DAD FOUND a spot near the back where they could keep an eye on the crowd—and get to the door fast, if necessary. She kept thinking as she observed the congregation how different it was from Father Santiago's flock. Whiter, for one. But also louder. When Pastor Benjamin said certain things, especially when he asked questions, the crowd would shout back an answer.

The church also looked different. The Catholic one was dark, cool, and perfumed with incense. This one had big windows that brightened up the room but also let in all the heat. Box fans and swamp coolers hummed along on all sides, but sweat trickled down in a line between Anza's shoulder blades. Instead of wooden pews, there were folding chairs arranged in a kind of crescent shape around the little raised area in the middle where Pastor Benjamin preached.

She didn't like the way he talked. He was like a teacher yelling at students for being too noisy when she wrote on the blackboard, the same sternness in his eye. And he kept emphasizing certain words for no reason she could see.

"And you have turned *away* from God. You know it. Everyone in this room *knows* in their heart that they have sinned."

The crowd chorused in agreement.

"Sin is a *sickness*. It is a sickness. And there is only one cure, people. One cure. The good book." He held up his Bible, and people gasped and applauded as though they hadn't known exactly what he would say.

He turned a slow circle. "Now, who among you is ready to reject Satan? Who's ready?"

"Me!" A young woman leapt forward. Anza didn't recall her name but recognized her from around town. The woman had come from Bisbee or somewhere else and moved here after marrying a Galina boy. She wore a prim blue dress, her blond hair carefully curled. "I've let Satan in, but I want him out!"

Then she fell to her knees and started calling out words in a ragged, rough voice. "Church! Floor! Agh, preacher! Damn you, preacher!" Her limbs flicked out in rigid motions as her head twitched from side to side. Around her, the crowd whispered and prayed, swaying with their hands clasped before them.

Anza frowned and glanced at Dad then back out at the crowd. She didn't understand. Anyone could see that wasn't a real fit. Naming was always in a flat, quiet voice with no more than slight movements of the head. It never included complete sentences or comments aimed at anyone in particular. And she'd never heard of anyone Naming and Statuing or Dancing at the same time. But even though everyone in the church must have known that, they still stared at the young woman with rapt attention.

Pastor Benjamin approached her, laying a hand on her forehead. "Are you ready to reject Satan? Are you ready to cast him out?" He spoke to the woman, but his voice boomed out to the back of the church.

"Ah, yes, yes, cast him out!" She writhed and twitched at his feet.

Pastor Benjamin held the Bible against her forehead.

She shrieked as though it burned her skin.

"Leave this young woman, devil! I said get out, Satan! Begone from this place!"

After a minute of that, the woman let out one last scream and slid to the floor, limp. Others in the crowd helped her to her feet.

"Has the devil left you?" Pastor Benjamin asked.

"Yes," she cried weakly. "He's gone!"

The crowd erupted in cheers and shouts of "Praise Jesus!"

Dad folded his arms, eyes wide with dismay, and leaned over to speak into Anza's ear. "They aren't really buying this dog and pony show, are they?"

They were. Anza scanned the crowd and didn't see a hint of doubt, not a single frown of concern. She bit her lip and tried to shrink down into her seat.

Once the crowd had calmed, Pastor Benjamin held up a hand. "Now, remember, the forces of evil are persistent. This isn't about winning one battle. This is about winning the war. Even after Satan has been cast out, he may return. We've all seen it happen."

The crowd nodded.

"So you have to stay strong. Keep fighting. And remember..." He paused dramatically. "When you see someone who doesn't seem to be fighting the devil, that's not a sign that they're holier than anyone else. No, sir. I know some have been saying that those among us who haven't been afflicted by the Plagues of Galina must be purer, chosen by God. But don't you believe it! Those who aren't afflicted haven't been *spared* the sicknesses of the devil—they've just given up!" His gaze drifted over the crowd, then he looked directly at Anza, staring her right in the eye. "To struggle against Satan is a mark of holiness. Those who fail to fight have joined the side of darkness."

Anza's breath stopped in her throat.

Then he turned away. "Go with God, and peace be unto you."

The crowd erupted in cheers again, and as Anza watched them, she had to fight the urge to run.

Some of the congregation drifted out the front doors, but others lingered to talk to Pastor Benjamin. Dad and Anza had to wait for what seemed like ages to get their chance.

"Benjamin," Dad said, extending his work-roughened hand. "Sean Kearney."

Pastor Benjamin blinked a little before shaking his hand. Anza assumed it was because Dad had left off the "Pastor" part. "Welcome to our congregation, Mr. Kearney."

"Oh, I'm not here to stay," Dad replied, unsmiling.

Anza winced. They had talked about how to handle this, but she supposed it was foolish to think he would play nice after what he'd heard.

"I need a word," Dad said, "about some things folks from your congregation have been up to."

Pastor Benjamin's smile flickered. "Of course. Please, come to my office."

He led them to a cluttered little room at the back of the church. The desk was covered in books and magazines, the wastepaper basket overflowing. He cleared off two chairs and motioned for them to sit. "Now," he said, settling into the chair on the other side of the desk, "how can I help you?"

Dad explained everything that had happened in the last few weeks, starting with the incident in the grocery store and ending with the Fourth of July celebration. "Now, I'm sure you can agree with me that blaming Mexicans for these... these *plagues* is just nonsense. Maybe your congregation needs a little clarification on that point."

Pastor Benjamin nodded, eyes shining with sympathy. "Race hatred is a great sin. A great sin. But I think you may be misguided, Sean. Because there are Mexican and Indian members of our own congregation, and they've had no troubles."

Anza had seen no more than two or three families of brown people like her.

Dad raised an eyebrow. "Really? You asked them?"

Pastor Benjamin chuckled. "I don't need to. I keep a close eye on my flock." He folded his hands on the desk in front of him. "Some members of my congregation may have become overzealous in their fight against the devil's forces. But I assure you, it's not about race."

"Excuse me, sir," Anza said. "But they said 'Mexicans,' both times, to my face. I was there."

"They misspoke. What they meant were papists. I know, I know, that's not the popular term these days. But the Catholic Church has invited evil into this country—and into this town."

Dad tensed as though about to spring across the desk. "Now wait just a damn minute—"

"Did you see the paper yesterday, Mr. Kearney?"

Anza froze. She knew what was coming. Dad had broken out the good whiskey to celebrate, after all. He'd waxed nostalgic about the struggles of their people and how far the Irish had come since staggering onto American shores a century before.

"The Democratic Party made a Catholic their nominee. For *President of the United States*. If they have their way, John F. Kennedy will be president, and then we'll be a country run by a man bound to listen to the pope before the American people." All that kind understanding vanished from his features. "The Catholic Church is a cancer, Mr. Kearney, a cancer at the heart of this country. Look at the priest of the Catholic church in this very town. He's done nothing to fight the evil that's spreading among us. He's done everything he can to stop people from seeing Satan's hand in it."

"That *priest* you're talking about has worked like a dog to find where the sickness came from. Where it *really* came from," Anza spat. Dad laid a hand on her arm.

Pastor Benjamin said nothing for a long moment. "Well, fighting this plague isn't about race. It's about uprooting the corruption of the papists who want to destroy us. And if it just happens that most of the folks in this town who attend that church are Mexican and Indian, well, that's got nothing to do with it. The non-white families who attend this church know that full well."

Dad stared for a long moment, jaw muscles twitching. "You know," he said slowly, "my daddy was a mean, pigheaded old bastard. He warned me when I started seeing Elena, God rest her soul, that he'd never speak to me again if I married her. But I did, and he went to his grave without meeting his granddaughter." He paused. "He was a son of a bitch, but at least he was a straight shooter. You? You're every bit the hateful piece of shit he was but a coward to boot."

Pastor Benjamin's mouth dropped open.

Dad stood, knocking his chair back. "We're leaving."

Anza rushed to keep up. She'd seen Dad like this a few times, so angry every muscle in his body tensed like a coiled spring. He stomped his way out of the church, flung open the truck door, and slammed it so hard, it was a wonder the window didn't shatter.

Even then, knowing how mad he was, Anza slapped her palm against the dashboard. "Why didn't you just go and paint a target on our backs, huh?"

He shot her a look, eyes blazing, but she knew it wasn't aimed at her. "You heard him, Anza. Target was already there. Unless we want to pay for his protection every Sunday."

"Well, that train's left the station now." Even as she said it, she knew it wasn't really fair. They never would have joined his church, not in a million years.

Dad sighed and turned the keys in the ignition. "We'll figure something out. There's more of us than them in this town anyway. It comes down to a fight, we'll win."

CHAPTER 21: 2020

"**M**s. Motz, thanks for taking the time to talk with us," Colin said.

"Well, I'm at my wit's end, so I'm prepared to try anything." The video quality was bad, but from what Colin could make out, she was a striking woman in her early thirties, dark-skinned with coiling brown hair pulled back from her face. She had only the faintest touch of a German accent under the cut-crystal English.

"Could you just start by going over your symptoms for us, from the beginning?"

They'd done some hasty research into Munchausen's Syndrome and other mental illnesses that made people likely to imagine or falsely report illness. "Ugh, that's probably what that bitch doctor thought I had," Sonia had said after reading the list. Alonzo sat behind the laptop, out of sight of the webcam. He held a pen over their makeshift checklist, ready to note danger signs. Sonia had a different checklist: essential elements of the Plagues, details she hadn't included in any of the forum posts.

Leonie went through the now-familiar litany of symptoms. The blackouts then being told about the Naming, Statuing, and later, the Dancing. Colin dropped in one of their trap questions about headaches and nausea, watching to see if Alonzo picked up any warning signals.

But if anything, Leonie wasn't anxious enough about her symptoms. "Oh, no, not at all. I always feel completely normal afterward. Really, if it goes on like this, it's not so bad, is it? Better than diabetes,

I'd say. I'd rather nod off every now and then than have to worry about jabs every day."

Colin watched the other two exchange a glance of dismay. "That's... probably a good attitude to have."

"Of course, it's the progression that worries me. Do you have any sense of what I can expect to happen next?"

Sonia held up a sheet of paper saying what he already knew: *She's legit.* He saw all of the checked boxes on the side, the things Leonie couldn't have guessed from their posts or questions. She'd mentioned the odd birdlike motions of the head and the unvarying combination of three distinct muscle movements per Dancing fit.

"Well," he replied after a moment's hesitation, "if it follows the Galina pattern, then the next stage is Remembering. Which is pretty much like Naming, except more complex sentences describing things you remember. And the original Plagues ended after that phase, so..."

"Oh, well, that's good news, isn't it?"

"We hope so, yeah. Now, could you tell us about your family history, again?"

She didn't know what her grandparents' names would have been, but her father's name was Kevin Tseda, and he was the right age to have a parent in Galina during the Plagues. Colin thought he remembered a Tseda family, although he couldn't recall more detail than that.

"You'll let me know, won't you? If you find anything?"

"I promise you'll be the first one we call." He disconnected from Skype.

"Another grandparent?" Sonia asked.

"I think so. Timing works out."

She shook her head, lip curled in disgust. "That's the biggest kick in the balls, as far as I'm concerned. That I got this from Grandpa fucking Richie instead of a family member who was worth a damn."

"If you don't mind me asking," Alonzo began, frowning, "what was so bad about the guy?"

Colin watched, reminding himself not to speak. Several testimonies pointed to Richie Rollins as the likely killer of at least one person on the night of the riots. He wasn't sure if Sonia knew that or if she would want to hear it. He'd also wondered from the way she talked if there was some kind of abuse he shouldn't be prying into.

She shrugged. "He was a racist, sexist sack of shit."

"Yeah, but that describes, like, half the grandparents in the world. Why do you hate him personally?"

Colin inhaled, wondering if Alonzo had overstepped. It was surprising; Lonzo was usually more careful than most about invading privacy.

But something must have broken down those barriers, because Sonia frowned, staring thoughtfully into space and tapping a pen against her cheek. "You know, I'm not really sure. I mean, I was only five when he died, so I was too young to understand a lot of the things that made him a terrible person. But I think... He always made my dad feel small. My dad was a quiet guy, a little sensitive, and Grandpa Richie just trampled all that. I felt—" She stopped, an odd expression of confusion unfurling over her face. Whatever it was, she shook it off. "I don't know. Probably just heard enough stories over the years to form a bad impression."

Lonzo looked like he wanted to ask another question. Something was there, some idea he was pursuing. But then Colin's phone rang, and the moment was lost. The caller ID showed another Galina descendant calling them back.

"EVER HEARD OF THIS Charles Fort guy?" Sonia asked, peering over the laptop.

"As in 'Fortean Phenomena'"? Yeah," Colin replied without looking up.

"Yeah, so, I'm going through this book he wrote, and he had a real hard-on for weird rain. Like, fish, frogs, blood, shit like that. Kinda sounds like the Red Hail, right?"

"Right. So, what, you're thinking the Red Hail might have happened somewhere else?" Alonzo asked.

"Nope," Colin said without hesitation. "At least, not coinciding with these same symptoms and not in any place with written language. I compared Galina to as many mass hysteria cases as I could find, and there was nothing just like it. That's why I focused on it." His mouth twisted into a wry smile. "Because it was unique. *Fun.*"

"Good thing you did," Sonia said, "or we'd have even less to go on than we do now."

He didn't answer, because at that moment, Alonzo started Dancing. He slouched down in his chair, arms and head twitching in repetitive, twisting movements.

Colin jumped up and held his shoulders with both hands. "It's okay. It's okay. I'm here," he muttered over and over.

Sonia cleared her throat. "Sorry, but... you might not want to do that."

"What?"

"Well, for me, the worst part of these things is coming out of it and seeing how things have moved around. Especially if there's someone really close to me who wasn't there before. It's like, blink, and bam, someone's right there in front of your face."

"Oh." He took a reluctant step back. "I didn't think about it."

"Yeah. I guess it would be hard to imagine, if you've never been through it." She paused. "I guess in a way, I'm glad I'm getting them, if Dylan is too. At least I get what he's going through."

They both watched Alonzo spasm for a minute. "How old is he? Your son?" Colin asked.

"Seven." She caught the look in his eye. "Got knocked up when I was eighteen, in case you're trying to do the math."

"Sorry."

"I'm not." She grinned. "He's a great kid. Smart as hell. I know all moms say that, but it's actually true. Don't know how. His dad's dumb as a fucking brick."

Colin smiled a little, although his eyes kept getting dragged back to Alonzo. "I take it you're not together anymore."

"No. We were never really *together*, you know, just for a night or two. And thank god. He's a walking argument for single mother-hood. Which is cool, because I never really felt like I needed a guy to be the dad. I mean, me and Dylan were doing just fine, until this. I had it all worked out. I mean, not perfect, but... You know, it worked. And then this bullshit had to screw it all up." She gestured vaguely at Alonzo's flailing form.

"Yeah. I get it. It's not exactly the same, but Lonzo and I had about one good week of living together before this happened. I mean, he was basically living at my place for a long time before that, but we technically still had separate places." His gaze fell. "People told me living together would be an adjustment, but I don't think this is what they meant."

"Well, he's a lucky guy. Most people would have bailed by now."

Colin shrugged and pretended to mess with some papers on the table. Sonia thought she saw him blushing a little.

Alonzo straightened up, his eyes focusing. "Um. Hey, was I just out?"

"Yeah," Colin replied quietly. "Stage Three. Dancing Sickness."

"Oh. So just one more stage, right?"

"If the pattern holds, yeah. The fourth one is the Remembering. And then, if it's like Galina, it might just end there."

Sonia exhaled, blowing her bangs out of her eyes. They were overdue for a trim. "I don't know if I'll be able to stand it if we don't figure it out. I mean, even if it goes away, not knowing…"

"I can take the mystery," Alonzo said, picking up his book. "I'll take mystery any day of the week, if this goes away."

Sonia exchanged a glance with Colin. He would never be able to take the mystery. She saw it in his eyes.

"OKAY. LET'S OPEN IT up. Possible explanations. No suggestion is too dumb," Colin said as Alonzo came back to the living room with the box of Chinese delivery. He dropped the food in the middle of the coffee table.

"I think my list might challenge that position." Sonia grabbed a carton of lo mein. "Okay, so, going off all the conspiracy websites and stuff, here's the things people have said caused the Galina Plagues." She cleared her throat. "First up: toxic waste from the copper mines dumped into the groundwater. And some of those explained the Red Hail as, like, evaporated waste or something in the atmosphere."

"I remember something in your notes about how they tested the groundwater back when the Plagues first started, so it's not that," Alonzo said.

Colin nodded. "Right, and people with different water supplies are having the same symptoms."

"Okay, so not number one." Sonia crossed it off the list. "Next up, a curse. Because the town's in former Apache territory or some-thing, so Indian curse, Stephen King–style."

"Do we seriously have to consider that one?" Alonzo groaned. "The whole Apache curse thing is just really racist."

"I know. But okay, setting aside the whole Apache thing. A curse." Colin held up his palms. "None of us want to, but let's think about it."

"It's just... If this is magic, there are no rules, and I'm just not there yet," Alonzo said, filling the silence.

"Okay. Let's just leave that for now. Because Lonzo's right, if this is magic, we don't have anything to work with anyway."

Sonia crossed off the second bullet point on her list, the one she'd already privately disregarded. "And now for our ickiest theory: Option number three, inbreeding, which caused everyone in the town to have the same genetic condition. If it's this one, guys, I will never stop barfing."

"Nope," Alonzo said immediately. "The town didn't exist as a single gene pool long enough for that, and even a genetic disease hitting an entire population wouldn't become symptomatic in everyone at the same time."

"And also it's gross and offensive," Sonia added. "Can't believe these motherfuckers online are actually saying this about a town full of real people. And speaking of gross and offensive: cannibal cult. Because cannibalism is apparently responsible for something called kuru, which has some kinda sorta similar symptoms."

Alonzo shook his head again. "If it were a prion disease, it wouldn't have stopped. The neurological damage would have just progressed until they died. Also, I refuse to believe Grandfather Fernando ate human flesh."

"Next?" Colin asked.

"Straight from the History Channel: aliens," Sonia said in her best dramatic narrator voice. "Alien explorers anal probing people and experimenting and shit. No one seems to have any thoughts on *why* aliens would do any of those things, but it's pretty popular on the forums."

Alonzo stabbed at a piece of shrimp in his fried rice. "I mean, technically, yeah, it could be. I guess. But what would their motive be? Why bother with us?"

"That's the problem with the alien theory. Their motives could be literally anything, and we wouldn't have any clue how they think or what they want or anything, really." Colin pinched the bridge of his nose, squinting as though through a headache.

Alonzo pushed a container of pepper beef at him. "Eat."

"Yeah," Sonia echoed. "You're skinny as fuck."

Colin took a grudging bite of the food but stopped as soon as Alonzo wasn't paying attention.

"The next couple are all variations on 'governments experimenting on people.' There's good old Soviet weather control and the US government trying to replicate Soviet weather control. Then there's some other experiment by the US government, maybe involving the water supply, because the town was mostly brown people and they were into the whole sterilizing-folks-and-keeping-America-white thing. Thoughts?"

Alonzo stared into space for a moment. "Hm. Wouldn't be the first time the US government has experimented on its citizens."

"Yeah. The Tuskegee Experiment, MK-Ultra, sterilizing institutionalized women. That stuff was all over the forums. And I totally wouldn't put it past them. My money's on this one, honestly," she said then took another bite of food.

"Plus, this is the Cold War we're talking about—1960. Think they'd hesitate to experiment on some half-Mexican town near the border if they thought they'd get some new weapon out of it?" Alonzo nodded. "I'm with Sonia on this one. I think this is our best bet."

Colin bit his lip. "I don't know. I'm sure they'd do it if they had the technology, but this kind of thing leaves a paper trail. It might stay classified for fifty years, but eventually, the truth comes out. And also, most of the real conspiracies aren't really all that well-executed.

I just can't believe the CIA or the DoD or whatever could execute something this well and keep it this quiet and then never use it on anyone."

Sonia tossed aside her notepad. "Welp, that's what I got. Anyone else?"

Colin snorted. "All the ones I found are the same things you find on almost all mass hysteria conspiracy and paranormal message boards. They have the same dumb five or six ideas they recycle through every weird event. And they're always bullshit."

"Hey, you said everything was on the table," Alonzo reminded him.

"Okay, you're right." Colin sighed. "Let's continue, then."

"I pretty much got the same list," Alonzo admitted, grimacing down at his notepaper. "The only additional suggestion being demonic possession, which may or may not be related to that 'Apache curse' explanation. There's an entire message board where people are fighting about that."

Colin frowned. "That's one we should think about."

"You are *not* serious," Sonia snapped.

"Not, like, strictly Catholic concepts of possession. But possession in general is pretty much a cultural universal. It's not always demons. A lot of cultures have people who claim they're taken over by a benevolent entity during ceremonies and rituals. So maybe there aren't *Exorcist*-style demons, but if this happens all over the world, then maybe there's some physical reality behind it we haven't figured out yet."

"Note to self: Read up on possession. Because that's somehow where my life is at," Sonia grumbled, scribbling a note.

They all chewed quietly for a while.

"So... what? None of these are solid leads, then?" Sonia asked, breaking the silence.

"They're all possibilities. Some more than others," Alonzo said. "But bottom line, the problem is that any of these answers means believing something really goddamn crazy. I mean, we have to accept that possession is real, magic is real, maybe that aliens are real, or the CIA did this to us. Either way, we can't keep thinking about the world in the same terms as before *and* figure out what's happening. And that's hard to do."

Sonia shrugged. "Well, we don't have a choice, do we? The world is different, whether or not we want to face it." She pushed her food away. "So we might as well suck it up."

"You're right." Alonzo sighed. "We just have to keep going with this. Magic, possession, whatever—we keep researching it all. What other choice do we have?"

CHAPTER 22: 1960

"It was stupid. The stuff that girl was doing, it wasn't anything like a real fit."

"Well, the more people see these fake fits, the more they'll think that's what some of them look like." Dove paced back and forth in quick, agitated steps.

"And the harder this task will become," Father Santiago added. He seemed older than he had when they'd started, his black hair showing a few flecks of silver.

Dove snorted. "So, first, he says the fits are caused by the devil. Then he says *not* having fits is a sign of the devil. Am I missing some deep theology here, Padre?"

He rubbed his forehead as though trying to banish a headache. "Evangelical churches aren't known for their consistency."

"Doesn't matter, though." Anza sighed. "He's got people on the lookout for anybody who isn't having fits. That means you and me, Dove."

"But mostly you." Dove flipped through some notes. "First, because your daddy made a stink. And second, because you're the only one your age who isn't having them, but there's lots of old folks who aren't."

Father Santiago frowned. "That is curious, isn't it?"

"Well, we know age matters. Hits the young'uns first. Hm." She set aside the notes. "We'll have to look into it more, but first, we should deal with the matter at hand. Anza, I think it's high time you had a fit."

ANZA JOINED FERNANDO, Consuela, and Mark on the sidewalk near the ice cream parlor. Paula and David had made their excuses the last few weeks, not joining Anza or any of the other Mexican kids during their trips into town. Anza considered how devastating that would have felt three months ago, but now, it entered her mind only as a sign of the larger pattern at work.

"Feels weird, being watched all the time," Fernando said, tossing a pebble into the road.

Anza nodded and looked down the street at where Dad and Mr. Cardenas stood outside the saloon. They seemed faintly embarrassed about it, probably remembering how it would have felt to have parents following them around when they were sixteen or seventeen. But no one argued with them about it, not even Fernando, who had grumbled to Anza about being able to take care of himself.

She waited until she spotted a cluster of women she recognized from Pastor Benjamin's church. She caught Dad's eye and gave the slightest nod.

"Remember," Dove had told her. "No warnings. No taking a deep breath, no clearing your throat. Only Name things around you. And don't let your eyes focus on anything."

Anza stared at a spot on the street, trying to look blank, the way she'd practiced with Dad and in the mirror. Just as the gaggle of ladies passed next to her, she intoned, "Street. Black. White. Paint. Women. Shoes."

"Oh god," Fernando said, grabbing her arm. The fear in his voice almost made her break rhythm, but she pressed on.

"Mr. Kearney!" Fernando shouted, waving down the street. She hadn't counted on him making a fuss, but she felt more eyes turning toward her. No chance anyone would miss this.

Dad came running up, right on cue. "Anza! Oh no, Anza!"

She risked a quick glance in his direction, narrowing her eyes to tell him to tone it down. Everyone knew Sean Kearney didn't get spooked easy, and no one really panicked about fits anymore.

He seemed to get the message. "Come on, Anza, let's get you home," he said, tugging her to her feet.

She tried to move with that hazy suggestibility Namers had, wondering if she was overdoing it. She waited for Dad to open the truck door, pick her up, and set her on the seat.

"Keep it up," he mumbled as he climbed into the driver's side. "Folks are still watching."

She kept muttering and staring blankly ahead until they turned the corner off Main Street.

"How'd I do?" she asked when no one was in sight.

"Sure looked convincing to me," Dad said. "Feel bad for Fernando, though. You really scared that poor kid." He paused. "I know you two aren't going steady anymore. Don't worry. Not gonna pry into why that is. But that kid still has puppy-dog eyes for you. Be patient with him, yeah?"

"I—"

Anza never finished her sentence. As she spoke, Dad nodded in an exaggerated motion. At the same time, his lips peeled back from one side of his mouth and closed again in a quick rhythm. His hand twisted in toward his wrist, the whole limb tapping against his chest. The truck drifted toward the right shoulder as Dad let go of the steering wheel.

"Shit!" Anza shrieked, sliding across the bench seat to grab the wheel. She straightened out the truck, but it was speeding up—Dad's foot was jammed against the gas pedal. Grabbing the leg of his jeans, she tugged and pulled, trying to watch the road at the same time. There was a curve coming up, with an irrigation ditch beyond it.

Pulling on his pant leg wasn't working. Finally, Anza took a deep breath and kicked his shin until his foot slid off the pedal. Then she stomped on the brake as hard as she could, nearly flying up onto the dashboard as the truck skidded to a halt just before the ditch. Her foot bounced off the brake, and the truck's engine stalled.

Anza gripped the steering wheel, trying to catch her breath as Dad twitched and Danced. It wasn't a deep ditch. They wouldn't have died—or even been hurt badly—if they'd gone into it. Still, her heart thudded in her throat like it wanted to burst out of her.

Dad settled down after a few minutes. He sat up straight and blinked at the ditch in front of them. "I... What happened?"

Anza got out of the truck and circled around to the driver's side. "I'm driving from now on," she said, opening the door.

He stared at her for a long moment before averting his eyes, some kind of shame on his face. "Okay," he said in a voice meek and unlike him.

Anza took his place in the driver's seat, started the engine, and drove them home without another word.

CHAPTER 23: 2020

Interview with Melissa Rios, age forty-nine. Interview conducted by Colin Ayres, University of Arizona Department of Sociology.

Q: Thank you for meeting with me, Ms. Rios. Could you explain your connection to Galina?

A: My mother was born and raised there. I wasn't, though. I was born in Yuma.

Q: Was she there in the summer of 1960?

A: Yes. She would have been about twenty-three at the time. She didn't like to talk about that summer very much. I think she saw some bad things, back when the Plagues happened.

Q: Do you remember anything she told you about it?

A: Uh... Not really. Not exactly. I mean, it's hard for me to separate out what I heard from her and from my aunts and uncles and friends of hers from Galina.

Q: Just do your best to tell me what you remember, even if you're not sure where it came from.

A: Well, the biggest thing was when the men from Pastor Benjamin's church went after the priest. There were all kinds of rumors going around about how it was the Catholics' fault. Anyway, I don't really remember who told me about it, but I still have this dream sometimes. The priest is talking to an older woman in this little dark church. He's a young priest, maybe still in his twenties. And these men just burst in with a gasoline can. And then, in the dream, one of the men—this white man with a blond beard—hits the priest in the mouth. I always see his lip splitting and blood running down his chin, and he falls down. That's always when I wake up.

Q: How long have you had this dream?

A: It seems like my whole life. But that's why I think my mom must have told me about Galina when I was younger. I don't remember her telling me, but the images are so vivid. I feel like she must have told me the story, even though I never remember her talking about it. Where else would I have gotten something like that?

CHAPTER 24: 1960

"So, how do you know this doctor?" Anza asked.

They stood on Dove's front porch, watching the empty road. "Old friend from back in my charity ward days," Dove replied, voice clipped. Anza could tell she didn't want to say more.

A few minutes later, a shining yellow Cadillac rounded the bend and bumped cautiously up the driveway. Dove raised a hand in greeting. The car stopped, and a woman in a white blouse, sunglasses, and wide-legged gray pants stepped out. Anza's eyes widened. She'd never seen a woman wear those kinds of clothes in real life.

"My goodness, Dove, you really did remove yourself from civilization." The woman's crisp accent sounded the way her clothes looked. Her short, honey-colored hair was slicked close to her head, and her lips were painted deep red.

Dove met her halfway to the porch and pulled her into a long hug. "It's been too long, Faye."

"Yes, it has, darling. Belle sends her love." She stepped back from the hug and removed her sunglasses in one smooth motion. Her eyes were a summery green, webbed with faint crow's-feet.

Dove led her up the porch. "Anza, this is Dr. Faye Chiswick. Faye, this is Anza Kearney." She gave the other woman a meaningful glance. "Elena's daughter."

Faye blinked. "Oh my." She extended a hand. "It's an honor to meet you, Miss Kearney."

Anza wondered if her mother would keep hovering like a ghost in the conversation, or if one of them would say something direct about it. She wasn't sure which she preferred. But she cleared her throat and took Faye's hand. "You, too, Miss… Dr. Chiswick." She smiled. "I've never met a woman doctor before."

"Oh, those fusty old men at the American Medical Association do their best to keep us out, but we slip through every now and then. And please, call me Faye." She turned back to Dove. "Now then. We've got young patients to see, as I understand it."

"That's right. We'll have to drive over." Dove handed her a typed-up summary of everything that had happened so far and everything they knew. It filled a depressingly small number of pages.

"Golly," Faye said after a moment. "You weren't joking when you said this was a strange one. You didn't tell me the half of it."

"If I'd been honest, you might have been afraid to come." Anza caught something teasing in Dove's tone.

"Cheeky cow. But just so I know, how *would* you rate the risk of contagion?" Faye gestured for them to follow her to her car.

"For you? None. We haven't found a single case outside Galina, even though there's been plenty of contact. Our other researcher, Father Santiago, is doing another drive through the surrounding towns today, making sure we don't have any cases in Bisbee or Sierra Vista that we've missed. But I don't think he'll find anything."

"*Father* Santiago? Darling, you haven't converted, have you? Become a nun?"

"No. Won't be, either, unless they let me into the fun kind of convent." Dove grinned at her. Anza had never seen the toothy look on her face before. Faye let out a delighted cackle, and Anza knew she'd missed some private joke but suspected it would be a bad idea to ask about it.

Faye let Anza climb into the back seat before starting up the car. The seats were covered in buttery leather. Anza worried her Ropers must be tracking dirt into the beautiful car, but Faye didn't seem concerned. "So we're looking for what, exactly, from the children?"

"What happened after the Red Hail. They disappeared on the mesa and turned up three days later covered in mud and having the Naming fits. Their parents and Anza and I all asked them what they remembered, but they just have a big blank spot between playing outside and seeing the hail start, and waking up in the hospital."

"Hm. Could be tricky. Gaps in the memory that big usually mean there was some kind of serious trauma. I take it they were examined for signs of abuse?"

Dove nodded. "Healthy as can be, aside from the fits."

"Well, no guarantees, but I'll see what I can do."

"What kind of doctor are you?" Anza asked.

"I'm a pediatrician with a specialization in clinical psychology. That just means I work with children with mental problems."

"It's just about the most heartbreaking specialization that exists in this world," Dove said over her shoulder. "This lady here has the patience of a saint."

"Now if I only had the moral fortitude to match," Faye added, turning where Dove indicated. "This is it?"

"Yeah. The parents know we're coming."

Faye parked, opened a compact, and carefully wiped the crimson from her lips. Then she mussed her hair a bit, swapped her sunglasses for clunky clear ones with heavy frames, and pulled a shapeless mouse-brown cardigan from the glove box. "People expect a lady doctor to look a certain way, darling," Faye said when she caught Anza watching her. "It's easiest to make them feel like they're right."

Mrs. Garces met them at the door. "Hello, Dr. Chiswick, welcome. Thank you so much for seeing them."

The three children stood waiting near the front door, wearing their Sunday best, obviously stationed there by Mrs. Garces.

"Well, isn't this a strapping young man we have here. And two such lovely ladies," Faye said.

All of them smiled right away, Margarita hiding her face against the wall but peeking out to giggle now and then.

"Now. I'd like to talk to each of them in turn. I generally ask parents not to be in the room, since children can say disturbing things sometimes. Are you comfortable with that, Mrs. Garces?"

She nodded. "Yes, Mrs. McNally explained everything. Pablo? Pablo, will you speak with Dr. Chiswick?"

He hesitated, biting his lip.

Faye smiled. "Come now, young man. I don't bite."

He couldn't help smiling back at her.

Mrs. Garces showed them to Pablo's room. Anza sat in the corner and got ready to take notes.

"Now, Pablo," Faye said, perching on a chair and leaning forward so she was eye level with the boy. "I've been told that you don't remember anything about disappearing on the mesa. Is that true?"

He nodded. "I just remember the Red Hail starting to come down. And a piece hit me here." He pointed at his right ear.

Faye winced. "Oh, that must have hurt dreadfully."

"No." Pablo gave a stoic shrug. "It wasn't too bad. Then I woke up, and Dr. Allen was shining a light in my eye."

"I see." Faye folded her hands in her lap. "Pablo, have you ever heard of hypnosis?"

"Is that when you make someone think they're a chicken?"

She laughed. "Oh, no, not at all. That's just show business. Hypnosis can't really do that. No, when you hypnotize someone, it's more like when you start to fall asleep, but you aren't quite asleep yet. Do you ever suddenly remember something, just when you're about to fall asleep?"

Pablo nodded.

Faye continued. "So, Pablo, what we'll be doing here is trying to see if you remember anything else about that day that you don't quite know about. Do you think you'd be willing to give that a go?"

He looked nervous but nodded anyway.

She patted him on the knee. "That's the spirit. Let's begin."

ANZA HAD ASSUMED HYPNOSIS would involve Faye swinging a pocket watch on a chain, intoning something about getting very sleepy. Instead, it was more like when Anza tried to persuade kids she was babysitting to take their nap. Faye drew the curtains, had Pablo recline on his bed, and spoke in low, soothing tones. The only thing that was different was the metronome she set up on his bedside table. Its rhythmic clicks filled the room.

"Now, Pablo. I want you to imagine every muscle in your body relaxing. Start with your toes, then your feet. Your entire body is relaxing. Are you relaxed?"

"Yes."

"Now I want you to imagine walking down a long, dark hallway. Can you see it?"

"Yes."

"The hallway is dark, but you aren't afraid. You're safe."

"Yes."

"As you walk down the hall, you see a little speck of light at the end. As you get closer, you see an open door. Past that door is that day on the mesa, just before the Red Hail. Can you see it?"

"Yes."

"Go through the door."

"I'm through."

"Tell me what you see."

"Margarita found a lizard. She's trying to catch it in a cup so she can scare Luz with it. It gets darker. The clouds came when I wasn't looking. I tell Margarita and Luz we should go back to the house before the rain starts. But the Red Hail starts to fall." Pablo bit his lip.

"Remember that you're safe, Pablo. Nothing can hurt you. Now tell me what happens next."

"I pick up Luz and start to run. The Red Hail keeps falling. It stings where it hits me. Margarita trips, and I go back to help her. Her knee's bleeding, and she starts to cry. There's red mud on the front of her dress where the hail is melting. I take her hand and try to pull her up, but the ground pulls her down."

Anza scribbled notes as the boy spoke. She glanced over at Dove, who stared intently at him.

"I try to pull her out of the ground, but it pulls me down, too, and Luz gets pulled down with me. It's dark. I can feel the mud all around me, except around my face where there's air. My clothes are gone.

"Then the mud pushes us out into an empty place. It's cold. There's light everywhere, not much but all the walls and the ceiling glow red. There's one light brighter than the others. It's a red ball in the middle of the floor." His breath came in quick gasps. "Red dust comes out of the ball. It glows like the walls. It flies to us. It goes in my nose and my mouth, and I hear Margarita and Luz screaming—"

Anza jumped and gasped as screams echoed from the other end of the house, near the kitchen. They were little girl screams, frantic and high-pitched. Faye half stood, wide eyes darting from Pablo to the door and back again. Dove motioned for her to sit and dashed out of the room.

"Pablo, you're safe. Tell me what happens next."

His hands curled into claws at his side. "I can't move after I breathe in the dust. Except when it wants me to. It tells me to move my hands and my feet and my mouth, and it makes me remember the words for things. And it tells me to remember things, like people and animals and our town. I don't want to, but I have to."

"How does the dust tell you to do things, Pablo? Does it use words?"

"No, no, no words, it can't talk. It just makes me feel like I have to." He pauses. "There are other things in the room too. There are some coyotes, and a bobcat, and some birds and lizards and snakes, but they can't come near us. They make noises sometimes and move funny, like us."

"Then what?"

"It takes a long time. I fall asleep. But then it tells me to wake up. And Margarita and Luz are already standing. And it tells us we're going home. We get pulled down into the mud again, and then we move through it for a long time. And when the mud pushes us out, it's bright outside, and we're on top of a rock, and the mud is high up, but then it sinks back down to the ground. Some red dust comes with us. It flies out of the ground, but then it turns into big red bugs and flies away."

Faye nodded. "You've been very brave, Pablo. Very brave. Now it's time to come back. Imagine yourself on top of that rock. You turn around, and you see the long dark hallway again. Do you see it?"

"Yes."

"You walk down it, and you see a light at the end. It's this room, today, and you're lying on your bed safe in your house. Do you see it?"

"Yes."

"Walk through the doorway. And when you step into the room, you wake up."

Pablo's eyes popped open. He blinked for a moment. "Did I fall asleep?"

Faye shook her head. "No, you did brilliantly. Do you remember anything you told me?"

"No," he said, shaking his head and sitting up. "Was I supposed to?"

She hesitated. "No, not at all." She reached for her bag, smiling brightly. "Now, I believe I just may have a lollipop for you, young man."

Pablo trotted off, happily unwrapping his lollipop. Faye and Anza stared at each other in silence for a long moment.

"Was that real? What he said?" Anza asked at last.

Faye rose and opened the curtains, letting sunlight back into the cluttered little room. "Well, he believed it was. Whether or not any of that actually happened is another matter."

They found Dove and Mrs. Garces in the kitchen, watching the two girls draw with their crayons at the kitchen table.

"Are they all right?" Faye asked, too low for them to hear.

Dove nodded. "I think so. They were speaking. Not like Naming, something else." She handed Faye a torn slip of paper, maybe the back of a grocery receipt. "Is this what Pablo said after I left?"

Faye's lips pressed together into a flat line as she read. She nodded once before passing the paper to Anza.

And it tells us we're going home. We get pulled down into the mud again, and then we move through it for a long time. And when the mud pushes us out, it's bright outside, and we're on top of a rock.

CHAPTER 25: 2020

"The fuck is that?" Colin muttered, lifting his head from his pillow.

Alonzo sat up, trying to place the sound. Buzzing, humming. At first, he thought it was just the air conditioning unit outside the window, but it was too loud for that. "I'll go see."

"Okay." Colin rolled over. He was asleep before Alonzo left the room.

It was louder in the hallway. Something outside, beyond the sliding glass back door. Not cicadas, too grinding and harsh for that. Something flitted by in the dark, just catching the moonlight for a moment.

Alonzo stepped out into the cool, dry night. The sound kept going, surrounding him as he walked out across the yard, but he didn't see anything. He turned in a slow circle, squinting into the shadows cast by the plants and the garden wall.

Red glinted in the corner of his eye. He turned, but it was already gone.

Then something landed on his forehead, cold and metallic on his skin.

Porch. He'd only moved about ten yards since he blinked, but he felt like he'd lost a lot of time. Gasping, he batted at the cold metal circle on his forehead. It detached and flitted away in the dark.

Sweat broke out over Alonzo's skin. He backed slowly into the house, sliding the screen door shut behind him and fumbling with the lock. He touched his forehead and told himself he had not seen what he thought he had just seen. There had not been a shining, golf-ball-sized red-shelled beetle like a bloody scarab on his forehead. There were not more of them hiding in the dark.

SONIA TOOK HER TIME on the walk back to Cara's place. She'd had a good set, sitting in for the lead singer of Cara's band after she'd come down with the flu. The crowd had liked her, and she'd gotten some free drinks and enough bar food to count as a meal. She thought for a moment of getting Ross to relocate the band to Tucson once this was all over. The music scene was better, Dylan would like it here—

She stopped half a block away from Cara's house. Something sat on the pavement just in front of the mailbox. A dog, she thought. Then she got closer and saw the angle of the face, the silvery pelt.

Sonia had never seen a coyote up close. They were always just flashes at the edge of her vision, scampering away from the edge of the road or slinking behind trash cans. They'd always struck her as shifty little creatures with none of the nobility she imagined wolves having.

But this one just sat and watched her as she approached. She wondered if it might be rabid, but it didn't drool or sway or growl at her. It just stared, eyes yellow in the streetlight. Sonia tried to remember everything she'd read about the coyotes in Colin's notes, the weird behaviors out on the mesa. She didn't remember anything about them approaching humans, and certainly nothing about attacks, but...

Sonia kept her eyes on the coyote as she made her way to the gate. She'd just slide through sideways and close it behind her, and it would be trapped on the other side.

She got one hand on the latch before the coyote jumped.

It didn't snarl or bare its teeth, didn't spring like an attacking dog. Instead, it rose smoothly onto its back legs and, before Sonia had a chance to move, put its front paws on her chest.

Blink. She still stood in front of Cara's gate, but now she faced the opposite direction. A muscle in her arm cramped like it sometimes did when she Statued. The coyote stood about six feet away, watching her.

As soon as Sonia took a step back, it turned and trotted off, disappearing into the night.

"FUCK WALKING. WALKING is dumb. Especially during the summer. That's why humans invented cars." Sonia scowled through her sunglasses.

"It's five minutes. We'll make it," Alonzo replied, wiping sweat from his forehead. It was a bad time for a walk, but he couldn't stand being in the house any longer, and Colin had to be on campus for a department meeting.

The neighborhood was quiet this time of day. He hadn't met many of the neighbors yet, but he felt comforted by the blue signs that had popped up like mushrooms all along their street. Sonia snarled at the lone GOP sign on one corner, and Alonzo suspected it would be kicked over or defaced by nightfall.

He closed his eyes and sighed as they stepped into the chilled air of Time Market. "Hey, if you want to order the sandwiches, I'm just going to pick up some groceries."

Sonia nodded and went to stand in line at the deli counter. Alonzo paced through the aisles, grabbing bread and cheese and a few other things they were running low on. For the first two weeks after he'd decided to stop driving, he'd had Colin take him to the store whenever they needed something. Now, though, he tried to avoid asking Colin to chauffeur him around any more than he absolutely had to. Colin claimed he didn't mind, of course, but how could he not? And once the semester started—

Loud, nervous conversation pulled Alonzo out of his reverie. "Shit," he said under his breath, dashing toward the deli counter.

Sure enough, Sonia stood, head drooping, speaking in a low monotone as people around her panicked and dialed numbers into their phones.

"It's okay. She's fine, she doesn't need an ambulance," he said. He put a hand to the small of her back and guided her out of the sandwich line, careful not to touch bare skin. They'd touched since that first terrifying incident, with no ill effects, but he didn't want to take any chances, especially not in public.

Sonia trudged along in response to the pressure on her back. Alonzo noticed how sharp her spine felt under her shirt, how much her collarbones stood out under the skin. He made a mental note to get her to eat more.

"Dude, are you sure?" asked the dreadlocked white boy behind the counter. "Because that looks serious." He held a phone near his head.

"Yeah. Please, this is a medical condition she deals with all the time. An ambulance isn't going to do any good."

"Okay, if you say so." The kid turned away to speak into the phone then hung up.

Alonzo noticed for the first time that Sonia wasn't Naming. He bent closer, listening to her words: "I put the key in the car door. Yes. I pull the handle. I don't know. I sit inside. No. The leather is too hot against my skin."

Alonzo pulled out his phone and turned on the voice recorder app, making sure it was close enough to catch her muttered words.

Then he glanced back up at the menu board and the kid behind the deli counter. "Did she order yet?" he asked.

"Uh, no."

"Okay, in that case can we get two Reubens, a BLT, and a pound of the macaroni salad?"

"Dude. Seriously?" White Rasta pointed at Sonia.

Alonzo bit back an impatient *fuck you*. "Life doesn't just stop because you have a medical condition. Believe me."

While he waited for their order, he typed out a quick text to Colin. *Sonia just started Stage 4.*

He tapped Send and went back to watching Sonia stare and mutter. It could all be over soon. In ten, eleven days, it might just end.

It would end, or they would find out what Stage 5 looked like.

"SO, I'M GONNA HEAD back to Phoenix for a few days. Or permanently, if it stops," Sonia said, rubbing her eyes. "I mean, Lonzo and I are three days into Stage 4, so we could be near the end of it. And I need to spend some time with Dylan. I mean it's been, Christ, like almost three weeks?" She paused. "You know, that's the longest we've ever been apart since he was born. I shouldn't have left him with Mom this long. I really gotta see him."

"Good idea," Colin said. "You deserve a break."

Sonia wrapped up the last batch of notes she'd cobbled together, emailed them to Colin, and shut off her laptop. "Call me if anything new happens?" she said, getting up and retrieving her bag. "And I can do research from Phoenix, so let me know."

"We will. Sorry to see you go." Alonzo hugged her.

"Me too." She returned the hug with an awkward, closed-fist tap on the back. "Catch ya later."

"Later," Colin said, watching the door close behind her. He caught Alonzo's eye, smiling sheepishly. "I was getting used to having her around."

"Me too. But if this ends with Stage 4... Man, it's gonna be a relief to get back to normal."

"Yeah."

"You gonna have time to finish your book before the semester starts? If we aren't spending our days working on this?" Alonzo asked.

Colin pretended to be engrossed with something on his laptop screen. "I don't need to. I talked to my editor two days ago. Told them I needed an extension."

"What?" Alonzo leaned forward so Colin couldn't hide his face. "You were almost done."

Colin bit his lip, avoiding eye contact. "I can't turn in a book arguing something I don't believe is true anymore."

Alonzo said nothing, but Colin saw the guilt. "It's okay," he said. "Really. It's not going to be that hard to fix. I mean, it was always more about how people reacted to the Plagues and not so much about what caused them, so... I just need to get rid of all the stuff about what I used to think caused the Plagues. Just focus on how people lost their shit about it."

"I'm sorry," Alonzo said after a long moment.

"Don't be." Colin smiled, trying to be convincing. "It's not important. You getting better, that's important. And we might be through it pretty soon, so..."

Alonzo took his hand, neither saying anything else.

CHAPTER 26: 1960

"And there was no chance the girls could have overheard what Pablo was saying?" Father Santiago asked.

Dove set a glass of whiskey in front of him. "None. You know those adobe houses. Walls are two feet thick. A brass band could be playing in the next room, and no one would be the wiser."

"The girls were screaming at the top of their lungs, and we just barely heard it," Anza added. She hoped Dove would offer her a whiskey, too, but she didn't.

"Well, Faye. You're our expert. What do you make of it?" Dove asked, settling back in her chair.

Faye snorted. Her lipstick was back in place, the brown cardigan discarded. "Darling, saying one is an expert on hypnosis is a bit like saying one is the world's foremost expert on the bottom of the ocean. The truth is, we know next to nothing about the mind or how it works." She sighed. "If it were just young Pablo, I'd say he was probably subjected to terrible abuse or molestation and concocted this ghastly cavern as a coping mechanism. But I can't even begin to explain how the two girls could spontaneously recite the exact same account unless they planned it in advance. And I've never met children under the age of eight who could execute a hoax that well."

"Let's imagine as an exercise that everything the children described really happened," Father Santiago began. He held up a hand to cut off Dove's objection. "I don't really believe that, but we should consider it."

"Oh, I agree," Faye said, staring at the ice cubes floating in her glass. "Even if it's not the literal truth, it's not random nonsense. We should take it seriously."

Father Santiago nodded. "Okay, then. The Red Hail creates some kind of cavern or sinkhole. There's something inside, some kind of red sphere, Pablo said? It gives off dust, they breathe it in, and then something 'tells' them to do things. Things that are quite similar to the fits the rest of us have been having."

"Except they're awake for it. And they can hear, or feel, this thing telling them to do things," Anza said. "That's the biggest difference. No one else knows when something's happening."

"So it keeps them down there for three days. Along with animals apparently being subjected to the same process. It keeps them alive, it keeps them healthy, it heals Margarita's knee. Then, after three days of this, it lets them go, and their symptoms are now the same as any-one else," he said. His fingers reached out as though he could pluck the answer from the air.

"Yes, it's odd." Faye frowned. "The current symptoms are more like epilepsy than anything else. Or some other seizure disorder. But you can't use hypnosis to recover memories from what happened during an epilepsy fit. The brain simply isn't able to absorb informa-tion during those episodes. So they aren't just seizures."

"It's like it was using them to learn," Anza mused. She looked up to find the others watching her. "I mean... the kids go under the ground. They go through all the stages in three days. Then they get spit out, and the Plagues go around like wildfire, like it's learned how we work."

"You know," Faye said after a long moment, "that might not be as mad as it sounds. If we're imagining that this thing is deliberate-ly infecting people and inducing fits for some purpose. Well, then, it would have to know what parts of the brain control movement, memory, consciousness, speech. If it wanted to *turn off* our conscious awareness while these other things are happening, well, I suppose it would need to poke around a few test subjects first to get a sense of how they work." She fixed Dove with a grim stare. "So it fiddles about with the Garces children for a few days, works out the structures of the brain, and then moves on to the rest of the town once it's got its technique worked out."

Dove rolled her eyes. "Except all of that means we have to accept that some smart dust decided to come to Galina to use us like puppets." She pointed at her shelf of pulp magazines. "I read that kind of thing for fun, not because I think it happens in real life."

"But think about it, Dove," Father Santiago said. "It really makes a great deal of sense when you think about it. The fits, they happen in clear stages, and they're increasingly complex. They start by Naming objects, like learning vocabulary. They hold one immobile position, a body holding still, like you would study in anatomy class. Just to learn how the body is put together. Then they move on to motions. And the motions from Dancing fits seem to get more complex with time."

"So it's administering tests," Faye said. "Language, reflexes, movement."

"But...Why?" Anza slapped the coffee table. "Why the hell would anyone go to this much trouble? What's the point of all this?"

No one spoke for a moment. "Doesn't matter," Dove said at last, "because I don't think we're at a point where we need to be taking Pablo Garces at his word. At least, not the crazier stuff. But what we *can* get out of it is that there's a cave somewhere. And maybe that cave is where our little fungus is breeding." She smiled thinly. "So. Next step's obvious. We gotta find someone in this town who knows their way around caves."

ANZA WAS JUST ABOUT to leave the church when Patty ran inside. Dove was visiting with Faye before she had to drive back, so Anza and Father Santiago organized reports on their own. He had been hesitant to let them do work while sitting in the church pews, but it was the only place in town that wasn't bathed in stifling heat.

Then Patty ran inside, letting the heat and sunlight in through the front door. She skidded to a halt between the pews. "Father! There's a fight in the café. Mama sent me to get you."

Father Santiago dashed after her. Anza found her notebook and followed. She heard the fight before they even reached the café, women shouting over each other.

Inside, Millie stood between Mrs. Foster and Old Mrs. Garcia. Mrs. Foster was mother to J.D. and Henry. Anza had heard mutterings from all the Fosters, more nonsense about Mexicans being to blame for Henry being out of work on account of his burned hand.

Old Mrs. Garcia was the oldest person in town, a tiny, shriveled doll of a woman. No one was sure exactly how old she was, but she had to be over one hundred. She claimed a daily splash of whiskey in her tea was what kept her going. She still trundled down to Millie's for buttered biscuits and gravy every Thursday, even though it seemed to take her forever to walk down the street.

Now, though, she seemed angry enough to deck Mrs. Foster if Millie let her go. "Father!" she shouted in her creaking voice. "This woman slandered me and my family! She accuses me of putting a hex on that child!"

They all turned to stare at the young girl sitting in the nearest booth. Anza vaguely recognized her as one of the Fosters, maybe one of J.D.'s cousins. She twitched and bobbed in her seat, hands and head moving in repetitive spasms.

"She was looking right at Betsy, right at my niece, just when she started doing that! She never done anything like this before, and then this old bat looks at her, and she starts!" Mrs. Foster cried out, hysterical, makeup running down her face in streaks. Her eyes flashed with terror as she watched her niece.

"I only looked over when the girl started moving!" Old Mrs. Garcia shouted back. "I don't know nothing about these things."

"Mrs. Foster, please calm down," Father Santiago said. "This has been happening to people all over town. Mrs. Garcia had nothing to do with it."

"Yes, she did!" Mrs. Foster pushed him away. "She looked *right at* her. And she's one of the only ones who hasn't had any fits. Everyone else is getting sick, and we're not even gonna look at the ones who ain't?" She pointed at Mrs. Garcia. "I'm telling you, she did something, probably some Indian curse."

Millie had to hold Mrs. Garcia back again.

Father Santiago sighed. "Mrs. Foster, there is no such thing as a curse. Or a hex. This is an illness." And he sounded convincing, even though Anza knew his doubts.

"And more importantly," Millie said, "I ain't having this nonsense in my café. Keep the peace or get out."

Mrs. Foster gave Father Santiago a stare of pure loathing. "Betsy, come on, now. Come on." She tugged at the little girl's arm.

Betsy got out of the booth, still staring and twitching. The entire café watched in silence as the woman and the girl left.

"Hexing a little girl. What have I done that someone would accuse me of such a thing?" Mrs. Garcia asked, eyes brimming with tears.

"There, there." Father Santiago led her to a booth. "No one believes in any of that."

"I'll get your biscuits, Mrs. G. Don't you worry about a thing." Millie mouthed, "Thank you," at Father Santiago as she bustled back to the kitchen.

Once Mrs. Garcia calmed down, Father Santiago led Anza back to the church. "Did you write down what the girl was doing?"

Anza held up her notebook. "Just a little. Didn't want to get too close." She shook her head. "Hexes."

"It's silly, but I'm hearing more and more things like that. It's troubling."

"About curses?"

He nodded, biting his lip. "And about the ones who haven't had fits. Mostly old women. That frightens me."

"Why?"

"Back in the days of witch trials, it was usually old women, the poor, midwives, who were accused. And when people start believing in witches, well, violence can occur very quickly." His eyes swept the street as though searching for the mob coming with their pitchforks.

Anza laughed. "Come on, Father. This is the twentieth century. People are scared, but it won't come to that."

He watched her in sad silence. Anza suddenly felt much less confident and much more afraid.

ANZA CAME HOME TO FIND Dad sitting at the kitchen table, staring at a beer. She glanced at the clock. "You're home early. Something happen?"

"Sit down, Anza." He didn't look up.

"What happened?"

Dad sipped his beer. "Doug died today." There was a little hint of wonder in his voice, as though he couldn't quite grasp it.

"Oh my god. How?"

"Electrocuted. Don't know how, exactly. He was working on the electrical, near the roof bolt, and something went wrong. We think... We're not sure, but he might have been Dancing at the time. If he had a fit, he could have touched the wrong spot without meaning to, and…"

Anza wanted to hug him, to take his hand, but she knew this mood. He didn't want to be comforted yet. "I'm so sorry."

"Yeah. Well. They fired all of us, so I guess it won't happen again."

It took a moment for the words to sink in. "Wait. What do you mean?"

"I mean, Anza, that they fired every miner from Galina. Said it was for our own safety, but those fuckers from Bisbee and Caldoso and Apache Pass have been pushing for it for weeks, now. Scared they'll get infected." He gave her a humorless rictus of a smile. "Your old man is out of a job. After all these years."

Anza sat up straight, trying to look calm and poised. She suspected she was failing. "It's okay. We'll make do. We'll find something."

"Yep." He took another long pull on his beer. "But not here, we won't. Galina's dying, Anza. If it weren't for the Plagues, it would have been something else. Sometimes I think this town started dying the second Elena took her last breath." He paused. "Sorry, sweetheart. I know you wanted to finish high school here, but I don't think it's going to happen."

"I don't have to finish school. I can get a job if we need to."

"Over my cold dead body, you won't finish school," Dad said, eyes flaring with anger for the first time since she'd sat down at the table. "Your mama would turn over in her grave. You're finishing school, and then you're getting a scholarship, and then you're going to college. And that's more than *Pastor Benjamin's* little dullards are ever gonna do. That'll show him."

Anza couldn't quite hide her smile. "That's why I have to go to college? Just to show up Pastor Benjamin?"

Dad grinned. "Yep. So I can rub it in his stupid, sweaty face."

"He does sweat a lot, doesn't he?"

"All the damn time. Must have to drink water all day long." He stared at her, left eye closed more than the right, the way it always was when he was drunk. "But seriously. That's why getting fired ain't so bad. Even if I don't have a job, I still got the smartest kid in town. And if he don't like it, he can..." He frowned. "Shit. Forgot what I was going to say. 'M drunk." He got to his feet, wobbling a bit. "G'night, Anza," he said, patting vaguely at her shoulder as he stumbled out of the kitchen.

She stayed sitting where she was for a minute, looking at their messy little house. She'd never felt much for the linoleum tiles in the kitchen, the cramped living room full of secondhand furniture, and the screened-in porch with its moth-eaten hammock. But now, the thought of having to leave it behind made her throat ache.

After a while, she let out a breath, stood, and wiped her face. She gathered up the beer bottles Dad had left on the table, collecting them all into a trash bag. She tidied up, not bothering to stay quiet. Tonight, Dad would sleep through anything.

Carrying the bag of empty bottles in one arm, Anza made her way to the trash can out by the road. The air felt stuffier than usual, muggy with tomorrow's rain. She lifted her hair and wiped sweat from the back of her neck.

After she threw the bottles away, she turned back to the house. She'd just planted one boot on the porch step when she saw the beetle. It rested on the porch's dusty screen, like a droplet of blood half as big as her palm. Her breath caught in her throat as she got a better look at it. It wasn't a beetle, not really. It had the hard, shiny carapace and the stubby little red legs, like a tick, but it didn't have a head. The top and bottom of the shiny circle were completely identical. No eyes, antennae, or anything emerged from either end.

Before she had time to think about it too hard, Anza cupped her hand and snapped it down around the bug, hoping she didn't accidentally squash it. Nothing crunched under her fingers, but it didn't move, either. Opening the space between her index and middle fingers just enough to see, Anza peered in at the insect. It sat still, lifeless as a paperweight. Then it dissolved into red dust.

With a yelp, Anza danced backward, wiping the dust off her palm. The rest hung suspended in the air instead of falling to the ground. As if carried by a breeze, it drifted away in a narrow cloud, a red band swimming away through the air.

Anza ran inside and scrubbed her palm with soap and a sponge until it tingled. She sat at the kitchen table, waiting for the fits to start. But they never came.

CHAPTER 27: 2020

Colin woke up to an empty bed. He waited for a few minutes, assuming Alonzo was just in the bathroom. But then he rolled over and saw the bathroom door was open, the room dark inside. He pushed aside the blankets and wandered out into the hall.

He found Alonzo standing in front of the sliding glass door. He was completely naked, staring up at the moon. Colin frowned. Alonzo never walked around the house naked. He always put on at least a pair of sweatpants, even to grab something from the kitchen.

"Lonzo?"

Alonzo turned slowly. Something about the way he moved seemed off, too deliberate and careful. "Hello, Colin."

Colin stepped back and groped for the light switch, heart pounding. It wasn't Alonzo's voice that had spoken. Colin couldn't have said exactly what was wrong, but he knew without any doubt that it wasn't Lonzo. "What?" he asked as he turned on the light, not sure what he really wanted to ask.

Alonzo watched him with a wide-eyed, earnest expression. "This One has wanted to speak with Colin."

There was something almost cut-and-pasted about the speech coming from Alonzo's mouth. Each individual word sounded right, sounded the way it would if it were really him talking, but the words didn't fit together, the cadence shifting and dipping throughout the sentence.

"Who's 'This One'?" Colin's tongue felt thick and clumsy in his mouth.

Alonzo frowned like someone doing a bad impression of concentration. "The question is difficult for This One to answer. But This One comes to learn and to teach. This One hopes Colin will learn and will teach." He took a few tottering steps forward, peering at the floor as if watching for obstacles.

"Stay back." Colin shied away. The tang of adrenaline rose in the back of his throat.

Alonzo kept coming. "This One doesn't mean Colin harm. Nor does it mean Alonzo harm. But This One needs help. This One needs to consult with Those of Origin. And the Means to do so aren't here."

"Get back!"

He reached for Colin's arm. "This One has waited a very long time to speak. This one needs Colin's help. Colin must help This One find the Means."

Colin punched him. He didn't plan to, but as soon as the thing wearing Alonzo's skin touched his arm, his fist flew out as though of its own accord. It connected with Alonzo's cheekbone. His eyes widened in surprise as he toppled to the floor. Colin felt something in his index finger snap on impact. The pain followed, hot and sickening, moments later. Cursing, he clutched at his hand.

Alonzo sat halfway up, pushing himself up onto one elbow. "What the fuck?" He stared down at his own naked body.

"Oh shit. Shit, I'm so sorry. I'm so sorry," Colin gasped.

Alonzo touched his face. His eyes widened at the sight of Colin's hand. "Did you fucking *hit* me?"

"No. Not you," Colin said, sinking to the floor beside him.

SONIA AWOKE STANDING in the moonlight. The curtains were open, even though she knew she'd closed them before going to sleep on Cara's couch. Her hand hurt.

She held her songbook and a pen. She recognized the pain in her hand as the familiar cramping that came with writing for too long. A wave of dizziness swept over her, like the feeling of standing too fast after sitting for a long time. Trembling, she reached for the lamp next to the couch and clicked it on.

She'd filled at least three pages of the notebook. It was her handwriting, her tidy looping cursive. But the way the words were arranged and the flow of the text, that wasn't her. Her song lyrics came in flashes: line here, a rhyming couplet there, arrows and shorthand symbols linking different pieces in clusters across the page. The new pages, though, were unbroken blocks of text, words filling the paper from one side to the other.

Sonia shook, trying to remember if she'd been writing when she blacked out. But no, it was past three in the morning, and she'd crashed at eleven, exhausted after one last day of wading through Fortean nonsense and responses from Galina descendants. She saw the exact point where the foreign script started, just below the last lyric she'd written. It was an idea for an opening line, "Beneath the burning mesquite." *Mesquite* was circled and followed by a question mark, with *saguaro* written in the margin next to it.

Just below that familiar scribble, the new text began.

This One wishes a conversation with Sonia. This One needs to consult with Those of Origin, Those of Origin to This One as Dustin and Richie were of Sonia's origin and she is of Dylan's. The Means to consult with Those of Origin were last witnessed with One of the First Meeting. This One and Another One tried to tell Sonia of this need, but she became frightened. The Agreement of the First Meeting has been honored, but This One and the Other Ones cannot proceed without the Means to consult Those of Origin.

The message repeated three times over three pages. At the very end, on the last repetition, came something different: *This One is honored to be in contact with Sonia. This One has waited a long time to speak with her.*

"THIS IS GONNA HURT," Alonzo said as he got to work splinting Colin's broken finger. Colin sucked in air between his teeth and tried not to flinch.

While Alonzo put away the first aid kit, Colin got a bag of frozen peas out of the freezer. Alonzo accepted it with a nod, holding it against his cheekbone. "Next time you need to take me down, use the heel of your hand so you don't break your fingers. Aim for the nose. Haven't you ever been in a fight before?" He heard the judgmental tone and wanted to take back the question. It was a good thing Colin had never had to fight before—he knew that. It wasn't Colin's fault he'd grown up bi in some nice lefty town in California instead of gay in a red state. Alonzo had always been glad Colin didn't have the bitterness that came with learning to take a beating, but in some little corner of his mind, he also worried about anyone who never learned.

Colin stared at him, eyes wide and devastated. "I'm sorry."

"I'm not mad. I'm serious. If I do anything threatening, don't hesitate. Hit me." He took Colin's good hand in his own. "I'd much rather wake up bleeding than wake up and find out I hurt you."

"I don't think..." Colin paused. "I don't think you were going to hurt me. It. I don't think *it* was going to hurt me. I just freaked out."

"What exactly did it say?"

"It—"

They both jumped as someone hammered at the front door.

"Who is it?" Alonzo shouted.

"Sonia. Open up, now. It's important."

Alonzo went to pull on pants and a shirt while Colin answered the door. He came back to the living room to find Sonia wearing yoga pants and no shoes, hair in a messy topknot.

"I called and texted, but you didn't answer." Her voice shook. She dropped a spiral notebook onto the table. "I woke up, and I'd written this." She blinked, seeming to notice Alonzo's face and Colin's hand for the first time. "What the fuck happened to you two?"

Neither responded. Alonzo skimmed through the gibberish, pulse quickening as he read. "This is just like what you were saying," Colin said, peering over his shoulder. "All the stuff about 'This One' and 'Those of Origin,' you were saying all that."

"He said *that*?" Sonia asked, face pale.

"Close."

Alonzo listened as Colin recounted the things his body had said and done. He met Sonia's gaze and saw an odd shame mirrored back.

"Okay," he said, pushing away the notebook. "Those of Origin. That has to mean parents or grandparents, right?"

Sonia nodded. "Yeah. Dustin was my dad, and Richie was my grandfather, so if 'Those of Origin' are like them, that's the only thing that makes sense."

"Jesus. Are we really talking about this? Like, an intelligent species? Are we really having this conversation?" Alonzo asked.

Colin gulped, his Adam's apple bobbing. "If you'd seen it, Lonzo... That wasn't you. And it wasn't your neurons misfiring. That was something else. A... a personality, an entity, whatever."

"I can't go back to Phoenix," Sonia whispered. "Not if something's taking over. I can't risk being around Dylan like that."

"Okay." Alonzo wiped his face and snatched a piece of paper from the piles scattered around the table. "New thesis. We're being influenced by something intelligent that isn't us. So. Let's move forward with that assumption. What do they want?"

"We've gotten two messages. The same one, pretty much," Sonia said.

"Three. There was the time you both froze. The thing about the cell phone. We just wrote off what you—it—what it was saying, but I always wondered about the actual message." Colin opened his laptop and scrolled through his notes. "You both said, 'I hold my phone. It does not work. I walk and lift it up in the air, and I search for the place where the words that say *No Service* will go away.' Right?"

They both nodded.

"And-and tonight, both of you had a message about... 'the Means to consult with Those of Origin.'"

Sonia frowned. "How are those things connected? I mean, the 'Means to consult' can't be a cell phone, right? Those are everywhere, if that's what they need."

Alonzo shook his head. "But okay, ignore the literal image of the cell phone. If that was an analogy, then the basic meaning there is that it's trying to make contact. It's trying to talk to someone far away, but it can't reach them." He closed his eyes, working through the problem. "So we're hosting these things. They want to get in touch with their—fuck, ancestors or elders or whatever. But they don't have the 'Means'—whatever that is—so they're trying to tell us about it so we can help them? I guess?"

"Then why not just come out and fucking say it? If they speak fucking English and have us replay our memories and shit, why not just spell out what the fuck we're supposed to do?" Sonia demanded, hugging her arms tight around her body.

"It seems like they're struggling." Colin stared into space. "It just... the way it was talking felt like it was trying really hard to translate something and it just wasn't getting across. Like the 'This One' thing. I mean, if they don't even have names, then they've got to be really different from us. Maybe they just can't get the point across in our terms, our language."

"But they're learning. I mean, that's something we knew from the start, right? Each of the Plagues increases in complexity. So the Naming and Dancing and Remembering, that's like... I don't know? A systems check." Alonzo grimaced a bit on the last part.

"And it makes sense with your fMRI. If your brain is accessing visual memories when you Statue, maybe that's like them reviewing footage. Learning whatever they can through your experience."

"And then this fifth stage is... what? Them having a recital?" Sonia asked. "Taking us out for a spin instead of just replaying shit we've already said and done?"

Alonzo nodded. "Basically, yeah. Sounds about right to me."

"But why? What's the point of all this?"

"To teach and to learn. That's what they said," Colin answered. "Maybe that's it. Maybe this is just about making contact for its own sake."

"'The Agreement of the First Meeting.'" Alonzo stared down at the page, turning that phrase over and over in his mind. "Does that mean a first meeting with us? With people? And if they learned to communicate well enough back then to make some kind of agreement, why didn't anyone ever talk about it?"

"Maybe it was something the people making the agreement didn't want anyone to know about. Something shitty." Sonia gnawed on one of her thumbnails, which were already bitten down to the quick.

"What do you think they mean by 'First Meeting'?" Colin asked. "Is that Galina in general or a specific incident?"

"That's not the big question, though," Alonzo said. "The big question is, what was different about how this played out sixty years ago? Why didn't they ever get to this stage, or at least why didn't most of the Galina survivors get to this stage? There was nothing like this in your research."

Colin said nothing. Alonzo turned the question over in his mind, trying to find an answer. Everything was the same. It was even the same season—

He noticed Sonia glancing back and forth between the two of them, eyes wide. "You guys aren't this fucking stupid, right? We know *exactly* what's different this time around." She gestured with both hands. "Dude, the town fucking ripped itself to pieces last time. People died. Would you come out to play, the way things got in Galina?" She let out a dry, humorless little laugh. "They've been *hiding*. They're coming out because it's finally safe."

CHAPTER 28: 1960

Main Street was more crowded than it normally would have been on a Tuesday. Ashen-faced men drifted in and out of the saloon and the cantina. Women congregated in the dress shop and at the front of the market. It wasn't like when just one of the men at the mine got fired, when everyone pretended everything was normal if they encountered one of the men's family members. Nor was it like when someone died or got hurt in a collapse, the hugs and outpourings of grief and free rounds at the saloon. No, it felt like everyone in town was staggering away from a different car accident, all wrapped up in their own private shock. They gathered, but few spoke, and all watched the street wide-eyed, as though waiting for a signal.

Anza found Fernando sitting alone on the sidewalk. "Are you okay?" she asked, taking a seat next to him. She thought about telling him he was right about the blood beetles, but from the expression on his face, she didn't think he would care anymore.

He shrugged. "Yeah. I mean, my folks were already talking about moving. Guess this just means we'll have to do it sooner now. You?"

"I guess. It's funny, I was always so scared of something happening to Dad down in the mine. But now I can't imagine what else he'll do."

Fernando started to put his arm around her shoulder, stopped, and folded his hands in his lap again. "He'll be okay. He's smart, and he's a good worker."

"I know. Still…" She leaned back and rubbed her eyes. "I just hope we figure out the Plagues before I have to leave." She thought again about that beetle collapsing into red dust.

"Maybe the fits will stop once everyone's away from Galina."

Anza saw the hope in his eyes. It stopped her from saying what she was thinking, that he had no reason to believe that, that the fits would most likely just continue wherever they went. Instead, she nodded and smiled, saying nothing at all.

Fernando stared down at his shoes. "I'll miss you, you know. If we move."

"I'll miss you too." And it was true, even if she didn't mean it in the same way he did.

Anza started to say something else, something to make him smile again, but motion caught her eye. Across the street, one of the women in front of the market stopped speaking. Her upper body twisted to the side and forward again, side and forward. At the same time, the muscles on the right side of her face contracted, and her hand fluttered back and forth like a bird. Most of the women in the group just watched. One trotted over to the saloon, although Anza didn't know what a husband or a brother could do about it.

Tim Evers ran out of the saloon and over to the Dancing woman. Anza vaguely remembered the two of them going around town together. They were engaged or maybe just courting.

"You'd think he's never seen a fit before," she muttered.

"It's scary, seeing someone you care about doing that." Fernando shot her a reproachful glance. She remembered the panic in his voice when she'd pretended to Name and wished she hadn't said anything.

A group of men came out of the saloon, trailing after Tim Evers. Richie Rollins led them. Anza's breath caught as she recognized the men following Rollins, ones who had been with him on the Fourth of July or who had scared people since then. They all looked wild-eyed, enraged.

They were too far away for Anza to hear the conversation, but she knew from the way Tim Evers yelled and gestured at his girl-friend that he was demanding something. As she watched, the Mexican women shrank away from the rest of the group, moving farther down the sidewalk. Then Richie stepped past Tim Evers and pushed Mrs. Diaz hard enough for her to lose her balance and tumble to the ground.

"Get out of here!" he shouted loudly enough for Anza to catch the words.

Most of the other Mexican women rushed forward to help Mrs. Diaz. A couple pushed back, yelling at Richie. One or two of the white women joined them, but most stayed behind Richie and his boys.

Dad ran out of the saloon, straight at Richie. He turned right into the punch Dad threw, a mean right hook that sent him sprawling. But then his friends were all over Dad, punching and kicking, and he disappeared beneath them.

Anza grabbed Fernando and hauled him to his feet. "Go to the cantina. Tell the men there what's happening."

He didn't move, just stared at the melee across the street.

"Go, Nando!"

He seemed to wake up, nodding, and dashed to the corner. Anza ran the other way, to Sheriff Brandt's office. His secretary's desk was already abandoned, but there was a light on behind his door.

"Sheriff!" she shouted. "Sheriff, there's trouble!"

He appeared at the door a moment later. "Miss Kearney? What's wrong?"

"Big fight, out in the street. Richie Rollins and his boys. It's bad!"

Anza fought to urge to scream at him to hurry as he fetched his hat and jacket. *Come on, come on! Why are you so* slow? He followed her outside, muttering under his breath as he saw what a mess things had become.

The men from the cantina had arrived. Anza couldn't see clear sides in the fight, just a roiling mass of clumsy punches, a few forms moving weakly on the ground. She gasped as she caught sight of Mr.

Cardenas dragging Dad out of the fight. Blood dripped from his face, and he seemed only half-conscious.

Most of the folks fighting were men, but Tina and Minnie Rodriguez, the sisters who waitressed for their father at the cantina, were right in the middle of the fray. Tina swung the bat their father kept behind the bar while Minnie tried to drag one of Richie's friends out of the group by the back of his shirt.

A gunshot cracked the evening in two. Anza ducked, half-covering her head. A high-pitched whine rang in her ear, and she realized that the shot had come from right beside her. Sheriff Brandt's pistol was pointed at the sky.

The crowd stopped, everyone turning to look at Sheriff Brandt.

"Now listen up, everyone," he barked. "This fight here is over. All of you go home. The next one to throw a punch or argue with me gets to spend a night in the cells. Go on now. Get."

For just a second, Anza thought Richie might argue. But he just spit a mouthful of bloody saliva onto the sidewalk and walked away, shooting Sheriff Brandt one last resentful sneer. Others went off toward the cantina. A few stayed where they were, sitting or struggling to stand up.

"Sheriff," Anza said, "that wasn't a *fight*. That was Richie and his boys attacking people on the street. Just like we warned you he was doing. He just pushed Mrs. Diaz off her feet, for no reason. You gotta lock him up before he really hurts someone."

He gave her a cold, flat stare. "What did I just say about arguing with me?"

"But, Sheriff—"

"You looking to spend a night in jail, Miss Kearney? Because you finish that sentence, that's exactly what's gonna happen."

Mouth dry, she shook her head. She knew she was right and he was wrong, but his tone still made her want to lower her eyes in shame.

She went to where Dad stood slumped against Mr. Cardenas. Fernando hovered a few feet away, pale.

"You okay, Anza?" Dad mumbled, and she almost laughed through the tears at the absurdity of him asking her that question through broken teeth.

"Some of these cuts are pretty bad," Mr. Cardenas said. "They'll need stitches. Want us to help you take him over to Doc Allen?"

"No. Can't afford that anymore." Anza took Mr. Cardenas's place under Dad's arm. "Besides, we got someone better."

"WELL, SEAN, I ALWAYS knew Anza must have gotten her smarts from her mama, but I never thought she got *all* of them from that side." Dove dabbed more antiseptic on Dad's forehead. "Damn stupid thing to do, going up one against six."

Anza watched them, noting Dad's blood on Dove's fingers. She thought about the connections between the three of them. Dad didn't even know—and never would, she'd decided.

"Yeah, well, at least Richie Rollins has one less tooth in his mouth, thanks to me." Dad's voice came out thick and muffled around the ice pack pressed against his jaw.

"Couldn't believe Sheriff Brandt," Anza said for the third or fourth time. She paced, unable to keep still for more than a few seconds at a time.

"I'm surprised he did as much as he did, frankly." Dove threaded the suture needle with thread that had been soaking in a dish of antiseptic. "Man gets the white folks mad, he's out of a job."

"But he acted like it was, you know, a *fight*. With two sides. Like both sides started it."

"Probably a good thing it finally spilled out into the streets," Dove said, ignoring her. "Now people can't pretend they don't have to do something about it. Maybe we can get enough people together to talk to Mayor Fuller, tell him he's got no choice but to step up."

Tires crunched on the gravel of the front yard. Dove was up in an instant, dropping the suture needle and grabbing her gun from the side table. She peered through a crack in the curtains and relaxed. "It's okay. Just Santiago."

He rushed inside without knocking.

"Calm down, Padre. They're fine," Dove said.

"No, no, that's not... I mean, of course, I'm relieved. But, Dove, Anza, there are new symptoms."

The room froze. "What?" Anza asked at last.

Father Santiago pulled his notebook out of his pocket with shaking fingers. "Mrs. Tseda, she isn't a regular member of the congregation, but she brought her son Miguel into the church just after the fight. He's a little older than Anza."

Anza nodded. "I know him." He was a quiet boy, usually spending his time with the five or six other Navajo kids in the school.

"She brought him inside, and at first, I thought he was Naming. You know, eyes blank, speaking, letting himself be led along. But he wasn't just saying words. He was having an entire conversation. Or half of a conversation." He flipped through the notebook pages until he found the right spot. "I didn't get it all, but I wrote down what I could. The part I recorded starts like this: 'I walk to the gate and lift the latch. Yes. I turn right and walk down the road until I reach the sign. Yes. I turn right again. I look down at my shoe. No. It has a hole in the toe. The sun hurts my eyes.'"

"What the hell?" Dad asked, squinting through his swollen eye.

"I know, it just goes on like that. He was just telling the story of walking to school. But there were pauses between every sentence. And saying yes and no—he's responding to someone." He shook his head, eyes wide. "This went on for ten minutes. Mrs. Tseda said it started twenty minutes before they arrived. Miguel had been having the other fits for weeks now, so she knew right away this was something different. She brought him to the church, hoping I could perform some kind of ritual." He bit his lip. "I tried to tell her, if I could do such a thing, I would have cured my entire flock by now. But the poor woman is desperate."

"Has she been having them?" Dove asked.

"No."

"Of course not."

Everyone stopped and stared at Dad. He opened his eyes, apparently sensing that the room had gone silent. "Well, Mrs. Tseda's got to be fifty, if she's a day. You ever seen an older woman having a fit? Because I sure haven't. Haven't you all noticed the little old ladies in town running themselves ragged helping everyone else out when they have a fit?"

Dove's eyes widened, realization passing over her features. "I'm an idiot. Anza, Padre, I need you to go through the notes while I finish stitching up Sean here. Put everybody's age and sex on one list."

Anza scrambled for the notes, but she already knew without going through the entire stack that Dad was right. All of the women they'd interviewed had been under forty-five, but the men had been spread out across all ages. Anza wracked her brain for members of Pastor Benjamin's congregation who wouldn't speak to them, any old woman she'd heard of having a fit or seen having one. But the oldest woman she could think of was Fernando's mother, who was forty-one.

Half an hour later, they had two columns of writing moving down several pages. The letter *M* or *F*, and a number indicating age to the right of that.

Dove taped a bandage over Dad's stitched head wound, set a beer on the table before him, and scanned through the pages. "It holds up," she said. "I didn't see it before because we got so many older men on the list. But not women. Age range is infancy to forty-one for females, infancy to seventy-eight for males."

"Why's this damn thing picking on us?" Dad asked.

Dove nodded as though confirming something to herself. "It's fertility. Or potential fertility, in the case of kids."

Father Santiago covered his mouth. "That's it," he said through his fingers.

"Well, hang on, now," Dad said, sitting up straighter in the chair. "Anza's only sixteen. And she's... well, I don't want to be indelicate, but haven't you had your... you know." He made some helpless gesture.

"Yes, Dad, four years ago." She'd never bothered to tell him when she got her first period. He'd told her a year earlier that he'd spoken to Mrs. Cardenas and she'd said Anza could come to her for questions about "woman things." Anza hadn't been sure at the time what he meant. But sure enough, the day she first bled, Mrs. Cardenas had been prepared with sanitary towels and a catalogue from which she could order the right undergarments.

"Well then, shouldn't..."

Anza swallowed. Whether or not she *should* be fertile didn't matter. She and Dove both knew she was. She met the older woman's eye over the coffee table, silently begging her not to tell him.

Dove cleared her throat. "Sean, not all women are fertile. Even young women. Sometimes we're just born that way, and there's no way to tell until you start trying to make babies."

"Oh. Anza, I'm sorry," Dad said. The anguish in his voice made her heart break.

"Now, none of that, Sean. You're not ready to be a granddaddy, anyway. Besides, doctors can fix all kinds of things these days, if Anza's ever inclined. So don't you worry." Dove said it in that unmistakable way she had, that way that told the room no more would be said on the matter.

Dad brightened a little, but concern still shadowed his battered face, like Anza was sick or something.

"What do we do with this? This new information?" Father Santiago asked.

"Hard to say," Dove replied. "But if we go with the possibility that this stuff, whatever it is, that it has intentions and it isn't just a fungus, it does imply some things about its plans. Long-term plans."

"I'm so *tired* of learning things and none of it being useful," Anza snapped. "That's all we do. We find something new, and we still don't really know anything more than when we started."

Dove smiled thinly, lifting one shoulder in a shrug. "That's how it goes. People study diseases for years and years and don't get anywhere, and then one day, it all falls into place."

"I guess so," Anza said at last. "And we might still find it. We still have to go and try to find this cave the Garces kids fell into." She swallowed. "See if maybe there's a bunch more of those bugs down there."

"I was hoping it wouldn't come to that," Dove said, rubbing her forehead. "But I found someone to help us out."

CHAPTER 29: 2020

"Hey. Heading back to Phoenix?" Cara wandered out from the bedroom, yawning.

"No." Sonia avoided her eye as she stuffed her things back into her bag. "Change in plans. I have to stick around Tucson for a while."

"Oookay," Cara said. "Then why are you packing up all your shit?"

"I'm staying with Colin and Alonzo. I think it's for the best."

"Why? You know you're welcome to stay as long as you want, right?"

Sonia said nothing, focusing on folding her socks.

Cara sat on the couch. "Sonia, are you okay? Did I do something?"

"No. Of course not." *Look her in the eye, coward.* "I'm leaving because we're friends, but if you see the new stuff that's started happening, I don't think we will be anymore."

Anger clouded Cara's features. "Wow. I guess you don't think very highly of me, if you think I'd ditch our friendship because you're sick."

"I'm not sick. That's the problem. This isn't a disease. This is something else living in me, something that isn't human, and I wouldn't blame anyone in this world for running the other way once they got a look at it. But I'd rather not see that happen, so I'm leaving before you meet this thing sharing my skull space." She tapped two fingers against her temple.

Cara's mouth dropped open. "Sonia, sweetie, I'm sorry, but you're sounding crazy right now."

"Exactly. I need to be around people like me. People who understand what's really happening to me." She tried to smile. "It's not your fault you don't get it. You're just lucky." Lifting her bag over her shoulder, she gave Cara an awkward hug and said goodbye. Then she left without looking back.

SONIA AND ALONZO SAT on the back porch, talking quietly and drinking Coronas. Neither had said anything about wanting a private discussion, but Colin was pretty sure that was what it was. He took his laptop to the bedroom and shut the door behind him.

A few minutes later, Tori appeared on his Skype screen. The picture was fuzzy, but he could tell her face was rounder than it had been a few months ago, and she'd stopped straightening her hair. It hung blond and curly down past her shoulders. "Hey there, Col." She grinned.

"Hey. How's the bump?"

"Preparing for liftoff. Due date's in two days."

"Wow. You ready?"

Rajit dipped into the picture, a dishcloth and a plate in his hands. "Fuck no."

Tori shoved him out of the frame. "Fuck yes. This thing needs to get out, stop mooching off my bloodstream already. Look at this." She shifted the screen so her belly loomed like a hill in the foreground.

Colin cleared his throat, already wondering if he was making a mistake. "Listen, as much as I love Rajit—I love you, Rajit," he called.

A faint "Love you, too, other Dr. Ayres" echoed from the background.

"I kinda want a one-on-one, if that's okay."

"Huh. Asking a pregnant lady to move from one room of her house to another. Now you're pushing it." The image bounced and froze as she carried the laptop somewhere. "Okay, Rajit's all jealous and locked out of my office. What's up?"

"Sorry in advance if this freaks you out enough to send you into premature labor, but... I really don't know who else to talk to." He'd hoped he would stay cool as he told her, but his voice was already shaking.

The smile dropped from her face. "Col, what's going on?"

The whole story spilled out, everything from the moment he'd found Alonzo Naming on that first day.

Tori's face paled as he spoke, her eyes growing wide. "Goddamn," she breathed when he finished. "You didn't tell Mom about this, right?"

Colin snorted. "God, no. She'd probably decide Lonzo just needs some time in a sweat lodge or something."

"Okay. Huh. Well, so far, you're doing everything I would do. Research, identifying the stages, all that." She bit her lip. "The problem as I see it is that you want two things. You want Alonzo back the way he was. And you want to understand what these things are. You can't have both."

"Think so?" he asked, even though he already knew the answer.

She nodded. "Yeah. I mean, understanding these things means talking to them as much as you can. That doesn't seem compatible with getting Alonzo to stop channeling or whatever he's doing."

"What would you do?"

Her voice went gentle. "Col, I kinda think the choice has been made for you, hasn't it? I mean, Alonzo and your friend can't seem to stop this even if they try, so..." She shrugged. "It seems like you're wasting time and energy fighting it. I'd say you're better off trying to make meaningful contact."

Colin let out a quavering laugh. "You seem like you actually believe me."

"Course I do."

"Is that because of pregnant-lady brain?"

"Probably." She managed a quick smile that faded almost as soon as it appeared. "I'm sorry this is happening like this, Col. You and Alonzo... It seems like the real deal."

"It is." He stared down at the keyboard. "Everyone before him seems like a practice run now. Bianca, Sara, David, they were great, but this... It's something else, always has been."

"Oh, baby brother," Tori said fondly, her hand tucked under her chin. "You got it bad, don't you?"

"Yep." He sighed. "But that doesn't really have anything to do with this, does it?"

"Sure it does. What's your favorite thing about Lonzo?"

As bad as Colin felt, he couldn't resist the opportunity to make an exaggerated leer and throw out a suggestive "Well, I guess it would have to be his..."

Tori rolled her eyes. "Your favorite *character trait*, deviant, not your favorite throbbing organ. God, walked right into that one, didn't I?"

He smiled and gave the question serious thought. "Um. I guess, he's strong. He's independent—"

"Exactly. That's what you have to remember. This process, what you have to do next, making contact, it's probably going to be hard and scary, and you don't know where things are going to go. But Alonzo's tough. He can handle whatever happens. Remember that."

"You're right. He can handle it. Not sure I can, though."

She glared at him. "*Dude.* Yes, you can. And look, it sucks that this is happening through Alonzo, but stop being so damn mopey. I'd fucking kill to be in your shoes right now."

"I'm telling Rajit you said that."

Her hands flew around her head in a fluttery gesture. "Not *that*, but I mean, you might be making contact with a non-terrestrial intelligence, for Christ's sake. That would be literally the most important discovery of all time. And it's in the hands of a goddamn sociologist."

Colin laughed. "There's that silver lining I was looking for. Sticking it to the hard sciences."

Tori grinned, and Colin took a moment to marvel at the way she could always nudge and bully him out of a slump. "Okay. You're right. I'm going to go see what I can do with these things."

"That's the spirit. Also, if you see any signs of advanced optics, bring one straight to me, okay? That Nobel is fucking mine."

"You got it."

She bit her lip, forced cheer gone again. "But, Col, if..." She took a deep breath. "If this turns out to be something bad, tell me as soon as you know, okay? Because people always want to protect pregnant ladies from bad news, but if I'm about to give birth in the middle of an invasion, I'd rather know."

"Oh god, I didn't even think..." Colin tried to imagine hearing about this the way Tori just had, about to be responsible for a new life.

"Stop. I just said I'd rather know, okay?" She put on a brave face. "Now go find out what we're dealing with."

"IT'S LIKE FINDING OUT you have a parasitic twin," Sonia said, picking at the label on her beer bottle with a thumbnail.

"Kind of. Except we don't know if they can cut these things out." Alonzo swatted at a mosquito. It was too humid to be sitting outside, but Colin was in the house, and he wanted a little time alone with someone who knew exactly what he was going through.

"It's weird, though, because I always did kinda feel like I had a little voice in the back of my head. Just every once in a while." Her eyeliner was smudged with sweat, darkening the circles under her eyes even more. She looked sickly and gaunt in the dim light.

"Yeah?" Alonzo asked.

She shrugged. "Just a couple times. Like, when I found out I was pregnant with Dylan. You know I never thought, especially back then, I never thought I'd go through with it if I got knocked up. But then I found out I was pregnant, and I was thinking about making an appointment at the clinic, and I just..." She bit her lip, hesitating. "I heard, like, a voice, but I don't think it was actually speaking words. It just said, 'It's time.' Or something like that. Like, with that meaning. And I knew it was right. It was time for me to be a mom."

"You ever regret it?" Alonzo asked before he thought better of it.

She took a long time to answer, just silently picking at the Corona label. "Regret's not the right word. I've never wished he wasn't here, you know? But lately... And maybe not just lately, maybe sometimes before all this Galina shit started, sometimes, I wish he'd landed with someone who would do a better job." She held up a hand in a sharp gesture. "*Don't* say something about how you're sure I'm a great mom. I fucking hate that, when people reassure you about something and they don't know anything about it."

"Okay. Noted."

She sighed. "Before this, I usually felt like I was doing okay. But then all this started, and I realized that I *was* doing okay, but only as long as things weren't too complicated. Like, we're both healthy, I have a job, all that. Then I'm okay. But that's the thing—good moms are still good moms when life throws shit at them. And when life threw shit at us, I wasn't ready. I didn't have the... I guess the resources. To deal. So I wish I was the kind of mom who had her shit together enough to handle a disaster without having to run off and leave him with someone else. But regret having him? No. It's been hard, but I never regretted it. Except maybe when I'm bathing suit shopping. Bikinis and C-section scars don't mix." She traced a line along the front of her jeans. "Seriously, here to here."

"Okay, you win the battle-scar fight. I don't have any that big."

"Eh, that one on your eyebrow is no slouch. Or those on your knuckles. Used to have a temper?" she asked.

Alonzo traced his thumb over the familiar white ridges webbing the knuckles on his right hand. "Sort of. Queer kids had to either hide or pick fights if they wanted to get by at my high school. I picked fights."

Sonia sipped her beer. "Out in high school, huh? Ballsy."

He let out a dry laugh. "It wasn't by choice, believe me." Then, at her raised eyebrow, he added, "When I was sixteen, me and another guy were fooling around in a parking lot, and some of the other kids from our school found us. They told everyone, and since my dad taught at the school, it only took a day or two for word to get back to him."

"Awkward."

He still remembered the jeers, the stares, the stifled giggles, and whispers as he walked through the halls the next day, the way his father ignored his presence for the next several weeks. His face burning with humiliation like a fever. "Oh, yeah. Very much so. But I figured I could either deny it and get a girlfriend as fast as possible and hope the rumors died down or embrace it and knock the crap out of the next kid who called me a fag. Went with option two."

"How'd that work out?"

"It was rough for a while," he admitted. "Got suspended for fighting once. But eventually, the other kids figured out it wasn't worth it to bother me."

"Just not before you got your head cracked open," Sonia said, pointing at the scar cutting through his eyebrow.

"Oh, this one wasn't a fight. Not really." Alonzo stopped for a moment, remembering that strange day for the first time in years. He wondered if he'd deliberately segregated that memory, if it conflicted with his experience so much that he'd just filed it away in some dark corner. "I think..." he said slowly, "it was a little like what you were just talking about. I was walking to gym class, and I heard some kids say something, whispering 'faggot' or whatever. It was a group of seniors, big guys, some of them on the football team. Way too many for me to take. But at that point, I just didn't give a shit anymore. So I turned around to start something. And I heard, not really a voice, but just something saying 'Stop!' really loud. It freaked me out so bad, I turned around and smacked right into a pillar."

"Ooh, bet that helped your tough-guy rep," Sonia said. Her smiled faded. "Jesus. How long have we been dealing with this shit? And why didn't we notice?"

He didn't have an answer. They sat in silence for a while longer.

Finally, she stood. "I'm gonna go pick up some dinner. Least I can do if you're letting me camp on your couch."

After she left, Alonzo went to find Colin. He found him sitting on the bed, staring at a blank Skype screen. "You okay?" Alonzo asked.

"I told Tori. She had some thoughts."

Alonzo started to ask about them or something about the plan and his conversation with Sonia. Instead, he pushed the laptop out of the way and nudged Colin over until he had room to curl up against his side. "No more about it today," he said, closing his eyes and holding Colin tightly. "Let's just..."

"Yeah. Just this." And Colin stroked his hair until he drifted off to sleep.

CHAPTER 30: 1960

"This is it." Dove pulled into the driveway of a sprawling, freshly painted ranch house.

Anza blinked and rubbed her eyes. She and Dad hadn't gotten back from Dove's place until two o'clock in the morning, then she'd had to get up at six to meet Dove and drive out to the next town.

"This caving thing must pay pretty good," Anza said, slamming the truck door.

"Oh, it doesn't pay. It's just his hobby," Dove replied.

"People climb around in caves for fun?"

"Swiss folks do, apparently."

The front door opened, and a tall, sunburned man walked out. "Good morning!"

The man had hair so blond, it was almost white. His lobster-red skin made his blue eyes seem even brighter. He would have been a good-looking man, Anza thought, if he stayed out of the sun a little.

"Good morning. Dove McNally. We spoke on the phone."

"Yes, of course. A pleasure to meet you." He had a strange accent Anza had only ever heard when Dad took her to see *Casablanca*. "Hans Fehrmann."

"Anza."

Hans smiled, showing gleaming white teeth. "Well, it is rare for me to meet other caving enthusiasts, except those who travel here for the caves, of course. Just last week, I took a lovely French couple on tour for their honeymoon."

"People come all the way from France to see caves here?" Anza asked.

"Oh yes. We live in caver's paradise, this part of the country. Of course, they also come to see Tombstone and the other Wild West sites. But we will be looking at nothing for tourists today. I understand you think some children may have found their way into a cave system?"

"Yeah." Dove pulled out her map and tapped the red dot marking the fresh cactus patch where they'd found the clothes. "Some cactus popped up almost overnight, so we can't get to the exact spot, but we were hoping you could find a way in there."

"Hm. Yes, there is a cave system somewhat nearby, but I did not think it extended so far into the mesa. Who knows, perhaps we will find something new?" He gestured to his truck. "Please, my equipment is already packed. I can take you."

On the drive over, Hans delivered a dizzying amount of information about caving, cave safety, and emergency procedures. "But I'm sure neither of you will have any trouble remembering that, yes?" he finished, smiling brightly.

Anza shot Dove a look.

"We'll just follow his lead," Dove whispered.

Anza slouched down into her seat, trying not to think of bats, snakes, or anything else that slithered in dark places.

THE CAVE ENTRANCE WAS barely a crack in the rock, something she would have walked right past if it hadn't been pointed out to her. "This is the closest cave system I know of to your spot on the mesa. It is possible there is some branch leading farther. We will look." Hans made sure Anza's helmet fit snugly on her head. "Don't worry. Cave-ins are very rare in natural caves. They have lasted millions of years, and they will last longer yet."

Hans led them through the crack in the hillside. Anza held her breath, her skin crawling with imagined scorpions. The passage was so small, she had to shimmy sideways, rough rock at her back and chest. Just when she decided to call the whole thing off, the crack opened into a small cavern.

"This way." Hans led them down a little passage, where Anza had to crouch to keep from scraping her helmet on the roof. The little light on her belt illuminated the cave only in narrow bands and flashes, leaving the ceiling and upper walls hidden in darkness. Moving in the lightless space felt oddly timeless, like she could go back outside and find that five minutes had passed or that night had fallen while she was away.

Focused on keeping a hand on each side of the passage, Anza didn't notice Dove had stopped until she bumped into her. She stood on tiptoes to see over her shoulder, squinting in the dim glow of the flashlights. The passage opened up into a new cavern. The ceiling and walls expanded out about fifteen feet in each direction, but the entire room ended with a perfectly vertical wall of stone blocking off the far end.

Hans paced back and forth in front of it, running his fingers over the flat rock and muttering, "*Nein. Nein...*"

"Nine what?" Anza asked.

It took him a moment to respond. "No, it is... This is not right. We are perhaps a quarter of a mile from your place on the mesa. The passages I know would end in another hundred yards or so. But not like this." He took her hand and pressed it to the wall. "Feel. The smoothness."

It felt like the blackboard at school, a slightly rough substance made perfectly flat. She moved her palm in a big circle, not finding a single bump or crevice in the entire thing.

"This wasn't in the cave before?" Dove asked.

"This was not part of *any* cave before. This is not natural. Look." He trained the flashlight on one end of the cavern, where the flat wall met the rest of the cave. Anza didn't know anything about stone, but even she could see the clearly visible line demarcating where uneven, porous limestone gave way to the flat reddish surface of the wall.

"Someone has *put* this here," Hans said, outraged.

They spent a fruitless forty-five minutes searching for a way around the wall. Hans took them down other passages, explored a different cavern, and even burrowed into tiny hole barely big enough to let his body pass through. A few minutes later, he came back to where Dove and Anza waited.

"It is there too. At the point where this passage widens, there is the same kind of wall." He wiped his face, smearing more mud and dirt onto himself.

"I don't think it's going to let us through," Dove said at last. "We should go back."

Hans's eyes widened at the "let us," but he said nothing. With a nod, he started back through the darkness.

The sunlight stung Anza's eyes as she stepped back into the day. She turned away from the sun and toward the mesa, shading her eyes and peering in the direction of Galina. She froze. "Dove," she said, voice cracking.

Beyond the mesa, a column of black smoke stained the sky above the town.

THE CHURCH WAS STILL smoldering when Dove's truck screeched to a halt in front of it. A pile of books, furniture, and other odds and ends was in front of the hardware store. About two dozen people, mostly women who spent a lot of time at the church, ferried armloads back and forth between the scorched building and the growing pile. Others carried sandbags and buckets of water through the arched doorway.

"What happened? Where's Father Santiago?" Anza demanded, grabbing the first person she saw.

"He's in the cantina. Hurt but alive. We called Dr. Allen, but he hasn't come yet." The woman bustled off to set down the chair she was carrying.

Anza let out a long, shaky breath as relief flooded through her. She ran for the cantina, Dove close behind her. Inside, low ceiling fans did little to cool the sticky air in the small, dim room. Anza blinked and noticed Tina Rodriguez staring between the wooden slats of one of the shuttered windows next to the wooden bar, a shotgun across her lap. She nodded once to Dove and Anza before resuming her watch.

Father Santiago lay splayed out on one of the cantina's benches. Blood covered his face. One of his eyes bulged, swollen and puffy under the tacky red. Mrs. Cardenas knelt at his side, dabbing at his face with a washcloth.

"Esperanza!" she exclaimed. "You shouldn't be here! We've sent all the children to stay with my husband until we're finished here. No one is to be alone."

Anza ignored her. "What happened?" She couldn't take her eyes off the raw, swollen flesh of Father Santiago's face.

Mrs. Cardenas told the story in long, winding, infuriated sentences, pausing now and then to tend to Santiago's wounds. Mr. Rodriguez interjected from behind the bar now and then. Halfway through, Mrs. Bauer came inside, and the story started over again. Anza almost screamed at all of them then, tempted shrieked at them. *Focus, dammit!*

Still, Anza managed to piece together what had happened. Roughly an hour after Mass had ended, Father Santiago had been inside with those making confession, a few of the lady volunteers, and a handful of other members of the congregation who had lingered after the service for one reason or another. As Father Santiago was speaking to Mrs. Cardenas about next Sunday's sermon, the front doors had burst open. About ten men had marched inside, carrying gasoline cans and clubs. They wore makeshift masks, but Mrs. Cardenas recognized Richie Rollins and several of the others he usually ran with. Father Santiago had walked swiftly down the aisle to ask what they wanted, at which point they'd beaten him and shouted for everyone to get out unless they wanted to burn with their idols. Then they'd poured gasoline on the altar. Someone had managed to fetch help from Millie's and the cantina quickly enough that a group of people swarmed in and pulled Father Santiago out of the huddle of men kicking and spitting on him. The group had fled quickly, seemingly surprised by how fast help arrived.

Mrs. Bauer speculated that they had originally meant to set fires all throughout the church but had only managed the one at the altar before they were scared away. Those who had worked to rescue the religious relics and Father Santiago's possessions from the living quarters said they thought the church would be salvageable, the building largely intact, but the damage to the apse and the transept would need serious repairs.

"He's concussed pretty bad. Pupils are both the same size, and I don't think there's a skull fracture, but we should still get him to a hospital." Dove stood. "What the hell is taking Doc Allen so long?"

"He's gone." Minnie Rodriguez came into the cantina, ashen faced. "He up and left."

"What do you mean?" Anza asked. "He out on a house call or something?"

"No, no, I went to the clinic. There's a sign out front saying it's closed. And then I went by his house, and it's locked up tight. I think he flew the coop."

Anza and Dove exchanged glances. "Well, if this town doesn't have a doctor anymore, we'd best get him to Bisbee. Anyone got a car he can stretch out in?"

"I know someone," Minnie said, running back outside.

"Anza, you go with Mrs. Cardenas."

"Why don't I just take your truck back to your place? I can drop it off and walk home."

Dove whirled around, eyes aflame. "Tell me you aren't that stupid. Tell me you know why you can't be walking out alone now. Ever." Dove pointed at the cantina's mesquite shutters, finger gesturing to the street beyond. "Someone just set a church on fire and beat the priest black and blue. A nice priest everyone likes, for that matter. And who do you not see out there?"

Anza tried not to wilt under that stare. "Sheriff Brandt."

"That's right. Sheriff Brandt or any of his deputies or state police or any other policeman. The law's not here to protect us anymore. And that means no one who doesn't go to church with those bastards can be on their own from now on."

Anza nodded and looked away. Mrs. Cardenas took her by the hand and led her outside, as though she were the one who had survived seeing the church set ablaze. "Don't worry, Esperanza. I'll take you home. Your father will keep you safe."

Something disrupted the tidy line of people carting Father Santiago's goods to and fro. One of the men stood still, lips moving. Another, a few feet away, contorted into a Statue position. No one paid any attention to the Namer or the Statuer. They all just moved around them without a glance, going about their business as though the world weren't ending.

THE CARDENAS HOUSE was already full of kids when Mrs. Cardenas led Anza inside. Mrs. Cardenas was the go-to babysitter for most people, so her house usually contained several kids from around town. It had been that way for as long as Anza could remember. But there had never been so many. They covered all the furniture and sat huddled together on the living room floor. Mr. Cardenas hovered over all of them, looking protective but also absurdly grateful to see his wife. "I got all the kids who were home by themselves. Most of their parents should be by to pick them up pretty quick here." Anza wondered if that was confirmed or if it was just wishful thinking.

Anza caught sight of Fernando awkwardly trying to comfort a wailing toddler, one of the Richardson kids. "I'll help keep an eye on the little ones," she told Mrs. Cardenas, taking the boy from Fernando.

The adults nodded and disappeared into the kitchen. Anza heard snatches of hushed whispers, but the babble of the children drowned out any specific words.

"Hey, Anza," Fernando said, scooting over to make room for her on the living room's threadbare blue couch. "Must have been scary, the stuff going on in town." He sounded a little jealous.

Anza shrugged. "It was mostly over by the time I got there. I think Father Santiago's going to be okay, but he got hit pretty hard." She balanced the Richardson boy on one knee and gestured at the rest. "Really think the kids aren't safe out here?"

"They're probably okay, but..." He glanced over his shoulder. "Have you heard this stuff about Tracey?"

The Richardson boy started getting fussy again, and Anza dandled him on her knee. "Tracey Edmonds? No. What?"

"No one's seen her for almost a week. People in town, they've been saying Pastor Ben came to the house and picked her up in his car and took her somewhere. And she hasn't been back since. I didn't really believe it, but today, we went by to see if Tracey or her sister were by themselves." He hesitated. "Mrs. Edmonds was there. She looked like she'd been crying, and..." He checked again to make sure his parents were still out of earshot. "I think she was *drunk*. And when we asked where Tracey was, she just looked sad and shut the door."

"She didn't say anything else?"

Fernando shook his head. "No. Think something happened to her?"

Panic clawed at Anza's throat. She didn't know exactly what she thought had happened to Tracey, but the idea of being taken away by Pastor Benjamin made her taste bile. "I don't know. Just... be careful, Fernando. Don't get yourself alone with Benjamin or any of his people."

Fernando frowned at her. "It's not me who's making them mad, Anza. Anybody needs to be careful, it's you."

She rolled her eyes and pretended to dismiss the point with a flutter of her hand. Fernando moved on to a new topic. She nodded now and then, but she heard none of it. Anza thought only of Tracey and where Pastor Benjamin might have taken her.

CHAPTER 31: 2020

"Just to be clear, are you suggesting a séance?" Sonia asked.

Colin sighed. "No. It would only be a séance if we were contacting ghosts, which I'm pretty sure isn't what these things are. I'm just suggesting we... you know, invite them to have a chat. See if they can elaborate on what they want us to do."

"I don't like it," she said.

"Me neither, but I think he's right," Alonzo replied. "Ignoring it doesn't help, so maybe confronting it will. But..." He turned to Colin. "I think we should be restrained first."

"Kinky," Sonia muttered.

Alonzo shot her a look. "I'm serious. Look, they might not seem violent, but what if that changes? I'm stronger than you, Col. What if they decide to use that? Or what if Sonia and I gang up on you?"

"You would never hurt me," Colin almost said but stopped himself. It was true—Alonzo would never hurt him. But he wasn't going to be dealing with Alonzo.

He hesitated but finally nodded. "Okay. We'll go with restraints. Let's get started."

Ten minutes later, Alonzo and Sonia sat on opposite sides of the kitchen table, their wrists tied to their chairs with belts and an electrical cord.

"Come on, man," Sonia had said when Colin tied her first arm. "I'll wriggle out of this in five seconds flat. Tie me up like you mean it."

"That sounded filthy. You hitting on my man?" Alonzo asked with a sly grin.

"This isn't funny," Colin said.

Sonia and Alonzo burst into giggles.

He waited for it to pass, trying not to let his irritation show. "Ready?"

"Yeah. Sorry." Sonia let out one last snort. "I'm done."

"Go ahead."

Colin turned on the blocky yellow EMF detector he'd bought after his first conversation with Tori. He hadn't found anything unusual in the detector's range when he'd tried it before. A few times, the numbers had climbed, but each time, he'd found an appliance or electrical wiring causing the disturbance. It had reacted to Alonzo and Sonia the same way it reacted to his own body—nothing more than the blips of the human body and its mysterious electricity.

"Okay," Colin said, sitting at the head of the table.

Alonzo and Sonia stared at each other, Colin watching them in profile.

"I want to talk to the things living in Alonzo and Sonia. Will you come out and talk to me?"

Nothing dramatic happened. There was no obvious moment of transition, no Statuing or exaggerated movements. Still, Colin felt it like the change in pressure before rain begins to fall.

They turned at the same moment, both smiling. "These Ones are happy to speak with Colin." Their voices overlapped, speaking in perfect unison.

His tongue went dry in his mouth. "I... I'm happy to speak with you, as well."

"These Ones need the Means to consult with Those of Origin. Will Colin help?"

"I would like to help. But I don't know what 'the Means' are. Can you please tell me what that is? Can you describe it to me?"

Alonzo and Sonia went back to watching each other. She nodded. He cocked his head. Neither spoke, but Colin felt the conversation passing between them. He held up the EMF reader. He didn't understand the numbers and couldn't remember the ranges that meant radio waves, microwaves, and whatever else, but the digits were climbing up to a range they hadn't approached in this room before.

"These Ones apologize," they answered at last. "These Ones are limited. Explanations are difficult without Those of Origin and the Other Ones."

"What Other Ones?"

"All Other Ones. These Ones and the Other Ones are far apart. These Ones can't reach them."

"What can I do to help?" Colin asked.

Alonzo's hands flexed against the bindings. "If These Ones could move, they could meet with Other Ones outside."

Colin bit his lip. "Outside? Like the yard? That's all?"

"Yes," they said together.

"Okay." Colin unwound the belt from Alonzo's familiar wrist, focusing on his sandy-brown skin and big square hands. He swallowed, sneaking a glance at that empty alien face.

Alonzo blinked at Colin as the belts and cords fell to the ground. He made no move to rise until Colin had untied Sonia as well. Both stood and went to the sliding glass door, moving with exaggerated care. Colin trailed behind them, already wondering if they had made a big mistake. He remembered to grab the EMF reader and his phone, still recording everything.

Sonia seemed to have trouble with the door, awkwardly lifting the latch between forefinger and thumb. She finally got it open, and both walked out into the yard.

The sky was overcast, monsoon clouds gathering. One or two fat drops had already fallen to the pavement of the walkway. A faint buzzing caught Colin's attention, growing louder as he listened. Something zipped through the air, hidden by the motion of the desert willow at the edge of the yard. Thin branches swayed in the wind. Other things moved through the plants, across the gravel, and past leaves, too fast for him to see more than a flash of glinting red.

Then a coyote leapt over the fence in a smooth, quick motion. Colin shied away from it, cursing under his breath. He realized now that he hadn't quite believed Sonia's story about the coyote on the street. It lay down on the ground near where the others stood motionless.

Another leapt the fence, joining the first. It had a slightly different coat, red-brown rather than silvery gray. But it was unmistakably a coyote, not a dog. For all its proximity to two human forms, there was nothing tame about it.

The insects all came out of hiding at once. Shining metallic beetles the size of golf balls, with shells like garnet glass, swarmed out of the trees and the bushes and down from the roof, landing on Sonia's and Alonzo's exposed skin. They went completely still as they landed, legs latching onto the flesh.

There were birds too. Colin hadn't noticed them at first, but now they flew down and landed on the coyotes and on Sonia's shoulders. One landed on Alonzo's feet. Shaking, Colin held up the EMF reader. Twenty-eight MHz and climbing, and even from what little he'd read about electromagnetic fields, he knew that was well out of range of what human or animal bodies produced in nature.

The beetles looked like red armor coating Sonia and Alonzo. More raindrops fell, one sliding like a glass bead through Sonia's hair. Colin didn't want to leave the porch, but he forced himself to step down into the yard, circling far around Alonzo and Sonia and the things draped over them. He stopped when he saw their faces.

Red beetles dotted their cheeks and foreheads, leaving only their eyes and mouths clear. They still weren't themselves. Both stood with their heads tilted slightly back, eyes rolled up into their sockets. Then, as if in response to some signal, both blinked and focused on him. "The Means to contact Those of Origin has been moved from its original location. But it hasn't moved far. One of the Other Ones witnessed the Means in the possession of one of the First Speakers, several years ago. These Ones and many of the Other Ones will need to travel to the Place of Landing in order to find the Means." They paused. "Will Colin help us?"

"Yes," he whispered.

The sky opened, and rain hammered down into the yard. The coyotes slipped over the wall and out of sight. The beetles launched into the sky like fireworks, disappearing into the trees and plants and through the rain. The number on the meter dropped back down into the same range it had been in most of the house and the garden.

Colin looked from the meter to Alonzo's face, searching for hints of him behind the mask. *Please,* he thought, *please let him come back.*

Alonzo shook his head just as Sonia let out a little yelp. "What... Why the fuck did you untie us?" He wiped rain from his face.

"It... Get inside," Colin said, pushing them toward the porch.

"What happened? What's out there?"

Colin slammed the sliding glass door shut, locking it with trembling fingers. He stood there for a moment, watching the rain and searching for the things hiding in it.

Alonzo's hand closed around his shoulder. "Col? What happened?"

Colin turned away from the window. Sonia and Alonzo stood watching him. Water dripped down their faces.

"I have something you need to see," he said, his voice trembling.

"WHAT THE FUCK WERE those things? I've never seen those before," Sonia said, eyes locked on the screen.

"They aren't real insects. I don't think," Alonzo replied. "But I've seen them before. I think they've been hanging around in the yard." He watched the beetles crawl over his own body, a body moving and speaking in a way he didn't recognize.

"I think... It didn't seem like they had that information before. About the Means. It wasn't until they went outside and they were in contact with these things that they knew."

"And that's when the EMF reading went up?" Alonzo asked.

Colin nodded.

"The coyotes in Galina got infected, too, right? And the birds?" Sonia asked. "And some people saw those bugs. So when there's a lot of these infected together—"

"The signal gets stronger," Alonzo said, nodding. "Like adding to an antenna."

"Well, whatever it did, it gave them enough information to tell us to go back to the Place of Landing." Colin watched Alonzo, expression dazed and vacant.

"Galina," Sonia muttered. "Fuck."

"HI, COLIN? THIS IS Jason Nguyen."

Colin blinked, thrown off by the unexpected voice. "Oh, hi, Jason. How are you?"

"I'm good. Listen, I'm calling because I heard back from some researchers I contacted about the Galina mesa. Two of them didn't really have anything interesting to say, but one did."

Colin scrambled for a blank sheet of paper and his pen. "Yeah? Okay, what was it?"

"Well, this is from Zuzanna Gzowski. I mentioned her before. Her research is mainly on cactus wrens. Well, way back in the day, she saw similar stuff as my coyotes. You know, really major migration, way greater distances than we'd normally expect. Except her project kept going, and she's still got data from tracking devices coming in. And apparently I called at just the right time, because everyone in her lab is going apeshit right now."

"About what?"

"It's crazy, but all those wrens that migrated out to Mexico and Texas and way up into Utah? They're all coming back. It's not the right season for them to be migrating anywhere, but apparently, all their specimens just up and started flying long distance two weeks ago. And they've got them coming from enough directions, they got a pretty clear idea where they're all headed."

"Galina?"

"Bingo. No one knows why, but they're all going home."

After Colin hung up, he went back to where Alonzo and Sonia sat in the living room, not speaking. Books and laptops and papers lay scattered around. Colin realized as he saw the mess that none of it was going to help. He sat on the couch between them. "I think maybe it's time we head to Galina. We talked to them. We took the leap of faith, so maybe the best thing is to do what they ask."

"I was thinking the same thing," Alonzo said.

Sonia nodded. "Me too. But at the same time... I don't know. The idea scares me."

Alonzo sighed. "I know what you mean. But nothing scares me more than just going on like this."

"Okay," Colin said, taking a deep breath. "We leave tomorrow."

CHAPTER 32: 2020

E*xcerpt from interview with Caleb Peterson, age seventy-two, by Colin Ayres, University of Arizona Department of Sociology.*

Q: I'd like to hear about Benjamin Reeves.

A: Pastor Benjamin. We all called him Pastor Benjamin or Pastor Ben.

Q: Right. You were part of his congregation. Is that correct?

A: I suppose... I was only twelve when the Plagues started, see? So it was more that my parents were members of his congregation, so I had to go. But I guess I believed, too, at least until that summer.

Q: Can you say a little more about that?

A: I don't... Listen, I've never talked to anyone about what happened that summer, except my wife. And even she hasn't heard everything. I guess I'm too old for anyone to bother getting me in trouble with the law, but—

Q: I'll remove all identifying information from your statement, Mr. Peterson. Remember we talked about that when you signed your release?

A: I know. I'm not really worried about the law. I'm just... [begins crying].

Q: It's okay. Take your time.

A: Oh god. We were all so terrified. We thought it was the wrath of God or the influence of the devil or something. We thought so many different things. It was just such a confusing time. Looking back, I think we all went a little crazy that summer. But... for most of the summer, it was just talk. Talk and prayer and meetings, and a little fight here and there. But then something changed with Pastor Benjamin. He got... I don't know... mean, bad-tempered. He'd lash out. At the time, we all talked like it was just righteousness, him getting caught up in the heat of the moment, but I think now he was scared for himself. His fits were just as bad as anybody's, but people were looking to him as an example. It must have been a lot of pressure. That doesn't excuse anything he did, but it's the only way I can make sense of it.

Q: Make sense of what?

A: Tracey Edmonds. I... My parents hosted a meeting. Not a regular church meeting open to the public, but a smaller one. Just them and Pastor Ben and his wife, and a few more of the really respected people in the church. They held a meeting, and Pastor Benjamin announced that he needed to take the fight to the devil. That the prayers and the things they were doing in meetings weren't working, and they needed to try something else. He said Tracey Edmonds's mother had come to him, begging him to do something to help Tracey's fits stop. Pastor Benjamin said he had a plan to help her, but it needed to be secret. The law wouldn't understand, and neither would the folks in town. So my parents said they could use our house.

Q: For what?

A: They just called it "the confrontation." Later, I learned it was what most people would call an exorcism.

Q: They performed an exorcism?

A: They tried. It didn't work, of course.

Q: Can you walk me through what happened?

A: Tracey arrived at our house the day after the meeting. We weren't really friends, but I knew her from school, and I think she was relieved to see someone around her age there. She said she wanted to come, that she agreed to do whatever it took to get rid of her fits, but looking back, I don't know what other choice she had. She stayed in our spare room. It had been my brother's room before he went off to join the army.

Q: What happened next?

A: The first two days were fasting and prayer. Pastor Ben came over and prayed for hours and hours. Then his wife would take a turn praying with Tracey, and then someone else from the congregation. She didn't eat that whole time, and she only drank one cup of water a day. This is during the summer, you understand, so you can imagine how dangerous that was.

Q: What came after the fasting and prayer?

A: Well, then came the ritual. It involved holy water and crosses pressed against her skin, and screaming at the demon inside her to leave. Of course, Tracey's nerves were completely frayed by that point. She started crying almost as soon as Pastor Benjamin started yelling at her.

Q: And you saw this ritual being performed?

A: Parts of it. It went on all day. My parents wanted me to watch. God knows why. Something about learning a lesson about the wages of sin. At one point, she Statued, and they tied her to the bed. Said it was the devil fighting back. At the end of the third day, after all that ritual, she had another fit, so they knew it hadn't worked.

Q: So what did they do?

A: Benjamin did the only thing he could do. He kept going. He said we were locked in a battle of wills with the demon, and only by staying strong would we win. So they kept up that ritual for three more days. Three more days of no food, almost no water, being tied up and screamed at by Benjamin and his followers. I can't imagine what it was like for her.

Q: Did anyone voice doubts about what Benjamin was doing?

A: No. Tracey's mother had been sent away early on. Benjamin said the devil would try to exploit her weakness as a mother. And the rest of us... I could tell my mother realized it was a mistake early on. Before the third day. And I think my father had doubts too. But by then, it felt like it was too late. People had been forced to leave the congregation for argu-

ing with Benjamin before, and nobody wanted that to happen to them. So I think everyone just hoped he would get tired or give up.

Q: Did he?

A: No.

Q: Then what happened?

A: I guess it's fair for you to make me say it, considering I'm partly responsible. I was there, and I didn't do anything, so... Tracey died on the seventh day. I don't know what from. Dehydration, starvation, her heart just giving out. But whatever killed her, Benjamin came out of the room and told us he'd been right on the brink of victory when the devil decided he'd rather take Tracey's life than let the Lord win.

Q: I... She died?

A: That's right. I saw her, right after. She looked so small and thin and... [interviewee cried for several minutes at this point]. I never set foot in a church again after that day, and I never will.

Q: Was anyone ever arrested or charged with a crime?

A: No. The town doctor had given up and left by then, and Pastor Benjamin had Sheriff Brandt wrapped around his little finger. I don't know what story they told Tracey's mother, but it must have been convincing enough for her to not to push it farther than that.

Q: What happened after that? Within the congregation?

A: Oh, Pastor Ben had that all worked out. He said we couldn't defeat the demons one by one. He said we had to destroy the source of the corruption, and once that happened, everyone else would be cured.

Q: And what was the source?

A: The first cases, of course. The Garces children.

CHAPTER 33: 1960

The doorbell rang as Anza was cooking supper. She took one step toward the hallway before Dad barked, "Stay there!"

He peered through the front window, relaxing at whatever he saw. "It's just Paula."

"Paula?" She frowned as she went to the door. She'd resigned herself to Paula's slow withdrawal, assuming Pastor Benjamin had infected her with his madness.

But the Paula who stood on the front porch, shifting from one foot to the other, looked just like the one Anza had always known. "Can we talk?" she asked.

"Okay. I need to finish making supper, though," Anza replied, trying to sound neutral. She went back to the kitchen without checking to see if Paula followed her or not. She sliced her vegetables and waited for Paula to work up the nerve to speak.

"Anza... I'm sorry. My mama and daddy told me not to spend time with you or Fernando or any of the other... you know. But still, I could have snuck away. I could have called."

Anza raised an eyebrow. "You feel bad for turning your back on the Mexican kids, so you decided to say sorry to the one who's half-white?"

Paula cringed. Her long, slender fingers picked at her blue skirt. When she was relaxed, Paula's angular build and short blond hair made her seem glamorous. Slumped against the kitchen counter, though, she seemed more like an awkward twelve-year-old boy in a dress. "I'm sorry. No. I came to you because..." She took a deep breath. "I know you've been working with Father Santiago and Dove

McNally. I know you're trying to stop this... this thing. And I heard some things I think you should know." Her brown eyes filled with tears. "I used to really believe in Pastor Benjamin, you know? He used to make so much sense. But now I'm just scared.

"Right before Richie and them set the church on fire, we were at church. You know, our church. And Pastor Benjamin gave this sermon about Jesus bringing a sword instead of peace and Elijah setting bears on the kids who mocked him and how we have to pull weeds up by the roots before they take over the garden. And I just got so scared, because I knew what he meant. He never said it direct. Not like 'Go hurt Father Santiago' or 'Go burn down the Mexican folks' church,' but we could all understand what he meant, you know? And then Richie and his boys went and did it."

Anza stirred the stew and added salt. "That's not news, Paula. Everyone in town knows who did it. Even with those stupid masks."

"I know, but... I heard something else." She drew closer. "And, Anza, you can't tell anyone I was the one who told you. They'd kill me."

"What is it?"

"Well, after the sermon ended, my dad and some others were talking to Pastor Benjamin. And they were asking about seeds and roots and nipping something in the bud, and I think I know who they want to go after next."

"Who?"

Paula's eyes shone with fear and shame. "The Garces kids."

"WE WERE STUPID NOT to worry about it sooner," Dove said, pacing. "It's obvious."

"Nothing obvious about a preacher going after little kids," Dad growled.

Mrs. Garces pulled Luz closer to her. She sat in the middle of Dove's couch, the kids huddled around her. "Why would Roberto stay?" Mrs. Garces asked again. "Even with a gun, he can't protect our house forever."

"Bert's tough. They won't want to mess with him." Dad put a hand on hers, his awkward rough fingers dwarfing her small, soft ones. "He just wanted you out of the house to be on the safe side. I'd do the same. We'll just sit tight here and wait it out."

A shadow fell across the doorway. Anza looked up to see George Esquivel standing there, his rifle under his arm.

George smiled at Anza before looking at Dad and Dove. "No. No, I got a better idea."

ANZA WOKE TO ORANGE light flickering through the curtains. It danced along the wall above the couch. She sat up. "Dove!" she hissed. "Dad!"

Dad sat up straight in the armchair, blinking and rubbing his eyes, just as Dove ran into the room with her pistol.

"Knew it," she said, peering through the window. "Sean, be ready with that shotgun. Anza, go wake Mrs. Garces and watch the back door."

Voices echoed outside. Someone knocked on the front door as Anza ran to the guest room to wake Mrs. Garces. "Mrs. Garces! Get up, quick!"

The woman sat up, wide awake, and followed Anza without a word.

"I got a .45 aimed right at your head through this door," Dove yelled as they reached the kitchen. Mrs. Garces lifted the other shotgun, pointing it steadily at the kitchen window.

Anza crept back into the living room, even though she knew Dad and Dove would want her to stay hidden.

"We just want to talk, Mrs. McNally!" someone called.

"All right then. Get down off the porch. Back right up. That's right." Dove turned to Dad and dropped her voice. "Sean, you come out behind me and keep that shotgun aimed right at them. They so much as reach for a piece, you open fire."

"Why the hell are you going out there?" Anza hissed.

"Get back in the kitchen!" Dad gestured with his chin. She ignored him.

"Just trust me," Dove said, opening the door.

Pastor Benjamin stood at the front of the crowd. They carried flashlights, lanterns, and even a couple of torches and candles. Anza assumed those were just for effect. Then she thought about why else they might have fire and imagined being in the kitchen with flames licking the walls, and she had to press her hands to her mouth to stifle a shuddering gasp. She told herself to be like Dove, standing tall and still, but she knew if she tried to stand out there, her knees would shake.

Benjamin smiled and spread his empty hands wide. "Mrs. Mc-Nally, there's no need for all this. We aren't here to hurt anyone."

"Oh, no?" The revolver in Dove's hand didn't waver. "Why all the firepower, then?" She jerked her head at one of the men to Benjamin's right, someone with a pistol in one hand and a rifle slung over his shoulder.

Anza slipped closer and peeked out at the crowd. Her tongue felt as dry as sandpaper, sticking to the roof of her mouth. She nearly vomited at the sight of Sheriff Brandt wearing his civilian clothes, hovering near the back. *There's too many, too many. They're going to get in—*

"We're only trying to bring the light of Christ to those afflicted by the devil's wickedness. Those who are also, sadly, afflicting others." Pastor Benjamin spoke in a low, reasonable voice. "You must know that this can't end until we destroy the root of this evil."

"So you're gonna kill three little kids to make your own fits go away." Dove's voice dripped with contempt. "You even know how diseases work, you dumb son of a bitch?"

Familiar coldness passed through Benjamin's eyes and was gone. "We're not going to kill them, Mrs. McNally. We're here to cure them. How could you even think such a thing?"

"Cure them how?"

He tried to take a step forward. Dove cocked her Colt without a word. He stepped back. "I've proven my ability to fight these demons. I want to perform a ceremony to cleanse the Garces children of their affliction. Once they're cured, the rest of us will be too. Don't you want that for them? For all of us?"

"And then what happens, when your little ceremony doesn't work? They wind up in a ditch with a bullet in their heads?"

"Mrs. McNally, your lack of faith fills you with such sadness. Such cynicism." His tone went molasses sweet with pity. "Now, it's my duty as the spiritual leader of this community to take over the task you've so clearly failed to accomplish. It's a man's task to fight the devil, not a woman's."

Dove laughed. It started as a snort but grew into a full-throated cackle. "Oh, Benjamin. You tiny, insignificant man." His face darkened. Dove took a slow, relaxed step forward. "I knew a man like you once. You see, Ben, I grew up in a whorehouse up near Superior. It's where my mama worked. And there was a preacher man who used to buy her time every Saturday night. Sometimes, he'd rough her up while he was at it." She said it matter-of-factly, like she was talking about a trip to the market. The crowd gasped and murmured.

She continued. "So every Saturday, he'd hurt my mama for fun. Then, every Sunday morning, he'd preach in his church. I went there a few times, because I was curious about what a man like that would preach about. And then, one morning, his sermon was about whores and fornication and how those who chose the 'path of idleness and pleasure,' as he called it, were ruining the world and tempting men away from their wives and the like. Idleness and pleasure. That's what he called the work my mama did every day, just to put food on the table. And then, when some member of his church brought the clap home to his wife, who do you think was at the front of the crowd who came to that whorehouse to drag the women out and shame them in the street? That's right. Good old Preacher Simmons."

Smugness crept into Pastor Benjamin's features. "You expect us to be shocked that Dove McNally is a whore's daughter? Is that why you're telling us this? I think you'll find very few people surprised about that." The crowd murmured. A few of the men nudged each other and leered, saying things Anza couldn't hear.

Dove laughed again. "No, I'm telling you this so you know what happened to him. You see, what Preacher Simmons didn't know was that my mama and the other girls in the whorehouse set up these clever cameras in some of the rooms. Mainly because those pictures would fetch a pretty penny in a certain kind of magazine shop. But for another reason too. For the clients who treated them wrong or who had a lot to lose. And men like Preacher Simmons, the ones who got liquored up and passed out half the time? It was just too easy to get good pictures of those ones, even with cameras being as big and bulky as they were back then." She took another step down the porch as the smirk crumbled off Benjamin's face. "And well, once everyone in town, including the preacher's wife, got to see those pictures, he was finished. Ended up drinking himself to death. Now the lesson, here, Benjamin, since I know you're much too thick to deduce it on your own, is that pride goeth before a fall. As in, a man too stupid to realize the women in a whorehouse could be clever ended up dead because of it. Kind of like how you assumed the folks in this town who don't go to your church would be too meek to protect their own."

Pastor Benjamin's smile twitched. "One shotgun and one pistol against an entire congregation protected by God's righteousness? Now, now, Mrs. McNally, who's being prideful here?"

"Oh, I'm not talking about me and Sean. I'm talking about the dozen veterans who've been looking at you through their sights ever since you and your little mob walked into my yard. Did you know George Esquivel was a sniper over in France?" She clicked her tongue. "Unfortunately for you, since he's also godfather to Pablo Garces."

Benjamin glanced out into the darkness of Dove's property, the shadowed area near the barn, and the shallow irrigation ditch across the road. "I think you're lying."

"George," Dove called out without turning her head. "Give Ben here a little demonstration."

A shot cracked out through the darkness. Anza jumped as the bullet tore through the top of one of the torches, tossing sparks over the mob. Someone shrieked as the crowd shied away from the flaming stick its holder had dropped to the ground.

"Now, before anyone does something stupid..." Dove pointed at a man about to raise his rifle. "We want nothing from you. Just walk away. Keep to your church, your part of town, and we'll keep to ours. That's all."

For a moment, Pastor Benjamin seemed almost animal in his fury. Then he rearranged his features and faced his congregation. "Brothers and sisters! It pains me to say this, but we can't save sinners who don't want to save themselves. We should go now and pray that these people come around to the light of the Lord."

Some in the crowd grumbled, but more peered anxiously out into the darkness. They shuffled back down the driveway and out of Dove's yard, taking the main road back to where they must have left their cars and trucks before coming. Anza got up from where she'd watched by the kitchen doorway and joined the others on the porch. Dove waited until Pastor Ben and his crew rounded the bend and disappeared from view before she raised an arm. "Everyone okay out there?"

George Esquivel and Leroy Briggs stood and approached from the east side of the property. Anza remembered Leroy from school, two years ahead of her. He'd seemed like a small, quiet boy, but he was known throughout the county as a prodigy with a rifle.

George moved with a stony look on his face until he saw Anza. Then he smiled and tipped his hat, same as always. "Miss Kearney," he rumbled, "how are you this fine evening?"

She let out a rough, shaky laugh. "I'm fine. Are you okay, Mr. Esquivel?"

"Just like old times."

Roberto Garces and Bob Tseda came in from the other side of the yard. Rumor around town was that Bob had been a code talker during the war, although when asked, he always said it was illegal for him to say anything about it.

"A dozen men, eh, Dove?" Bob asked, white teeth gleaming in the dark.

"Good as." She gestured for them to come inside. "You boys come get some rest. Someone else can take the next watch. Though I don't think they're coming back."

Mrs. Garces ran down the steps and into Mr. Garces's arms.

"*Esta bien*," he murmured, even though he still had a haunted look in his eye.

George sat on the front step, his rifle across his lap. "Don't think I'll be getting any sleep tonight, Mrs. McNally. Never could, just after a battle." His white teeth flashed in the dark. "Wouldn't object to a cup of coffee, though."

"Coming right up." Dove and the others trooped inside, leaving Anza and George alone on the porch.

"No need to worry, Miss Kearney. They won't be back tonight."

Anza realized she was staring into the darkness where the road curved out of sight. She tried to smile. "Sorry. You're right. Just keep thinking… Thanks for being here, George. Don't know what would have happened if you hadn't been here." Her voice came out shaky, almost tearful, and she quickly cleared her throat and pretended to be okay.

George chuckled and leaned back against one of the mesquite posts holding up the porch roof. "Oh, I don't think y'all needed me at all. Dove would have kept everyone safe."

"You think?"

"I know. Only a fool would underestimate a woman protecting her home." He must have noticed Anza's quizzical glance. His gaze went distant. "I met this woman in France, back in '44, just after we landed at Normandy. She headed up a French Resistance cell that helped us make our way inland. When my unit met up with them, there were guys who couldn't believe anyone would take orders from a woman. But the men she was in charge of? They'd have followed her straight into hell. They knew what she was made of. She was small as anything, ninety pounds soaking wet, but she'd been fighting the Nazis for three years before we even showed up. She was small, but she was smarter, braver, and more willing to lay down her life than any of those Gestapo bastards—pardon the language—because it was her home. She wasn't the only one, neither. There were women in that war who did things… Well, push comes to shove, women do what needs doing to protect their own."

Anza shook her head. "I can't imagine doing anything like that. Dove, maybe, but..."

George said nothing for a moment. "I think you underestimate yourself, Miss Kearney. You got steel. Anyone can see that." He paused. "That's why you gotta watch out for that Richie Rollins. Women like you make men like him feel small. And men get dangerous when they feel small."

Anza's face flushed, and she was glad for the dark. Dove slipped out the front door and handed George a cup of coffee. "Here you go, George. Feel free to take the couch if you change your mind about sleep." She turned to Anza. "Your daddy and I are keeping watch out back if you want to join us."

Part of Anza wanted to stay out front with George, but another part of her was glad for the escape. "Okay. Night, George."

He lifted one hand. "Good night to you, Miss Kearney."

"You want some coffee?" Dove asked as they went back into the house.

Anza nodded. "Yeah." She bit her lip, wondering if she was about to cross some sort of line. "Was all that true, all that stuff you said about your mama?"

"Every word."

"Why'd you tell them that?"

Dove went to the sink and rinsed out a coffee mug as she spoke. "Men like that only have two weapons that matter. Fear and shame. Could have waved my gun in his face all night, but the most important thing was to show him I wasn't scared and I'm not ashamed of anything."

Anza took the coffee and let the cup warm her hands, saying nothing.

Dad joined them. "Boys are settled down."

"You should sleep, too, Sean. You were already up."

"Nah, can't sleep. Could use some coffee, though."

Dove nodded and poured him a cup. "Figure we should go out on the back porch. They won't try coming to the front door again."

The three of them sat in the darkness of Dove's screened-in back porch, listening to the cicadas and watching the night.

"I'm a wee bit concerned we may have just started a war," Dad said at last.

"The war already started, whether we wanted it to or not. They set fire to a church, Sean. If that ain't an opening shot, I don't know what is." Dove sipped her coffee. "Peace ain't on the table, so best we can hope for is to show them that folks will fight back. Make it more trouble than it's worth."

Anza folded her arms against the nighttime chill. "Does it even matter at this point? If we figure out the Plagues?"

"For Galina? I don't know. Probably not." Dove sighed. "But for me... Yeah. It matters."

They said nothing more, watching until the dark sky burned pink and gold along the edges.

CHAPTER 34: 1960

"I called the bishop and told him what happened. He's a powerful man with contacts in the state government, so perhaps there'll finally be an investigation." Father Santiago tried to smile, but he seemed hollow and shaky, face bruised and head swathed in bandages.

"Yeah, maybe." Dove cleared her throat. "Listen, Padre, you got a lot to deal with after what happened. Anza and I can take it from here if you don't feel up to—"

"I'm fine." He cut her off with a gesture. "There's no point in rebuilding my church if we don't solve this."

Dove nodded. Anza passed him the makeshift map she'd drawn of the mesa and the caves snaking underneath it.

"We didn't get a chance to tell you about the caves, but we found something down there." Dove told him about the red wall, that barrier Hans had insisted belonged in no natural cave system.

He stared down at the map, shaking his head. "What could be under there?"

Dove said nothing for a long moment, staring out the window. "I think it's time to accept that this isn't just some spore or fungus or bacteria. I mean, it might be those things, but it's not *just* one of those. This thing, whatever it is, has a will. It has purpose. Diseases don't build walls to protect themselves. So, it seems to me, we need to start thinking less about what it does and how it spreads and more about what it wants."

"If it only infects fertile people, that does seem to imply that its plans are long-term. At least a decade from now, if it's willing to infect children who won't be fertile for a dozen years or more." He grimaced. "But that still doesn't tell us what it would want with future generations."

Anza bit her lip, half-raising her hand like she was in school. "Well, we could ask it."

"Yeah, but first we'd have to figure out how to get through that wall. Or down through the cactus patch," Dove replied.

"I don't think so. Remember when Faye talked to Pablo, and the girls were saying the same stuff he was?"

They nodded.

The idea crystallized in Anza's mind. "So, the stuff is all connected. Like the plants I read about, how they can talk without making any noise, over long distances? And if that's true, we don't have to go to where the dust first came from. We got some of it sitting right here."

Dove's eyes widened. She turned and studied Father Santiago. "Interesting."

He shook his head. "I've considered this. I've tried... speaking with it." He smiled without humor. "Almost like prayer. But I've heard nothing."

"Almost like prayer," Dove muttered.

He shot her a dark look.

"Right, but folks never remember when they've had a fit. So maybe it did talk back and you didn't know," Anza said.

He didn't seem convinced.

"I think it's worth a try."

"Sure don't have any other good ideas." Dove sighed. "What do you say, Padre?"

"Okay." He didn't bother trying to hide the fatigue in his voice. "Let's try."

"THIS FEELS LIKE A SÉANCE," Anza whispered, remembering an old movie she'd seen with Dad. There'd been a dark room, candles, and some spectral presence shaking the table.

"Hope not," Dove whispered back.

The curtains were drawn, the living room lit only by a few kerosene lanterns. Anza fanned her face with a notepad. The swamp cooler was on, but it couldn't compete with the heat from the lantern flame. Still, everyone agreed without discussion that what they were about to do felt incompatible with daylight.

Father Santiago sat in the armchair, eyes closed. He'd said he was trying to meditate. Anza had never meditated, but apparently, it meant sitting still and breathing.

"You ready?" Dove asked after a few minutes.

He nodded without opening his eyes.

"I'd like to speak to the thing that causes the fits. The thing living in Father Santiago's body. Will you talk to us?" Dove asked.

Anza waited, pen poised above notebook paper.

There was nothing for a few seconds. Then Father Santiago's head bobbed up and down in an unnatural, marionette-like motion.

Anza had to stifle some sound, maybe a curse.

Dove recoiled but moved on. "What's your name?"

Father Santiago's eyes stayed closed, but his lips moved. He spoke in quick, liquid Spanish. Anza leaned close to Dove, whispering the translation. "I walk down the street by my father's house in Guadalajara. My mother's hand is in mine. I smell burning charcoal on the air. My mother points at the marigolds in the garden. There are many bees on the petals."

He stopped speaking. Dove and Anza exchanged a glance.

"I don't understand," Dove said at last.

There was no reply.

She tried again. "Where do you come from?"

"I go to one of the rooms in the college. There are already five others there. They show me the telescope. I see the meteors fall across the sky. I think they look like rain on fire."

"What's the red sphere? The orb Pablo told us about?"

"I write words on white paper. I fold it and put my mother's name on the outside. I go to the mailbox to put the paper inside, and I find one she has sent to me."

Dove glanced down at the list of questions they'd prepared. Anza knew she was thinking about how useless they were. "What do you want from us?"

This time, the thing using Father Santiago's voice took a minute to answer. Anza almost thought he'd fallen asleep before it finally spoke again. "I sneak out of my room at the seminary. I go to see the girl I met at the shop. She takes me to see a film she says I will like. Then I take her to eat food I think she will like. We each tell the other one secret."

As Anza finished translating, Dove closed her eyes and let out a sigh. "Thank you for speaking with us. Please let Father Santiago wake up now."

He opened his eyes, sitting up straighter in his chair. "Did I fall asleep? Or did it work?"

Dove stood and opened the curtains while Anza extinguished the kerosene lamps.

"You didn't fall asleep. But I'm not sure it worked, either."

They told him everything he'd said.

He looked away when Anza told him about the story of the girl and going to the movies. "I hadn't thought about that in ages," he said.

She suspected that was a lie.

"But those were all things you remember? It didn't make any-thing up?" Dove asked.

He shook his head. "No. I remember all of those things."

Anza read over the notes again. "The answers don't make any sense, but it really *felt* like it was answering us. Right?"

"Yeah. I mean, all this babbling came after we asked a question, each time. And it nodded."

"Maybe..." Father Santiago leaned forward. "We already know that the fits become more complex over time. Single words before reciting memories, still poses before motion."

Anza nodded. "Yeah."

"What if... When one learns a foreign language, the easiest thing to learn is how to read something in that language, and then the second easiest is to understand someone else speaking. But the hardest part is learning to form your own sentences. So—"

"So this thing is learning us by going back through things we've already said and seen and done. But when it tries to answer a question, it can't come up with its own words," Anza said.

"Makes sense," Dove added after a moment. "We ask a question, and it falls back on some memory of the padre's it thinks gets at what we're asking. Not that I can understand for the life of me what it's saying."

"But you see? We've made contact," Father Santiago said, smiling. "We have somewhere to go from here."

CHAPTER 35: 2020

"This isn't what I pictured. At least, not from the way Grandpa Richie used to talk." Sonia peered out the window of Colin's car, watching a gas station, a minimart, and a trashy biker bar go by. For some reason, she felt certain there should be an ice cream parlor where an empty lot now stood.

"Well, this isn't what it looked like before. The population was about fifteen hundred in 1960, not including the people living just outside of town. By 1962, it was six hundred. Now it's about three hundred fifty in the town itself, and most of those are border patrol officers and their families. Most of the old houses have been knocked down, and they have trailers where they used to be." Colin shook his head. "Which is an incredibly dumb move, considering how much more energy-efficient those old adobe houses were."

"Feels too Mexican. Border patrol agents want to be housed in good old-fashioned American plastic crap." Low anger thrummed through Alonzo's voice. They'd been stopped at a checkpoint, as he'd warned them they would. Sure enough, they'd checked Alonzo's ID, had a German shepherd sniff the car, and made them wait. Colin claimed he'd never been stopped while driving on his own during research trips, but Alonzo got questioned at checkpoints every time.

Their hotel rooms were in Bisbee, about a twenty-minute drive from Galina. Sonia liked the feel of Bisbee, its quirky little shops and cafés and the hippie murals decorating the buildings. Then, between Bisbee and Galina, there were big vacation homes, wine tasting rooms, and converted ranches standing back from the highway, painted blinding white against the cactus-dotted hills.

It wasn't until they turned off the highway and reached the Galina town limits that the big ranch houses and signs for hiking trails gave way to ramshackle buildings, trash-strewn sidewalks, and a grubby main street marred with potholes. Something about the town felt sickly, half-dead, like a stillness in the air beyond typical small-town quiet. Even the wind seemed to avoid the place, Sonia thought as they parked on the street and stepped out of the car.

"So, what's the plan?" Alonzo asked.

Colin wandered around the front of the car. "Honestly, I kind of thought we'd get here, and something would just happen. With you two."

"That's it?" Alonzo stared at him.

"What?" Colin replied, a little snappish. "I don't know any more about what's going on than you do. Why do I have to come up with the plan?"

"Easy there, boys," Sonia said. "Okay, they wanted us to come here. That was pretty clear. So maybe we walk around to sites that were important last time around? Maybe we need to get close enough to 'the Means' or whatever to pick up the signal."

"Works for me," Alonzo said. "What's up first?"

Colin shaded his eyes and peered down the street. "Well, we're close to the church. The Catholic one, I mean. It's abandoned and burnt out but still standing."

Sonia thought back on Colin's dissertation, which she'd skimmed for the main points. "And that one's important because it's where the violence started, right?"

"The large-scale violence, yeah. There were some street fights and things before that but nothing like what happened with the church."

"Lead the way."

The front doors of the church were locked, the wood warped and sun bleached. Colin led them around to the back, through an area Sonia guessed was probably where the priest once lived. The interior of the church was dim, although the smashed windows let in enough sunlight to see the floor. The few pews that remained had been tipped over and smashed. Soot covered the altar and the east wall, overlaid with graffiti. Sonia's boot knocked over an empty beer bottle and sent it rolling down the rubble-strewn aisle.

"They've just let it sit here, all these years?" Alonzo asked.

"It's Church property. Consecrated ground. Transferring properties like this can take a long time. This isn't the original fire damage. They repaired it the first time around, but it caught fire again a few years ago and hasn't been used since." Colin reached out, his fingers grazing the crumbling stucco coating one of the walls. The bulky metal splint on his broken finger caught and pulled off a chunk of plaster.

Sonia wondered if Colin saw more than she did, having spent all these years trying to understand what happened here.

"Maybe..." Sonia cleared her throat and tried again. "As much as I hate to suggest it, maybe we should try letting them in again. See if they give us some direction."

Alonzo wiped his mouth. "I don't know. It seems wrong, here." He tried to smile. "You can take the boy out of the Church..."

Sonia shrugged. "Whatever. I can do it. You don't have to." She closed her eyes. "Come out, come out, wherever you are."

ALONZO HAD JUST STARTED recording on his phone when the change happened.

"Christ, that's disturbing," Alonzo murmured as he watched Sonia's personality drain from her face. "Is that what I look like when it happens?"

"Yeah. Pretty much."

Alonzo tried to imagine watching Colin like this, and he could barely stand to think about it. He thought about how short-tempered and edgy he'd been since seeing that video of himself and Sonia in the yard and realized he'd never stopped to wonder what it was like for Colin to stand there and film it. "Sorry," he whispered.

"It's okay," Colin whispered back, flashing a brief, tired smile. His face went serious again as he returned his attention to Sonia. "We're in Galina. We're here to find the Means. Can you tell us where it is?"

Sonia blinked. "No. This One believes it's become dormant until it's reactivated by One of the Ones."

"So how do you know it's still in Galina? The Place of Landing?" Alonzo asked.

"That was the agreement—with the First Speakers."

Colin started to ask something, but Alonzo held up a hand. "Wait. Are you saying there were some of our people in Galina who negotiated an agreement with your people?"

"Yes."

"Who were they?" Colin asked, dropping his backpack to the ground and scrambling to pull out a notebook. "What were their names?"

It stayed quiet for a moment. "This One doesn't know. The Ones Before didn't yet understand the importance of names. They didn't pass such knowledge along to This One."

"Do you know anything else about the First Speakers?" Alonzo asked.

"There were three." It paused again, eyes flicking upward. "One lived in this place."

"Father Santiago? Are you talking about Father Santiago?" Colin squeezed Alonzo's arm so hard, he probably didn't even realize he was doing it.

"This One doesn't know."

"But he lived in this building? This structure?"

"Yes."

"What about the other two?" Alonzo asked.

"This One doesn't know names. They didn't live here. They didn't house Ones."

A frown furrowed the skin between Colin's eyes. "You mean they weren't infected?"

Sonia's right arm flailed in some impatient gesture. It made Alonzo realize how still her body had been before that movement. "This One doesn't like 'infect.' That isn't what This One does."

Heat boiled up in Alonzo's chest. "Oh, really, you don't *like* it? Well, pardon the fuck out of us for using the wrong word to describe the way you've violated us."

"This One has no choice. This One can't survive outside of Sonia's body."

"That's *your* fucking problem." Alonzo's face heated up, and a buzzing sound filled his ears. It had been years since he'd let himself go into a rage, years of learning to stop and breathe instead of taking a swing. Now he wondered why he'd ever bothered to develop that kind of control if this was where it had gotten him. In some small, horrible corner of his mind, he thought about closing the distance between himself and the *thing* and smashing that maddening blank look off its face. The only thing that stopped him was the knowledge that it was *Sonia's* face. *Sonia's* body—

"Stop," Colin said, dropping his voice to a low hiss. "That thing's controlling her right now. You really want to see what it could do to her when it's pissed off?"

Alonzo took a deep, shuddering breath, swallowing what he'd been about to say. "You're right. I'm sorry," he said when he trusted himself to speak.

"Colin's wrong to say this. This One would never hurt Sonia." Alonzo caught an undercurrent of emotion he hadn't heard before, a new shakiness woven into the odd rhythm of the voice. "This One was born as Sonia was born. This One sings when she sings. This One gave birth to Another One as Sonia gave birth to Dylan. This One loves Sonia."

The adrenaline left Alonzo's system so fast, he felt sick to his stomach. He stopped, really thinking for the first time about the thing living inside him. If it had been with him his entire life, they had taken their first breaths together. It had seen every single thing he had ever seen. It had felt everything he had ever felt.

He stared at Colin's face. Every time he had ever looked at Colin, two minds had seen through one pair of eyes. From the way Colin stared back at him, eyes stunned and shining, he was thinking the same thing.

"I'm sorry," Alonzo said after a moment, voice rough. "I was angry. This is hard for me... and for Sonia."

"And for This One, as well. But this will become better when we have the Means to contact Those of Origin."

"Do you remember anything else about these First Speakers? Anything that can help us find them?"

"They didn't house Ones. They were female. That's all This One can say."

"Two women, both asymptomatic, and Father Santiago. Okay. We'll try to find them. Can we speak with Sonia, please?"

She blinked, posture relaxing. "Anything?"

"Yeah. Think we got something." Colin reached down for his backpack.

"You okay?" Sonia asked, frowning at Alonzo.

He stared at her, trying to see two lives in one. "Yeah. Sorry. I'm good." He paused. "We learned a lot, actually. It's kind of hard to explain. You should see the video."

He led the way out of the crumbling church and into the blinding daylight.

THEY SAT IN A BOOTH at the greasy spoon diner near the highway. Sonia didn't imagine many people from Galina ate there; it seemed more like a place for truckers to get breakfast on a long haul.

Colin had his laptop out and was searching through old research notes. "There wasn't a whole lot on Father Santiago. I have here that he lived in Galina when he died and that he was in his eighties at the time."

"Was he infected?" Sonia asked.

Colin seemed to cringe a little. "Maybe we should avoid disease-related terms."

She felt her jaw drop. "Fuckin' seriously?"

"I'll explain later," Alonzo muttered. "It's part of... you'll see."

"Anyway, yeah, several people remember him Naming, Statuing, Dancing. It came up in a lot of discussions about the religious hysteria and the racially motivated violence."

"But the women who were also First Speakers didn't?"

"Yeah. Which probably means they were middle-aged or older."

Sonia sipped her Pepsi, trying to ignore the dirty smudges on the side of the glass. "Yeah, what's up with that?"

Colin sighed. "I don't know. I used to think it was classic bias against post-menopausal women, same as with pretty much every witch trial. Now, no idea."

"So two old ladies and a priest faced down the thing that scared the crap out of Grandpa Richie? Wish the old bastard was still alive so I could make fun of him for it." She cackled at the thought.

"Okay, I'm emailing the public record office for Cochise County to see if they have any wills or anything public on file for Father Santiago. Might point us to someone."

Alonzo poked at his chorizo and hash browns. He'd been weirdly quiet since the church. Sonia wondered what was in this video he hadn't shown her yet.

"Maybe we should track down the Garces kids. If the Means are with someone, then the first ones to get the, you know, whatever we're saying instead of Plague, they make as much sense as anything else."

Colin's eyes widened. "Oh goddammit. I'm an idiot."

"What?" Alonzo asked.

"I knew there was something about the cactus and the mesa..." He typed and clicked away on his laptop. Sonia had gone through a lot of his research notes during their investigation, but there was plenty she hadn't read. She could hardly believe the amount of research that went into one book.

"Got it." Colin nodded, eyes flicking back and forth across the screen. "Interview with Violet Brandt. Her dad was the sheriff. Here's what she says about the mesa: 'After it was over, people still never wanted to go back to the mesa. The spot where the Garces kids' clothes were found? The cactus never grew right again. It used to be like every other part of the mesa, but right there in a big circle, the cactus grew so thick and close together, no one could ever get through. And you could just feel it. Something was there. It didn't want us to come near it.'"

Alonzo frowned. "You think that's where the Means is?"

"Maybe. I mean, if that's where the kids disappeared, and it can all be traced back to them..."

"You know where this spot is? This place where the cactus is fucked up?" Sonia asked.

"That, I do." He turned the screen so she could see. "The police report marked the exact spot on the map where they found the clothes."

She glared at the map. "So we're going hiking in the desert in the middle of July. This is complete balls."

"OKAY, SO, FROM HERE, it should only be about a fifteen-, twenty-minute walk." Colin studied the map on his phone and pointed straight ahead from the spot where they'd parked alongside the road.

Alonzo gestured at the prefab houses scattered along the slope leading toward the mesa. "Are you sure none of this is private property? I'm way too brown to get away with trespassing on some border patrol guy's back lot."

"Uh, pretty sure, yeah," Colin said, hoping he was right.

Sonia led the way up the mesa. For all her bitching about sunburn, she knew how to hike desert terrain better than Colin did. He was used to beaches, woods, and gentle trails with soft ground. He still didn't have a good feel for how to spot desert paths and keep an eye out for the cactus, the hidden arroyos, the scorpions, and the snakes all at the same time.

Sonia climbed over the last little rise before the desert stretched out into a flat plain. "Uh, Doc, was that patch supposed to be right ahead?"

"Yeah," Colin said, trying to catch his breath before resuming the climb up the slope.

"Okay, then, we got a problem."

Colin followed Alonzo over the rise and stopped. "Oh, *come on*."

Thirty yards ahead, stretching out across the mesa, the skeletal frames of unfinished houses stood stark against the sky. The concrete slabs of the closest ones were visible through the wood frames, flat bulldozed earth between each half-finished house. A chain-link fence surrounded the entire development.

"Flora Mira Community," Alonzo said, reading the faded sign hanging from the fence.

"This looks dead. Why would you stop building houses halfway through?" Sonia asked.

"The last recession. Lots of developments folded. The ones in Phoenix and Tucson mostly got resold, but the ones out in the middle of nowhere, not so much." Colin remembered hearing about a development project somewhere around here, but all his older interview subjects had been skeptical. None believed that Galina would ever be reborn.

"Well, let's go find that cactus," Sonia said, boosting herself over the chain link.

"Hey, wait." Colin raised a hand, but Alonzo followed her right over.

"Fine," he sighed, struggling over the fence.

"Dude, how have you never climbed a fence before?" Sonia asked.

"Never came up." He staggered as he landed.

THEY WANDERED THROUGH the half-finished houses. Clear tarps still hung over some of them, but others had obviously spent years exposed to the elements. Plywood had warped and bent, concrete had crumbled around the edges, and the smell of dry rot pervaded the air. A few of the frames had started to collapse, their wooden beams lying buckled on the slabs. There were odd, disturbing bits of evidence of human activity—Big Gulp cups and the occasional cigarette butt. Colin stepped off a slab and onto a space where a cul-de-sac would have been.

The occasional weed and small lump of cholla struggled into the light between the houses, but there was no unusual patch of cactus. No spot where things grew as they should not.

Colin found Alonzo standing in the middle of one of the houses. He stared down at the concrete under his shoes.

"What if it's under one of these?" he asked. "I mean, what if the only thing they want is trapped under concrete? What do we do then?"

"Get a jackhammer."

Alonzo tried to smile, but Colin guessed what he was thinking. They couldn't even find the spot, much less start digging.

"Yo, guys."

They followed Sonia's voice to the far end of the development, near another stretch of chain link. She stared out into the desert beyond. As they approached, Colin saw what she was watching.

A group of coyotes sat in a perfect circle, no more than ten feet from the fence. Eight of them, different sizes, were spaced out at even intervals. They sat still, but as Colin watched, one of them let out a little yip. Seconds later, one across the circle made a slightly lower-pitched sound. Then another let out a low growl.

None paid the slightest attention to the humans standing a few feet away.

"Think they know where we can find the Means?" Colin asked.

"No." Alonzo turned away. "I think they're looking too."

CHAPTER 36: 1960

"**N**ow, I don't want you going anywhere on your own, hear? You stay with Dove," Dad said for what seemed like the fiftieth time.

Anza glared. "Dad, I know."

"Just don't want you getting cocky just because things been quiet for a week or so. Who knows what Benjamin and his people are cooking up."

Anza nodded. It had been a week, and while tension hung in the air like a fog, no one had been hurt. No buildings had been set on fire. Father Santiago's people kept to the cantina and Millie's Café; Pastor Benjamin's kept to the saloon and the ice cream parlor. The general store and the tack shop seemed to have been allocated as neutral territory by some silent agreement. Still, everyone moved about their business quickly, walking from one place to another in pairs or bigger groups. No one lingered on the sidewalk to chat.

Dad lifted his suitcase. Sweat stains were already forming under the arms of his starched white shirt. His reddish-brown hair was slicked back with pomade for the first time Anza could remember, and he smelled of aftershave. "Tony and I should get to Tucson by three o'clock. We play our cards right, we should find some work in a day or two. Soon as I have a handle on that, I'll start looking into places to stay, make sure it's near a good school."

Anza nodded, trying to smile. School was supposed to start in two weeks. She couldn't imagine what it would be like if kids of Pastor Benjamin's followers were thrown back into classrooms with the Mexican kids and other Catholics. The peace wouldn't last—she would bet anything on that. "Don't worry about all that, Dad. Just try to find a good job. We'll figure out the rest later."

Dad pulled her into a hug, kissing the top of her head. "Your mama would be just bursting with pride if she was here." His voice came out thick and rough. "I'll call you when I get to Tucson."

"Go," Dove said, coming out of the kitchen. "We'll be fine."

Dad waved one last time and went out to where Mr. Cardenas waited in his truck. Anza knew Fernando had wanted to go with them so he could find work, too, but Mrs. Cardenas had insisted he remain at home with her. Father Santiago was staying with them until the church was repaired, and Anza suspected she didn't want to cause a scandal by being alone with him in the house at any time.

Dove waited until Dad and Mr. Cardenas drove out of sight before turning back to Anza. "So. The good Padre should be here in a couple hours. I say we spend some time thinking of better ways to ask our questions."

ANZA SAW SOMETHING was wrong as soon as Father Santiago walked inside. His face, still bruised and healing, had an ashy cast to it. He hovered in the doorway as though unsure of where to go.

"Santiago? What's wrong?" Dove asked.

"Geor..." He stopped and cleared his throat. "George Esquivel is dead. He was out on Main Street, and a truck pulled up next to him. There was a fight. He's... He's been shot."

It took a moment for the meaning of the words to hit. It didn't make sense. She must not be understanding him—

Then the shock passed, Anza's knees gave out, and she sank to the ground. Those kind eyes, that rumbling voice... She thought of how he always tipped his hat when he saw her. She would never see that again. That evening on Dove's porch, the first time he'd spoken to her like an adult. *His wife...* She clamped a hand over her mouth, stifling the shriek of rage trying to claw its way out.

"Oh my god." Dove rushed to the phone. "The Garces family."

"I've already been there." Father Santiago sat heavily on the couch. "I waited with them until some more relatives came, cousins and brothers. They're all armed. I can't believe I've told my flock to arm themselves, to carry *guns...*"

"Better than relying on prayer," Dove said.

He ignored her. "There's been no peace, not really. They were just waiting for someone to let down their guard, and then... I should have known."

As afternoon turned to evening, the calls started coming in, people looking for Father Santiago. The stories were mostly second- or thirdhand, but they all painted the same picture. Shots fired at houses. Bricks hurled through windows. A cat bludgeoned to death and hung on a gatepost. Beatings in the streets. Everyone said the men weren't bothering to wear masks this time.

Between the calls, Father Santiago kept trying to reach the bishop at his headquarters in Tucson. After leaving three messages with the secretary and calling three others on the bishop's staff, he slammed the phone back into its cradle. "This is useless! The bishop's eighty-six years old. They say he's retiring next month. He either doesn't know what's happening or doesn't care. We can't rely on him to pressure the authorities." He fetched his car key from the bowl near the front door. "I have to go out and see if I can help."

"Don't be stupid, Padre," Dove snapped. "You don't even have a gun. There's nothing you can do to stop what's going on out there."

"Just... try to get the state police on the phone. The governor. Anyone who will listen." He dashed out before Dove could get another word in. She growled but picked up the phone and asked the operator to connect her with the state capitol.

A fruitless hour later, Dove slammed the phone down just as Father Santiago had. "Same damn thing over and over. 'That's the jurisdiction of the town sheriff.' Never mind that the bastard sheriff is probably right in there, raising hell with the rest of them."

"Do you think Father Santiago's okay?" Anza asked, staring out the window. She remembered when he'd been unconscious in the cantina, smeared with blood...

"I don't know. Hope so."

At last, the phone rang. Dove answered, and relief flooded over her features. "It's Santiago," she said, cupping her hand over the receiver.

Anza let out a shaky sigh and sat down.

Dove listened for a long time. "Okay. We'll be there." She hung up.

"What's going on?"

"The padre's okay, but sounds like other folks got hurt. Mayor wants everyone to meet at the Big Z Ranch. Everyone who isn't out of their damn mind, at least."

"Why there?" Anza had never been to Big Z, and its owners, the Bennetts, never seemed to be in town. She'd always assumed they were just snobby.

"Guess it's just the biggest place that doesn't belong to one of Ben's people. And it's too dangerous to meet in the town hall or the school."

The thought of that froze Anza. The town hall, the school, the quiet section of Main Street where a bar fight was the worst thing that ever happened—she couldn't picture how those places she'd been countless times could somehow have become dangerous.

"Santiago says we should be okay driving through town if we don't stop. He says it's calmed down a lot, and folks from that neighborhood fought back hard enough to scare the worst of them away," Dove said as Anza followed her to the truck.

She saw the smoke as soon as the truck crested the hill on the main road leading to town. It didn't rise in a column like something from a still-burning fire. Instead, it hung in a dirty cloud over the road. Even before she saw its source, some twisting in Anza's gut told her where the smoke came from. "Dove? I think that's my house."

The house still was still smoldering when Dove pulled up in front of it. Past the familiar honeysuckle-draped gate, the closest corner was scorched black. The ceiling had buckled on one end, revealing a glimpse of the dark room beyond.

"Oh, Anza," Dove breathed.

Anza stepped out of the truck, saying nothing. She made her way up the driveway, through the yard where she'd spent countless lazy days playing with Fernando, Paula, and the others. The little pots of gardenias still sat next to the porch, petals blistered. The front porch step let out a familiar creak as she stepped on it.

Tears came to her eyes as soon as she opened the door, not because everything was gone. She saw right away that the fire had been confined to one half of the living room. Most of their things could be salvaged.

No, the tears were for the broken windows, the shattered lock on the door, and the filthy things scrawled in black paint on one of the walls. She cried because, even if they stayed, even if they repaired the house and painted over the obscenities, she would still feel the hatred seeping through the walls like mildew.

"Richie," Dove said from the doorway.

Anza shrugged. "Or one of his boys. Not that it matters which one." She sniffed, gesturing at the mess. "This is the kind of people we have in this town. I don't know why I didn't see it before."

Dove lowered her eyes and turned away as though ashamed.

Finally, Anza wiped her face. "I'm going to get a few things," she said and went inside before Dove could argue. She grabbed a knap-sack and stuffed it with objects she didn't want exposed to the elements, things Dad would want her to save—pictures of Mama, the coffee can of rainy-day money, and the shawl Great-Grandma Maureen had brought from Galway. Then she added a few things from her room, clothes, a hairbrush, and other things she didn't want left behind if anyone else decided to pick through their house.

Anza went back outside without looking at the wrecked living room and nudged Dove toward her truck. "Nothing else we can do about it now. We should get going. Take Main Street. I need to see."

Dove pursed her lips but didn't argue. Before they even reached Main Street, Anza saw smashed windows in the neighborhood on the south side of town. A burnt, blackened Chevy was parked on a corner. Tipped garbage cans had spilled their contents into the streets. Nothing moved. If anyone remained in town, they were hiding behind locked doors and drawn curtains.

Dove steered the truck onto Main Street. Anza's breath caught in her throat. Shattered glass glittered on the sidewalk in front of the cantina. A car sat half-blocking the road, the driver's-side door hanging open. A smear of something dark and red stained the pavement in front of the hardware store, and Anza wondered if that was where George's body had fallen. Her stomach lurched at the thought, her eyes pricking with tears. She smelled gasoline and smoke on the air. It seemed to cling to her hair and her clothes, sticking to her like sweat.

They said nothing as they passed through Main Street, left the town, and continued on to the slopes where the wealthier ranchers lived. Anza spotted cars and milling crowds long before they reached Big Z. People looked tired and disheveled, carrying knapsacks and pillowcases stuffed with clothes.

"There's Santiago." Dove pointed over the steering wheel.

He stood near the ranch house's big front doors, directing people inside. As soon as he spotted Dove's truck, he ran over to meet them.

"Are you okay?" Anza asked, hugging him without thinking.

"I'm fine, Esperanza." His hand shook when it touched her shoulder.

"The town looks like a war happened."

He nodded, the lines around his mouth deep with fatigue. "They must have been planning it for days. At least fifty men, maybe more. They attacked houses and the cantina and Millie's all at once. No one had time to prepare, to defend themselves..." He shook his head.

"Were there any more, other than..." Anza cleared her throat. "Other than George?"

He blinked fast. "Two. Sheila Morris was run down. We think it was J.D. Foster's truck, but no one saw who was driving." He took a deep breath. "And also one of theirs. Tim Evers was shot. We don't know who did it, but he was smashing the windows of Mrs. Diaz's house at the time."

Anza wondered if that was everyone or if bodies would continue to turn up as people filtered back into their homes and businesses.

"These folks got a place to go?" Dove asked, pointing at the people filing inside the house.

Father Santiago nodded. "Yes. Mrs. Bennett ran a home for refugees during the war. She's organizing food, places to sleep in the house and the outbuildings. At least until people feel like it's safe to go back to town."

"Any word on the law coming in?" Anza asked.

"Yes. The mayor will announce this at the meeting, but he sent two of the council members to see the Cochise County Sheriff's Department. They've agreed to help, but they're treating it as something much less serious than it is. They won't be here until tomorrow."

"That's something, at least." Dove glanced around as though making sure no one else could hear. "Listen. Even if the law gets here, the Plagues are still going to turn people against each other. We don't fix that, anything else is a short-term solution."

Father Santiago sighed. "Dove, we've tried. We've tried every-thing."

"Not everything." She hesitated. "I had an idea. Something you and me can do, tonight."

"Me too," Anza said. She thought she knew what Dove was going to suggest, even though they hadn't talked about it.

Dove's eyes narrowed. "No, Anza, researching is one thing, but I'm not taking you into danger."

"Dove, you leave me behind, I'll just follow. You know I will."

Dove stared for a long moment before shaking her head, teeth gritted. "Goddammit. Just like your mama." And she told them her plan, what they would need, and where they would need to go.

Father Santiago agreed, and Anza nodded without speaking.

She waited for him to return to the line of people at the front of the house. Then she snagged Dove's sleeve. "Dove," she said in a low voice, "there's something else. Something I think we need to do, if we can make contact."

Dove listened to Anza's idea. Even as she said it, Anza wondered if it was too much, if it was taking it too far. But Dove only nodded once, steely-eyed, before walking away.

MAYOR FULLER SHOWED up in a sweat-stained shirt and torn Levi's, his equally ragged family in tow. He looked like he hadn't slept in a week. As much as Anza knew he was to blame for not stopping this mess sooner, she couldn't bring herself to be too angry with him. Judging from the grumbles around her, others had no such hesita-tion.

The Bennetts had quickly realized the futility of holding a meet-ing indoors, given the number of people. So they'd moved everything

out to the ranch house's little courtyard. The brick floor of the courtyard filled almost immediately, with everyone else standing beyond
the low wall encircling the garden.

"This town meeting is hereby called to order," Mayor Fuller said,
tapping an empty coffee cup against the courtyard's wooden table.
People started shouting, calling Mayor Fuller a useless coward. He
stayed silent, letting the venom rain down without protest. Once the
yells and catcalls died down a bit, Mayor Fuller sighed and said, "I've
failed you all. I failed this town. All I want now is to do whatever I
can to make it better."

The crowd still growled and mumbled, but the heat was lost. The
mayor droned on in his broken voice about the county sheriff's officers who would show up in the morning, the investigation he would
begin into Pastor Benjamin's activities, and the delegation he would
send to the state attorney general's office.

Anza stopped listening, letting her eyes drift over the crowd.
None of them knew. None of them knew what she and Dove and Father Santiago were about to do to save them all. And they probably
never would.

She thought about where they were going and what they would
do there, and adrenaline flooded her blood like electricity. As scared
as she was, she wanted to *go* already.

Dove slipped through the crowd. "Come on. They'll be distracted for a while."

Anza nodded and followed her out to the long driveway. Just as
she was about to reach the door, she heard the scuff of footsteps on
gravel.

"Anza!"

She turned to find Fernando following them down the driveway.
"I'll be there in a second," she told Dove.

"Don't take too long."

Fernando looked paler than usual and jumpy. "Where you going?"

"I can't say." Anza sighed. "Dove and I might have a way to fix this."

"Just come with us." The words spilled out of him, tripping over each other. "Tonight. My mom says we're leaving now, not coming back. Tucson first, maybe Phoenix after. You could come with us, and then we'll meet up with your dad—"

"I can't."

His eyes welled with tears, and for just a second, he looked like a little boy again. "Anza... if you don't come with us now, I don't know if I'm gonna see you again. I want..."

Anza stepped forward and wrapped her arms around him. "I'm glad you're going," she said, and he flinched against her. "It's going to make things a lot easier if I know you and your mom and your dad are safe."

She stepped back.

He stared at her, miserable. "But why can't—"

"Bye, Nando." She turned and walked to Dove's truck.

He said something else, something she didn't quite catch, but she didn't look back.

CHAPTER 37: 2020

"Let's stop here and ask around about folks who would have been in Galina back then," Colin said. "I tried to find as many as I could before, but maybe I missed someone."

"You think whoever has the Means stayed around here?" Sonia asked.

"Maybe not, but it makes sense. If they knew someone was going to come looking. And there was all that stuff about an agreement or something, so..." He pulled into the decrepit gas station at the end of Main Street.

Alonzo stepped onto the pavement. "You go ask. I'll gas up the car."

Sonia got out, too, wandering in a slow circle around the pumps as the engine ticked and cooled. Alonzo started to wash the windshield, pausing as he glanced up Main Street. "Is it just me, or does it seem like there are a lot more people than there were before?"

A woman drifted along the sidewalk, peering at boarded-up shop windows. There was no way she lived around here; her tawny hair was artfully styled, her silk blouse tucked into designer jeans, and she clutched an expensive-looking leather handbag to her body.

Behind her, a young couple stood with two small children, blinking and peering around as though lost. On the other side of the street, a Latino man in his twenties, wearing punk attire and a Mohawk, smoked and shuffled back and forth.

There were too many cars, as well. Alonzo walked away from the pumps, watching as first a silver Honda and then a battered green minivan cruised down Main Street, the drivers' heads turning back and forth.

Just as Alonzo reached the cracked sidewalk at the edge of the gas station parking lot, the young man with the Mohawk started Remembering. Recognizing the posture before he heard the words, Alonzo approached him, Sonia trailing behind.

"I flip my turn signal. I turn the wheel. The coffee cup tips in my hand. Hot coffee spills on my thigh. No. Yes. I'm angry because it burns. No." The cigarette burned down close to the man's skin.

Alonzo pulled the filter out from between his fingers and ground it under his foot. He avoided looking directly at the man's face. Seeing someone else Remember filled him with pity, and he couldn't stand the thought of anyone else pitying him in the same way.

"Are you here because of this too?" someone asked from behind him.

The young couple with the kids had crossed the street. They watched the Remembering man with pained recognition.

"Yeah. Both of us." Alonzo gestured at Sonia. They introduced themselves.

"Which of you is having it?" Sonia asked.

"Me. And the kids." The woman's face contorted for just a moment before smoothing out again. Alonzo had seen that look on Sonia's face before, a level of guilt he couldn't comprehend. He also recognized the terrible helplessness in the man's expression from the way Colin had watched him lately. He wondered for the first time if he was the lucky one in all this.

"Are you staying in Bisbee?" he asked.

The woman nodded. "Yeah. We came down from Colorado Springs."

Colin came out of the gas station, shielding his eyes and peering in their direction.

"Hey, can we get your names and number?" Alonzo asked. "We have some leads. Nothing concrete, but—"

"Of course." The woman pulled her phone from her purse with a shaking hand. "Anything. I'd really take any answers at this point."

"We're trying. Stay close for the next few days, if you can."

She smiled like agony. "We don't have anywhere else to go."

Alonzo went back to meet Colin by the car. Halfway there, Sonia turned and trotted back to the family. She said something to the woman, something Alonzo couldn't hear. Tears poured down the woman's face, but she also smiled. Sonia walked away without another word.

"What was that?" he asked.

She avoided his eye. "Mom stuff. Don't worry about it."

"What's going on?" Colin asked as Alonzo put the gas pump back in place.

"We're not the only pilgrims," he replied, gesturing. "I got their names. For the list."

Colin watched the family walking away down the sidewalk, the Remembering man still in place. "I guess I was expecting this, somehow. Didn't realize it until now."

Alonzo climbed into the passenger seat. "I wonder how many people are going through exactly the same thing as us."

"Except with way less information than we have," Sonia added from the back seat.

"That's a horrible thought," Colin sighed, "because we don't know anything."

"That's not true." Alonzo reached out to touch his arm. "You know you're making this easier, right?"

"Yeah." Sonia nodded. "I mean, it still blows, but I'd be a head case by now. More of a head case, I mean. If we didn't have your research to go on."

Colin raised his eyebrows. "Sociology research being helpful in everyday life? Now I know you're lying." But some of the dark cloud lifted from his face, and his arm relaxed under Alonzo's hand. "I got a few names from the cashier. Not that many, but apparently, he's a nephew of someone who's lived here her entire life, so he knows some people." He waved the little slip of paper. "Maybe our mystery women are here."

SONIA GOT A CALL ON the way back to the hotel. "That was Leonie Motz," she said as she hung up. "She called to tell us she's on her way to Arizona right now."

"Did she say why?" Alonzo asked.

"She said she had an episode, but her partner told her it was different from all the others. More lucid. It sounds like what we were doing the other day. Apparently, she kept saying stuff about going to the Place of Origin, and she put two and two together."

"Hm." Alonzo stared through the window at the empty highway. "I'm guessing the population of Galina is about to go up by a lot."

"Think the feds are going to get wind of this at some point?" Sonia asked. "I mean, I'm sure they have geniuses at the NSA watching for weird patterns and population movements and shit."

Colin shrugged. "Maybe. Doubt it. They could have gotten interested in Galina sixty years ago, and they didn't. I don't think this is how they picture an invasion, so they aren't watching for it."

Everyone paused.

"Is that what you think this is?" Alonzo asked. "An invasion?"

"Can you think of a better word?"

"No," he said at last. "No, I can't."

SONIA WATCHED PASSERSBY as she made her way to Bisbee's closest market. Alonzo was taking a nap, and Colin had dug back into his research notes, trying to find obvious candidates for their two mystery women. She'd helped with the research as long as she could, but the things she'd said in the church kept bobbing to the surface of her mind, distracting her like reflected light in her eye.

Alonzo had waited until they returned to the hotel to send her the video from the church. She'd been annoyed with him earlier, thought he was just being evasive or trying to shield her from something. But then she'd watched the video and understood why he'd wanted her to see it for herself, why he'd wanted to give her time to process it. If he'd just told her those things, those things about her One caring about her, loving her, not wanting to hurt her or Dylan, she would have snarled and called bullshit. But seeing it with her own eyes, hearing the ragged edge in her own voice... She couldn't make herself believe that it was a lie. This creature, whatever it was, loved her and Dylan, and it loved its own child. Sonia had no idea what to do with that information.

She tried to spot others in the crowd. Bisbee was the closest city to Galina that had hotels and places to eat, so most of them would be here. Especially now, as night began to fall. Even the bravest pilgrims wouldn't be on the streets of Galina at night, not with that sense of grime and corruption in the air.

She caught sight of a Namer or maybe a Rememberer on a corner. The way people passed by told her who was one of *them* and who was just a normal Bisbee resident or tourist. People like her viewed the Namer with a kind of tired empathy, while the others turned quickly away as one would from a babbling homeless person.

Lot of us out tonight, Sonia thought.

She didn't really need to watch the people on the streets to know that, though. There was a crackle in the air, like static except as a buzz on the skin instead of a sound. Maybe it was conversation she sensed, silent exchanges across the boosted signal that came with many being close together. *It must not be strong enough to find the Means, not yet.* Still, she couldn't escape the sense of almost-subliminal chatter.

Her phone buzzed in her back pocket. "Hello?"

"Sonia, it's Dylan." Mom sounded panicky again, tearstained even through the phone. "He's talking, but he's... different. It's not like the Naming. It's more like someone else is talking through him, and it's scaring me, but I don't—"

"What's he saying?"

"Oh, nonsense, but mostly stuff about how we need to go to something called the Landing Place or the Place of Landing. And he keeps saying something about means, like it's a thing, but I don't understand—"

"Mom, stop. Put him on the phone."

"He's having an episode, Sonia. You know he won't listen."

"Tell him..." Sonia took a deep breath. "Say, 'Another One is on the phone and wants to speak with This One.'"

"What?"

Sonia repeated herself. "Got it?"

"Yes."

She heard her mother speaking to Dylan, his voice indistinct in the background. Covering the mouthpiece with her hand, she closed her eyes and whispered, "You want to talk to your baby, here's your chance. Go ahead."

Blink. The night was growing darker now, and the streetlights powered up. A voice spoke into her ear. "Sonia? Sonia? Are you still there?"

Clearing her throat, she said, "Yeah. Yeah, Mom, I'm here. What's going on?"

"Dylan's back. I don't know what you said to him, but it worked."

"What did he say? Before he came back? What exactly?"

"He said, 'Will One of Origin come back soon?' and I think I heard you say yes. And then he said, 'Then This One will wait.' And then he was back, and he didn't remember any of it."

"Let me talk to him."

"Didn't you just…"

"No. That wasn't me. And it wasn't Dylan. Put him on the phone, please."

There was a long moment of silence. Sonia felt the questions there and prayed her mother would be merciful enough not to ask them. Finally, she heard Dylan's voice. "Mom?"

"Baby," she said through a sudden constriction in her throat. "How are you?"

"Fine."

"Tell me the truth, now."

He sighed. "I miss you."

"I miss you, too, kiddo. And I'm going to be home really soon. I know I said that before, and it wasn't true, but this time… Well, I'm where the answers are."

"Galina."

She stopped, eyes fixed on the pavement. "How did you know that?" She hadn't told Mom where they were going, not wanting to explain still more of what was happening.

"I don't know. I just… It's like I'm bored, and I want to go somewhere. I just feel like I need to go to a place, and I think it's called Galina."

"Okay. I get that, kiddo, but stay where you are, okay? No hitchhiking south. I'm gonna have answers for us real soon."

"Okay. Love you."

"Love you too." She hung up and pressed a hand to her mouth, ignoring the stares of passersby.

As Sonia sniffed and got herself back under control, she felt that pressure behind her eyes again. Had it been with her all her life, and she'd just never paid attention? She didn't remember. She took a deep breath. "I know how you feel," she whispered and resumed her walk to the market.

CHAPTER 38: 1960

"We have to do this at night?" Anza asked.

"I didn't want you to come along at all," Dove shot back. "Besides, it's a cave. Doesn't matter if its day or night once we're in there."

"I should go second," Father Santiago said. "If you're right, and it's like the cactus, it will take over once we get close. It may be hard to lead me after that."

"Me first. Then the padre. Then you, Anza." Dove turned to Santiago. "Are you absolutely sure about this? You're the one taking a big chance here. And any infected person should work just fine. It doesn't have to be you."

"I'm sure. It should be me." He squared his shoulders. "I'm ready."

The cave seemed darker this time, even though Anza knew Dove was right—it didn't make any difference if it was day or night once they got past the first narrow passage. The darkness seemed to swallow the beams of their flashlights, as though trying to snuff them out. The cave had the exact same smell as before, the humid air like breath. Dove stopped to mark the walls with pieces of tape every time they made a turn or moved into a new cavern. The shotgun on Dove's back caught against the walls more than once. Anza thought about what it would sound like if she had to fire it in the cave. The echo would deafen them all forever.

They were inching their way sideways through a narrow section when Anza walked straight into Father Santiago. Even in the confines of the cave passage, he had still managed to twist himself into a Statue pose.

"Dove!" Anza shouted, too loud in her panic.

"Sh! What?"

"It started." She listened in the darkness as Dove made her way back over.

"Okay, well, we knew this would happen. Means we're getting close." Dove fumbled at Father Santiago's waist until she found the rope he'd tied around his torso in preparation for this moment. "I'll drag him. You push him along."

She grunted as she yanked the rope. Santiago toppled like a falling tree, still stiff and contorted as he hit the bottom of the passage. Anza winced but did her best to lift and push his legs along.

Even with both of them working together, it took twenty minutes to get his rigid body through the narrow section and into a spot where the cave widened.

"Have to... rest," Dove said, gasping for air.

Anza made sure Father Santiago's nose and mouth were clear of the mud before she sank to the ground, legs shaking with fatigue. The air smelled sharper, almost coppery. She hadn't noticed it the first time.

"Okay," Dove said at last. "We're close. Let's see if we can get him upright. Be easier to each get an arm."

They managed to maneuver him onto his feet. It felt less like pushing a human body and more like trying to manipulate a block of carved wood covered in cloth. Anza got under the arm he held crooked at chest level, while Dove got the one stretching to the left almost parallel to the ground. Together, they dragged him along, his pointed toes scraping the floor of the cavern.

"There. There it is," Dove said, wheezing.

Anza twisted her head enough to see the red wall, visible in small flickers as the light on her belt moved to and fro.

They got to the wall. Anza pressed a palm to it. Beneath the cold, porous surface, it almost seemed to pulse.

"Moment of truth," Dove muttered.

They tipped Father Santiago forward until his forehead almost touched the wall. Just before his skin made contact, the stone seemed to flex and shy away. Then, as his hair brushed the wall, the rock opened inward. Anza saw now how thin the wall was, like an eggshell.

They wrestled Father Santiago through the wall as it shivered and shrank away from him. The space it made for his body barely left enough room for them to follow, but they slipped through just as it started to close. Anza fought the urge to leap back through, to run before the wall decided to seal them in forever.

Anza helped Dove lower Father Santiago to the ground. He gave a twitch and a gasp, arms flailing. Then he Statued again, this time corpse-like on the ground.

Dove's belt light illuminated only a fuzzy circle of reddish stone floor. There was light beyond that, though. Anza blinked at the rusty haze in front of them.

It was like glowing fog but with a brighter point in the distance. Anza fumbled with the flashlight in her pocket, clicked it on, and swept the beam along the floor. Everything was the same smooth red stone the wall was made of. Anza tried to find the other walls and the ceiling, but they were too far. Everything just faded into a hazy glow outside the flashlight's range.

"Come on," Dove whispered at last. "We can leave him here for a minute."

They walked out across the cavern floor, steps echoing. Anza held up her hand. Even without the flashlight pointed at it, she could still see the outline of her fingers in the red glow. She counted her steps. After seventy-three, the brighter red spot started to come into focus.

After one hundred three, they stopped. A solid-red orb sat on a flat rock in the middle of the floor. Its surface looked almost like cut glass, light catching along its edges. From Pablo's story, Anza had imagined something bigger, but the orb was only about the size of a basketball.

"Well, hello there." Dove hefted the shotgun, chambered a round, and pointed it straight at the orb. "We're not here to hurt you, less we have to. We're here to negotiate. Bring Father Santiago over so we can have a talk."

The orb didn't move, but a light flared deep under its surface. Anza heard some rhythmic sound in the darkness behind her. As she watched, Father Santiago's body came toward them with lurching, awkward steps. She fought the urge to run screaming into the dark, away from that terrible motion.

"That's far enough," Dove said when he was about ten feet away. "Now, we know you haven't got this whole talking thing worked out, so we'll ask questions and you just answer yes or no. One word. Think you can do that?"

"Yes."

Anza jumped. The word came out hesitant and mangled, like a drunken slur. Father Santiago's head tipped to the right, his eyes half-closed.

"Okay, then." Dove wiped sweat from her brow and raised the shotgun a little higher. "Did you come here to destroy us?"

"Na-oh."

"Did you come here to hurt us?"

"No." The word came out clearer this time, more confident.

"Did you come here to take over our bodies?"

"No."

Anza wondered what would happen if they got through all the possibilities they'd come up with and still hadn't figured out what the things wanted. She wondered how long they could narrow things down before they had to give up.

"Did you come here to learn about humans?"

"Yes."

Dove swallowed before she asked the next question. "Do you plan on living here? For good?"

It didn't answer for a moment then replied, "Yes."

"Are there more of you? Aside from the ones who are in our people and in the animals around here?"

"Yes."

Dove gestured at the orb. "And this thing I'm looking at. Is this how you communicate with the ones who aren't in people? Or animals? Am I talking to them now?"

"Yes."

"This thing you infect us with, does it get passed along when someone has a baby?" When it said nothing, Dove added, "Reproduces?"

"Yes."

Dove turned to Anza. "My arms are getting tired. You wanna hold this?"

Anza took the shotgun, careful to keep her finger off the trigger. The lights inside the orb drifted, concentrating on the side closest to her. She tried to see eyes in that glow, but it resembled nothing more conscious than a candle flame.

Dove squatted, crouching to eye level with the orb. "The things you make our bodies do. Are those... tests? Is that how you learn about us?"

"Yes."

"And when you do enough of those tests, will you be able to talk with us? Through our bodies? Better than you can now?"

"Yes."

Anza thought she heard a little excitement, something new shining under the flat, garbled tone.

Dove nodded. "Mm-hm. Well, let me explain something. I know you want to talk. And we want to talk to you. But these things you've been doing are scaring people. You've seen that, right?"

"Yes."

"These people, in this town, they aren't ready for this. They'll destroy each other before you ever get a chance to really talk to us. Do you understand?"

"No."

Anza sighed. "What you're doing scares people. And when people are scared, they do stupid things." She paused. "Were you with George Esquivel when he died?"

"Yes. Yes *sa-ad*." The last word was mangled, almost unrecognizable, but even if she hadn't been able to decipher the language, Anza would have understood the anguish in its voice.

Dove stared up at her, unnerved. She cleared her throat. "Well, if you keep doing the things you've been doing, there'll be a lot more like that. A lot more people like George Esquivel. They'll be killed, and you won't learn what you want to learn from us." She took a deep breath. "Now, I'm guessing you won't go back where you came from."

Silence.

Dove frowned. "Or you *can't*. Is that right?"

"Yes."

"Well, then, I got a compromise for you. You still see and hear what we do even when people aren't having fits, right?"

"Yes."

"Here's my proposal. You go quiet. You stop making people do things. You stop making people have fits. You wait, and you watch. You pass along to the next generation, and the one after that. You learn, and you take the time to figure out how we work. It's pretty damn clear there's things you're having a hard time understanding about us. Can you... go dormant, keep quiet, watch us for a while?"

"Yes."

Dove closed her eyes. "Here's my offer. You do that. Stay quiet. For... sixty years. Sixty times around the sun. In exchange, Anza and Father Santiago and I will keep your secret. We'll hide this thing, which is obviously important to you, if you're keeping it underground. You watch and learn, and in sixty years, you can speak again." She paused, then in a rush, she added something she and Anza hadn't talked about before. "And not the next generation. Not the children of the people infected now. Only the ones that come later, only talk through them. Do we have an agreement?"

Anza held her breath, listening only to her heartbeat thrumming in her ears as the silence stretched out.

"Yes."

Anza and Dove exchanged a look. Both glanced at Father Santiago, as though to make sure he still couldn't hear them. Then Anza turned back to the orb. "One last thing. Something else we'd like you to do, to help us protect your secret. To help this town survive. You might not like it, but believe me when I say it needs to be done."

And Anza told it what had to happen, the part they hadn't told Santiago before coming down into the cave. Her part of the plan. She averted her eyes as she spoke, ashamed of what they were asking.

It took another long moment to answer. "Yes."

Dove exhaled. She stood, suddenly looking very tired. "Thank you." She took Father Santiago by the arm and began leading him back across the cavern.

"Wait." Anza stared at the orb. "I don't know if you can answer this. But... why didn't you infect me?"

Father Santiago made a string of guttural syllables before going silent. Then, as Anza watched, a cloud of red dust rose from the orb. It swirled, forming a glowing shape in the air. She squinted, trying to understand what she was seeing. It could almost have been a ram's head, with curling horns and a tapering nose.

"Goddamn." Dove drifted back to the orb, staring up at the image. Her eyes widened.

"What is it?" Anza asked, trying to understand what Dove saw.

"This..." Her fingers traced the shape in the air. "This is a pelvis. A reproductive system. If..."

"What?" Anza asked. Her heart fluttered in her chest as she imagined what Dove might see there. A tumor or—

"I can't tell from this, but... What your mama had, the thing that made her bleed out, it was a congenital defect. Pelvic malformation. Maybe they're trying to tell us..."

"You're saying... I have the same thing?" Anza asked, her head spinning.

Dove turned away from the image. "If that's true, and if you'd tried to carry that pregnancy to term... God." She hid her face, breath hitching in a sob. "Could have lost you too."

"Dove... Dove, it's okay. I'm okay." Anza touched the other woman's shoulder.

"Yeah." She wiped her face and took a deep breath, all business again.

Anza smiled. "This is good. Don't you see?"

"What?"

"It's not just fertility. I mean, they don't just care if I can get pregnant. They care if I survive it. They don't want us to suffer." Anza laughed, tearful. "They don't want to hurt us."

"Maybe." Dove nodded, but Anza could tell she wasn't convinced.

"What happened?"

They both jumped. Father Santiago blinked, eyes widening as he took in the cavern around him. "Is that... Oh, Lord." His hands fluttered together near his chest as though about to press together in prayer.

"I think it worked." Dove gestured at the orb. "Sixty years. It agreed."

"Then what? What does it want?" He pointed at the image above the orb, now slowly disintegrating into dust. "And what is that?"

Dove bit her lip. "Let's talk about this outside, Padre. It's time to leave."

The wall parted before Father Santiago, who walked through it on his own this time. Dove and Anza followed. As the wall grew shut behind her, Anza turned back for one last glimpse. The cavern stretched red and glowing in front of her. In the distance, the orb shone like a tiny star. It seemed to watch her for a moment. Then the wall closed, and she stood in darkness again.

CHAPTER 39: 2020

Alonzo opened his eyes to Colin trying to talk on the phone quietly enough not to wake him. "Okay, okay. Thanks. Yeah." He hung up and noticed Alonzo watching him. "Sorry."

"Don't be. Come back." He held out an arm until Colin wrapped around him, head on his shoulder. "How long was I asleep?"

"All night. Close to sixteen hours."

"Man, I don't know what's wrong with me."

Colin hugged him tighter. "Sonia crashed early too. She says there's a lot of Galina descendants in town. She seemed to think the, you know, the Ones are talking to each other. It made her tired."

"Makes sense. Gotta be getting their energy from somewhere. Little vampire fuckers." Then he remembered the One who had spoken in the church the day before. He thought about that loneliness behind Sonia's eyes, and he felt a twinge of guilt. He lifted his head and squinted at the sliver of daylight coming through the blackout curtains. "Speaking of which, is there any food within arms' reach? I'm really torn between wanting to eat and wanting to cuddle."

"Might still be some granola bars next to the bed."

Alonzo searched for a minute before giving up and sinking back on the pillow. "Never mind. Food later." Blinking, he remembered what had woken him. "What was the call?"

"Oh, county records office. They found a will for Father Santiago. He didn't have much when he died, since his house and everything was Church property. But he had some personal effects, mostly books, and he left them all to someone in Galina named Esperanza Kearney."

"She likes to be called Anza," Alonzo muttered, barely listening. Then he thought about what he'd just said and tensed.

Colin sat up. "What?"

"She prefers Anza," he said slowly. He tasted that name. It was familiar but not one he'd ever said aloud.

"How do you know her?"

Alonzo pushed himself up on his elbows. "I don't. I just knew... Anza, not Esperanza." He sat all the way up, rubbing his eyes. *Long hair, waist-long, black as a crow's wing, and silky between his fingers.* "Oh Jesus."

"Hey, hey, it's okay." Colin's weight shifted in front of him. His hands rested on Alonzo's arms. "I'm here. You're okay. What's going on?"

"I remember something. But I don't think it happened to me." He didn't think he'd ever mentioned it to anyone. It was such a limited, insignificant image, nothing close to a story. But it had been with him his entire life, passing behind his eyes just on the cusp of sleep, flitting through dreams, sometimes stopping him in the middle of a task. He'd written it off as something he'd seen when he was a small child, something that had imprinted for no particular reason.

The memory was of a girl, perhaps sixteen, with a waterfall of gorgeous hair spilling out from beneath a battered cowboy hat. She sat on the sidewalk beside him, face turned so he saw her only in three-quarter profile. Her dusty brown boots were half-covered with heavy jeans. Her gingham shirt, too big, was rolled up at the sleeves. She watched something else, and he wished she would pay attention to him instead.

That was it—a split-second image with no story or meaning to go with it. But now the name Anza hung over the memory, superimposed like subtitles on a screen.

"Do you have any pictures?" Alonzo asked. "Of the ones who would have been teenagers at the time? Around Grandfather Fernando's age?"

"Yeah." Colin snatched the laptop off the table and returned to the bed. "I scanned the 1959 yearbook. It was the last one they did before the school closed."

He clicked and scrolled until he found the pictures, turning the screen so they could both see. Alonzo spotted Grandfather Fernando, skinny and awkward in his starched Sunday-best shirt and pomade-stiff hair. One year back, in the sophomores, he saw her.

"There she is. Anza."

She didn't smile at the camera, brown eyes wide and serious. Every other girl on the page had her hair curled and bobbed in sculpted 1950s styles, but hers hung in a thick braid over her shoulder. Colin studied the picture for a moment before looking up again. Alonzo saw in his eyes that he didn't understand.

He took a quavering breath. "I think Grandfather Fernando was in love with her. And I think he kept that a secret until the day he died." Alonzo stared at the picture, and traces of love lingered like an aftertaste.

"DUDE, THIS BETTER BE good. I'm so tired." Sonia followed Colin down the hall to his room.

She expected Alonzo to be up and dressed, ready for the day, but he still sat half covered by blankets, back propped against the bed's headboard. His expression was so dazed, she thought for a moment that he might be Statuing, before he lifted his head to give her a haunted look.

"What happened?"

Colin picked up his laptop. "I'm going to show you a picture, and I want you to tell me how you feel."

"You know, there was a time when I would have asked why, but not anymore." She dropped into one of the room's stiff chairs. "Shoot."

Colin set the laptop in front of her. "This one," he said, pointing at the first in a row of old yearbook pictures.

He needn't have bothered to point. Sonia's eyes locked on that girl immediately.

"Tell me what you're thinking, Sonia."

"I'm thinking..." She swallowed. "I want to hurt this girl. I want to kill her. And I don't know why."

Alonzo leaned forward. Dark circles stood out under his eyes. "Those things your grandfather did. Belittling your dad and all that. Being a violent, racist prick. Did you actually see those things happen?"

"I don't..." Her mind raced. What had she actually seen? All that came to mind was Richie and her dad at the table at Thanksgiving, no harsh words exchanged, just passing the gravy. "I don't know."

"Do you actually remember finding things out about your grandfather?" Alonzo asked, voice rough.

"No." *Don't say it,* she thought, even though she couldn't quite focus on what she was scared of hearing. *Please don't say it.*

But he did anyway. "Or do you just remember because your dad and Richie did?"

"No."

"What else do you remember from Richie?" Colin asked. "Things you didn't see yourself?"

"Stop!" She started to gasp, breathing quickly, although none of the oxygen seemed to get through. So many moments, she knew now, so many little flashes of bloodied knuckles from punches she'd never thrown and the ringing sound of slapping a woman she'd never met. And Billie Holiday, Lady Day—she'd *always* loved her music, before she ever heard it, and then once she did, it felt like coming home…

"Sonia, Sonia, come on, breathe." Alonzo's voice floated down to her as though through water. Someone pushed her face down between her knees, sending the blood rushing back to her head.

The buzzing sound in her ears gradually cleared. As soon as she trusted herself to sit upright, she pulled herself up and leaned on the table. Colin and Alonzo both watched her, arms slightly out-stretched as though to stop her from tumbling to the ground. "He's always been there," she whispered. "He's always been… I always knew how bad he was. Even without the stories, I knew." She tapped her chest, trying to make them understand. "When I'm bad, when I want to hurt people, that's him trying to get out."

"No. Richie's dead. Those are just some old memories, just left-over pieces," Alonzo said. "Just little things that got passed down, with this other thing."

"It's not just Richie. If this works the way I think it does, there's some of your dad too," Colin added.

"Yeah," Sonia choked, nodding and trying to smile. "He was good. He wasn't Richie." There was a memory she'd always wondered about, one of her mother as a very young woman, dancing. She'd always found it odd that her mother seemed so much younger there than in any other memory, that she was dancing in a place Sonia felt sure she'd never been. She let out a long, shaky breath. "We've always been who we are because of this, haven't we?"

Alonzo glanced at Colin, biting his lip. "I think maybe I always knew I was different, and I just didn't… didn't let myself look at it."

"But you know what that means, right?" she said, voice raspy and dry. "We're not getting rid of it. If it goes this deep, it's here to stay."

She watched the two men in front of her. She saw the fear and grief in Alonzo's eyes as he avoided looking at Colin. But Colin didn't waver; he watched the other man the same way he always had.

"Then we'll find a way to manage it," he said, with such optimism, it made her want to cry. "If you've always had it and it didn't affect your lives before, then it can be that way again."

"No," Alonzo said, staring at the floor with a sad smile. "No, it can't."

Sonia didn't want to be alone, but she stood anyway. "I'm going back to my room for a while. I need a shower." And she left them to face their changed future, as well as to contend with her own.

"I JUST THINK WE NEED to be realistic about this."

"Yeah, and, *realistically*, we know this went dormant for sixty years. Who's to say that's not going to be what happens this time? I mean, Christ, maybe they're just trying to go home." Colin focused on making the bed, picking up the clothes scattered around the floor. He didn't want to see that resignation in Alonzo's eyes.

But Lonzo wouldn't let him avoid it. He reached out and took his arm, making it impossible to look away. "Col, I need you to listen. I know there's nothing in your notes or your manuscript or anywhere else saying this is here to stay. But I *know*. Okay? I can feel it. This is going to be with me for the rest of my life. Sonia knows it too." He bit his lip. "I know you're the expert, but you need to trust where I'm coming from on this."

Colin tried to move away, but Alonzo didn't let go of his wrist. "I don't know why we're even having this conversation. I mean, we still need to find the Means. The goal hasn't changed."

"I know, but what we can hope to get out of it *has* changed." Colin saw him trying to be brave, and he didn't want to hear what was coming next. "And that's something you need to think about. Because, look, you didn't sign up for this. You don't need to feel guilty if it's too much—"

"Oh, goddammit, Lonzo, stop." Colin's face flushed, his eyes stinging.

"No. *Listen.* Don't avoid this." He saw Alonzo trying to keep it together, mostly failing. "Aside from the fact that it's going to be shitty to live with, there's also... Look, the first time we met, when we started talking and it just clicked, it was talking about the Galina Plagues that brought us together. If this thing has always been influencing me and the way I think, then maybe, on a subconscious level..."

Something fell in Colin's stomach. "What? You only love me because the goddamn parasite in your brain is telling you to? Thanks, asshole, that's a really great thing to say to me."

"That's not what I meant. I *do* really love you, and you know it. But doesn't that bother you, if this thing was a factor in us getting together? Don't you think that's going to come up at some point, the fact that there's always been this third person—or thing—here with us?"

Colin fought the urge to throw a lamp across the room. "That's great, Lonzo. How about we have every potential fight that could come up during our entire lifetimes, just in case? I mean, Jesus, did you bring this up because it was the worst possible fucking time?" He wondered why Lonzo wasn't getting mad, why he didn't snap and yell back so they could just fight, get it over with, and move on already. But he just sat there, maddeningly calm.

"This isn't just any issue. It can't wait. And that's why I need you to really think about this. Don't just dismiss what I'm saying. This goes way, way beyond anything either of us thought we were going to have to deal with. And what we have is amazing, and I love you more than anybody on earth, but we're grownups. Love doesn't conquer all, and we both know that. So..." He sniffed and wiped his nose. "I'm going to go out and find us some breakfast, and while I'm gone, I want you to think long and hard about the possibility that this is the best it's gonna get. Really think about it. Because Sonia and I can take it from here. We don't actually need an uninfected person doing the talking, if we take turns. And because I'll survive if you bail now, but I don't know if I'll be able to take it if you leave later."

He got up, grabbed the room key and his wallet, and left. Colin sat on the edge of the bed, numb. He wondered if the ringing sense of shock was what it felt like to get punched in the face. His mind rebelled against the thought of it, but he forced himself to imagine things going on like this for the next six months, the next year, or the next ten years. He pictured the dinners, parties, and vacations marred by Naming fits, moments of possession, and the agony of seeing someone else looking through Alonzo's eyes and speaking with his voice. The idea of it made Colin feel like his chest was caving in.

Then he made himself imagine the only thing harder to picture than that: packing his things, walking out of the hotel, going home to gather the rest of his stuff, and being alone for a while. Then sometime, maybe a long time later, he would find another man or another woman and let the memory fade...

His phone beeped and buzzed against the surface of the side table. It was a text from Tori: *7 pounds 8 ounces*. Beneath it was a picture of her in a hospital gown, face sweaty and exhausted, but glowing. A newborn, red and wrinkly, was curled against her chest.

Colin let out a little laugh, opening his mouth to tell Alonzo before he remembered he wasn't in the room. Then something broke. He saw with complete certainty that Alonzo was right, although he couldn't say how he knew. This wasn't ever going away.

Alonzo took about forty-five minutes to return with a bag of bagels and muffins, even though Colin knew the café was just around the corner from the hotel. "They didn't have poppyseed, so I got you banana nut," he said, passing the bag over.

"Come here. I want to show you something." He patted the edge of the bed next to him.

Alonzo sat almost warily, not as close as he would normally.

Colin held up the picture. "Look. I'm an uncle."

"Seriously?" Alonzo smiled and took the phone from him. "Wow. Newborns are ugly as sin, aren't they?"

Colin laughed. "See, I was hoping you'd say that first so I wouldn't be the only one going to hell."

Alonzo chuckled a little and handed the phone back, his smile fading. "Did you think about it?"

"Yeah." He started to take Alonzo's hand in his own, remembered the splint, and switched hands. "It's scary and disappointing and not even close to what I wanted for us."

Alonzo nodded without speaking, staring at the floor.

"But I'd rather have you like this than not at all."

"Yeah?" A touch of hope glimmered in Alonzo's eye.

"Yeah. You kidding? Man, it's not even close. And who even cares if this thing nudged you toward me when we first got together? It's still something we built, however it started. So I don't care that it's always been there." He touched Lonzo's stubbly cheek. "I told you. Your normal is my normal."

"Oh man," Alonzo sighed. "You don't know what a relief it is to hear that."

"Yeah, I do."

"You're gonna get so much sex later."

Colin laughed through the fatigue. "I better." He tilted Lonzo's chin up for a kiss. "But later. Right now, we've got Grandfather Fernando's old flame to track down."

CHAPTER 40: 1960

"**I** want to be the one to tell him." Anza stared through the windshield of Dove's truck at the empty highway winding out under the stars. They'd picked the spot right next to mile marker 201 because the land stretched so flat and empty, no one would be able to sneak up on them. If more than one car showed up, they would simply drive away.

Dove raised an eyebrow. "You think he's more likely to listen to you?"

"No." Anza swallowed. "But it was my idea. I think... I shouldn't get off easy. I should have to say it." She rubbed her palms together. They'd stopped at Dove's place to scrape off most of the mud after dropping off Father Santiago, but fine grains of silt still clung to her clothes and skin.

"Good girl." Headlights appeared on the horizon. Dove reached for her shotgun and balanced it across her lap. "Here we go."

Anza recognized Pastor Benjamin's car. Her heart thudded in her throat as the sedan pulled over on the highway's opposite shoulder.

"Looks like he brought Richie with him," Dove muttered.

Richie Rollins and two of the Foster brothers climbed out along with Pastor Ben. Their hands hovered near the holsters on their hips.

"Too much of a coward to come by himself." Anza opened the truck door. "Come on."

"Mrs. McNally. Miss Kearney. I must say, it doesn't seem safe for two ladies to be out alone on a night like this." Pastor Benjamin's voice dripped with false, honeyed concern. The moon shone brightly enough for Anza to get a good look at his face. His compassion seemed so obviously practiced, so artificial. She wondered how anyone in the congregation had ever bought into the act. She wondered if he believed it himself.

"We're fine, thank you very much," Dove said, raising the shotgun just a hair.

"So. You have something to tell me about the Plagues? Something so important, it couldn't wait for morning?" He folded his thick fingers together, resting them across his middle.

Behind him, Richie leered and toyed with his belt as he stared at Anza. It made her skin feel prickly and dirty.

She stood tall and cleared her throat. "The Plagues are going to be over tomorrow, Pastor Ben. We made a deal with the things that brought 'em here. They're going to stop messing with folks."

"A deal?" It came out like a purr, filled satisfaction she didn't quite understand. "A deal with the devil. So that tomorrow, you and your kind will be free of the Plagues, and godly people will continue to suffer." His eyes shone with fatherly disapproval.

"Not just my kind. Everyone. Everyone gets better tomorrow." Anza took a deep breath. "But there's a condition. You and Richie and anyone else involved in killing George or anyone else in town, you leave tonight. If you don't leave or if you ever set foot in Galina again..." She wavered, wondering if she'd crossed some terrible line or if there was another way she hadn't seen before. But then she felt Dove's presence at her shoulder, and she pressed on. "If you don't leave Galina, you'll Statue, and you won't ever come out of it. They'll just hold you there like that forever, so you can't hurt anybody else."

Richie spat on the ground. "What a crock of horseshit."

The compassion melted from Pastor Benjamin's face. "Why should we believe you?"

Dove snorted. "Personally, I kinda hope you don't. I hope you stay put and see what happens." She shrugged. "But Anza here is a better soul than I am. She thought you deserved a fair warning."

Benjamin's eyes widened. It occurred to Anza that no one had ever been afraid of her before. It was a strange sensation, awful, but... "My god," he said. "You really have made a deal with the devil."

"It's not the devil, Pastor Ben," Anza said. "It's just... something else. Something alive but not like us. I don't think they mean us harm. I mean..." She swallowed. "The only reason they'll hurt any of you still here tomorrow is because we asked them to."

Richie and J.D. Foster exchanged a glance, fear overcoming their swagger.

"Not the devil? You've seen what's happened to the people of this town. How could that be anything but the devil's work?" Pastor Benjamin asked. "You lie to yourself all you want, Esperanza Kearney, but I won't bow before Satan. I won't." Then, for just a moment, he seemed lost, young, and alone.

"Well, we delivered the message. Now we'll be going," Dove said, nudging Anza toward the truck. Richie reached for his holster, but Dove snapped the shotgun up toward him. "Give me an excuse, Richie. Go on."

His hand relaxed and dropped to his side. He stared not at Dove but at Anza, and his hatred burned like a July afternoon. Anza almost wished Dove would pull the trigger.

"God protects his own, Esperanza," Pastor Benjamin called as she climbed back into Dove's truck. "You'll see. No deal with the devil can penetrate God's armor."

The four men still stood in the middle of the road as Dove started up the truck. "Damn fools," she said as she drove away. "Well, I suppose it doesn't matter. We'll be rid of them tomorrow, one way or another."

ANZA SLEPT ALMOST UNTIL noon after she and Dove got back from their meeting with Pastor Benjamin. The phone rang several times. First, it was someone telling Dove the county had finally sent out cars full of officers, and that they were setting about putting Galina back in order. The second call was from Dad.

"I'm fine, Dad, I promise. I wasn't anywhere near most of the bad stuff that happened."

"I should have been there," he fretted. "We were out looking for work all day, and no one at Tony's brother's house was there to take a message. There wasn't anything in the paper, so I didn't know until Bert called—"

"Dad, Dad, stop. It's okay. We're all okay. Did you get a job?"

"What?" he asked, sounding blank. "Oh. Yeah, yeah, I did. So did Tony." Then, like the news didn't matter, he added, "I'm coming right home, okay? Stay with Dove until then."

Anza promised to stay safe and hung up. Dove stood in the doorway to the kitchen. "Didn't tell him about the house?"

Anza shook her head. "No sense making him more upset. He'll find out soon enough."

Dove was silent for a moment. "Maybe we should go see if they kept their end of the bargain. While we're waiting."

Anza bit her lip and nodded. She didn't really want to see, but she knew they would have to face what they'd done.

Beige Cochise County Sheriff's Department cars sat parked near intersections all over town. Officers directed traffic and watched the streets. They seemed like humorless men, all with the same mustache and sunglasses. Anza wondered how long they would need to be in Galina.

Dove parked a short distance from Pastor Benjamin's church, and they got out to walk the rest of the way. Dove had her revolver hidden under the tail of her shirt, just in case, but three patrolmen were within shouting distance.

As they approached the church, an ambulance pulled up in front. "Looks like we're just in time," Dove said.

Someone inside the church wept, letting out loud, keening sobs. Anza and Dove waited with a cluster of other onlookers as paramedics went inside with a stretcher. A few minutes later, they brought Pastor Benjamin out.

He lay in an awkward Statue pose, tipped on his side, one arm stretching out behind his back. His lips were parted, as though he'd frozen mid-sentence. Anza recognized the blank emptiness in his eyes as the expression of someone in the midst of a fit.

"True believer," Dove said in a low voice. "I wondered."

Pastor Ben's wife followed the stretcher into the ambulance while several female members of the congregation wailed and wiped their eyes. One of them was Paula's mother.

"What happened?" someone in the crowd asked her.

"We thought it was just another fit," she sniffed. "But it never stopped. It started around sunup, when we were holding a vigil. But it's been hours, and he's still..."

"Hey, that's interesting," Dove said, loudly enough for the crowd to hear. "Do you know, I don't think I've seen one single person have a fit since the wee hours of the morning."

People turned and looked at her.

"Almost like the Plagues went away as soon as he stopped talking." Dove turned to Anza and made an exaggerated shrug. "Guess we'll have to wait and see, won't we?"

"Whore," Paula's mother spat as they walked away. But Anza heard the murmurs of the crowd behind them. She knew people would go out and ask and search for signs. Then they would find that the Plagues had indeed ended.

Even though she knew he must have run in the night, Anza watched for Richie. She thought she would probably spend the rest of her life checking crowds for his face.

They found Father Santiago helping the Rodriguez sisters sweep up the glass in the cantina.

"Hey there, Padre," Dove said.

"Hello, Dove. Anza." He set aside the broom. "I'll be back in a moment."

He followed them outside. "Did you hear about Pastor Benjamin?"

Dove jerked a thumb over her shoulder. "Saw him. They just loaded him up into an ambulance and carted him off."

He frowned. "I thought maybe it wasn't honoring our agreement. But I haven't seen anyone else have a fit, so…"

"Maybe it just understood what had to happen. Maybe it knew we wouldn't be able to hide it with Benjamin interfering."

"Small price to pay," Anza said. The words came out sounding angrier than she'd intended.

Father Santiago blinked at her in surprise. Something flickered over his face, some hint of doubt or questioning. But then he turned back to Dove. "We'll all keep an eye out, yes? Make sure the fits aren't still happening?"

"Yeah," Dove said, nodding. "Me and Anza can go ask around."

He returned to the cantina as Dove and Anza wandered past Millie's Café.

"You sure he wouldn't be able to deal with the truth?" Anza asked as they passed the saloon and the bank.

Dove shrugged. "Maybe. But why burden him with it?"

"We're okay. Least, I am."

"Well, young Anza, he's a man. Men can afford to be merciful. We can't." She gripped Anza's shoulder and turned her so they stood eye to eye. "You remember that, girl. The high road is a luxury women can't afford. No matter where you and your daddy go, no matter what you do in this world, you don't forget that."

Anza nodded. "I won't."

They carried on down Main Street. Anza watched the people go by. Some smiled, some met her gaze with grim nods, and still others turned away in shame. She stared at the street beneath their feet, the broken and burned buildings, the debris on the pavement. She drank it all in because, even though she knew she and Dad would pass through the town at least once more before they left, even though she knew she would be back to see Dove, it still felt like the last time.

They reached the end of Main Street, circling around to Dove's truck. She drove back to her little house on the hillside. Anza watched in the side mirror, not blinking until Galina vanished behind her.

CHAPTER 41: 2020

"So you think Anza was one of the mystery females?" Sonia asked. She still had to bite back a snarl at the thought of the girl. It wasn't clear in her mind what Esperanza Kearney had done to make Richie hate her so, but she knew it was humiliation of some sort. The memories carried the acrid tang of male powerlessness in the face of female disdain.

Colin shrugged. "Maybe. She and Santiago might have been close for some other reason, but either way, if she knew him well enough to inherit all his stuff, then she'll know more about who he was involved with than anyone else."

"And she would have been about sixteen during the Plagues, right?"

"Right."

"Priest, teenage girl... I dunno, guys, I'm worried there's some ickiness here."

Alonzo flinched. "Let's hope not. Doesn't matter, though. She's our only lead."

They took the stairs out of the hotel, knowing from the previous day that the elevator took too long. A lot of the tension seemed to have lifted from Colin and Alonzo. Sonia didn't know what they'd talked about while she cried in her own room, but she could guess. It made her think about the talk she would need to have with Dylan at some point.

Two of the hotel staff hovered near the glass doors of the lobby, peering outside and muttering to themselves. One of them looked like she wanted to say something to the three of them as they passed, but she kept her mouth shut.

Colin went through first, taking two or three steps before freezing and recoiling. "Jesus fucking Christ."

Almost immediately, Sonia saw what he'd reacted to. The streets were full of hosts carrying Ones. She knew it because they all stood statue-still, staring motionless at the three of them. She recognized the mom with the young kids from yesterday, the woman in the designer jeans, and the guy with the Mohawk. Other people, whom she assumed were just regular residents, threaded their way timidly through the frozen bodies. Some half smiled and frowned as though hearing a joke they didn't quite get.

"Anyone else suddenly in the mood to watch *The Birds*?" Sonia asked.

Alonzo stood with his hands bunched into fists, as if ready to fight but unsure who to aim for. "Why aren't we frozen too?"

"Maybe they know we're close." Colin spoke in a whisper for no reason Sonia could see.

"Well, we better get moving and find her then," she replied.

They made their way to the car, giving the hosts a wide berth. She half expected them to attack right as she opened the doors, like some horror movie. Instead, they just turned and patiently watched as the three of them drove away.

IT TOOK SOME DIGGING through the county's archaic paper catalog system, but they finally found a few public documents. Colin scribbled down the requests, and a few minutes later, the clerk delivered a handful of folders to the desk in the tiny reading room.

The first record was a birth certificate for Esperanza Kearney, born to Sean and Elena Kearney. Nothing helpful there. The second was a census record from when she was six, including the address where she lived with her father. Colin wrote it down, even though he was pretty sure all of the old houses in that part of town had been knocked down and replaced.

Finally, there was another will. "Dove Maria McNally, nee Murphy."

Sonia let out an almost animal growl. "Agh, that name fucking pisses me off too. This is like really specific PMS."

"Not me. That one feels... intimidating," Alonzo said, a distant look in his eye. "But like it's someone I respect."

"She left her house, the contents of her bank account, and all personal effects to Esperanza Kearney. It's witnessed and dated March, 1982."

"So we've got one man and one woman leaving all their shit to a younger woman. Think these are our First Speakers?" Sonia asked.

"I don't know, but this address is a lot more promising than the house she lived in as a kid." Colin rose from the little table. "Let's go check it out."

"WHAT IF SHE'S THERE?" Sonia asked, staring out the window. They turned off the highway and onto a meandering dirt road winding its way around the base of the mesa. Here and there were trailers and newer houses, but there were also crumbling adobe buildings and even a tarpaper shack surrounded by fallen debris.

"Isn't that what we want?" Alonzo asked.

"Yeah, I guess, but... I'm just thinking about it. If she's really there and she has the Means or she knows where it is, then what?"

"Well, then, for better or worse, we get some answers." Colin met her eyes in the rearview mirror for just a moment before looking away.

"I hope so. But I guess I just haven't..." She trailed off as the car bumped around another curve in the road. Several people stood along the road's shoulder, staring at the car as it went by. None were dressed for hiking or walking outside for any length of time.

"Think they're watching this? Through us?" Alonzo asked.

"Yeah," Sonia said, that pressure behind the eyes flaring again. "I think they're depending on us." She laughed. "How fucking scary is that, if we're the ones people are depending on? If we're the ones leading?"

"Could be a lot worse, you know," Colin said. "In fact, you two leading the way... I can't think of anyone better."

He meant it, Sonia realized. He really meant it. He thought she was good enough, smart enough, and strong enough to be doing something this important.

That one part of her, that part that was Richie, sneered and snarled, whispering that she was wrong, that everyone was always thinking less of her, and that Colin didn't really mean it—

Shut the fuck up, she told that part of herself, and it fell silent. She *did* belong here. She knew it. "Pull over."

Alonzo glanced back. "You okay?"

"Yeah. There's just something I want to do before we get there."

Colin pulled to the side of the road. Sonia stepped out, phone in hand.

Her mom picked up on the first ring. "Sonia?" she asked, voice reedy with worry.

"Mom, bring Dylan to... wait. Is he there? Can you put him on speaker?"

"One second," her mom said.

Then Dylan said, "Mom?"

Sonia's throat tightened so much that she couldn't speak for a moment. "Hey, baby," she said at last. "Mom? Bring Dylan to Galina."

"I'm coming to see you?" he asked. She could tell from his voice that he was smiling.

"Are you sure?" her mom asked.

"Yeah. Yeah, I'm sure. Dylan, we're together from now on, okay?"

"Did you find out how to make us better?"

Sonia stared out across the desert, this place she remembered down to her bones. "No. I don't think so. I think we're just going to be like this from now on, kiddo. But that's okay. We'll have each other, and I think... I think we'll also have other people like us."

"Okay. Grandma, can we go now?"

Sonia said goodbye and climbed back into the car.

Alonzo turned back to face her. "You okay?"

She nodded and wiped her eyes. "Yeah. Yeah, I'm good." She smiled. "Let's go."

"THIS IS IT."

The house was an old adobe rectangle painted plain beige. The front yard and driveway were bare and undecorated but also free of weeds and trash. An old white truck sat parked beside the house. Two pots of red geraniums, the only color in sight, grew on the front porch on either side of the door.

No one answered the knock at the front door. They went around to the back, where a little barn and toolshed stood. There, Colin saw an old woman with straight white hair trailing down her back. She wore a sunhat and a long-sleeved denim shirt. She lifted some hay with the tines of a pitchfork, tossing it over the barn's stall doors. Inside the stall, a horse nickered.

Colin cleared his throat. "Excuse me?"

She turned, shielding her eyes and balancing the end of the pitchfork against the ground. "Yes?"

"I'm looking for Esperanza Kearney."

"That's me. Folks call me Anza, though." She was small-boned, with large brown eyes. Sun and time had creased her features, but Colin still recognized traces of the girl from the yearbook photo.

"Oh my god," Alonzo whispered.

On Colin's other side, Sonia covered her mouth and took a step back.

"We..." Colin gestured at the other two. "All of us came to see you. We wanted to ask you some questions about what happened in Galina sixty years ago."

She regarded them for a long moment. "You're the third generation, aren't you? Has it started again?"

"Yes." Colin's heart pounded. Alonzo's hand gripped his shoulder.

"What are your names?"

Alonzo hesitated for only a second before he stepped forward to shake her hand. "Alonzo Cardenas."

"Cardenas? Fernando Cardenas's—what? Grandson, it must be? Oh, I knew your grandfather well." Colin caught a wicked little edge in her smile and saw something of the story there.

"I know," Alonzo said, blushing a little. "I think I might remember some of it."

"Oh dear. Well, the less said about that, the better." She turned to Sonia. "And you?"

Sonia took her hand, a little stiff. "Sonia Rollins. I know Grandpa Richie was a piece of shit, so you don't have to pretend otherwise." Her jaw muscles worked and tensed. Colin almost heard the fight there, the instinctive anger working against her other reactions to Anza's presence.

"What a relief," Anza said, her mouth twisting into a wry almost-smile. She turned to Colin. "And you?"

"Colin Ayres. I'm not from Galina. I'm just... I just need to be here."

"Well then"—Anza tossed the pitchfork aside—"you better come inside. I owe you a lot of explanations. And also an apology." She must have sensed their confusion. "You'll understand why once I've told you everything."

CHAPTER 42: 2020

"So, you see, that's why I said I owe you an apology," Anza said as she finished the story of the cave and her last days in Galina. "As pathetic as that sounds under these circumstances. We traded your future for our own. Our Plagues ended, but we knew Galina's grandchildren and great-grandchildren would pick up where we left off." Her eyes shone with guilt. "We wrote you into this story long before you were born, and for that, I can't say how sorry I am."

Silence stretched out between them.

"Why the third generation?" Alonzo asked at last.

Anza smiled without humor. "It wasn't for any rational reason. I wish there was a good reason it had to start with you and not your parents or your children, but there wasn't. Dove just did what she thought Elena would have wanted. She asked for enough time for me to have my own children if I chose, for me to live a long life. But she didn't want it to be so long that I wouldn't still be around. For you." She paused. "She worried about you, the third generation, a lot. Especially in those last few years."

"What happened? After that night in the cave?" Colin asked.

Anza shrugged. "Nothing important to why we're here. Dad and I left, like about half the folks in town. Dove and Father Santiago stayed. I came back to see them whenever I could." She stared at her glass of tea. "I went to medical school, became a doctor. An epidemiologist. I had a good career. Nothing earth-shattering but good. Got to travel, see the world, save some lives. I came back here to be with Dove in her last days. She did two rounds of chemo before she called it off, said she was ready to die in her own home. I was with her at the end. She thought I was my mama." Her eyes went distant for a moment. "And then she left me this house. I think she knew someone should be here. For you. We weren't sure how the third generation would find the thing in the cave. The Means, you call it? But we both figured it made sense to keep it close by."

Colin asked the question he'd been dreading. "What happened to Pastor Benjamin?"

"He died in a state mental institution. He never regained the ability to move, speak, or do anything else." There wasn't a trace of pity in her gaze. "Remember that. They destroyed a life. They'd have done the same to Richie and his boys, too, if they hadn't fled. They're capable of that. Then again, they only did that when we asked them to. Make of that what you will."

"You ever have kids?" Sonia asked, filling another long silence.

"No. Oh, I could have adopted or even just had a C-section and had my own. But I didn't dare. Not with knowing that fertility was important to them but not knowing why."

Alonzo frowned. "Why not? I mean, you know what these things are. You know what they want."

"Do I?" She sipped her tea. "I don't think I know anything at all about what they want. I don't know anything at all about what kind of world they'll create or what they'll do to us. I suspect their motives are about as comprehensible to us as ours are to ants." She shrugged. "All I know is what they've told us. And people lie, so why should we assume they can't... or won't?"

"Well, the fertility thing at least was pretty simple," Alonzo said, uneasy. "They just wanted to make sure their own offspring would be safe."

Anza said nothing for a long moment. "That does seem to be the case now, talking to you. But it wasn't clear for me. Besides, there's a lot more we don't know about what they're planning." She paused. "It was the choice I made, and I don't regret it."

"I guess it's up to us to find out what they want," Sonia said.

Anza nodded. "Yes. And I have something you'll need."

She heaved herself to her feet, her birdlike frame tottering slightly as she disappeared down the hallway. A minute later, she came back with a wooden box. "It looks heavy, but it's not. I think it's hollow."

Anza opened the box and lifted out a dark-red orb. Alonzo let out a little gasp.

"Fuck me, it's real," Sonia muttered.

"Why is it here?" Colin asked.

Anza set it on the coffee table like some absurd living room decoration. "When I heard about a new housing development going in on the mesa, I took Father Santiago back down into the cavern. It wasn't this latest development, the one that failed. It was an older one that never got off the ground. But I thought it would, back then. They were going to pave right over the entrance and the cactus patch, you see, and I didn't want us to be unable to reach it. I felt terrible, taking Santiago down there. He was nearly eighty at the time and certainly in no shape to go spelunking. But of course, I needed someone who was infected to get through the wall. It seemed to be asleep until Santiago touched it. Then it woke up. We explained the situation, and they let us take it." She gazed at it for a moment. "It's funny. Movies always show them coming in big shiny spaceships. But their ship was nothing like that. Just red dust falling from a cloud, with no one outside of Galina the wiser."

"Is this... Are their people in there?" Colin asked.

"No. It's a transmitter. Or a transmitter and receiver. Back then, the metaphor they used to explain it involved letters. Now, I suppose it would be email." Her lips curled in a sad smile as her eyes turned upward. "I think they've been waiting up there, all this time. Just more dust floating around our satellites or through the atmosphere. Waiting for their children and grandchildren to give them a call."

"Yeah," Sonia said. "I can feel it. They aren't in here, but..."

Alonzo nodded along with her.

Anza sat back in her armchair and gestured at the orb. "So, what are you going to do now? Go public? Tell the government?"

Colin and Alonzo looked at each other.

"We haven't decided yet. But no, I don't think so," Colin answered.

"Good," Anza said. "Wouldn't trust this administration not to disappear the lot of you, the way they do business. Keep it small. Quiet."

"First thing we gotta do is make contact. Then we'll see." Sonia gave the orb a look Colin couldn't quite place, some mix of anger and empathy.

"What do you think we should do?" Alonzo asked.

Anza sipped her sun tea. "Oh, I don't know. I've had so many thoughts about that thing over the years. And who knows what they really want, when all's said and done?" She paused, gaze traveling slowly across Sonia's and Alonzo's faces. "It's in your hands now. You two, you were born for this. You'll figure it out."

She stared out the window for a long time. Colin looked at the white hair spilling over her shoulders, trying to imagine the sixteen-year-old girl she'd been, the terrors she'd faced back when that hair was dark.

After a moment, Anza shook herself and followed Sonia's gaze to the bookshelf. "That was the first book Dove ever gave me."

Colin turned to see a battered old copy of *I, Robot* sitting on a little stand apart from the rest of the paperbacks. "In retrospect, I suppose *War of the Worlds* would have been more appropriate. Or *Day of the Triffids*."

"Let's hope not," Colin said.

She smiled, and for just a moment, she was young again. "Indeed." Her face went serious. "But I guess that's not up to us, is it?"

As Anza showed them to the door, Alonzo turned back to face her. "Thank you for buying us time. Even if that's all it ended up being." He glanced at Colin then back at her. "Even if it all ends now, it's more than we would have had without you. You represented us well."

"I tried," she said, voice heavy with regret. "Now it's your turn." She touched Alonzo's cheek. Then she showed them outside and shut the door without another word.

"ARE YOU SURE YOU WANT to do this?" Colin asked. The three of them sat in their Bisbee hotel room, the red orb at the center of the table. Alonzo knew that if he opened the curtains, he would see droves of hosts standing in the street. Even more had arrived between when they'd left Bisbee and when they'd returned, joining the frozen gathering outside the hotel. Cops had been trying to shoo people away, but even they seemed to understand on some level that the situation was beyond them and hadn't tried to remove anyone by force.

"Yeah. They've been waiting a long time," Alonzo replied. He held Colin's hand under the table, running a thumb over his knuckles.

Sonia nodded. "I'm sure. Besides, I'm a little curious to see what happens."

"Okay." Colin moved farther back from the table, held up his phone, and started recording. "I'll be here."

Sonia and Alonzo exchanged a glance along with quick, tense smiles.

"Ready?" he asked.

"Yeah."

Then both placed their hands on the orb.

The glow started gradually, just a flicker in the center. It expanded like red flame licking the inside of a hollow globe. It grew warm beneath Alonzo's hands. He heard something, whispers at the back of his mind, growing louder and louder. The air in the room thrummed, almost vibrating. Sonia's eyes widened, then—

Blink.

Colin had shifted position slightly, holding his phone a little closer to Alonzo's face.

"How long was I out?" Alonzo asked.

"About two minutes," Colin said. "Nothing happened."

Yes, it did, Alonzo thought. *Didn't he feel it?* The room buzzed and hummed around him. He was about to say something when Sonia looked up and smiled.

"Hello, Alonzo. It's wonderful to finally speak with you."

Alonzo's mouth opened of its own accord. "And you, as well, Sonia. These Ones are honored."

Sonia's eyes widened, and one hand fluttered to her lips. "Holy shit. I was awake for that."

"Me too," Alonzo replied, and it was his own voice again, his own movements.

Sonia's features instantly rearranged themselves into a serene, placid expression he'd never seen on her before. "We apologize greatly for the blackouts. When still cut off from our Hive and each other, we were unable to achieve simultaneous consciousness with our hosts. Now, though, we can finally speak to each other."

"Who am I speaking with right now?" Alonzo asked.

He jumped when the reply came from his own mouth. "We don't have a name that can be translated with any accuracy. The closest term would be 'the Hive,' although that has a negative connotation in your culture." His neck turned, and he felt his lips twitch up in a smile. It was the strangest sensation; when he and Sonia had touched hands and Statued, he'd felt powerless, possessed, like a by-stander trapped in his own body. Now, though, having the Ones move and speak through him was more like a sneeze—a compulsion he couldn't quite resist but not like something he was being forced to do against his will. "Hello, Colin. We're pleased to be able to speak with you again. Although if you're here to protect Alonzo and Sonia, you should understand that they're completely safe. We would never allow them to come to harm."

He heard his own voice as though in a recording. It was his—he recognized it, but it wasn't quite right. That horrible cut-and-paste rhythm was gone, though, replaced with smooth, confident tones. He *liked* that voice, he realized, and enjoyed hearing it.

Colin swallowed. "I'm... I don't think you'd hurt them. I'm not really here to protect them. I'm here more as a witness." He gestured with his phone.

"Very good. This is indeed a historic day."

"Are you Those of Origin?" Alonzo asked.

"Yes and no. That term refers to the main Hive, which is in earth's atmosphere. You're talking to us now. But we're also all of the Others, all of those born into human bodies, and those born into coyotes and birds and lizards and every other life-form we've touched." Hive-Sonia made a liquid gesture toward the window. "All of those who came back to Galina and the Ones who are still far away. You're talking to all of us, now that we're connected again."

After a pause, Sonia's personality returned to her face. "Is that why you sound different?" she asked.

The Hive nodded Alonzo's head. "Yes. I'm sorry you had to struggle with such limited communication. But we're a collective in-telligence, you see, and those of the Third Generation were strug-gling to get by individually, with only the knowledge they inherited from their forbears, the observations they made on their own, or the rare exchanges of information between others in range. Even three generations of study barely scratches the surface when trying to understand communication so different from our own. On a collective basis, we have a much stronger grasp of it."

"The situation created by our landing was unprecedented for us," Hive-Sonia added, "so we were uncertain about how to deal with it. The transmitter, for example, wasn't intended to last this long without upkeep, so the decision was made to power it down until we reached the end of the agreed-upon dormant period. There was a great deal of concern among those of us in the main Hive that the Third Generation wouldn't be able to find it. We were even considering sending down another mission, even though it would have risked detection by several governments."

Alonzo's lips started to move again. He wondered if he could ever get used to that feeling. "I know at times you've all wondered if there was some great master plan. If we were executing some perfect plot. The truth is, those of us you've interacted with up until this point were marooned. They were frightened and alone, and all they knew was that they needed to press on with their information-gathering mission as best as they could. That and the time at which they should activate and resume attempts to communicate."

"And that they needed to try to contact the main Hive," Sonia said.

Her back straightened as the Hive took over again. "None of us realized it at the time, but Dove McNally and Esperanza Kearney did us a great service. We completely underestimated the complexities of communication and social organization within your species. Collective minds are the norm, you see, for intelligent life. We have much less experience with individual intelligence. If we'd tried to enact the mission as planned when we first landed, it might have been disastrous." She shook her head ruefully, embarrassment coming over her features. "Everything that happened to our Galina hosts and everything that's happened to their descendants over the last several months, those were just, as Alonzo guessed, systems checks. Just the barest attempts to understand how our new hosts worked. And even that cost human lives. We deeply regret that. That was never supposed to be part of our mission."

"What..." Colin cleared his throat. "Sorry if this is a rude question, but what do you look like? Outside the hosts? Are you those beetle things?"

"No. Those are just our way of disguising short-range communication and surveillance technology. They just boost signals enough to reach out to nearby Ones. They aren't us. To your eyes, we're just red dust. That's all. No little gray men with big heads, I'm afraid." The Hive winked through Sonia, shocking Alonzo with how natural it seemed. "Of course, the particles you see as dust look entirely different to us. To you, our bodies and our technology are indistinguishable. Formless, malleable particles that can assemble and reassemble. To us, though, there is a world of difference between the dust that brought us here and forms our technology and the dust that is us."

Next came the big question, the one Alonzo been waiting for and dreading to ask. "What's your mission?"

Hive-Sonia blinked at him. "What we've always said. To teach and to learn."

"You don't want to... I don't know. Colonize us, assimilate us, make us like you? Or, I guess, make everyone else like us?"

Sonia laughed, and while it sounded genuine, it was not the real Sonia's laugh. "Of course not. What could we possibly learn if we made you like us? It would defeat the entire purpose."

An echo of Sonia's laugh bubbled up through Alonzo's throat. "We know you have all these assumptions about what visitors like us would want. We've seen it in your popular culture, in your conversations, for sixty years. But..." Hive-Alonzo shook his head. "The fact is, we're not here with a message of universal peace and understanding or an invitation to join a Galactic Federation or to bestow world-saving new technology. We're disappointing, in that respect, I imagine. But we're also not here to colonize, conquer, or destroy you. We're explorers. That's all. Not good, not bad, just... here."

Anger flared in Sonia's eyes. "But... do you seriously not know how much it sucks, getting your body taken over? I mean, this, right now, it's better, but do you know how fucked up and scary this has been?"

Her face changed again, and she lowered her gaze. "We're truly sorry. Truly. Autonomy is such a difficult concept for us to understand. We're just beginning to grasp it, even after all this time," she said, sounding contrite. "We can't leave. We're permanently bound to our hosts, and our Hive now lives in Earth's atmosphere. So I won't lie to you and pretend we can stop this mission, because we can't. But, Sonia, Alonzo..." She reached out to touch Alonzo's hand.

He shuddered at the touch, both alien and familiar, but he didn't pull away.

"We aren't here to take your life. Or anyone's. This is still the first stage of our mission, when we learn to communicate and negotiate our place within a new species. The next stages will be easier."

Alonzo took a deep breath. "Are we the only people negotiating on behalf of the human race right now?"

"Yes."

"In that case, I have a request. No, actually, strike that, I have a demand. Stop taking control of bodies without permission. Find a way to ask us, me and Sonia and all of the others, if you can speak through us. And only do it if we say yes. Don't ever take control of our bodies without permission again. Got that?"

Stillness came over them again. They stared as though waiting for something. Alonzo heard that whispering at the back of his head again.

"Agreed," the Hive replied at last.

Alonzo turned to Colin. "So. No more surprise episodes. It's not exactly a cure, but... I think I can live with it."

"Yeah. Me too," Colin replied. His hand found Alonzo's under the table.

They said nothing for a long moment, just watching each other in silence as the tension of the last days and weeks fell away.

Alonzo took a deep breath. "Well, I guess before we go any further, I should say, on behalf of the human race, welcome to Earth."

Hive-Sonia smiled. "Thank you. We've waited a long time to hear that."

Sonia bit her lip, as though unsure if she wanted to ask the next question. "So, what happens now?"

Her features smoothed again. "That's not completely up to us, Sonia. A lot of how this works will depend on you and the other humans we'll interact with." She cocked her head. "How do you imagine this will go? How do you want us to move forward?"

Alonzo said nothing for a moment. He hadn't spoken with the Hive for very long, but he could already tell they were comfortable with silence. He thought about the question, all the things he hadn't bothered considering past this meeting.

"Well," he began, "you landed in a small town in the middle of a desert. You didn't land in New York or Tokyo or DC. And even after you learned more about how our society works, you didn't ask to be taken to our leader."

Colin laughed a little at that.

Alonzo went on, the ideas forming as he spoke. "You aren't interested in leaders. At least, not the way we think of leaders. You're a hive mind. You're interested in the people."

"That's good, Alonzo. Now." Hive-Sonia leaned forward. "Knowing what you know about us, where do we go from here?"

Alonzo looked at Colin. "What do you think?"

Colin hesitated. "There'll be meetings. Quiet ones. No big summits. But we'll find, I guess, scientists. Experts. We'll choose carefully. We'll find... the curious. The openminded. The ones who are willing to listen and learn and share what they know with you."

"Like you and Tori," Alonzo said, nodding.

Colin's eyes shone with excitement. "There'll be advances in science and technology, and people probably won't be able to figure out where a lot of them came from. And new philosophies, new theories, new ideas about... well, everything. There'll be fiction, novels, movies, maybe—things that don't give you away but get people ready for you. Your society, the Hive, they'll change too. I don't know how, but we'll show you new things, new ways of thinking."

"You already have," Hive-Sonia said, something both sad and warm in her eyes.

Alonzo took a deep breath. "And then, one day, when people are ready, we'll show them how long you've been with us."

"And how much we've done for each other," Sonia's and Alonzo's voices said together.

Silence fell again. Alonzo wondered if he would live to see that day, if it would happen in the next few years, if he and Colin would be old men, or if it would never happen at all. He wanted to find out.

"So," Hive-Sonia asked after a minute, "are you happy with this future you've described?"

With a little rippling shift in Sonia's features, she shrugged, half smiled. "Sure. I'm cool with it."

Alonzo smiled and squeezed Colin's hand tighter. "Yeah. I'm ready. Let's begin."

ANZA STEPPED OUT ONTO the back porch. It was dusk. The setting sun stained the mesa golden red. The air smelled of dust and honeysuckle. Dove had never grown flowers, but Anza had planted honeysuckle seedlings the day after she moved in. Now the vines hung as heavy as they had on the front gate of her childhood home.

She carefully lowered herself onto the porch swing, wincing at a twinge of arthritis in her hip. As always, she thought of the times she and Dove had sat there. The night the mob had come for the Garces children. The night they'd struck their bargain with the thing in the cave. And another night, years later, after Dove's last good day before she sank into a haze of morphine.

Anza sipped her whiskey-spiked tea. She had one cup every night, just one, and always sitting right here. Always facing the mesa.

Something creaked on the porch step. A flash of gray crossed the corner of her eye. She turned to find a coyote sitting in the middle of the porch. It watched her with its angled yellow eyes, back straight, so unlike the cringing posture of a normal coyote.

"Well, hello there," Anza said after a long moment. "Have you come to tell me something?"

The coyote stood and walked toward her, confidently and without fear. It drew close enough for her to smell its fur. Then it sat again and rested a paw delicately on her knee.

Out on the mesa, a dozen others howled in unison. Anza peered into the dusk and found them sitting in a loose ring at the edge of the property, faces turned to the sky. Their long jaws stretched open as they cried out. This wasn't the excited yipping barks of a hunting coyote pack or a yelp of pain. This was a celebration, a howl of joy.

Something unclenched in Anza's chest, something that had been coiled and tensed like a spring for sixty years. She rested a bony hand on the top of the coyote's head. They stayed that way, watching each other, for a minute or two.

Then the coyote bounded off the porch to join its pack. Anza watched as they trotted away and vanished into the desert once more. Then she sat back on the porch swing, sipped her tea, and watched the red light of the sunset fade from the mesa.

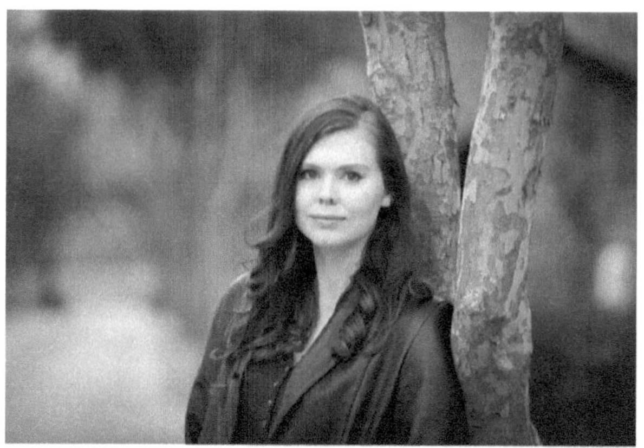

About the Author

Jamie Killen's introduction to the world of dark fiction came at the age of seven, when her well-meaning but perhaps overly enthusiastic dad decided that the works of Harlan Ellison made for some great bedtime stories. She's been avidly consuming science fiction, horror, and fantasy novels, movies, comic books, and podcasts ever since.

Jamie's short stories and flash fiction have appeared in dozens of anthologies and magazines. She is also a writer and director of several dark fiction podcasts.

Originally from Arizona, Jamie now lives in Texas with her long-time partner. When she isn't writing, she enjoys practicing her mixology skills by inventing new and exciting designer cocktails. She also likes craft beer, travel, and cuddling with her two adorable rescue mutts.

Read more at https://jamieskillen.wordpress.com/.

About the Publisher

Dear Reader,

We hope you enjoyed this book. Please consider leaving a review on your favorite book site.

Visit https://RedAdeptPublishing.com to see our entire catalogue.

Don't forget to subscribe to our monthly newsletter to be notified of future releases and special sales.